IN THE NAME OF GOD

Based on True Stories

DOMINIK POLESKI

In the Name of God

ISBN
978-1-960197-73-3 (Paperback)
978-1-960197-74-0 (eBook)
978-1-960197-72-6 (Hardcover)

IN THE NAME OF GOD

CHAPTER 1

THE SLIM, BLACK silhouette of Aleksander Brodski was clearly and unmistakably recognizable even from a considerable distance; the characteristic lanky, bent forward figure, the long arms swaying alongside his disproportionately long legs, as that of a typical tall teenager, giving an impression of utter awkwardness. He walked quickly, as if deliberately trying to avoid looking around or being seen, seemingly oblivious of the passers-by and few indifferent onlookers, and only occasionally lifted his head up to scan the path in front of him. Once satisfied, he bowed his head again and surged forward, engrossed in his thoughts. Alek, as he was commonly called, had a habit, or quite possibly out of necessity wearing what seemed like the same clothes day in and day out. Black, baggy trousers and white shirt with rolled up sleeves up to his elbows on most sunny days, but on a day like this, his usual attire was complemented by a dark, well-worn out jacket over a similar shirt, and of colour that was rather hard to define, but which must have been white once. On his feet was a pair of always the same, worn-out, dark old leather shoes, and as everything else on his thin frame, they too seemed oversized. The day like any other day seemed typical, uneventful and eerily quiet. It was the end of September 1967 and the gloomy weather announced fast approaching of a different season, and that was to be expected in these parts at this time of the year. Several large patches of heavy, cumulous clouds hanged low, as if just above the rooftops of the small town, only to be dispersed from time to time by a sudden gust of cold, easterly wind, carrying scarce, large drops of rain mingled and falling with a kaleidoscope of colourful early autumn leaves, swirling down in a familiar perennial pattern, and then slowly lying down to eternal rest on the wet ground below. Occasionally, Alek walked right into a puddle left by the rain in the cracked and uneven surface of the gray, concrete tile sidewalk. That didn't disturb him at all, his pale face didn't seem to betray any emotions, and if anything at all, just an intense concentration on the pathway below his feet. Rarely a passerby would notice a faint, barely discernable smile on his face, when for a second or two he reluctantly lifted it up to look ahead. As always, he was in a hurry, intent on doing his usual errands as quickly as possible, and then getting back home without any incident, that would disturb his usual routine and peace of mind. Alek usually stopped at one or two stores in the commercial part of town, for he always knew exactly what he wanted. He didn't say much, seldom spoke more than few words besides the polite, customary greetings, and only asked for whatever he came for. Those were just the usual household necessities, nothing special, nothing fancy, mostly the basics, like bread, milk, cheese, fruit jam, flower or grits and again quickly lowered his head down, waited for the products to arrive on the counter, as the store clerk hurriedly retrieved the goods. Alek would then nervously put the money down without much thought, usually all he had, then he would take the change, or sometimes quite surprisingly or perhaps absentmindedly even without waiting for it, just as quickly turned around and left the store, although knowing well that in his household every small coin counted. It wouldn't be the first time Alek left the female clerk dismayed, bewildered and shaking her head, followed by a deep sigh, and looking at the young lad, as he was walking away, without turning back. Alek didn't waste any time going back home; his humped, slim figure moving swiftly, measuring out those familiar long strides along the gray, uneven pavement. His mother was anxiously waiting for him at home, as she always did with uncertainty, deeply concerned whenever her only son didn't come back within what she thought was a reasonable amount of time. That day she took a day off work due to an unpleasant case of a common cold she unexpectedly caught. At this time of the year and the months ahead, unfortunately it became a usual occurrence, after a back-breaking toil at a local fruit processing plant, one of the town's major employers. Constantly bending down, lifting fruit or vegetable-loaded thick cardboard boxes or wooden crates, moving and pacing the wet concrete floor between unheated, dump concrete block walls of the main processing and production hall. The entire room was filled with stifling sour air of a mixture of seasonally fresh and variety of already rotting fruits and vegetables, well past their prime, piled up here and there or scattered around. Several large, vertically rectangular and barred windows, perhaps dating back decades, with dirty, fogged-up cracked thick-glass panes and numerous small holes, provided little protection from the outside elements, and only added to the dreary, repugnant atmosphere inside. That was her unforgiving reality, and she considered herself lucky to have a job to go to, at least five or six months a year.

Alek soon passed the commercial section of town and continued till it changed into a straight raw of dilapidated, residential two-story communal housing on both sides of the road, one not much different from the other. Alek then turned into a familiar, narrow cobblestone side street, which he crossed few times before without an incident. Yet, he momentarily stiffened and hesitated, and then quickened his pace, since it seemed deserted and a little darker here, as if the gloomy clouds above have found their destination, trapped between the dark walls of the surrounding buildings. Alek barely made some thirty or forty steps, when a sudden violent jolt, unexpected brute force threw him against a side wall of one of the residential structures, almost knocking him down. A pair of strange, strong hands tightly clenching the shirt around his thin neck, shook him violently and repeatedly thrashed his frail body against the building.

"Watch where you're going, idiot! Can't you see? What's the matter with you? Are you blind?" growled the angry young man with a disdainful grimace on his face, pinning Alek to the wall.

"I'm sorry, I'm really sorry…I didn't mean to…I didn't see you," Alek in complete shock, pale with fear and trembling began to plead with the stranger; his scrawny body as if a deformed gnat sprawled on the wall behind. Instantly, he thought he must have accidentally ran into a local pedestrian, which in fact wouldn't be the first time, but if that was the case, it was nothing more but an honest misunderstanding. He soon realized that the young man had absolutely no intention of letting him go, not just yet, when he bellowed, turning to his accomplices, presence of which wasn't immediately apparent.

"Did you hear this? You just listen to him. He didn't see me. Try keeping your head up, stupid," said the man, turning his head sideways, as if talking to one of his companions, while pushing Alek forcefully against his chest with a clenched fist, with that characteristic smug expression of complete dominance. Alek gave out a low groan, as he caught a glimpse of two other teenage boys, perhaps between sixteen or seventeen years of age, coming out from around the corner of the building. They approached slowly, nonchalantly, looking at Alek intently, with the same disdainful smirks on their faces, and took positions on both sides, closing in a semi-circle with Alek in the middle, surrounded on all sides and up against the wall. He was trapped. A paralyzing fear engulfed his frail body, and his legs began to shake uncontrollably, making it difficult to stand, and every passing second seemed at least like an unusually long minute. There was no way out and no one around to help; the street was deserted. The young man in front of Alek's face, perhaps no older than eighteen, held his shirt with his right hand tight under Alek's chin. The unexpected tormentor grinned with obnoxious self-confidence of someone who was waiting for this moment for a long, long time, and wasn't about to let his pray get away easily, as if this was his time to shine, to enjoy every second of it.

"You're a fucking Jew, aren't you?" asked one of the other two with visible contempt, and stepping up to Alek even closer, adding his filthy paw in pushing him against the wall, while the eldest was still holding him by the shirt in a fistful, tightly twisted into a knot under Alek's chin. They didn't expect an answer, for they all knew very well who Alek was. Yes, they've all seen him few times before, if they happened to pay any attention, hurriedly walking the same streets, never looking sideways, and ignoring them. They didn't like being ignored, certainly not by someone like the Jew, in the small world of strictly defined and upheld range of their daily activities. It seemed nothing more than aimlessly roaming the streets like a pack of hungry, vagrant dogs, staking out their sovereignty over the streets at least in their immediate neighbourhood, looking for an opportunity to cause disturbance, senseless vandalism and exert their authority. Alek stricken with an overwhelming fear turned pale, and with his back clinging to the wall couldn't utter a word, his blue lips trembling, as his dark eyes began to swell with tears, and each passing second was turning into a horrific nightmare, ominously unfolding and not ending soon.

"What the hell are you doing around here? Didn't you know, you couldn't walk this way? This area is off limits for suckers like you. Didn't you know that?" continued the eldest of the three.

"No, I didn't, I'm sorry…I didn't mean it, I'll never do it again, I promise," Alek began to plead as panic was setting in.

"What's your name?" asked one of the other, younger boys.

"It's Alek."

"Alek who?"

"Alek Brodski. Please let me go… I'm sorry. I was just on my way home. Please, I assure you, you'll never see me here again", he replied in a low voice, with a painful grimace of complete helplessness on his pale, fright-stricken face.

"Jew, what's in that bag you're carrying?" asked the eldest, shoving Alek back again, hard against the wall of the building. Alek didn't say a word, just opened his trembling hand and dropped the bag to the ground. They all looked down. The canvas bag opened up as it fell down, and the meager contents spilled on the ground, plainly visible. It was immediately obvious, the young thugs were not interested in what was in there. There was nothing in it they could use, nothing of real value to them and they were clearly disappointed.

"Do you have any money?" asked the purported leader again.

"No, I don't have any left, just a few small coins, nothing really", answered Alek, barely audible, his lips quivering, and his thin frame slightly curled up inwards, as if in a self-protecting mode facing the attackers. Their demeanor and aggressive postures suggested that a blow could come at any time, as they moved their arms erratically. The mob mentality was clearly on display each one of them fueled the other, nudging and trying to impress each other in a pathetic display of phony courage.

"So, you don't have money, and you're walking here where you're not supposed to walk, and saying that you didn't know any better, and now you just want to go home, right? Did you hear this, guys? What should we do with him? Should we just let him go?" continued the eldest and suddenly slapped Alek casually on a side of his head.

"Not so fast, he's got to learn a lesson. Give it to him, what are you waiting for?" immediately intervened one of the others, looking around as if making sure there wasn't anyone else in the vicinity watching or rushing to the scene. He then grabbed Alek fistful by the hair and shook it violently few times. Alek gave out a sharp cry of pain, and without resistance, with his back still against the wall, began to slide down, as if seeking refuge on the ground below, or perhaps hoping it would part beneath them and swallow up the tormentors to end the ordeal.

The attackers took it as a sign of weakness and just the right time to jump into action without reservations. If any doubts they still had, at that moment they were all dissipated at once. They knew Alek would not resist, much less defend himself. They had him at their mercy. The three young hoodlums already formed a semi-circle around their helpless victim, and so encouraged by the lack of any signs of resistance and apparent resignation, they started to push, slap and punch Alek randomly, as if it were a lifeless object. Although somewhat hesitatingly at first, it soon turned into a barrage of blows, supposedly to teach the accidental intruder a lesson. Each one of them eager to impress the other, to leave his own indelible mark on the victim, as if to make a statement to his companions, that he was certainly a member of the band in good standing.

Instinctively Alek made a feeble, awkward attempt to protect himself as best he could, shielding his face, waving his thin, long arms clumsily, as if attempting to drive off a swarm of bees, but to no avail. From his mouth a torrent of strange, almost inhuman sounds was pouring out, as if from a desperate animal being slaughtered and about to give out its last breath, yet still conscious, clinging to the remnants of its life. It was a shrill, wailing voice of an unbelievable, horrifying anguish and sheer terror, while the attackers pummeled and spewed obscenities at him. Never in his life had he faced such unprovoked attack and for no apparent reason at all. Somewhere form a distance a sudden scream and yelling rang out.

"Stop! Stop! In the name of God, stop it right now!" Then few seconds later it went off again this time much closer: "Stop it! Leave him alone, do you hear? You hooligans, you bandits!"

The eyes of the attackers turned in the direction of the menacing yells, closing in with every second. There was an elderly, stout woman with a sinister expression on her face, running slowly towards them from the main street, but quickly closing the distance, swaying heavily from side to side, waving her arms, armed with a packed black purse, tightly clenched in her right fist. The boys must have sensed the fury of the oncoming, fearless and obviously determined woman and didn't want to take any chances at the unexpected and looming real confrontation within just several seconds. That's not what they had in mind, that wasn't planned. They all stepped back from Alek, visibly baffled by the sudden turn of events, and just looked as if mesmerized at the heavy, elderly old woman recklessly charging forward.

"Let's split." That's the old hag Pavloska, I know her, and I've seen her before.

"She's crazy", shouted one of them.

"Are you sure? How do you know her?" asked the other, obviously hesitating, unsure what to do next, and all three of them reluctant to give up easily. Before they could make a reasonable assessment of the unexpected change of event, when quite possibly they all would be on the receiving end of Pavloska's fury, the old woman was within only several meters. They all could see fire in her eyes, clearly hear her mumbling something haltingly and incoherently, her words hindered by shortness of breath, but surely, she was intimidating and unstoppable in her surge forward. They all looked at each other for a split second, and now they knew well what to do, as if they had it all rehearsed many times before. Flight was the only reasonable option. Before Pavloska even got close enough to be of any serious threat, they all took off almost unanimously and quickly dispersed, each in his own direction, and like ghosts disappeared in between the gray, dilapidated buildings of the old communal subdivision. The exhausted old woman, barely moving her feet forward, staggering, breathing heavily and gasping for air reached Alek crouching by the wall, covering his face in his folded arms over his bent knees and sobbing. Pavloska tried to say something, but couldn't utter a word, holding her left hand on her rising chest, taking deep breaths, as if in the midst of a heart attack. Soon however she was able to collect herself somewhat, and bent over Alek with considerable effort, visibly straining herself, then muttered out panting:

"Are you hurt? Are you hurt, young man?"

She received no response, but the young man below briefly lifted his head up and looked at the old woman above him, and just as quickly lowered it down, back to his previous pose. Don't be afraid my dear, those bandits are gone now, you're safe. Poor boy…nobody deserves this, nobody", and she reached down with her hand to take Alek under his arm. He forcefully shrugged it off without looking, pushing it backwards, leaving the old woman somewhat taken aback by the young man's reaction, but she was not discouraged in the least.

"Are you all right, are you hurt?" Pavloska repeated again.

Suddenly and again from that curled up, thin body on the ground below, exited a most horrific cry. It was a choked up, pent-up raspy wailing squeal, as if a one those horrifying sounds one could perhaps hear only at a slaughterhouse, before the helpless animal gave out its last. Frightened, the old woman took two steps back.

"Are you all right, child?", she asked again, and added as if to herself: "They must have done something terrible to him. Oh Jesus…What in the name of God is this world coming to? They must have hurt him badly, those bandits!"

Alek was still crouching down, sobbing quietly with face down, covered in between his arms, resting on his knees. The shopping bag, loaf of bread, and a paper package of grits lay scattered on the wet ground nearby.

"I promise you, this crime will not go unpunished for as long as I live. You don't have to be afraid now, everything will be all right, it will. I'll walk you home, come with me young man, come with me. Where do you live?" continued Pavloska. Alek slowly lifted his head up and looked around bewildered. A narrow streak of blood from his nose was making its way into his swollen, trembling lips. His tearful, deeply set black eyes still betraying obvious fear and pain, were noticeably bruised all-around the sockets. Pavloska again bent down and hesitatingly put her hand under Alek's left arm and pulling gently upwards, tried to encourage him to get up. Alek resisted at first, but then with difficulty he started to stretch his legs slowly and slide up with his back still against the wall, strenuously lifting the weight of his entire aching body.

"That's good my dear, that's good...You're such a fine young man. Don't be afraid now. As long as I'm here, nothing will happen to you, you can be sure of that", said the old woman, as she continued to pull Alek gently by his arm.

"Leave me alone!" snapped Alek, shrugging off her hand again, while already standing on his feet, looking around, although still somewhat dazed and confused. Few strained spasmodic sobs escaped his swollen, bloodied lips, but he was slowly regaining his composure with each passing second, and clearly had no interest in talking to Pavloska. She looked at him with great concern, as if he were her own son, but was lost for words by Alek's hostile reaction. The old woman hesitated and made an effort not to impose her will and frighten the boy in his fragile state even more and waited for Alek to make the next move. Dejected, he looked down at the ground below, at the few scattered belongings, and then glanced sideways, down the alley to the main street that he came from just several minutes ago, barely fifty paces or so away, clearly visible at the darkened entrance to this dingy, secluded area of poor, working-class, dilapidated neighbourhood. Right there Alek noticed a boy of about twelve or thirteen years old, just standing there and looking with intense interest at the whole scene unfolding. Perhaps he just happened to come by at that particular moment, or else unnoticed he had seen it all. Although still greatly distraught, Alek had a sense he had seen the boy somewhere before, as their eyes met for a split second. Alek then reluctantly glanced at Pavloska, somewhat embarrassed by her personal, almost motherly overtures, this strange, overweight elderly woman, who suddenly appeared out of nowhere. Alek hesitant, made a few shaky steps in the direction of the main street, followed by several quick, long strides, and then he started to run slowly at first, and soon picked up the speed. It was an unexpected dash with a characteristic awkwardness of an overgrown adolescent, alternately stretching his long, thin legs up front, and then extending them back, as if momentarily leaving one leg behind. The startled old woman barely had time to react, made a few clumsy steps to follow him, but just as quickly gave up, pleading:

"Stop, please stop. Wait a second, wait for me! Stop!"

Alek ran, ran as fast as he could, without looking back, occasionally swerving sharply to avoid a rare passer-by or a puddle, and continued to run through mostly deserted streets leading to his home. He soon reached the familiar courtyard and burst through the front door.

CHAPTER 2

MRS. BRODSKI SEEMED to sense that something awful must have happened, long before he appeared at the door, as she was pacing around the kitchen, since Alek was out much longer than usual. By then she already stood waiting just inside, in the short hallway leading to the kitchen. She literally threw herself at her son, as soon as he appeared, and cried out with horror.

"Oh my God! What happened to you? Alek, what happened?"

"Nothing Mom, nothing really. I'm fine… I mean, I'll be alright, don't worry." Alek reluctantly freed himself for his mother's embrace, and in a few strides quickly crossed the kitchen and into the living room, reached the sofa and sank into it, or rather dropped down with a full impact of his weight. His mother followed right behind and without hesitation sat next to him, as he was clenching his delicate, thin and blood-smeared hands.

"Alek who did this to you? Tell me now, what happened?"

"Oh, it's nothing…Please just leave me alone, Mom. I want to be alone."

"Don't tell me it's nothing. And it's not the time to be alone. I can see what happened. Who did this to you?"

"Mom please, it's nothing, really. I'll be all-right."

"I knew it, I just knew this was bound to happen one day. Alek, for God's sake tell me, what happened?"

"Mom, I'll be all right, I need some rest, just leave me alone now, please."

"No, I won't leave you alone. Tell me everything that happened; I want to know. I'm your mother, Alek. I love you, son."

Alek sat there silently with his head down, unable to utter a word. Mrs. Brodski realized, she was powerless to extract anything out of him, and just looked at her son with profound sadness, as bitter tears started streaming down her pale cheeks, silently, incessantly. Despite the mournful atmosphere all-around, Mrs. Brodski tried hard to maintain her composure, to keep it all together, as not to show her weakness and despair. There were just the two of them, a family of two in this small communal home, without relatives in the entire neighborhood, in this God-forsaken town and this whole poor country, still not quite recovered from the ravages of WWII. They had no one else they could rely on, without family or close friends, only few casual acquaintances and immediate neighbors in this old two-story crumbling building, housing several crammed families on both floors, most of whom they hardly knew. The further from their doorstep, the fewer people they knew, whom they could even call neighbours, and certainly not friends. They had only each other. Mrs. Brodski exasperated, looked at her son with a heavy heart, taking deep breaths and sighing, then looking around the room for no apparent reason, as if looking for solace and hope in the furniture, few family pictures on the walls and several different objects scattered around the room. It seemed there weren't even the faintest traces of life, other than the two of them, engrossed in a profound sadness. There was nothing, only eerie silence, punctuated by an old, solitary, dark wooden clock on the opposite wall with a pendulum, which seemed to throb louder and louder, faster and faster with each passing second the more she looked at it. In the silence that engulfed the room, the sound of the clock was becoming unnerving, disturbing, racing like palpitations of a sick heart in its last throes, just before bursting open and spilling all its worn-out parts onto the floor below, unable to go on forever as if nothing happened, and then the time would stand still. If there was ever a time for the God Almighty to reveal itself, to intervene, having failed so miserably just over two decades before, when the horror of WWII engulfed the continent, for them the time was now. The family of two, mother and son just sat there hunched, impassively with sullen, hidden faces, their heavy heads turned down, each one unable to utter a word, overcome with emotions, paralyzed by sorrow, engrossed in that eerie silence, only broken up by the sound of the clock on the wall, rhythmically measuring out those long, painful seconds, and they were both profoundly sad. Mrs. Brodski temporarily lost in thought, after a brief pause suddenly awakened from the abandonment, quietly got up and went into the kitchen. She poured warm water into a large porcelain bowl, took out a small towel, and came right back into the living room. Alek was still sitting there on the sofa, just as she left him, absorbed in his own thoughts, staring down at the worn-out wooden floor, which lost its luster long time ago, marked with few sizeable patches of bare, decaying wood. The narrow longitudinal planks still mostly covered with dark, old varnish, spanned in the direction of the longer side of the rectangular room. The entire home consisted of a short corridor from the outside entrance door to the kitchen, a small two-piece bathroom, and one other bigger room, which served as a living room and at night turned into a common bedroom for both of them. The kitchen was quite spacious, although badly outdated, as everything else in this home, with a single window right onto a gray, high wooden weathered fence, dividing the two adjacent courtyards of dilapidated communal housing, as if of two different worlds. For whatever reason, it was generally agreed that the people on the other side of the fence were better off and envied. The main fixtures of the kitchen were a large cast-iron stove, burning coal and wood or whatever was available at the time, and an old, rather long, but free-standing faded-white cupboard, which also served as a storage for pots and pans in its lower sections, china and cutlery higher up, and a small pantry behind the upper doors. The whole unit was lined up almost against the entire longest wall of the kitchen, but seemed to permanently lean backwards, which was immediately noticeable. The rest of the kitchen was complemented by a small rectangular wooden table near the window, with three simple wooden chairs. The fogged-up, single pane window had a double, flimsy curtain, parting in the middle, stretched on a sagging thin string across the window frame, about two thirds of the height up. The worn-out, faded fabric with flowery, mostly pale blue and red pattern showed all the signs of age, just like the surrounding off-white walls, marked with patches of bulging and peeling paint over uneven layers of plaster, that must have been applied there over the years at least few times before, one on top of the other, and all of it now adorned with few brown-yellowish, irregular stains, crossing over from the ceiling above, giving it an impression of an unwanted permanence. Like all the floors in this communal apartment building, the small, crammed private quarters and common areas were covered with similar long, solid-wood planks marked with several cracks, small holes and indentations, some filled with spots of uneven, hardened wood filler and of everlasting grime in between, as a result of continued usage over the years and decades, and colour of which by now was impossible to define. All the floors must have been painted and re-painted at least few times before, but certainly the last time must have been long, long time ago. The Brodski's living room gave the impression of being crammed with several old pieces of furniture without any particular order or style, all accumulated over several years from different sources, and was not about to be disposed anytime soon. Beside the sofa, it contained a single bed in the furthest corner of the room, by the small and only window, then a large, rectangular table of rather fine antique quality, situated closer to the center of the room, surrounded by six matching chairs and a big area rug under them. The rug was covered in a myriad of faded colours, vaguely resembling the famed Persian rugs, as it was probably originally intended to be, but of course it must have been of Russian origin. Along one of the walls stood a brown, wooden drawer chest with a polished brass menorah on top of it, and a little further to the side, and also dark brown armoire, with age and design similarities of the featured table. Along the other wall stood a brown, wooden bookshelf with neatly stacked rows of books of mostly standard sizes, but all seemed to be bound in dark burgundy or brown hardcovers. The furnishings collection was completed by two odd night tables, one by the sofa, and one by the single bed. Three of the walls were sparsely decorated with framed black and white family photographs. The biggest and most prominent picture was a rather large wedding photograph of Jakub and Zofia Brodski.

The walls themselves, just as in the kitchen were now badly faded and stained, especially below the ceiling along the outside wall, the one with the window in it, and showed obvious signs of leaking roof in the past and possibly quite recently, and it too was covered by patches of thick, discoloured peeling paint and plaster crudely applied there few times, one layer on top of the other.

Mrs. Brodski placed the bowl of warm water on a chair beside the sofa, sat down near Alek with a look of painful concern, and with trembling hands began to gently wipe away traces of dried-up blood off his visibly bruised face. His blue lips were cut and swollen, and there was a small cut above his left swollen, bloodshot eye, with a dark-red welt beneath it. Alek's head jerked backwards and sideways with a grimace of pain on his face, as he gave out a long and hissing sound every time his mother touched one of the cuts with the water-soaked towel.

"Sit still, please", whispered his mother.

"But it hurts", snapped Alek impatiently, raising his voice.

"I know it does. I'm trying to be as gentle as I can. I think we might have to go to the clinic, and have a doctor look at it."

"No Mom, I'm not going anywhere. I'm staying right here. I will get over it, I'll be fine."

"I'm not so sure about that my son, we'll shall see. I know, it's quite a distance to walk, especially for you in this condition. I can't count on the neighbours, you know, I don't know them that well. They all don't seem to be very happy about us living here, some outright resent us for whatever reason. Unfortunately, as far as I know, we're the only Jewish family in this town, if one can call us a family."

"No Mom, they hate us here, I know it."

"That's what I just said, some do resent us", corrected Mrs. Brodski. "Now tell me, who did this to you? Were they the same boys who pushed you around and taunted before?"

"Yeah, the same three. I know now, that one of them, the eldest, is a son of the chief policeman here in town", said Alek.

"How do you know that? Are you sure?" asked his mom in disbelief.

"Oh, I've seen him before a couple of times walking with his dad, and he was a policeman, the chief of police. Everyone knows him."

"Alek, are you sure?"

"Yes Mom, I'm sure."

"Well then, in this case I have to pay him a visit at the police station, tomorrow." she said angrily, as if she has already made up her mind.

"I don't want you to go Mom, there is no use. I don't want any trouble. It won't do us any good."

"There will be no trouble son. Enough is enough! I have my own reason to file a complaint too. Something I haven't told you about. It has not been easy for me here either, the way I've been treated around the town."

"I didn't know that, Mom."

"I didn't tell you this Alek, because I didn't want you to worry, but that's not a big deal. What they did to you is just too much for me. It's not going to get any better, I'm sure. It has to stop; I must put an end to it. We can't live like this any longer and doing nothing now is not an option. After all, we've been doing nothing for the past few years, naively thinking it would change, it would get better, and it's not getting any better."

"Do you want me to go with you, Mom?" inquired Alek.

"No, not this time. I'd rather you stay home and rest. I don't know what's going to happen at the police station, At any rate, I don't want you to go through more aggravation. Although, it might turn out you'll have to go there with me eventually, only time will tell. Son, has anyone else seen this? I mean, were there any witnesses?"

"Yes Mom. Thanks to this old woman who showed up out of nowhere and chased them off and later stayed with me; it could have been much worse. I don't know her, but I think she is local. I must I've seen here before somewhere, but don't recall it now. There was also this strange boy, standing at a distance and staring at us. I've seen him before a few times, I'm sure. He was just standing there and looking."

"Good," that's good Alek, at least we have witnesses, if need be. It could be a problem locating them, but that's another matter.

CHAPTER 3

THE BUILDING HOUSING the local police, or Citizens' Militia, as it was officially called in the new socialist Polish People's Republic was located in an old, two- story concrete building, right in the town's commercial centre. It was actually at the end of one long row of several buildings spanning two entire blocks, home to many shops and small government businesses. Private enterprises were strictly forbidden in the blooming socialist republic, except for small segment of most common services; one man or woman operations, and even those were severely limited. The police station was located on the second floor, at the eastern end of this dilapidated, crumbling and gray concrete structure. The double, slightly ajar, wooden entrance door led inside the building's ground-floor vestibule, ending with a steep staircase to the upper floor. Everything around this place, right from the entrance was in a condition of total neglect and disrepair. Peeling paint, rusting metal balustrades, rotting wooden doors and few small window frames with cracked windowpanes and crossed with round metal bars. Once inside the ground- floor, dimly lit, damp entrance-hall, one was struck with an unbearable stench of rot, urine and possibly human excrement. If anyone was to venture a little closer, just out of curiosity on a round tour just within the confines of this room, unknowingly into the furthest corners, below the flight of stairs, one would have been struck by many other colourful adornments abundantly splattered around, crude graffiti and a stray patron's vomit on full display like a sumptuous platter, on a tiled floor with worn out black and white squares. There it was, perhaps for the past few days already, undigested vegetable salad, given back in a torturous agony for no other reason, than his body's assimilation problems. Partially dried up puddles of urine and few feces were still there, obscured in the darkened corners, most likely the aftermath of a typical rowdy night at the local popular drinking hangout, about two hundred meters to the west, in the same row of buildings. After hours, late at night the police station's ground floor vestibule had a dual purpose, for some, a handy and quick convenience outlet when everything else was closed, and of course a place to express utter contempt for the uniformed authority above, on the way back home. All this went on with almost assured impunity, while the officers, the guardians of the law, preferred the relative comfort of the second-floor office, and rarely ventured downstairs, especially on any cold or rainy day, year-around. Whoever ventured in here on a legitimate business, was also struck by unusual, and quite original mural artwork in the corners of the filthy concrete walls, left there by few drunken "artists", who obviously were not expected to carry a roll of toilet paper, and used their fingers as a paint brush, and the excrement as an artistic medium. This whole place emanated the most repulsive and creepy feeling, and it was a known fact, that many legitimate visitors once inside, had a change of heart, turned around and just as quickly left the building, never looking back. The common perception in town was, that the personnel of this proud law enforcement unit in the name of People's Republic of Poland, had little more than elementary school education. Education was not the most desirable attribute to possess, certainly not for this job, but rather your average police force member ideally had to be big, strong and stupid. Conformity was an indispensable virtue for the lawmen, and the law was first of all what the unit commandant said, then the local secretary of Polish United Workers' Party, then the district Party chapter head, and so it went up the party ranks right to the first secretary, comrade Wladyslav Gomulka in the county's capital. The country was in the Party's iron grip, and the police was its faithful arm, its essential extension. All the men in uniforms went through a basic indoctrination course in socialist ideology, the fundamental tenets of Marxism carefully tailored to their cognitive capacities, with periodic follow-ups in the following years. Not enough of the Marxist doctrine to make up for the gaps in the standard socialist education from elementary school and up, and thus proper understanding of the whole revolutionary philosophy was deemed dangerous, since it could encourage independent thinking, and thus undesirable conclusions. In the opposite spectrum, too much of socialist ideology could inflict an unnecessary strain on the poor fellow's limited mental capacity, and confuse him completely, which of course was not the ultimate aim. As grandpa Karl Marx so precisely stated in his immortal words back then and for posterity: "From each according to his ability, to each according to his needs." Under the circumstances, who in his right mind could argue with that?

Mrs. Brodski stood in front of the double entrance door, hesitating briefly, then she looked up at the red and white, metal plaque on the wall above, and holding the handle tightly, slowly pushed the heavy door inwards with a considerable effort. Once inside, she approached the staircase, looking around, up and down. The smell and what she has just seen after scaling just a few steps, must have taken away whatever courage she had. She paused and looked back, holding the handrail tightly. The door was now closed behind her. Profound feeling of fear and nausea gripped her body, as she was dragging her leaden legs behind her, and momentarily wanted to turn back. Loud banging and raspy, agonizing screams from above reached the bottom of the stairs, which only magnified Mrs. Brodski's fright and hesitation, but determined she kept climbing the steep stairs and slowly made it to the first landing. There were two intermediate landings to the high second floor militia headquarters. She mumbled something to herself evoking god's mercy, as the banging became louder and louder with each step. It seemed to be coming from a jail cell adjacent to the main police quarters, separated by thick concrete walls.

The main office of the police headquarters was surprisingly quite spacious, with a long counter just past the front door, then behind it three cluttered wooden desks in no particular order, several chairs, some filing cabinets, a wooden coat hanger, two black telephones and a rather large radio on top of one of the cabinets. High up on the main wall, directly across the entrance door hang three portraits, a standard feature of all the government offices. The first one to the left was a bold, oversized head of the First Secretary of the United Workers' Party, Comrade Gomulka, peering down at all below. Then in the middle, just slightly higher, hanged a picture of a white eagle on red background, Poland's national symbol. The portrait to the right, at the same height as Comrade Gomulka's, was equally bold likeness of the second communist in command, Comrade Jozef Cyrankiewicz, the country's Prime Minister, a Jew and a former Auschwitz prisoner. The air inside the office was stifling and reeked of tobacco, sweat, grime and unmistakably of cheap Russian cologne in various proportions, and only added to the whole unsettling atmosphere of the place. There were two policemen on duty in the office at this time. One of them of medium height but obviously fat specimen, and the other exactly opposite, tall and skinny. Both cops had a characteristic small mustache, as if it were a code requirement, and both were absorbed doing some paperwork, undoubtedly a very important task in their daily routine, and which must have strained those feeble brains to the limits. They didn't even notice Mrs. Brodski quietly standing there behind the counter.

"Good morning!" she said again with a particular emphasis.

Few seconds later, but what seemed more like minutes, the fat one sitting behind a desk slowly raised his head looking perplexed or annoyed but didn't utter a word. The other cop went about his business, looking for something in the filing cabinet, and without even a glance in direction of the counter, said rather loudly:

"Kovaluk, there is a woman standing at the front. Go and see what she wants."

The fat one immediately became animated, as if awoke suddenly and looked up, rolled his eyes and lifted his heavy ass slowly, then unceremoniously walked over to the front counter with his eyes firmly fixed on Mrs. Brodski.

There was an unmistakable aura of importance on his greasy, red, and rather ugly face, with acharacteristic nonchalant, condescending expression.

"What can we do for you Mrs.?" asked officer Kovaluk, once he reached the destination.

Mrs. Brodski hesitated and could not utter a word. She just stood there paralyzed by the overwhelming fear and uncertainty, then looked sideways. For a moment she seemed disoriented or completely lost. Her mind raced through, unable to recover any traces of rational thought, as if she was unsure where she was or why? She wanted to say something, moved her lips, but uttered no sound. The police officer visibly impatient, repeated:

"Mrs. what can we do for you?"

Mrs. Brodski shuddered, looked back at the entrance door, and back again at the burly man in front of her. Slowly it all began to fall into focus. She snapped out of the brief amnesia and the overwhelming fear of this office, the People's Militia, as it was formally known, the seat of the omnipotent authority, or the law.

"Oh, yes, yes…I'm sorry. I wasn't sure you see…I'm actually not sure if I'm at the right place."

"Just tell me, what seems to be the problem?" asked the cop somewhat irritated.

"I'd like to talk to the Commandant, if I may," she said finally regaining some of her lost composure.

"I'm afraid that's impossible. He's busy, as you can see. I'm sure I can take care of this", snapped back officer Kovaluk.

"I think it would be better if I talk to the Commandant myself", she continued.

At that moment the other policeman in the back of the room lifted his head up, and looked sternly in the direction of Mrs. Brodski. Their eyes met for a split second, but she lowered her gaze just as quickly, and looked back again at officer Kovaluk standing impatiently in front of her, behind the counter.

"So, what is it, Mrs.?" asked the officer.

"My name is..." started Mrs. Brodski, but was quickly interrupted.

"We know who you are. Everybody in town knows who you are. The question is, what did you come here for? What do you want? You either tell me now, or don't waste our time."

"I'm sorry for all the trouble I'm causing you. I came here to file a complaint", she said shyly.

"A complaint?" asked Kovaluk, raising his eyebrows, as if taken completely by surprise, and then added impatiently and with a visible agitation: "What complaint? Against whom?"

"You see Sir, my son Alek was beaten up by some hooligans on the street the other day."

"To file a complaint? Mrs. Brodski, things like these happen all the time. It is nothings serious, a child's play. We don't deal here with matters of this nature. You came to the wrong place. You should talk to their parents, or go to their school, maybe talk to their teachers, not us."

"I'm afraid it's more serious than that. Alek sustained some injuries to his face, chest and arms. He was roughed up and pushed around by the same bunch twice before. Things have been escalating for some time now. We need to put an end to it. We cannot live like this any longer. Alek told me that one of the young men is a son of ...", and she abruptly stopped in the middle of the sentence, lowering her head.

"Whose son is he? Tell me, please. Don't be afraid", asked the policeman sarcastically with a faint smile on his face. Mrs. Brodski stood there in silence, looking helplessly at officer Kovaluk with her big, frightened black eyes.

"Well, are you going to tell me, or are you just going to stand there and waste my precious time?"

"Alek said that he recognized one of the attackers. He is a son of..." Again, she stopped in mid-sentence.

"Oh, for heaven's sake, whose son is he?"

The Commandant's", she finally blurted it out hastily, looking in the direction of the police officer sitting behind the desk in the back of the room.

"What? Are you out of your mind, Mrs.? That is a very serious accusation. For your sake I hope you know what you're saying", said the policeman with dismissive, derisive smile and obvious contempt splashed across his fat, greasy face, and turning around, asked the other officer.

"Edward, did you hear what she just said?"

"No, I didn't. What did she say?"

"She said that your son apparently with his friends beat up her boy," Alek.

"What? She must be crazy. She doesn't know what she's talking about", snapped the exasperated station Commandant, as he quickly approached the front counter. There was a moment of silence, as the three of them looked incredulously at each other in turns, as the two lawmen were caught in total disbelief. Captain Sokolowski's facial expression and sudden abrupt gestures with his long, thin arms left no doubt that he didn't take Mrs. Brodski's daring statement lightly and was more than just visibly irritated. In this border town he was the omnipotent authority. He was the law, and anyone who dared to question or oppose that, would be met with a full force of his wrath. By now, it was a well- known and established fact. He came to town with his family just about three years before, with a task of introducing exactly that, law and order, "to clean up" this God-forsaken place. At forty-five he was the youngest in the detachment of four, the most educated of them all, with a middle school diploma and energy of a maniacal zealot, giving him a feeling of invincibility, as he dutifully embarked on his mission, knowingly trying to leave an indelible mark on this town and the surrounding villages for many years to come. Officially, the common perception was that Sokolowski was virtually incorruptible, and the perception was, that those who tried regretted it dearly and never tried again.

"So, you're saying, my boy Adam assaulted your son. Is that right?", the captain turned to Mrs. Brodski with a cynical, mocking tone in his voice, and a particularly cold and penetrating look in his steely eyes, both of which by now became his well-known trademarks. Mrs. Brodski once again hesitated, looked sideways, and down at the front counter, rather than face the obvious annoyance in Sokolowski's shallow, cold eyes and those narrow lips of his, already twisted in contemptuous, vengeful grimace, which seemed to be permanently affixed to his placid facial expression. His efforts at professional civility were just a futile attempt to conceal his real character, so easily discernable once confronted with something he felt strongly about, or had personal interest in.

"Did I hear you right, Mrs.? My son and some others assaulted your son, or am I delusional?"repeated the Commandant with increasing agitation.

"Yes", said Mrs. Brodski in a barely audible, soft voice.

"Yes?"

"Yes!" repeated Mrs. Brodski.

"When did it happen?"

"A couple of days ago."

"Where?"

"On a small side street, just off the Red Army Street, and few blocks away from the town's centre."

"Were there any witnesses?"

"Yes, my son said there was an old woman who intervened and chased those hooligans away, and a boy standing nearby, who just happened to be there."

"Any names?"

"I'm afraid, I don't know their names."

"So, no names, but there were witnesses. That's interesting..."

"You see officer, we hardly know anybody here."

"Why didn't you come here immediately?" the Commandant continued his interrogation.

"I wasn't sure what to do?" Mrs. Brodski answered politely.

"What is your son's name?"

"Aleksander Brodski."

"I think I've heard this name before. How old is your son?"

"He's fifteen years old."

"Where is your son now?"

"At home. I didn't let him go to school today. I'm afraid he's still not well." The Commandant was writing it all down on a piece of paper, then stopped and looked at it for several seconds, but what seemed like several minutes. A deep silence engulfed the room. The three of them stood there as if frozen, giving it an inhospitable and strangely surreal feeling. Sudden outburst of banging came from adjacent jail cell, accompanied by somewhat muted cries for help. A persistent series of "thud...thud...thud..." at equal intervals against a heavy steel door and sent a cascading echo bouncing off the thick, concrete walls of the entire building.

"Help, help! Help me!" cried out the man inside and then again after a brief intermission: "thud...thud...thud..."

Commandant Sokolowki abruptly lifted his head up in a gesture of obvious exasperation and an expression that he has finally lost patience. He literally shouted to his subordinate: "Kovaluk, go and shut that son of a bitch up once and for all!"

"Not a problem, chief", said the chubby policeman with an air of authority and confidence embarking on an important mission, and with a quick, instinctive movement of his plump hands checked if his gun and baton were still at his waist, then with a few rapid strides stepped out the door. What followed shortly after, somewhere on the other side of the door and still quite audible, was a barrage of the most obscene and incomprehensible tirade of profanities one could imagine. Then a menacing avalanche of threats to top it off, in what seemed like a well-rehearsed and frequently applied repertoire of abundant, but less known vocabulary of at least three akin Slavic languages, coupled with a few baton strikes across the metal bars. It had its desired effect, and must have stunned the poor soul behind, inside the cell like an electric jolt, which left him numb and silent. Kovaluk rushed back into the office slamming the door behind him, and with his hands still shaking, pulled out a package of cigarettes from his uniform's side pocket. He took one cigarette out, rolled it between his fingers twice, lit it up, inhaled deeply, and then nervously exhaled, blowing the thick, white smoke up in the air. His normally red cheeks, enhanced by regular dosage of vodka, were now pale, as the smoke rose into the air above their heads, and an overwhelming sense of pride and accomplishment he could barely contain, was written all over constable Kovaluk's face. Commandant Sokolowski meanwhile looked at his deputy with pity, and without saying a word, let out a strange growl, as a faint, sarcastic smirk flashed across his face. Mrs. Brodski felt trapped, helpless and all she could think about, was getting out of this place, back home where Alek was waiting and where within their small, crammed living quarters they could still find peace and tranquility, just the two of them together. Her apprehension before coming here now appeared to be fully justified, for she could have anticipated little sympathy, but a rather malicious interrogation at the hands of guardians of law and order in this town. The Commandant turned to Mrs. Brodski again, frowning and with the same cold demeanor.

"You were saying that my son and some others assaulted your son Alek. Normally I wouldn't bother with things of this nature, but since you're making this rather serious accusation, I will look into it. I will investigate this thoroughly. As much as it seems unthinkable, I'll talk to my son. You must understand, we deal here with matters of vital importance, not some child's play gone wrong. Like that drunkard in the cell, you know what he's done?"

Mrs. Brodski just shook her head, looking shyly at Sokolowski, who continued his arguments.

"Let me tell you. Last night he got drank out of his mind, and then started yelling publicly all those profanities and slanders against our First Secretary of the Party, Comrade Gomulka, our Prime Minister Cyrankiewicz, The Party, and against our dear friend and neighbour, the Soviet Union. I can understand someone can have on occasion too much to drink, with all honesty we all do, but to shoot your mouth off like that, and in public for all to hear, that's crossing the boundary. It must be dealt with accordingly and decisively to the full extent of the law. We won't tolerate open contempt, opposition, incitement and subversion of the worst kind. Enemies of the state will be eliminated. Apparently, it wasn't the first time he had done that. Besides, lately we've had reports of intensified spying activities along the border nearby. We suspect they work with local collaborators. These are dangerous times we live in Mrs. Brodski. The enemy never sleeps, trying to undermine our socialist motherland, which came to existence at such a great cost. We must be vigilant and always ready to defend against the evil forces of western imperialism."

Mrs. Brodski had difficulty listening to the Commandant's unexpected tirade, most likely taken right out of some mandated regional party's indoctrination session, an obligatory curriculum for all those in position of any authority. Socialism, imperialism, spying, subversion were such fantastic and irrelevant concepts to her now, that it only magnified her feeling of frustration and helplessness. She almost broke down, barely maintaining her composure, although the temptation to lash out and relieve the mounting anger was hard to restrain. She turned to Sokolowski, and looking him straight in the eyes said:

"I'm so sorry for taking up your valuable time, gentlemen. I know you have more important things to do, so I'll just go now."

"I assure you, I'm all for the rule of law. As I said, I will talk to my son and get to the bottom of this. One way or another, we'll let you know", added the Commandant with a dismissive tone.

Mrs. Brodski looked at them both for a few seconds, barely able to control her tears, then turned around, and without a word left the station as quickly as she only could, all the way down the steep concrete steps holding tight onto the handrail. The whole experience left her in such emotional distress, that once outside, she could not control herself any longer, and bitter tears trickled down her painfully sad face. In a state of almost complete despair, but angry and still with unwavering determination, she stepped onto the sidewalk, temporarily blinded by the daylight. Without as much as a glance at the surroundings, she hurried back home. Despite what seemed like vague assurances from the Commandant, she had no regrets, not in the least. As soon as she stepped over the threshold, knowing well that Alek was waiting anxiously, she was greatly relieved to be back home, and immediately conveyed to him some carefully chosen details of what had transpired at the police station. More so, she tried to reassure her son of her motherly boundless resourcefulness, strength, and protective instincts, and at the same time sparing him any new emotional burden with her own frustration and doubts. Alek remained in a pensive and reflective mood hearing the story from the police station, and then for most of the day he barely uttered several words, and even that with clearly audible agitation. He didn't eat much, didn't do much, just lied down on the sofa for most of the day. He briefly got up from time to time, made several steps aimlessly around the room, then back on the sofa, lied down again, then walked into the kitchen or the bathroom a few times, and looked out the window a couple of times without any particular interest.

An unexpected knock on the door few days later, early in the evening spoiled the silence, just in time and when things were slowly getting back to normal. Maria Pavloska stood there unannounced, introduced herself with polite bow and a smile and asked if she could come in, she'd like to talk. Mrs. Brodski greeted her warmly, happy to see her. Although somewhat surprised, she immediately recognized in the old woman a kind and gentle spirit, a good-natured demeanour and humility, that seemed to emanate from her like a living saint. Pavloska brought with her a small package of coffee beans as a gift. Her husband Stanislav, although close to retirement, but still working for the National Railways on freight trains and traveled frequently to the Soviet Union. Many staples there were readily available, but for whatever reason quite scarce in this part of the country, just across the border, such as coffee or black tea from Russian Republic of Azerbaijan with such intense aroma that could rival the best teas in the world. Among the other popular commodities scarce here, were also oranges, lemons, spices, Russian cigarettes and perfumes. The fashionable local women wore the perfumes in abundance, the smells of which in fact were easily detectable, even from considerable distance. Short on delicate balance and refinement, they emitted such a strong and pervasive sweet flowery smell, that it was impossible to mistake their origin.

The two women sat in the dimly lit room, chatted amicably, sipping the freshly brewed coffee, while Alek sat at the kitchen table presumably doing his homework. Mrs. Pavloska related her side of the story of attack on Alek and with such passion and attention to detail, as if she were talking about her own son. Mrs. Brodsky in turn shared the story of her visit to the police station, pausing from time to time, sighing, and taking deep breaths. Her facial expressions reflected that most unpleasant event as the story went on. On occasion her eyes stricken with painful sadness, swelled with tears from time to time, and she reached for a white handkerchief in the left pocket of her hand–made brown, wool sweater. Mrs. Pavloska listened patiently and attentively, seldom interrupting, mostly with affirmative "aha, aha", or "yes, yes my dear", or "those monsters!" Then in the end, she summed up the whole incident with absolute certainty: "The Almighty God has seen it all and will not be so gracious when the time comes to stand before him on judgement day, let me assure you of that". As the time went on, Mrs. Brodski managed a few barely discernible smiles in the corners of her lips, especially when recalling the Commandant's impassionate speech on merits of the Party, its leadership or the friendship of the good, benevolent big brother across the river, the Soviet Union. Pavloska leaned over occasionally and touched the slim hands of Mrs. Brodski in a gesture of sincere empathy, support and unwavering unity. The women became quite fond of each other during the short time they spent together sipping coffee and talking. True to her initial impression, Pavloska seemed the most decent and pious woman Mrs. Brodski has met in a long time. Such manifestations of kindness seldom came her way, as far as she could recall and ever since she moved here with her late husband Jakub. Although in the beginning of their amicable conversation Mrs. Brodski was inconsolable, with time she regained much of her confidence, natural dignity and determination. In the end she eagerly shared some personal details of her early life, right after they crossed the border from the former Polish eastern territories, before World War II, heading west with several groups of other migrants, before the border was closed by the Soviet Union for good, ending the mass migrations, dividing ethnic groups and cutting off families. However, thousands of displaced families from the east managed to re-settle within then present borders of the country in the first few years after the war, before the Soviets relishing in its insatiable expansionist appetite, decided to keep what they conquered following their invasion of the country on September 17, 1939. Poland lost about a third of its land mass and a substantial part of its population. There was no turning the clock back, at least not for a foreseeable future. So it was, Mr. and Mrs. Brodski temporarily settled in this small, quiet town, hoping to move further west shortly after, or out of the country, once contacts with any remaining close or extended family members were established. Credible scraps of information were very hard to obtain either from private sources or government agencies. Slowly they reconciled with a belief that, most of their known family members or friends had likely perished in the concentration camps, or perhaps managed to break through and left the country by now and settled in Western Europe, Israel or the USA. It was soon known that survivors of the once large Jewish population of war devastated Europe were making their way to Israel, especially following the official country's establishment on May 14, 1948, and then its official recognition by the United Nations. Jakub Brodski however, fell victim to rather unfortunate circumstances, he had little control over. When making inquiries at the neighboring county town about the whereabouts of his family members, he came across a rather inquisitive Party apparatchik. The bureaucrat upon learning that Mr. Brodski was a former middle school history teacher and an accomplished musician from Lvov in the current Soviet Republic of Ukraine, formerly part of Poland, insisted that Jakub stay here, at least for a few years to fill the void. There was a great need for all professionals whose ranks were so decimated and displaced by the war and teachers among them. Jakub Brodski was literally assigned a post in one particular secondary school and given no choice. Soon his new personal identification document was made out to the address which was to be only temporary, but soon it became permanent, and that was the end of his traveling plans. Many other people were met with the same fate, not only teachers, but some doctors, dentists, army officers, skilled tradesmen and ordinary bureaucrats found themselves "assigned" to posts around the nearest provinces in a massive and ambitious effort by the Party to maximize resources in an effort to rebuild the country from the ruins and backwardness as soon as possible.

Mrs. Brodski continued with carefully selected pieces of her life's story, until it became quite late in the evening. Both women enjoyed each other's company immensely and vowed to continue with a much closer relationship in the days and months to come. Actually, they've had a nodding acquaintance, or known each other by sight for a few years now, since the town is so small, eventually one is bound to see the same faces here and there going about their business. Thus, in the past Mrs. Brodski and Maria Pavloska ran into each other sporadically in the streets or in the shops, had they happened to be there at the same time, but it never went past just the basic cordial bows and greetings. Mrs. Pavloska promised to make every effort to help resolve the issue with Alek, and what now became a personal matter with Commandant Sokolowski, possibly with far-reaching implications.

CHAPTER 4

ALEK SPENT MOST of that time sitting at the kitchen table, pretending to study, but in fact trying to listen in on the conversation in the living room, which he suspected much of it was about him. He heard some of it, but not all and that made him uncomfortable, he didn't like being talked about. After all, many of the things he overheard, he's never heard before directly from his own mother and he felt disappointed, almost betrayed. Few times he got up and walked into the living room under a pretext of looking for something, circled around and then quickly disappeared again without a word. All he managed to elicit, were few meaningful glances and warm smiles from both ladies. The conversation went on and the tone varied with the subject discussed. At times it was lively, then followed by more somber and subdued periods, and then occasionally spaces of complete silence, perhaps moments of reflection. The two women made a commitment to keep in touch more often, as they finally bid farewell and parted at the door. Despite their age differences, the mutual affinity between them was unmistakable, and a beginning of a rare friendship was forged.

Mrs. Brodski stayed up well into the night immersed in her thoughts, pondering their future and regressing back into the past, the time when her husband Jakub was still alive. Life was different then, they all felt safe, there was hope. With his untimely death, all that fell apart, and with it their hopes and dreams of a better life, like a proverbial house of cards. Mrs. Brodski sat impassively on the sofa in the dimly lit room, surrounded only by a profound, undisturbed, almost divine silence. Instinctively she caught a glimpse of Alek standing, leaning against the kitchen door frame. He just stood there looking at his mother with all his usual intensity and those big, black eyes, without saying a word. It seemed as if the time stood still, and an overbearing feeling of sadness descended upon the household and permeated every corner of their small home. Since the death of Alek's father, whom he only vaguely remembered now, he learned to completely rely on his mother. She was his best friend, defendant, protector and closest confidante, and Alek was absolutely sure, he could always count on her. He understood well by now the struggles she went through to put food on the table, to buy the clothes he wore, or even the basic school supplies. It all came at a great personal sacrifice, although she rarely talked about it, in fact she always tried to maintain a positive attitude, and as if purposely, in spite of it all, keep a pleasant smile on her face whenever their eyes met. The meagre, monthly state pension allocated to her by the state after Jakub's death, most months didn't go nearly enough to cover the basic food necessities, let alone anything beyond that, which were considered luxuries. She supplemented the pension as a part-time, seasonal employee at the local fruit and vegetable processing plant, and occasional housekeeper for families that were better off and could afford it. Nevertheless, it all added up to manageable subsistence, in fact no better or worse than most folks in town, the only reassuring reality, but under any normal circumstances would be regarded as abject poverty.

The most vivid example that Alek could remember when things boiled over, his mom broke her silence and in a rare departure from the norm, shared a most disturbing event, which in a way became a turning point in her shopping routine. The one particular event that she related to Alek, must have had a great impact on her, since she talked about it with obvious pain in her voice, and which took place at one of the stores on her usual shopping errands, before in time the task officially became mainly Alek's responsibility. It happened at the old dairy store, when she was met with rude and spiteful remarks from other shoppers and one of the two clerks, as if in planned and coordinated group collusion. As she stood in the crowded and crammed to capacity store, which had just received a new delivery of several products, she had a feeling that there was a gentle sway of the throng, mostly local women, which grew into a push from the back. It then intensified, almost like a domino effect directed specifically at her. She quickly realized, and it seemed like it was not an accident, but a deliberate offence at her and no one else. The overwhelmingly female crowd, suddenly roused from their typically expressionless demeanor and sullen, vacant faces, burst out laughing. Mrs. Brodski didn't find it amusing at all, on the contrary, she was startled at first, then shocked, and once she fully realized what had just happened, her instinctive reaction was to leave the awful place immediately. Some of the shoppers found it infinitely amusing, and others made little attempt to hide their hostile feelings, when "that Jewess!" was heard uttered with contempt and reached Mrs. Brodski's ears somewhere from the back. Despite her attempt to free herself, she stood helpless, jammed between the mass of strange bodies, unable to retreat, even if she wanted to. When she finally got close to the counter, after a prolonged wait in among the multitude with no apparent, discernable queue, a disorder which only the locals seemed to understand, she was met with a disrespectful and provocative: "What do you want?" from one of the two boorish stout, red cheeked, past-middle-aged women behind the counter. At that moment Mrs. Brodski felt like the only thing she could think of saying, the only thing she could think of was: "Nothing, I don't want anything from you", and then squeezed herself through to the exit and just disappeared. Stories like these increasingly had a profound and lasting effect on young Alek, and with time only added to his sense of aloofness and estrangement. He found life around town difficult to understand and adjust to, either among his peers, who somehow knew it better and had no problem accepting things as they were, or among the general population, since one could never know how to react or what to expect. Yet, everyday life in town seemed to have its own deeply entrenched arrangements, its own peculiar motion, or rhythm and logic that the locals understood well, and "that's how it has always been around here", if one was to ask. For example, common was a practice of labour exchange, or "favours", among acquaintances, friends, close or distant family members or even strangers, since common services were almost non-existent, and money was always in short supply. Equally common was small scale bribery, either in a form of rare and valuable goods, or money, but mostly among those who had some to spare. "Greasing the wheels" of course produced immediate and favourable results. In time, Alek began to notice things he didn't see before, and hear things he had never heard before, all those little things that seemed to be the essence of life around here. Equally hard to understand were the customs at local social gatherings and celebrations, whether "men only" or conjugal. The frequently tossed around saying: *"Woman, wine and song"* almost always found its way to the table among a particularly festive crowd indoors or rapturous evening garden parties, but somehow the "wine"part remained a mystery to him and many others, but never seriously questioned, when the drink of choice was always vodka, and very seldom anything else. Particularly among the working class, simple folks, the more vodka flowed, the more singing there was, and in time little mattered whose woman it was, that a particular reveler had his eyes firmly fixed on, usually in the latter parts of the party. With each passing minute the fun-loving man was certainly more interested in the women sitting nearby, or directly across, but not necessarily his own wife, regardless how disinterested, unattractive or intoxicated the other woman was in comparison to his own wife. The missus sat there as if she didn't exist, or similarly was a subject of someone else's advances, and the husband was either already sloshed out of his mind or couldn't care less. To people in these parts that was the magic of vodka intake in appropriate amounts, sometimes in moderation, but usually meant to be enjoyed as the custom and tradition prescribed, that is in heavier doses, or until all the bottles were empty. The clear liquid just seemed to work its magic, never failed, just blurred vision and senses enough to make *"the grass look greener on the other side of the fence"*, and always true to the old, popular saying: *"Vodka warms you up, vodka cools you down, vodka will never do you harm"*. The familiar and frequent ring of vodka filled small shooter glasses bridged any social and ethnic divides, if only for the night, in uninhibited display of rare happiness in the midst of what seemed like a perpetual misery. Occasionally, someone brought out an accordion and tried his best to entertain the gathered crowd with his repertoire, while his fingers were still relatively agile and mind still able to recall the chords in a proper sequence. What followed was a mix of the most soulful Polish and Russian ballades, with the other partygoers soon joining in with their vocal accompaniment. The parties were becoming noisier and nosier as the time went on, frequently punctuated with a customary cry of delight, each time they raised the toast, exclaimed by one and followed by the rest: "*One hundred* years!" they shouted as an enduring wish for longevity, or *"Na zdrowie!"*, simply "To health!", and again usually initiated spontaneously by someone from the gathered group, and then shouted in unison by the rest, and it went on and on most of the night. By the end of the feast, any common etiquette inspired notions of civilized behaviour were dropped in lieu of more unpretentious norms of the wide-open swaths of eastern steppe, as the influence of the East was present in many aspects of their lives. One might say a temporary uninhibited relapse into "the way things have always been". That too of course, was an unequivocal testament to the proportional ethnic representation of the festive bunch. There was no telling though, when the jovial mood would take just as easily a somber turn, especially when vodka induced patriotic sentiments suddenly surfaced, and the toasts exalted the undeniable historical greatness of their respective nations, or prominent national heroes, dead or alive. Finally, what a good and friendly get-together would be without bringing up the present, and the customary litany of appropriate epithets hurled towards the omnipotent, ever-present and supposedly benevolent ruling Party, and its top apparatchiks, from the General Secretary and down to the local party scumbags, who liked to portray themselves as exceptionally compassionate, generous, almost philanthropic father-like figures. The usual celebratory festivities for whatever reason, were so foreign to Mrs. Brodski and Alek, that she made up her mind long ago to have no part in the social scene of the town, and never let her son anywhere near them, and thus increasing their isolation. It didn't go unnoticed, viewed with suspicion and itself became the subject of malicious speculations among the locals. Alek was beginning to recognize, that he reached a different point in his life, when with his rapid physical changes came a sudden realization, although disheartening and unnerving, that he disagreed with them all, even his own mother, and developed a somewhat hostile attitude towards anyone who happened to cross his path in a verbal confrontation. It suddenly dawned on him that he wasn't a little child anymore, and his problems were his own, of his own creation, and most likely beyond his mother's capacity to solve them. For years she was always there to intercede on his behalf when things got out of hand in his infrequent interactions with peers and adults alike. But now, what is she to do? She'd have to deal with the local thugs roaming the streets out of sheer idleness and boredom, like a pack hangry young wolves descending on unsuspecting pray, and it mattered little whether provoked or unprovoked, a reason could always be found. It was hardly a coincidence, but it seemed that rather by the law of mutual attraction they stuck together, growing up through childhood, adolescence and eventually adulthood.

Most townsfolks were well aware of the different small groups at various stages of their maturity and distressing existence and tried to live around them as best they could.

Alek with his usual serious demeanor looked at his mother with a strange curiosity, seemingly detached from the proximity of her presence, the necessary interaction and the usual emotional bonds that have bound them together for as long as he could remember. In a strange way he was mesmerized by her silhouette, as she was sitting there silently on the sofa, without a slightest movement, as if frozen in time. He admired her tall, slim and uniquely graceful figure, her refined profile and that sophisticated poise, even while sitting, that reminded him of the biggest film stars of the day, foreign and domestic he had heard about or seen in magazines.

The shoulder-length wavy, black hair, big dark eyes with long eyelashes, her nose with a slightly high bridge, and full lips which so often smiled back at him when their eyes met. The whole figure emanated an aura of a truly superior woman. Alek for the first time found himself looking at his mother differently, not so much as her small child, but rather as a man would look at a beautiful, newly met woman, with a fascination he had never experienced before. He was equally curious and embarrassed about it, with an accompanied profound feeling that she somehow knew what he was thinking, which ignited a rare blushing on his otherwise pale face. "Dad was a lucky man", a thought crossed his mind, "too bad he hadn't lived long enough to see mother now. He would have been very happy. They all would have been happy." That followed by a brief mental probe into eternal mystery, why good people die? Just when they still have most of their lives ahead of them, suddenly cut short, leaving their loved ones in grief that never goes away.

They both were deeply absorbed in their thoughts and reluctant to disturb the vail of magical and mutually understood silence, when already so much has been said, a space was needed and perhaps it was better to leave some things unsaid. The higher providence overseeing it all, must do its sacred work, if one is to believe what was written in the supposedly divinely inspired texts, passed on for generations, deeply entrenched in all Western societies, unfailingly reminded of and reinforced by the Christian Church for several centuries. Sadly, in the past, the doubters, dissenters, idolaters, and unbelievers were met with clergy's wrath and paid the ultimate price by the millions, filling with its shamefull stories the indelible pages of true history books.

In the following days and weeks, a period of relative quiet set in the neighborhood. Any given day resembled the next uneventful day, and all seemed to fall into its own repetitious pattern, like a great circle that could not be altered, as if living through the same days and months over and over again. The weather was particularly uncooperative, but as expected in these parts at this time of the year. The nights were cold, marred by increasingly hard ground frost, and the days had their generous dose of bone chilling rain, often mixed with heavy, large flakes of wet snow. Gusts of bitter arctic air carried by relentless wind from the east, as always invited the customary comments among the town's folks: *"Nothing good has ever come to us from the east"*, meaning the big, always vigilant brother to the east, the Soviet Union, spanning two hemispheres and eleven time zones. The town's streets and sidewalks were quickly covered with overflowing rainwater and a layer of slush, in places virtually impassible at many surface indentations and potholes scattered about most sidewalks and streets, for years left in a state of utter disrepair, due to lack of funds and perhaps lack of will in equal measure. Occasionally someone's foot would fall one of the water-filled potholes disguised in the slush, and then a litany of curses and profanities usually followed, and so it went, day in day out.

"When the only whore in town had a toothache, the nightlife died down", townsfolks used to say jokingly on days like these, as a cynical, but possibly a quite accurate testimony to the town's

size, isolation and backwardness. Seven or eight thousand people, and no one seemed to know exactly, inhabited this God-forsaken place year-round, which swelled regularly every Thursday for the farmers' market day, yearly church fair day, or May 1, otherwise known as The May Day, or International Workers' Day, or days just before Christmas or Easter holidays.

After the war, when the newly re-drawn borders were shut for good by 1948, the town's population was about equally split between Poles, Ukrainians and Byelorussians, or Russians as they were generally viewed, since nobody quite knew what the difference between them was anyway. They all seemed to live peacefully together in this small, decrepit border town, one might say, bound by the Slavic peoples' common threads: family, hard labour, women, music, good sense of humour and vodka, lots of vodka...Probably the only staple in plentiful supply in these parts. The local ruling authorities undoubtedly thought, as long as those simpletons had plenty of cheap vodka, they'd be happy and keep quiet in a perpetual cycle of spirits induced happiness on Saturday or Sunday night, or even an odd day in between, and naturally a nasty hangover recovery the next day, with severely diminished cognitive faculties. Although, the drinking for the most part was a weekend tradition, many dwellers especially of the lowest social class were seldom seen sober between the weekends, and left those who few who were strictly abstinent, or mostly sober or pretended to be, scratching their heads; "When do they work?", "How do they work?". "How can they work?" Well, somehow they did it, trudging along at half capacity, as not to exert themselves, carefully nursing their indispositions, with seriously dulled senses and diminished physical faculties, hopeless and apathetic, seemingly just like the rest and everything and just about everyone else in this bloody country.

The tallest building in town was the church, a house of God, with a steeple in a shape of a square cube at the base and a higher pyramid-shaped upper part, crowned with a metal cross. The tower housed a large brass bell that rang often, every day, even few times a day, and no one quite knew, why the hell it rang so often? Some folks, definitely a slim minority, would curse and spit whenever that big, hollow monster rang out, especially those who couldn't care less about The Church, its teachings, and everything else it stood for. As for the baptisms, marriage vows or the last rights, they thought they could do without them and would do just fine, and if anything, over the years would save themselves a significant amount of hard-earned money.

The congregation was mostly Polish, the faith Roman Catholic, and at the head of the St. John's parish was Father Antoni Pukalski, one of town's best known dwellers, and without a doubt its undisputed moral authority, at least among majority of Poles. He was well known for his occasional fiery homilies on the sins of the flesh, which sparked passionate debates among some faithful, or equally dismissive derision among the others, quick to point out Father Antoni's presumed hypocrisy. Father Antoni was a man in early sixties, although appeared much younger, never having to do an honest day's work in his entire adult life in a traditional sense. He was of middle height and build, somewhat larger arround his waist, with lively dark eyes that seemed to dance around, as if constantly on a prowl, and then suddenly stop and stare with piercing intensity at the object of his newly found interest, or desire. His most prominent facial feature was a rather big, crooked and red nose that protruded from his pale cheeks like sacristy's old, deformed door handle. That nose alone was a frequent object of mockery among the parishioners, those who cared enough to even notice. Some folks even swore on their ancestors' graves that they knew or had seen "the red nose" gulping sacrificial wine in the back rooms of the compound's quarters. The sessions, although supposedly infrequent, lasted well into the night, apparently sometimes in the company of his devoted Miss Klementyna, an eager servant and maid, frolicking and mischievously playing hide-and-seek like a child with the playful priest. She actually lived on the premises, in one of the adjacent small, but tidy and cozy rooms, dividing her time between the seemingly never-ending chores and prayer. The story had it that, Miss Klementyna, now in her mid-forties, had succumbed to temptations of the flesh at a young age of just 16. Allegedly, the culprit was her distant, much older cousin. Those were the times when girls whose innocence was so suddenly and irrevocably pierced, were disowned by their families, especially in profoundly devout, conservative circles, and thrown out of the house to restore the family's honour. From that time on, Miss Klementyna decided to devote her life to God and vowed to modesty, chastity and obedience, in accordance with strict Catholic guidelines of former generations. Although she had earnestly tried as a novice to a convent, she didn't actually last there more than a year for an unknown reason, since she has never wanted to talk about and thus has not revealed the cause, at least publicly. The good, pious woman eventually somehow ended up as a joyful, deeply religious and entirely devoted housekeeper, servant and companion to the parish priest Father Antoni Pukalski and his much younger assistant, Father Feliks Babinski. Yes, a bundle of joy she was; cheerful, bubbly, although a little on a plump side, but still quite attractive and desirable by any standard. According to great many familiar with the intimate workings of The Church, being close to the parish priest, meant being as close to God as one could get, at least in this town. The other house of warship, but a little less prominent of course, in the eastern part of town, closer to the Soviet Union border, was the Eastern Orthodox Church, which catered to the Russian and Ukrainian faithful. The parish priest Vladimir, or "The Pope" as he was most commonly called for some reason, a good friend of Father Antoni from the Catholic diocese, was a man of about fifty, or perhaps just a year or two older, and unquestionably the biggest inconspicuous womanizer this town has ever seen. In fact, his reputation was by then well established in the entire county. It was rumored that Pope Vladimir's clandestine holy services were in considerable demand among devout parishioners of female gender. Many folks openly and sarcastically speculated, that he was "dipping his aspergillum" in some "unholy waters" and wielding it indiscriminately. It was a fact, that Greek Orthodox priests, unlike their Catholic counterparts were allowed to marry and some did so, preferring stability of a family life, lest they be tempted by the devil and succumb to the weakness and temptations of the flesh. The majority of the Greek Orthodox clergy however didn't marry and for all the right reasons. It must be said, those were true believers, who wholeheartedly devoted their lives to Christ and his teachings. Still there were those among them, who preferred to stay single, but it didn't mean celibate, oh no...The priesthood gave Father Vladimir and his Catholic counterpart a unique opportunity for a close, devotional contact with many young and middle-aged discreet and eager women in town and its outskirts and the surrounding villages, who craved the special, personal attention bestowed upon them by the good shepherds. Among them were many women terribly mistreated and neglected by their own hard-working men, gone for most of the day or "indisposed" on any given day, and who'd rather tenderly caress their ploughing horses, but completely forget about their wives' big, firm and bouncy bosoms in desperate need of at least some attention. Besides, those big, hard and insensitive hands with abundance of furrows and crevices were not something to look forward to for any woman, in case the busy farmer eventually noticed his wife's existence. It must be added however, that few female parishioners upon whom was bestowed the privilege of an intimate encounter, felt a pressing need to brag about being uniquely selected by either of the two men of God for a special blessing, a personal consecration one might say. In this world and in these parts, it was an honour indeed, to be able to say at the end of their miserable, tumultuous lives with unwavering pride and a hint of nostalgia when old, nearing the end, bent in half and trembling: “I’m happy to say, I was consecrated by his Excellency Pope Vladimir, or Father Antoni himself.”

Pope Vladimir fell into the category of a married man with a family, whether by design or accident, it was impossible to tell. His own greatly pious wife Kalyna was rather unattractive, stout and perfectly domesticated woman, whose dedication to her husband was unwavering, in spite of abundant unmistakable signs and echoes of his occasional transgressions. Kalyna, an all-around sickly woman, looked old and worn out for her age, with signs of constant worry and distress on her plain and pale face. One might even feel some understanding and sympathy for the poor preacher, if sex was the last thing on his mind, if and when it came to it, when paralyzed with fear, as she dropped her dentures in a glass and turned off the lights. The pride of the family, Kalyna’s total devotion and pre-occupation were two pretty teenage daughters. Especially the elder one, Tamara was a frequent object of attention of many mostly dim-witted local boys, some clearly on a brink of mental retardation, showering her with whistles and stupid, lewd remarks. Tamara wasn’t the only one given this special attention, in fact any reasonably attractive girl in their view, that came upon this group of idle misfits, was certain to be met with the same fate. There always seemed to be few small groups of those local thugs here and there, standing around for no apparent reason, or playing some kind of game with small coins, or just walking somewhere, but certainly not in the direction of school. Few younger ones, those in the latter years of childhood were walking around with slingshots and mindlessly shooting at anything that moved; birds, cats, dogs, and sometimes even windowpanes of randomly selected homes just to have a little fun. Then the little rascals ran away laughing, as if what it was the most amusing prank under the sun. Other boys and teenagers unassociated with these small gangs were equally susceptible to the bullying and harassment and got out of their way the best they could. Over the years these teenage hooligans, as they grew in age and experience would become the town's fearsome, well-seasoned criminals, and to be avoided. They were all officially unemployed and had absolutely no intention of even looking for a meaningful employment but lived off and with their aging or old parents and supplemented their subsistence with petty crime. The hoodlums had connections with like-minded thugs in the district town, and on occasion in a coordinated effort embarked on a bigger score, a hit to be celebrated and made them proud. Needless to say, soon the bandits were bragging about it. Naturally some ended up in jail at one time or another, and disappeared from the scene for several months, a year or a few, but there were always the younger ones coming up the ranks to fill the void, and so it went on in never-ending cycles for generations.

Thursdays was a farmers' market day in town, and it was always held at the same location for as long as anybody could remember. It was at the end of a short cobblestone side street, near the town's centre, which at its very end flared into a sizable unpaved lot, resembling a large cul-de-sac, and adjacent to a small, overgrown, and perennially neglected city park. It was an ideal location for an open-air market of this kind. Many peasants, farmers and tradesmen from surrounding villages, poured into town by bus, by train, on foot, horse drawn carriages, or some the obviously well to do, by their own automobiles staffed beyond capacity with goods and wares for sale or barter. Many locals also joined in these weekly affairs peddling the fruits of their labour, their services, or variety of manufactured, home-made products to the extent that the local authorities would allow such private enterprises, or goods brought from across the border, the Soviet Union. It was a much anticipated, feverish event, fulfilling the basic needs of the people, since the state-ran stores and services were always lacking, with chronic shortages of the basic necessities. The town came alive on those days, and inhospitable weather had little or no effect on attendance. They were all used to it and well prepared. Nevertheless, the people knew what to expect, were well bundled up and adapted to sustain themselves even in the worst of conditions, with a little help of few shots of vodka, with flasks hidden in in the thick layers of their heavy overcoats. There was always the option of a quick dash to a nearby restaurant, well stocked with their own supply of vodka bottles for the weekly occasion. For many participants, mostly locals, the market day was not only an occasion to buy many much-needed high quality organic foods, but also a day to socialize, meet friends and acquaintances, smoke cigarettes, drink and talk while moving and stomping their feet, while frantically rubbing hands to avert the advance of the penetrating, bone chilling cold. There was the ever-present vapour mixed with cigarette smoke hovering around small groups of men standing around, engrossed in animated conversations, occasionally punctuated with outbursts of profanities or a loud laughter. The market displayed a colourful array of fruits and vegetables, good selection of dairy products, and always visibly restless chickens, turkeys, ducks, geese, rabbits, and piglets in wooden crates awaiting their fate. The market provided a great opportunity for local as well as visiting craftsmen and tradesmen from around the county to display their various products, such as stools, chairs, little tables, chests, cutting boards, rolling pins, tools and ladders to be bought or sold. At this time of the year, always present were fur pelts and new or hardly worn full length fur coats. The toymakers were also in full force on most Thursdays with their wooden blocks, clocks, simple trucks, wagons and figurines of various shapes and sizes. Also, there were usually few sellers of toys from the Soviet Union; ingenious state made products, which were actually in great demand. Their toys were quite different and had that distinctive, unmistakable Russian appearance, and above all were not readily available at any state shops in Poland's eastern peripheries. The most popular among the boys were toy guns, which had everything one could wish for; the detailed look, battery operated function, colour, emitting realistic sound, often accompanied by bursts of flashing red lights. Those were single-shot handguns or automatic multi-shot rifles, spitting plastic pellets or little plastic-tipped darts at a touch of a trigger, while producing those unmistakable bullet discharging sounds with rapid red flashes. For the girls, Russian dolls were a must. Not only that they closely resembled real babies or downsized little girls in their actual appearance, but they also closed and opened their eyes, moved their lips, arms and feet, and best of all, were able to make few basic universal sounds, like "Mama", or "Papa," or just a simple one-word greeting. The dolls' apparel was of the finest kind; exquisitely tailored colourful dresses, little socks and shoes. Every boy who had a sister, and who had one of those dolls, was sure to know the more intimate parts of her wardrobe, as well as what was underneath the underwear, and thus the first venture into the world of female anatomy was born. When disappointed by what wasn't there, was made up by imagination. The impressions were then sometimes eagerly shared with other boys in the neighbourhood. Some who seemed to know it all, or got carried away by their fantasies, or simply pretended to be more perceptive, who had an aura of experience around them and proclaimed to see a little more than others, perhaps fueled by their own experiences, could only utter with utmost certainty: "There is nothing there!"

The market was a welcome alternative to depleted and scarcely stocked government stores, and still met tacit, although somewhat reluctant approval of the authorities. Any independent activity, which in any way resembled capitalist form of production or manufacturing on a larger scale was not tolerated and was promptly shut down. The open-air market, and with it a small food growing, or manufacturing sectors was the limit of their tolerance and purported benevolence for the benefit of all. The Party knew increasingly well, they could not feed the populace under collective farm system in the essential food production chain or emulate the painfully obvious example of failure in the Soviet Union. Equally apparent was shortage of basic everyday services and availability of the most indispensable manufactured products. To avoid the most acute shortages, and in effect possibly a general discontent, The Party let the small markets flourish in their limited scope for the time being. It was universally understood that the time would undoubtedly come, and in fact many were absolutely certain, especially the government bureaucrats, that in not-to-distant future, the country would become the land of plenty under the expert guidance of the infallible Party. The abundance would flow like torrents of mighty rivers, flooding the countryside and the cities, to the envy of all the poor souls on the other side of the iron curtain and beyond. For once, the sacred communist credo: *"From each according to his abilities, to each according to his needs"* would be fulfilled and see the day of glory as proclaimed by Karl Marx. Those that doubted or opposed, would find themselves on the wrong side of history, and forever condemned literally and swiftly or eliminated. Those that eagerly embraced the ideology would be vindicated and prosper in the new progressive world order on epochal march towards new Enlightenment, liberation of the masses and workers' paradise. Although the paranoid authorities were concerned about even the slightest displays of public dissent, they had no reason to worry in this small town. People went about their lives preoccupied with hardships of everyday existence, and had little desire to trouble themselves with strange concepts of coming luminous future prophesized by that good, old, bearded man called Karl Marx. Very few people actually understood and even fewer took seriously his elevated ideology, although it's been a part of the latter years of elementary and middle school curriculum for two decades now. The proletariat, bourgeois or class straggles rang hollow and was the last thing on people's mind. One thing they all seemed to understand though, the right to private property, regardless of the communist propaganda, and considered it a God-given right, and they were prepared to defend it, if needed. Unlike their eastern Soviet neighbours across the border, who were stripped of all land in a massive collectivization and nationalization effort during Stalin's reign, Polish farmers enjoyed a substantial degree of autonomy. Here they were in force, every Thursday selling the fruits of their labour, and in return generate a modest income, or some, the most industrious among them, the daring and unapologetic risk takers, a rather significant income, which would allow them to buy much needed goods or services in return that the town had to offer and much more. Those few were in a position to acquire some generally considered luxury goods, big- budget items, like home appliances, motorcycles or vehicles. At those times, the government stores and services in the vicinity did their own brisk business, as the crowds swelled, causing long line-ups everywhere and naturally frictions among the locals and out of town folks. There was an undercurrent of subtle resentment directed towards the visitors from the villages, and occasionally tempers flared. The most common, perhaps spiteful, but largely unsubstantiated perception was that the "peasants" had no manners, wore old, tattered clothes, often muddy boots, and worst of all, they smelled of manure. There were also other points of contention, which many locals found irritating to say the least, like the fact that the outsiders seemed to have more money, or even a simple, quite irrelevant and trivial fact that many country folks flashed a line of supposedly gold or silver teeth every time they opened their mouths, and smiled or laughed wholeheartedly. Although, the town was small, but nevertheless it was incorporated in 1779, and the locals considered themselves a superior breed, city dwellers, despite the fact, that the town could hardly be called a city. Others found an issue with their horses, or rather what the animals always left behind, usually along the long stretch of the main street leading to the marketplace. It began from a large, empty lot near the church, which doubled as a parking lot and a resting place for the farmers with various horse carriages. The farmers, usually those with heavier loads unloaded first at the market, and then led the horse-drawn carriages back to the parking lot, often leaving a trail of steaming horse manure behind them, which needless to say, was so frowned upon and resented by town's folks. The others with lighter loads, or relatively fewer goods to sell, parked first and then carried their merchandise on foot the relatively short distance of about five hundred meters or so to the marketplace. The delivery often required making two trips, while somebody else was watching over the goods when they were gone, once at the market and then at the parking lot. Most of those with cars, trailers or modified wagons of all sorts, usually parked nearby on one of the town's side streets, and few vendors even at the marketplace itself, right behind their stalls and occupied privileged spots with a preferential exposure. That's just the way it has always been here, and nobody has ever questioned the natural order of things. The market beside its purpose as a commercial trading place, also served the locals and visitors alike as a place for interaction on a larger scale, and with it an invaluable source of information. One could often hear a lively conversation on variety of topics, from land cultivation, raising cattle, crops, availability of certain products, services or prices. Sometimes the subject of conversation was clearly on a lighter side, as participants swapped jokes, gossip or family stories. There were also groups of people who ventured into what was generally considered a "forbidden zone", and that was politics. Their understanding and interpretation of events, or people in the news was for the most part seriously lacking in substance and utterly naïve, in essence harmless. Most often than not, by the time the stories got to the market, they were most likely old news, or recycled several times since the original source, and Radio Free Europe was most likely the source. Eventually it would be so distorted and devoid of and credible information and valuable substance, it could be dismissed as mostly fiction or pure nonsense.

CHAPTER 5

MISS KLEMENTYNA, THE devout priest's servant and maid never missed the weekly farmers' market and enjoyed the atmosphere and its plentiful reservoir of goods. It was her weekly chance to get away from the highly regimented and often uncomfortable environment at the presbytery. She hurriedly scoured the stalls, knowing well what Father Antoni and his assistant Father Feliks particularly liked, and both of them were known for good appetite, especially Father Antoni. It was a challenge sometimes to satisfy the two gluttons and their visitors, some infrequent notable locals, clerics and visiting nuns from out of town. While hosting the visitors at various times, Miss Klementyna had her hands full trying to maintain, within reason of course, specific days of religious observations, as prescribed by The Church, besides the usual Christmas and Easter, but also everything in between and with it, periodic fasting. However, Miss Klementyna and the parish priest had a special understanding, and money was no object; there was plenty of it in the church's coffers. Ironically, quite often the same peasants dutifully coming to town for Sunday mass, and generously adding to the collection basket, were getting some of that money back from the purchases made by the church. Miss Klementyna supplied only the immediately needed goods for current consumption of the clerics, visitors, and of her own. However, the bulk of provisions were supplied by the farmers themselves, delivered and unloaded directly at the church compound. For the farmers, it wasn't just a convenient business arrangement, where the prices were usually fixed, with little room for negotiation, and Father Antoni more than willing to oblige without objection. For the suppliers, it was also a privilege to serve the town's highest and undisputed moral authorities, and in a process do good deeds, which certainly would not go unnoticed in heaven.

Mrs. Brodski too was out that day and mingled carefully among the folks at the unusually crowded market, despite the bad weather. As always, she was somewhat self- conscious and aware of the curious onlookers, either real or imagined. She thought that people stared at her for no apparent reason. At least the out-of-town folks couldn't have known her, she reasoned, so why had their eyes followed her, as she passed by? "Was it her obsession or paranoia?", she asked herself. She wasn't sure about it and many other things lately. She knew she looked differently than most other women in town, at least all those she had seen, or so she thought. On the other hand, there were many Jewish families living here before the war, and at least during its first two years of that horrible conflict. "Have they all forgotten them? Have they all erased memory of their neighbours and friends by now?"

Mrs. Brodski sometimes questioned, knowing well, she would never know the answer. Zofia was tall for a woman, and at forty-two years of age very slim, even skinny or bony one could say, but very agile. She moved with dignified, carefully measured strides, occasionally looking down at the path in front of her and sideways with her head held high, skillfully navigating between throngs of people standing or moving around in different directions. She was wearing a long black overcoat, the same she has worn for many years now, but it was still in a relatively good condition. Over her head she had a gray, thick wool shawl, and on her feet black, half-length boots, which although polished, betrayed considerable amount of time in faithful service. The weather was most unpleasant, dark, and gloomy with a mixture of bone-chilling, occasional drizzle and a light snow falling from the heavy, dark sky, with the temperature hovering just above freezing.

Mrs. Brodski went about her business, stopping for few necessities carefully planned in advance and within her means for the day, for there was no time for spontaneous negotiation, although it was almost always possible to bargain with the sellers. Nothing was written in stone. Soon she already had everything she needed but was still walking slowly and looking around for nothing in particular, but out of curiosity. This Thursday Mrs. Brodski was not in a hurry to get back home yet, it was barely past noon, and she still had plenty of time before Alek would get back home from school. Unexpectedly she ran into Maria Pavloska and was happy to see the old woman and her seemingly always smiling and radiant face. Mrs. Pavloska was equally happy to see Mrs. Brodski. They greeted and hugged each other warmly and planted kisses on both cheeks, as was the custom in these parts between family members or close friends. Although, they've known each other for quite some time now, bound together by the tragic incident with Alek, but in fact, it was just a courteous, casual acquaintance from the streets, which was sometimes impossible to avoid in this small town. Of course, there was a significant age difference between the two women. However, since Pavloska's visit, following that unfortunate event with Alek, there was an obvious affinity between them, much closer bond and understanding, almost like between two close friends indeed. They just stood there for a few minutes briefly exchanging polite remarks, then the latest family news, and eventually vowed to meet again soon, in private, preferably in Mrs. Brodski's home and parted with great sympathy.

When least expected, Mrs. Brodski felt somebody's hand slip under her left arm and forcefully grab her wrist. Frightened, she cried out and turned around abruptly. Instinctively, she jerked her arm back, trying to shake off the culprit, but she met the steely blue eyes of Commandant Sokolowski from the local police headquarters. He was dressed in full uniform, with a cigarette in his mouth, and like a repulsive lizard wrapped his cold fingers around her thin wrist even tighter. His narrow lips under a characteristic, small brown-reddish mustache, twisted in a stupid, disparaging smirk, as he cynically uttered:

"Good day! I hope I haven't frightened you, Mrs. Brodski. Don't be afraid, let's just go for a little walk. I'd like to talk to you. Shall we?"

"Let go of my arm, please," she snapped back at him decisively. Sokolowski visibly content with himself, completely ignoring what she just said, and in what would in fact appear from a distance a gentlemanly manner, steered her out of the market, and onto the street.

"Sir, what do you want from me? Let me go, please let go of my arm", insisted Mrs. Brodski with increasing irritation.

"Please don't be concerned, do not be afraid, madam. We must talk in private. There were too many people at the market."

"I'm not interested in anything you have to say, Sir"

"Oh, please don't say that Mrs. What I have to tell you is important, and not only concerns your son Alek, but you as well."

"But please let go of my arm; it hurts", she said with anguish in her voice.

"I'm sorry Mrs. I didn't mean to hurt you, just let us go out a little further", said the Commandant and then released her arm. Mrs. Brodski sighed with relief, slowed down, switched hands carrying the canvas bag with the goods she bought at the market to the just freed hand, and looked at Sokolowski with anticipation.

"Let's keep walking, Mrs. You should not be afraid; I just want to talk to you. I'd like to tell you something you might be interested in. I'm not your enemy, and actually you will be surprised if I tell you, I'm on your side. I sympathize with you Mrs. Brodski a great deal and I'd like to think, I know what you're going through."

"You? What are you saying?"

"Yes, I am very sympathetic to your situation", assured Sokolowski again.

"What do you know about me? What do you know about my situation? I'm afraid you have no idea what you're talking about", she countered right back.

"I know a lot more than you think, Mrs. Let me explain...You see I thought you'd come back to the station, you know, following your visit, but you never did. Frankly, I don't blame you either. It must be quite difficult for someone like you to deal with matters of this nature, and with the police in general. I understand."

They walked slowly in silence, arm in arm for several more meters, before the Commandant looking to the side at Mrs. Brodski picked up the conversation again.

"First of all, in the matter concerning your son Alek, I want to assure you, I treat this most unfortunate incident, if I may call it so, very, very seriously. I've personally conducted a full and thorough investigation. I've talked to my son at length, and so did my wife. I've talked to his friends, all those that could possibly hang out with Adam, and lastly, I've talked to their parents. I'm sorry to tell you this, but they all say, they all had nothing to do with assaulting your son. They don't even know Alek, they don't have the slightest idea who he is, or where you both live. Believe me Mrs. Brodski, I'm a father and I care about my son, and the last thing I want, is to raise a hooligan, a bandit under my roof, especially being in the law enforcement myself. I'm so sorry about this, but I'm sure I've left no stone unturned."

Mrs. Brodski suddenly stopped, her thin arms stretched down, disheartened and disappointed, but still holding the shopping bag in one hand, her shoulders fell forward and head slightly bent to one side, her sullen pale face stricken with profound sadness sank in resignation, and those big, dark eyes swelled with tears, looking helplessly at the Commandant. She then slowly turned sideways and looked ahead, towards some unknown, distant point where her anguished mind had just escaped. Sokolowski sensed her absence and disappointment, touched her arm and gently squeezed it, trying to regain her attention and tried to explain.

"Mrs. Brodski, you must understand, I know my son well. He can stir some trouble from time to time. Believe me, I and my wife had our hands full more than once. Let there be no mistake, he can cause some mischief, as any teenager would, but nothing really serious, you know young people nowadays, but nothing of the kind you told us. No, never anything like that. Adam would never physically assault anybody, especially a younger boy. No, never. His friends are not the kind either. I know them well; they are good kids. There must be a mistake; your son must have mistaken them for someone else."

Mrs. Brodski resumed walking. Sokolowski followed her instinctively and quickly caught up with her in a few long strides. Some passers-by looked at them indifferently and continued on their way. Just the sight of the police Commandant attracted attention here. They walked again side by side in silence for several more meters, both engrossed in their own thoughts.

"I knew it, I just knew it", said Mrs. Brodski quietly, as if to herself.

"What did you say, Mrs.?"

"Did I? Oh no, nothing in particular."

"I'm sorry," but you've just said something, I didn't quite catch that. Could you repeat it please, inquired the Commandant again.

"You know Mr. Sokolowski, I had a feeling this would happen. I should have listened to Alek. He wanted to go with me to the station that day I visited you, but I didn't want him to go through all this testimony and questioning; he had suffered enough. He's still just a boy. Sir, let me ask you this, do you want a confrontation with my son in the presence of your son and those other boys? Would you like us to face them in your presence?"

"No, no, that won't be necessary and completely counterproductive. I don't see how it could help matters in any way. In the absence of any witnesses, it would be your son's word against my son's word, or their word, and in the end wouldn't solve anything. Frankly Mrs., I consider this case closed."

"Mr. Sokolowski, how can you say that? What makes you so sure there weren't any witnesses?"

"Witnesses? Mrs. Brodski, for your sake, for our sake, let's just leave it at that, please. Trust me, it'll be better for all of us. Let's put it all behind us and move on. I'm really sorry that such a terrible thing happened to Alek, right here in our small, peaceful community."

The Commandant made an impression that he wanted to add something else but paused to let Mrs. Brodski respond. She didn't say anything, just looked ahead, out in the distance, while measuring out those equal slow paces on the uneven, gray, tiled sidewalk, as they walked hand in hand. All around seemed gray to her; the sky, the street, the buildings, the trees and even the people hurriedly moving in both directions, as if in some pre-conceived, obscure pattern. It all weighed heavily on Mrs. Brodski's already somber mood, as she tried to digest the cruel reality of what Commandant Sokolowski had just said, and to maintain an impression of a placid composure, as not to show him any weakness. The Commandant looked at her momentarily and acutely, as if trying to assess her state of mind, and now with a noticeably subdued and much gentler, almost concerned tone began again.

"The other thing I wanted to tell you is rather of a delicate nature, and I'm only going to tell you this, or rather make a friendly suggestion, because in spite of what you may think about me, or perhaps have heard of me, I actually sincerely do care about people. Frankly, I don't even know how to tell you this. I'm afraid you might take it the wrong way. Nevertheless, please don't be offended, I'm really concerned about you and your son, of course."

"I have no idea what you're trying to tell me Sir, but do not worry, I won't be offended, and I won't hasten to judge", said Mrs. Brodski.

"Well then, I dare to think I know how you've been struggling on your own over the years as a single mother in this town. Opportunities are few, and let's face it, life is not easy around here. I fact it is hard, not only for you, but for all of us, I must confess. I should not be telling you this, but there are days I'm disillusioned myself, as much as I'm trying to be hopeful and believe what we're all told by our government. What I want to ask you in all sincerity Mrs. Brodski, have you ever given a thought about adding a man to your life, like a companion you know, like meeting someone?"

"No, I haven't, and I don't think I will. This is the last thing on my mind. Why the hell would I want a man in my life? You've said it yourself, life is hard around here. Why would I want to complicate it even more than it already is? I appreciate your concerns, and I trust you're sincere in what you're saying, but in spite what you're thinking, I'm doing fine on my own, or let's just say, I manage."

"Please madam, don't be defensive, it's just a suggestion. You seem to be implying that a man in woman's life is nothing but a burden, if I understand you correctly. How is that?" asked Sokolowski curiously, surprised by Mrs. Brodski's decisive answer.

"Sir, I haven't seen another man since my husband's Jakub's death about six, seven years ago, and I certainly don't intend to now. Yes, I'll be honest, I've struggled at times financially and in many other respects. I know perfectly well that my son needs a father, a role model, especially now in his adolescence. I just cannot imagine a local Gentile man within intimate proximity, if you know what I mean. It's out of the question."

"Mrs. Brodski, I'm afraid this is not how I see things, on the contrary, this is exactly what you need. I know what you're saying about your son in need of a male role model in his life. I and my wife have it all, and I think we're a good, close family, but I'd be lying, if I say it's all nice and easy with our two boys. We have our challenges, like this alleged recent incident with your son, just to name one, but I'm absolutely convinced it is much better to share support and responsibilities between the two of us. I don't know what it is with you people about someone being a Gentile, as if it is a curse? Is that how you see us? How does it change anything? Does it really matter?"

"Maybe to you Sir it doesn't, but to me it makes a world of difference. The prospect of a middle-age Jewish widow being seen with a local Slavic man is just unthinkable. What would people think? What would they say? Have you thought about that?"

"I think you're exaggerating and needlessly concerned about that. There are few eligible man of your age around town, who are interesting and would be interested, I'm sure. Why not open to the possibilities, and give it chance?" continued Commandant Sokolowski.

"There might be possibilities, but there is only one certainty in my opinion, none of those men you're talking about is suitable; all religious beliefs aside, as far as I'm concerned," responded Mrs. Brodski.

"I'd respectfully disagree with you here. I know there are few respectable widowers, just like you are, and there are few old bachelors, who for whatever reason never married, and few widowers that I came across. They are basically good, hardworking men. Some of them in fact are professional, descent men, with good positions and salaries and their own homes."

"Well, I haven't heard of or seen any men that you've just described. Besides, as I said, I'm not interested, and that's the end of it."

"You haven't seen any good men, and you won't meet any if spend most of your time at home. There are different social functions around town from time to time for different occasions, you know. It's not only the church that people go to. As a matter of fact, I don't go to church myself, and not only because of my position or beliefs, but that's a different story."

They walked in silence for two or three minutes, passing some old, decrepit, gray buildings, passersby going about their business, the church, and a small group of people near the entrance to the church compound, who looked at them with interest. They all politely bowed their heads with respect at the sight of Commandant Sokolowski and greeted the couple courteously. The Commandant reciprocated kindly, and seemed to relish the attention given him, however brief it was. It only added to his aura of his importance, which was only too visible in his manner, head held high, and a meaningful smile on radiant face. Soon the Commandant picked up the conversation where they left off.

"I just want to add something Mrs. Brodski, so there are no misunderstandings. Everything that I've said to you today stays between us, so please don't share it with anybody, not even your own son Alek. Do you understand? It is a very delicate matter, as I said before, and we don't want any trouble. We're practically neighbours, it's such a small town…I wish you well, I truly do, Mrs. Brodski. I hope you'll take my advice, at least give it some serious thought, if you know what I mean. As for your son, I'm sorry once again, but there is nothing I can do. I've done all I could, to be fair. If there is anything else I can do for you, or help you with, I'll be happy to. You know where to find me."

"Mr. Commandant Sokolowki, I must tell you, I'm greatly disappointed. I don't think justice has been served or ever will be. I've realized more than ever, we cannot count on anyone here, not even the police to protect us from the ongoing harassment. I had hoped that some measure at least would be taken by the police. Obviously, I was mistaken; I can only blame myself for being so naïve. In retrospect, I should have never gone to the police station in the first place," summed up Mrs. Brodski bitterly.

"I'm sorry you feel that way. There is nothing I can add to that, but I assure you Mrs. Brodski, I have a great empathy for what you're going through as woman and a single mother. You're perhaps angry, and frankly I don't blame you. I'm sure you wish things would be easier, but don't we all? If one was to believe what the priests are preaching, it will be easier for some, a paradise in the afterlife. Of course, not for someone like me, a habitual sinner, a tormentor, if one was to believe what's been said about me, but certainly a saintly character like you."

The Commandant then looked curiously sideways at Mrs. Brodski and a managed a forced, ironic smile. He then quickly added: "Please take into serious consideration all that I've said to you today, and as I said before, please keep it all to yourself. Good day, Mrs. Brodski!"

Commandant Sokolowski then turned around abruptly, and hastily walked away in the direction they came from. Mrs. Brodski somewhat stunned by the sudden end to their conversation, made a half turn and looked at the quickly distancing tall figure, and quietly said: "Good day…" She stood there for a few seconds motionless, as if frozen, unable to move and to make any sense of what had just happened, then just as quickly composed herself looked around and she too walked away. She hurried back home, where Alek was most likely back from school and as always, anxiously waiting in anticipation of mother's return. Over time it became a routine, both were worried if either one of them wasn't home at the expected time, knowing well, either one or the other could have been an object of an unpleasant incident, whether in fact real or imagined, they were worried, nevertheless. Over the course of just the past year, mother and son experienced their share of indignities at the hands of neighbours and strangers alike, as if just the daily grind of life itself wasn't enough. It was however not that unusual for anyone else to experience similar episodes, for such was the reality of life in these parts; unforgiving, with all its hardships in the daily struggle for survival.

The weather was quickly turning into a full-blown winter with increasingly bitterly cold air and accompanying penetrating, easterly wind with a usual almost daily dose of light snowfall, which within just a few days covered the town and country fields with a thick white blanket and transformed life for its dwellers into a survival mode even more so. It was as if a tradition among the folks here at about this time and every year, when people expressed their surprise at the early onslaught of winter, its particular intensity, and as always summed it up with the same familiar line: *"Nothing good ever came to us from the east."* All-around the town and villages the preparations for Christmas were in full swing. Miraculously the stores appeared to be better stocked than usually, at any other time of the year. Surprisingly, the assortment of goods was noticeably wider than before, as if by a well-planned, premeditated government policy, coordinated with the local administration, to project indisputable image of The Party's wisdom, benevolence and an infallible economic policy in achieving another successful, consecutive five-year plan. Meanwhile, along the way, carefully cultivating the image of resultant growing prosperity in every corner of the new socialist motherland.

Despite the increasingly colder weather, the town became considerably livelier. It seemed there were significantly more people on the sidewalks and in the stores, more horse drawn carriages, cars and supply trucks on the streets and of course the farmers' market was also busier than ever. As always, freshly cut natural Christmas trees, spruce or young fir were in great demand. The trees emitted such strong, unmistakable aroma of the forest, that it instantly brought back memories and nostalgia of the past Christmas celebrations in the buyers, sellers and onlookers alike. Just the smell of the trees alone could elicit sighs and smiles on peoples' faces, as they changed hands. As always, at this time of the year, there were also few enterprising vendors and small manufacturers who defied the set rules, in a country that officially banned capitalist-style private enterprise of any size. Those merchants produced and sold products that were not readily available, or scarce in the government ran stores, and thus were met with a tacit acceptance by the authorities. Chronic shortages over the years were the norm, at times rampant and acute, to a point of becoming a fact of life, rather than an exception. Especially the eastern outskirts of the country, including these parts, were particularly affected, in fact neglected as most people felt, perhaps not even taken into account in any centralized economic plan of the ruling Party. People quickly learned to fend for themselves and fill the void. Ingenuity turned into action, and a significant sector of private small enterprises flourished, right under the radar of The Party bureaucrats and its extension, the guardians of law and order, the People's Militia. The weekly market was the best example of that unofficial transformation, from dogmatic socialism as the basis of economic development, under the banner of collective control of the means of production and self- sufficiency, to a vibrant sector of small private entrepreneurship. Especially the last two Thursdays and the last few days before Christmas the market was overflowing with farmers' goods, manufactured products and variety of small livestock dead or alive, poultry, fish, fruits, vegetables, furs coats, pelts, hats, mittens, toys, and of course wide variety of colourful Christmas ornaments or gifts. Shopping at the market during those days was more than just a necessity, it was an unforgettable experience and not to be missed. In fact, it became as if an extended holiday season, leading to and culminating in an ancient Slavic Catholic tradition of Christmas Eve on December 24. Very little has changed in these parts over the years. The whole town in this God-forsaken part of the world had its own truly special flavour, a taste and smell unlike anywhere else, where its inhabitants lived for better or worse from birth till death.

CHAPTER 6

THE MIDDLE OF December 1967, just like the year before, was a unique and much anticipated occasion to buy and sell, to browse, socialize, to see and to be seen, to present oneself to the community, or to meet people otherwise rarely seen, if that's what one wished for, or perhaps unintentionally could not avoid at any rate, and later was glad to see them, nevertheless. Even the sizable population of Orthodox Christians of Ukrainian and Russian descent were out in full force taking advantage of the opportunity for their own upcoming Christmas celebrations shortly after the New Year, on January 7. People were buying, bartering and haggling over prices, standing around in pairs or small groups and talking loudly, whispering or bursting with laughter while flashing their precious gold or silver dentures, as was the trend of the day. Out in the cold December air, clouds of vapour and cigarette smoke hovered above people's heads as they intermingled, bartered, talked and socialized. The atmosphere and smell of the entire market and much of the town's centre in those days was truly unique and irresistible. For many folks the yearly event has become an integral part of their existence, a temporary reprieve from the otherwise hopeless misery. Every moment to be enjoyed and savoured, like a rare, exquisite delicacy, and then warmly remembered and talked about for several weeks after.

In the evenings, lights on Christmas trees started to appear in the windows of many homes, adding charm and mystery to the aura of this festive holiday season, especially when the town was quiet by then, people were back in their homes after a day full of activities, and a light snow was falling from the sky, sparkling in the dim, yellow streetlights perched high above on tall, wooden lamp posts, lined up along few major streets, while the rest of town was drenched in almost total darkness.

Alek liked this time of the year, not because they celebrated Christmas in any particular and meaningful way in his household, being Jews, but it was impossible not to be affected by all that was happening around town. Other than his grade eight classmates at school, outside he didn't have anyone he could call a true friend. His school relationships didn't translate into friendships in his private life after school, not for lack of trying, but mainly because it seemed, he had so little in common with them, and vice versa. Somehow most of the school friendships were already formed, and he was left out once again, as every year. Alek didn't attend any regular religious studies or seminars organized by the church, and which most of the boys and girls dutifully attended as an extracurricular subject. He didn't go to either one of the two Christian churches in town, and he didn't celebrate any of the Christian holidays, particularly Christmas and Easter, and neither anything in between. The school was out usually few days before Christmas, but there was always a rather well celebrated yearly event for children of grades five to eight at the school he attended, and grade eight being the last year before graduating and moving on to middle school. This social event was usually referred to as "Winter Ball", although some called a Christmas Dance, in spite of the strictly secular system of education in the country. Every year it was held at about the same time, give or take a few days, Saturday or Sunday, followed by a general dismissal for the winter break. For many boys and growing teenagers it was a much anticipated event, which gave them a first closer look at girls long secretly admired in classrooms, but now dressed for the occasion in pretty new dresses and looking their absolutely best. It was a chance to make first awkward advances and stake out their claims, since more than one teenage boy was always interested in the same girl. The girls certainly relished the attention, but also had their own favourites as well, secretly whispering amongst themselves and exchanging furtive glances. Those that were reluctantly hauled to these events by one or both of their proud parents were visibly embarrassed by the fact, and once they found themselves in the main room where most of the festivities took place, which was the school gymnasium, they eagerly grouped with other boys and girls, desperately trying to avoid their parents throughout the evening. Quite often it was not an easy task, since some parents were equally determined to see their offspring dance with a boy or a girl, and if possible, to take a precious photograph, and that was the last thing the children wanted, especially the boys. It meant a total humiliation, that would linger on in their memories for months. Traditionally, a live band composed of local talent played the current, most popular pop tunes while the children ate snacks, drank soda and danced or pretended to dance the best they could, often encouraged by their snooping and intrusive parents, or even overzealous teachers. For many children it was their first attempt at dancing with the opposite sex, and at that particular, although fleeting moment, the most important event in their short lives, to be remembered for many years to come, or perhaps even lifetimes. To touch a girl, other than one's sister, and to feel the warmth of her hands and breath, closeness of her young body, stirring the most intimate senses and the smell of her hair was nothing short of a miracle, a dream fulfilled, almost the ultimate experience. Many, who before had only seen their parents in similar circumstances, regarded the ball as the first steps into adulthood, a source of pride or embarrassment for some, depending on one's performance dancing or making a meaningful conversation, and in effect a connection with the opposite sex.

Alek attended the Winter Ball only once in the past, but found it too crowded and most uncomfortable, left early with a negative experience and never returned. He was well aware he didn't quite fit in that environment and asked his mother not to pressure him to socialize with fellow students. Mrs. Brodski understood well her son's apprehension and never mentioned his need for attendance at the ball again, at least the last two years. However, Alek had a routine uniquely his own, he usually went out for an evening stroll alone, along the better lit streets, rarely venturing beyond the areas he has walked many times before. It was one of his favourite pastimes, his way of connection with the town and its dwellers, whenever he felt confident, safe and curiosity was impossible to resist, he just walked. Whenever Alek ventured outside, he had a strange habit of looking in the windows of people's homes, mostly from a reasonably safe distance and at nighttime, when the lights inside were on, and the curtains happened to be parted, or there were none at all. He could see everything what was going on inside, an inconspicuous peek into their lives, without them even knowing it. Occasionally he approached the windows closer whenever he noticed from a distance a real family drama unfolding, right in front of his eyes. He looked curiously inside for a few seconds, and then crouched just below the windowsill for fear of his presence being detected, the consequences of which could be most unpleasant.

Most men in town and surrounding villages seemed rather short, as if they had their growth stunted in early childhood, and then could never catch up. To make the matters worse, for many their physical development in some mysterious way was often paired up with their mental progress as well. One would be mistaken though, to think: "harmless little fools they were." Undoubtedly some were fools, but even fools have their peculiar wisdom, and they were anything but harmless, and definitely not cowards. They were cocky little bastards, they were scrappers and ready to take on a man of almost twice their size, if such a man should unknowingly stray into town looking for adventure. A liberal dose of vodka gave that extra edge in courage, while subduing any remnants of rational thought. Any woman who had a misfortune to be married to such an abominable earthly creature could attest to that.

All those bloody-blue bruises, black, half-shut eyes, swollen and bloodied lips spoke for themselves. Alek has seen his share of domestic violence on his night excursions. He had seen and heard loud sobbing, wailing and outright screams of women being reprimanded by their drunken, out of control men for what was commonly referred to as "insubordination", and which usually happened at regular intervals. The women desperately pleaded: "Please, for God's sake stop it. Please don't…I beg you in the name of God. Oh please, for the children…please stop. I'm sorry, I'm so sorry…Do you hear?"

Those pleadings, those desperate cries only riled up the all-powerful beast even more, and a barrage of fists followed in a rapid succession.

"Shut up, I said shut the fuck up or I'll kill you, you stupid bitch", shouted the man as he pounded his helpless pray with his dirty fists. Such generous methods of dispensing marital love and affection were not unusual in these parts in certain mostly working-class circles, a bold and unequivocal statement who was the boss, and who was in charge around the house, lest it be forgotten.

On the day of the school Winter Ball, Alek decided to actually come near the school, the curiosity was overwhelming; he just couldn't resist the temptation of seeing for himself, what he's been missing for the past few years. It was a rather mild night for this time of the year with a steady, light snowfall, but he was bundled up well for the weather and not worried in the least. He stopped from time to time to listen for any sounds, if he wasn't being followed, but couldn't hear a thing and moved on. The snow crunched and squeaked beneath his heavy winter boots, as he left behind a trail of footprints in the fresh, white powder. Once near vicinity of the school building, he walked slowly, he didn't want to be seen, ready to hide in case the door swung open when someone entered or left the school unexpectedly. Alek came close to the gymnasium and circled around, listening to the music and muffled, incomprehensible voices coming from inside, and he felt sad. He looked high up and inside through a row of small, barred windows, but they were too high above the ground, and the only thing he could see, were dimmed lights and a kaleidoscope of reflected shadows, dancing around the ceiling. He moved away from the gymnasium, and slowly walked along the main wing of the building, housing several classrooms. Most of them were dark inside with lights turned off, but Alek was particularly drawn to those two that had lights on, casting yellowish beams onto the snow-covered ground just outside. He looked inside one room, but there was no one inside, just the rows of student desks and empty chairs, then a large teacher's desk upfront, and two blackboards behind it on the main wall, with something still written on them with white chalk. It had a surreal, eerie feeling, so Alek moved on, passing few dark classrooms, then almost at the end, another classroom with the lights on. There were two figures inside, a man and a woman. She was sitting on the teacher's desk with her legs crossed and he was standing near her, with an accordion in his hands, strapped over his right shoulder, and the man was quietly playing a most soulful ballade. Alek was startled by what he had seen, and impulsively ducked just below the windowsill, breathing heavily. He recovered quickly and slowly lifted himself up, just enough to see inside, without being seen himself. He recognized the faces; she was none other than Ms. Lubinska, the young and well-liked math teacher, consistently judged by male students as the most beautiful female teacher of the school, and quite possibly, one of the most beautiful women in town. His name was Mr. Buzynski; a rather handsome, old bachelor and a music teacher, who treated his job and the subject he thought as the most important of them all. Alek, standing on his toes, with both hands held onto a cold, thick and disfigured sheet-metal windowsill, which was rolled into a small half-tube at the end and covered with snow and ice. Ms. Lubinska was well dressed in a fashionable and quite daring for the occasion red dress, with a long cut along her right leg, right up to mid-thigh and a pair of gleaming black high heels. Mr. Buzynski wore a black suit, a white dress shirt and a necktie. They both must have taken a break from all the activities and commotion in the gymnasium and hid away, oblivious of the outside world. He played the accordion with utmost devotion, occasionally swaying gently from side to side, looking straight into Ms. Lubinska's eyes with a shy, but sincere smile on his lips, such that left no doubt, it came right from his heart. She was visibly moved, almost aroused, looking straight back at him, and she was blushing, overtaken by emotion. Alek looked at them for a moment as if mesmerized, then quickly moved to the side, away from the window, with his back against the cold concrete building wall, breathing heavily, looking ahead, thinking and observing the vapor coming out of his open mouth, as his eyes swelled with tears, and he was sad. He couldn't move for a minute or two, and just stayed there in the shadow, listening to the quiet sound of the accordion, but did not dare to look inside the classroom again. Alek looked around and there was absolutely not a soul around to be seen, just a few yellowish lights glistening in the distance, in the windows of residential houses along the nearest street about a block away, right across the schoolyard. The light snow was falling gently and quietly adding to Alek's strange, surreal feeling of despondency and loneliness. There was a pungent smell of burnt wood in the air, most likely coming from the chimneys of the dark houses across, with barely distinguishable outlines, which except for few low, old huts with lights on, didn't show any signs of life. It was time to move on and head back home Alek thought, where his mother was certainly concerned and waiting anxiously in anticipation of his imminent return, as usual whenever he went out and was absent longer than usual. Along the way Alek passed by a group of Christmas carol singers, who went from home to home, spreading the holiday cheer by singing joyfully by the front windows or near the doors of homes along the main residential streets of town, waiting for a gesture of best Christmas wishes, or good will from the occupants in a form of a small monetary donation towards a good cause, to the benefit of the most unfortunate in the community. It was a long-held tradition and always expected at this time of the year, as if it were an integral part of Christmas celebrations, leading up to Christmas Eve. The Church too had its tradition of visiting homes, with one priest going around town, taking well-known, most profitable routes, always accompanied by a devout altar boy, and the other priest in a hired automobile with a driver servicing the surrounding villages. A typical house call was usually short, taking just few minutes, unless prior special arrangements were made with Father Antoni for a longer stay. The priest mumbled few, barely comprehensible lines of prayer, blessed the home and its inhabitants with a sign of the cross, and a gentle, mischievous smile to the children, if they were present, then gave out to them small, coloured, flimsy pictures of Jesus, Virgin Mary with baby Jesus, the current Pope in the Vatican, or some other unknown, bearded saint, or a humble female saint wrapped in headscarf. An unwritten law, or a common understanding for as long as this tradition went on and anyone could remember, was that the visiting priest was to be rewarded with money, presumably as much as the family could afford, however most of those visited never had much money to spare. The visiting cleric by his simple verses of incomprehensible short prayer, meant to intercede with God on behalf of the visited family, then a sign of the cross and other awkward hand motions implied blessing of the household. The outcome, at least at that moment was never in doubt. The family was again in God's grace and abundance would flow into their lives like a torrent of pure mountain spring, from that day forward. The amount given, or "donation" as it was preferably called by the clerics, varied and perceived to be entirely voluntary. It of course depended on material wellbeing of the inhabitants, whose family name the priest knew in advance, and if not, just one look around the home was enough to know what to expect. Usually, the amount was an equivalent of about one half-day's work, or average day's wages, or in some rare cases in well-to-do families it could go up to one week's earnings, those who could certainly afford it and eagerly wanted to assure their place in heaven. In the poorer families, usually several coins were dropped into an open palm of the smiling priest's hand. If for whatever reason the inhabitants wanted the priest to stay a little longer, the noble visitor was invited to sit down, have a snack, a cup of tea or a quick shot of vodka "for the road", and with it the amount of "donation" went up from there. The stopover went on smoothly, as if a well-rehearsed procedure with mutually understood glances, bows, nodding and gestures, culminating with the priest finally taking the money, and like a skilled magician, drawing aside his long, black overcoat, underneath which he wore a black cassock and slip the money below it, into a specially made deep sack, hanging alongside and fastened tightly around his waist. Then the door, but just before leaving, followed the final wishes of Merry Christmas, Happy New Year and good night. It was not unusual for an argument to ensue following the priest's visit, when mostly the husband usurped the right to the name of a rational thinker in the family, and lashed out at his well-meaning, generous, perhaps a little naïve and unsuspecting wife: *"Wanda, you stupid woman, why the hell did you give that scoundrel so much?"* The anger had its roots in the wildly known teachings of the priests themselves, while preaching temperance, that poverty was noble, and a blessing, somehow it all didn't add up, considering the clergy's own, relatively opulent lifestyles.

The priests never visited the Brodski household, for they knew well, they were poor Jews, and as such lived in their own small world, which had very little in common with the prevailing Christian beliefs. Nobody quite understood, why the Jews didn't believe the origins of God and the whole Christian doctrine based on The New Testament, when in fact the writings derived from the Holy Land and that ancient Jewish tribe in the Middle East. The entire Christmas tradition as celebrated in this small part of the world only contributed to Alek's feeling of alienation from the life of the community, not only at this time of the year, but throughout other months, when so much revolved around observances of the Catholic Church's liturgical calendar of events.

Christmas was a time when the residents went to church at least once, mostly twice, almost certainly on December 24-Christmas Eve, and usually the next day on Christmas Day. Alek and his mother never went to church, and there was no synagogue left in the entire county and hardly any Jews survived. The few synagogues that existed in these parts before, were burned by the Germans during WWII and the Jews exterminated. Although, over the years some well-wishers suggested to Mrs. Brodski in no uncertain terms more than once, that it couldn't hurt, after all "We all believe in the same God", and "It would look good" and "People would notice", so went the arguments, but unconvinced they still stayed away. Similarly, they did not participate in any social gatherings or functions, since they were only a family of two and didn't have any close friends, and certainly no relatives. The people they knew were mostly acquaintances and neighbours, except perhaps for the recent addition of Mrs. Pavloska, which seemed promising. Family and close friends dominated the social scene at the time of Christmas, especially on Christmas Eve and Christmas Day, December 25. Traditional meals consisting of few or several dishes were served, depending on family's financial situation, supplemented with lively conversation, some Christmas carol singing, or listening to commercial recordings carried over seemingly endless flow of refreshments. Christmas Eve was always celebrated within the closest and extended family, if they happened to live in town, or few invited long-time friends considered a family. Very little alcohol, if any was consumed on Christmas Eve, since a tiring midnight mass was still awaiting them. The focal point of this gathering was breaking and sharing of thin, white rectangular wafers, signifying the body of Christ and exchange of best wishes by all and to all participants.

Mrs. Brodski and Alek spent those days at home, although on few occasions in the past they were invited to some of the neighbours' homes, and either declined, or went there for just a brief visit, sampled foods, exchanged good wishes, and went right back home. Perhaps three or four times since they came here, they were pleasantly surprised by a neighbour's knock on the door, who brought over some traditional Christmas food and best wishes to share. The time before Christmas and leading up to New Year was a time of intensified activity in the two government ran liquor stores, as well as clandestine booze distributing pit stop of Ivan Kurvichenko, also known locally as "Ivan the Terrible". This older, small-time bootlegger and a hermit was a bundle of unkempt hair, lips twisted in a menacing snare of a primitive, carnivorous primate with blood-shot, fogged up eyes and just a few teeth left. Despite his unsavory appearance, in reality Ivan was a good man, a gentle soul, leading an ascetic life, minding his own business, and doing a brisk business at Christmas time, while serving the community in his own way. He used to say with pride: "for domestic consumption only", but that's how it all started, and to his surprise the word got around, the business picked up, Ivan had to diversify and sell the overproduction of his hand-crafted, throat and gut-burning potions, with significantly higher alcohol content than the vodka sold in the government ran liquor stores. Over time Ivan perfected his formula and his equipment, added few flavours to the otherwise pure, twice distilled alcohol. Christmas was a time of the greatest demand, especially for the flavoured spirits like raspberry, cherry, honey or lemon. He didn't drink much himself, but if he happened to taste his own concoctions, mostly on special occasions, when he had unexpected visitors, or a regular customer who came just at the right moment when Ivan was in especially celebratory mood for no apparent reason, or the customer had an urgent need to share something "very important" with the secretive bootlegger. Those were indeed rare moments when Ivan opened up about his own past, although never revealed much, beside few general details about a great deal of suffering he went through in the past at the hands of NKVD, the Soviet secret police. He seldom smiled, and if, it was a reserved, barely discernable smile, but almost never laughed, at least nobody could actually recall seeing him laughing. Despite his rather serious demeanor, Ivan was a good-natured, serene man. Perhaps apart from the moonshine, he was best known locally for his wood carvings of sombre figurines of hunched, visibly distraught and suffering people. The subjects of his art were mostly peasants, beggars and martyred heroes who fought and died for a righteous cause, or few tragic patron-saints with what seemed like pained expressions on their contorted faces. Ivan's favourite, often repeated phrase was: *"The world changes in front of my eyes. Time is not on my side. I've lost and suffered much in the past and cannot afford to let anger and hatred consume the last years of my life."*

The other well-known, small local entrepreneur of a different kind was a long-haired mystic, a naturopathic doctor and healer, a long-time resident from the east, Afanasy Pizdogryzov. It was said, that his grandfather married to a Polish woman of noble descent, was exiled by the late and last Tsar Nicholas II to the furthest depths of Siberia for revolutionary and subversive activities against the state. Afanasy somehow managed to find his way to the eastern outskirts of Poland in the aftermath of World War II confusion, where just across the river to the east, there was nothing but the Soviet Union for thousands of kilometers, spanning two continents and nine time zones. The inherently adventurous man as Afanasy was, apparently had enough of the happiness in the land of his grandfather and decided to try his luck in the land of his grandmother. His supposedly God-given healing powers were first applied quite successfully on farm animals, and miraculously apparently, they were healed. Soon he discovered, there was a big demand for his services among the people, especially women. Naturally then, he moved into a more rewarding practice, laying his miraculous hands on their aching and ailing bodies, and as the word got out, they flocked to him like flies. In time, the healer became part of the local small, but tightly knit society, consisting mainly of town administrators, bureaucrats and their spouses, few teachers, a medical doctor and few shrewd small businesspeople. The business elite in fact were smugglers, engaged in officially banned for profit commodity trading, mostly precious stones, gold coins and furs, but also more common and affordable gold and silver jewelry, watches, cigarettes, tea, coffee and toys from the "land of plenty," from the Soviet Union to Poland and sometimes on to other neighbouring socialist countries, where supplies were scarce and demand great. The healer lived in a modest home, but large for a single man living in an old communal housing on the western side of town, in somewhat secluded, wooded area. Over theyears Afanasy managed to assemble an admirable collection of antique Russian icons, Orthodox crosses, Bibles, and variety of other religious artifacts, which were a reflection of this outwardly profoundly pious man's true character and interests.

December 27, a day after the second day Christmas coincided with 25th day of Hebrew month Kislev, the beginning of Hanukkah, or the feast of lights. Preparations were underway at Alex's home actually at sunset the day before, Tuesday December 26. His mother had done some final cleaning and cooking. The table was covered with clean, white cloth and the ritual nine-branched candelabrum, the menorah was in place, along with big, white plates, wide soup bowls on top of them and cutlery. It was set for three people.

"Who is the third one for, Mom?" asked Alek

"Mrs. Pavloska will be coming tonight", she answered.

She barely finished her sentence, when there was a knock on the front door, and sure enough Mrs. Maria Pavloska was standing there in the dark, all bundled up. Mrs. Brodski quickly turned on the outside light, nestled just above the door, and there she was smiling warmly, stretching out her arms in a friendly gesture of greeting, as if between old friends. Mrs. Brodski threw her arms around the old woman, planted a kiss on both of her cheeks and pulled her right in. Once inside, Pavloska removed her overcoat, fur hat and a shawl and with a purse on her arm proceeded further inside, enthusiastically encouraged by the happy host. Alek got up from the sofa and without hesitation approached Mrs. Pavloska, greeting her courteously and respectfully, like a well-mannered, young man should. She pulled out a small box out of her purse, handed it to Alex, and said:

"This is for you, young man."

"Thank you, thank you so much Mrs.," replied Alek, taking the little box hesitatingly in his right hand, with obviously surprised look on his face. Then he looked at his mother for a sign of approval, but she just smiled without saying a word, which he understood as a consent. Mrs. Brodski invited Pawloska to sit down on the sofa, while she still had some work to do in the kitchen, informing them both that the dinner would be served shortly.

"Do you need any help with it, Zofia?" asked the guest.

"Thank you dear, but I'll manage. I've got almost everything ready. I don't have anything extraordinary prepared, just the usual, but I hope you'll like it."

"Don't worry about me, do what you have to," said Pavloska, and then took a place at one end of the sofa, and furtively looked around the room with interest. Mrs. Brodski was in and out of the kitchen, pacing quickly and still managed to exchange few words with Maria. She then removed some dishes out of the living room cabinet and added few things onto the table. An intense, pleasant aroma of cooked food filled the entire living quarters, adding to the already cozy and rather joyful atmosphere of the home. Alek also made few trips to the kitchen, checking impatiently on the state of the dinner to be served, or perhaps to avoid being left alone with Mrs. Pavloska, and be engaged in an uncomfortable conversation, or subjected to questioning, as was usually the case with adults pretending to be interested in all the details of children's lives. Most teenagers found this so irritating, avoiding it at all costs, under any pretext, however feeble, and at the same time trying to maintain an impression of civility, politeness, and reciprocate with equally pretended interest in the lives of adults. Soon a large bowl of chicken soup arrived, and Mrs. Brodski invited them both to take a chair at the table and indicating that she would like to recite a quick prayer before they'd begin the feast, and added that it would be perfectly acceptable to remain seated in this informal setting. She then bowed her head down and proceeded with the following words: *"Blessed are You, ruler of the universe, who* has *sanctified us with his commandments, and commanded us to kindle the Hanukkah light. Blessed are you, Lord our God, ruler of the universe, who performed miracles for our forefathers in those days, at this time. Blessed are you, Lord our God, ruler of the universe, who has granted us life, sustained us, and enabled us to reach this occasion."*

Before they proceeded to eat, Mrs. Brodski asked Alek to light up the first candle on the menorah. He eagerly pulled out a box of matches from the top drawer of the cabinet the candelabrum was sitting on, and struck the first match, but was unable to light it up. He then repeatedly struck it few more times, until it broke. He was visibly embarrassed and unhappy with himself and nervously pulled out another match, struck it against the small box twice, and to his relief, it lit up. He had difficulty lighting up the candle, only succeeding almost at the last second, when the match between his fingers was already at its end, like a twisted, burnt little stick with flickering, dying flame. The all looked at the candle for several seconds, for it seemed at first that its small flame was about to die, but after the initial doubts, it slowly regained its strength and burst into full unhindered glow. They immediately began to eat the chicken soup with delight, the guests expressing much appreciation for culinary prowess of the host. Mrs. Pavloska gave a brief summary of Christmas celebrations with her family in the previous few days. Mrs. Brodski and Alek listened to it with genuine and sincere interest. Following the soup, Mrs. Brodski served the traditional potato pancakes, called "latkas", which she had already fried before, and kept them warmed up and ready on the stove. At one point and as every year Alek asked his mother for the story behind Hanukkah celebration, since he could never remember all the historical details anymore, and which seemed to him so distant and fantastic, almost like a fairy-tale, a good bed- time story. She reluctantly agreed, but didn't want to impose on Mrs. Pavloska, unsure how she would react to it, assuming she probably had little interest in the obscure, most likely fictional Jewish story. Nevertheless, Mrs. Brodski actually wanted to relate everything and what little she knew, well aware how lacking her knowledge of the history of her nation was. In the past she learned to rely on her husband Jakub when he was still alive, but since his untimely death, she and Alek were on their own, fending for themselves the best they could. Mrs. Brodski picked up the mostly empty dishes from the table, took them back to the kitchen, and came back with a pot of tea and a plate of biscuits. She then returned with teacups and small dessert plates, poured the fresh tea into each cup while standing, then sat down and slowly began the story.

"I'm not really good at this, but what I know is that it was a period in our history during Greek domination and influence in virtually every aspect of life of Judea. In 175 BC Antiochus, an Athens-born warrior ascended the throne, established dominion over Judea, and Jerusalem was converted into Greek city. A proclamation was issued that forced all citizens to follow Greek religion, including pagan religious rituals. Soon, even the temple was used to slaughter of pigs on its altar. In 168 BC, in the marketplace of a small town called Modein, northwest of Jerusalem, Syrian soldiers erected an altar. The soldiers' captain ordered Mattathias from the men assembled, a Jewish

priest and elder to sacrifice a pig to Jupiter in honour of Antiochus. He didn't move, but another man came forward, offering to perform the sacrifice. The intention of the soldiers was to execute those who would refuse to eat the meat of the pig. Mattathias snatched the sward from the captain, killed the traitor who offered to perform the sacrifice, then killed the captain. Mattathias's sons surrounded him and together with their followers fled to the hills. It was the beginning of so-called Maccabee uprising, during which a decision was made to temporarily suspend the ordinance against fighting on Sabbath, giving them a military advantage over the unsuspecting enemies. In four years, the Maccabbees' victories brought them back to Jerusalem, where their immediate task was to re-consecrate the Temple, by removing the stones that had been used for pagan sacrifices, and they built a new altar. On the 25 day of Kislev, 165 BC, they lit the sacred lamp, but realized that they had enough oil for only one day, so horsemen were dispatched in every direction to find more lamp oil. After eight days someone had finally returned, but remarkably, the lamp had continued to burn with what was initially though only one day's supply. Hanukkah as a holiday for us commemorates re-consecration of the Temple, and the miracle of the lasting oil."

Mrs. Brodski stopped abruptly the narrative and looked at her son and Mrs. Pavloska, as a sign that it was indeed the end of the story, after which a period of silence followed. To break the silence, she invited them to have some more tea and biscuits, and then asked Alek to open the gift he received from Mrs. Pavloska. He got up eagerly, walked over to the small stand beside the sofa, picked up the small package, returned to the table and began unpacking it at once. Alek's eyes lit up and a big smile appeared on his face. It was a fashionable man's wristwatch with a black leather strap. He thanked Mrs. Pavloska for the gift with a visible delight and emotion in his voice. She explained that the credit should rather go to her husband Stanislav, who still works for the National Railways and rides regularly the passenger trains to the Soviet Union and back as a conductor. He quite often brought back with him goods and products in short supply and quite costly on this side of the border, but on the other side they were readily available and inexpensive. As once before, the first time they talked at length, Mrs. Pavloska offered Mrs.Brodski an array of goods, if she ever were in need of such things, at substantially discounted prices, of course. Mrs. Brodski thank her for the offer, and expressed her gratitude for Alek's present and for her unwavering support. In the meantime, Alek excused himself from the table and moved back to the sofa, where he began looking over his new watch, now his most prized possession, and tried to set the dials to the current time, while the two women continued with their amicable conversation. At one point, and quite unexpectedly, Mrs. Pavloska asked hesitatingly in a subdued voice.

"Zofia, have you ever given a thought to possibly having Alek baptized?"

"Baptized?" repeated Mrs. Brodski, taken totally aback. "What in the world are you saying? You cannot be serious, my friend."

"Oh yes, I am. I have to admit, I was a bit afraid to bring this up, I wasn't sure how you'd react, but please think about it. It would solve many problems, it wouldn't hurt, it could only help you both. You know as well as I do, people around here are not very understanding, and baptizing Alek here, in our church would certainly help a great deal, it would make your lives easier. We're all children of the same God, and after all, our faith derives from your faith, and most importantly the Son of God was one of your people. I'm sure our parish priest, Father Antoni would welcome you both with open arms. Then the people would come around too, just a matter of time. Please give it some thought, my dear. I'm sorry if I hurt your feelings in any way, I didn't mean to. I'm suggesting this as a solution to help you. You know, I care deeply about both of you."

"Yes, yes, I know. Don't worry, I'm not offended at all. At first, I was quite shocked, but I'll think about it.", replied Mrs. Brodski, making an impression she'd rather change the subject. Never in her whole life, not even for a split second had she ever thought about abandoning what was dearest to her heart, her faith and her Jewish traditions, just to gain wider acceptance in the community, or "make lives easier", as Mrs. Pavloska said. The idea of Christian, especially Catholic baptism seemed absolutely inconceivable to her. She wondered about the old woman's motives, or whether it was entirely her own idea, or there was someone else behind it and the old woman was just a messenger? Soon, Mrs. Brodski would be left only with her thoughts and impressions of Mrs. Pavloska's visit, since it wasn't long before she got up and Mrs. Brodski accompanied her guest to the front door. Mrs. Pavloska hugged her host and bid farewell to them both, then stepped outside into the cold night. Mrs. Brodski and Alek stood there at the door for several seconds shivering, and looked at the quickly departing silhouette, and only went back inside and closed the door when the old woman disappeared from sight, around the corner of the adjacent building.

Soon the country, Europe and much of the world would be swept by unprecedented chain of events, shaking up the whole decaying socio-political order, just over twenty after the greatest military conflict humanity has even known – World War II.

Early in the New Year, on January 6, 1968, the government-ran daily newspapers, in a short, front-page articles announced unexpected and sudden change in the leadership of the Czechoslovak Communist Party, without giving any specific reasons. The newspapers described the event as welcome and necessary for the country's future, economic and social development within the socialist framework of reforms, and unshakable allegiance to Marxism-Leninism. Antonin Novotny was voted out, and Alexander Dubcek, a Slovak with a liberal reputation replaced him as the First Secretary of the Communist Party. Many considered the shakeup inevitable and yet highly suspicious. Czechoslovakia a friendly country on Poland's southern border in the brotherhood of Eastern Europe's Warsaw Pact nations was generally viewed here as an orthodox, tightly controlled communist state. People craving more information than the official media could provide, once again were glued to their short-wave radios, listening to every word of Radio Free Europe unceasing reports. The news then was exchanged and recycled amongst the general population, with much speculation of what was really happening in the highest echelons of power, and what it all meant for rest of the Soviet bloc countries? Although most of the reports beamed incessantly by Radio Free Europe were considered as trustworthy among ordinary folks, yet there were those who refused to believe what they heard and dismissed them as a subversive western propaganda.

The Vietnam War at the time was also the major topic of numerous television reports, radio broadcasts and newspaper articles, and particularly intensified shortly after the New Year with an unexpected attack on the US Army base by the Vietnam People's Army and the Viet Cong on January 1, 1968. In the officially sanctioned statements, the government expressed its jubilation at the early successes of the Vietnamese and its unwavering support for that country's brave people, fighting the overwhelmingly superior invading American imperialist forces. The country that has a revealing and powerful motto on its currency: "In God We Trust", attacked an impoverished, tiny country Vietnam in south-east Asia, carpet-bombing it continuously, destroying its infrastructure and killing the country's people my all means at their disposal, apparently to liberate them from the evils of communism in the name of God. Sadly and similarly, so were bloody Christian Crusades to the Holly Land, in a span of about two hundred years, between 1095-1291.

The national government took this opportunity to announce new, vigorous efforts to help the Vietnamese with supplies of food and medicine, and appealed to the people for financial donations thorough a network of collection centres in all cities and towns across the country; at post offices, banks, schools, most places of employment, libraries and most stores. Alek, as all the students donated his nominal obligatory share at school, for which he received a small pocket-size, single-page 1968 calendar. His mother was asked to contribute few times at institutions she happened to visit at the time, and dutifully donated her nominal amount to avoid controversy and suspicion with her reluctance, although in their household every coin counted. The almost incessant informational campaign in the mass media on the current course and details of the Vietnam War began to worry the people, for whom the World War II was still fresh in their minds. Following the unprecedented Vietnamese offensive in the first two weeks of the New Year, mass shelling of district and provincial capitals in South Vietnam, was reported as an imminent victory not only militarily, but ideologically as well, over the decadent imperialism of the USA. The communist North Vietnam's assault, aided by the Soviet Union at the end of the month, known as the Tet Offensive, was particularly widely reported and analyzed by the government's tightly controlled media. It was the final, triumphant, nearing end to the American aggression and undisputed victory and a source of pride for the forces of communism over the imperialist USA. Great many folks in town turned to Radio Free Europe for alternative source of information, and thus equipped with their own perception of unfolding events, although with somewhat limited knowledge of the entire conflict, engaged in heated, impassioned debates as to who was right and who was wrong, and what it all meant for the country, Europe and the world. There were those, albeit minority, who viewed the Vietnamese advances as undisputed example of strength of the unstoppable forces of communism on the right side of history, on its march towards liberating their country from imperialist aggressor and imminent ultimate global triumph of *"liberty, equality, fraternity."* They argued, perhaps not without merit, that after centuries lived under the boot of monarchs, aristocrats and ruling parasitic bourgeois classes, there is nothing more equitable and appealing, than the new world order according to Marx: *"From each according to his abilities, to each according to his needs."*

The prevailing opinion however, and equally strong conviction, was that the "red plague" or the "Red menace" had to be stopped once and for all, and if it is in the Far East, then we're all that much better off. Let them square it off, and we too will reap the benefits.

At the end of January, Poland's communist authorities announced removal from the National Theatre in Warsaw of the popular play Forefathers' Eve by the country's IXX century national poet Adam Mickiewicz, and the last appearance was set for January 30, 1968. Initially, the play began in November of 1967 and was meant to commemorate the fiftieth anniversary of the Russian Revolution of 1917. The play in its new version was deemed subversive with decidedly anti- Soviet accents, prompting some in the audience to disrupt the show with verbal outbursts of hostile sentiments toward the Soviet Union. Immediately following the last scheduled performance, much of the audience in a seemingly spontaneous show of defiance, some with unfurled banners with decidedly anti-government and anti-Soviet slogans, then marched towards the monument of Adam Mickiewicz to picket and demonstrate against the play's suspension, demanding its reinstatement and "freedom of artistic expression." In the following days, two of the demonstration organizers, University of Warsaw students Milnik and Szeifer were relegated and arrested. In their defense, fellow university students organized a petition with a few thousand signatures, submitted to the parliament, demanding their re-instatement. Simultaneously, an unprecedented campaign of fliers was orchestrated at the university, further voicing demands for liberalization of educational system, politics of the central government, respect for freedom and democracy, repeated calls for reinstatement of relegated students and direct talks with the minister of education and rector of the university. The circulated campaign of words intensified with time, and still unknown opposition fractions joined in with their own agenda, directly challenging the legitimacy of the ruling Party, and calling for its overthrow. It all culminated on March 8, at the university's central square, where a few thousand students gathered in a mass display of defiance, listening to student speakers reading out resolutions explicitly calling for democracy and liberalization of public life and politics, freedom of expression, and demands for reinstatement of other relegated student leaders involved in the flier campaign and petition, namely Kantor and Modelski, incidentally all of them of Jewish ancestry. When busloads of plain-clothes and uniformed policemen along with dozens of secret agents pulled up and surrounded the protesting students, it was just a matter of time, before tempers flared. Overtly aggressive behaviour of the police was met with passive opposition from the students, beginning to disperse, once guaranteed by the university's administrative personnel the next peaceful rally, without outside interference. Unexpectedly, the police began their brutal, coordinated assault and mass arrests. Scores of students were injured, some severely, and the main leaders and instigators were dragged away to awaiting police vans, as onlookers chanted: "Gestapo! Gestapo! Gestapo!" In the following days more arrests followed, as the student rallies spread to other universities all over the country in solidarity with the students at the University of Warsaw. The news of the protest spread like a wildfire, and soon reached almost every corner of the country, including its eastern outskirts, often derisively called Poland-B. The press at first reported only sketchy course of events, minimizing their significance and scope, but it soon became apparent that, the news could no longer be contained or stifled. The protests were just too widespread to ignore, even in the police-state with tightly controlled media, it was no longer an option. On

March 11, the ruling Party's daily, People's Tribune published the official government version of events under a heading, "Around the events at the University of Warsaw." The article placed the blame for the demonstrations squarely on students of Jewish descent, a privileged class of students, branded "Banana Youth", which suddenly came out of the woods and with such highly visible presence.

In the Brodski household the Jewish holiday of Purim, which fell on Sunday, March 14 was a welcome break from increasingly politicized life in the neighbourhood and on the streets. The student protests became the favourite topic of quiet discussions and fervent speculations among family, friends and neighbours. The ever watchful and well-informed Radio Free Europe did not disappoint with their around the clock broadcasts, while the authorities were doing their best to jam them, but with mixed results at best. Mrs. Brodski and Alek didn't share the excitement of the general population, and didn't quite understand or didn't want to, the significance of it all, which almost everybody else seemed to attribute to major ideological conflict between East and West, and possibly looming WWIII. After a few days, following the initial wave, they became rather indifferent to all the attention given to some student protests in the capital; they had other things to worry about.

In the morning Mrs. Brodski asked Alek to read the story of Esther from their copy of Christian Old Testament, the only Bible they had. She didn't want to wait for the evening, had other things planned for the day and wanted to keep Alek occupied. She was disappointed with Alek's lack of enthusiasm, but not entirely surprised. Over the years he displayed ever increasing resistance to observance, much less celebrations of any Jewish holidays in an environment where the vast majority of his peers were devout Christians, or so it seemed, and there was no room for anything else. Being distinctly different in one's beliefs was not an asset, on the contrary. Alek read the bible aloud and reluctantly, as it related a story of a Hebrew orphan girl in Persia, known as Esther, and who became a queen of Persia on the throne of king Ahasuerus, and through unexpected turn of events prevented the genocide of her people at the hands of king's scheming viceroy Haman. While listening sporadically listening to her son's reading, Mrs. Brodski was busy making the traditional "hamantashen"; small, triangular pastry filled with fruit preserves, which she always prepared in small quantities each summer. She was planning to surprise Maria Pavloska and her husband Stanislav with these tasty treats later in the day. For his efforts Alek was rewarded with several coins, despite his lackluster reading, which at times was becoming torturous, but his mom being in a particularly good mood that day, just rolled her eyes and smiled.

CHAPTER 7

ON MARCH 19, 1968, the unthinkable happened. The conference of the Warsaw branch of The Party, chaired by the First Secretary of the Polish United Workers' Party, Wladyslav Gomulka, and was transmitted nationally by the state radio and television. In his lengthy speech, Gomulka outlined the genesis and course of the student protests, alluding to active "revisionist-Zionist" opposition, and described the instigators in the following words: "In the recent events that took place, actively participated university students of Jewish descent or nationality. Parents of these young people occupy responsible and high positions in our country." Gomulka then emphasized that, although there is certainly presence of Zionist nationalists in those circles, and whose interests do not necessarily coincide with those of the country, they do not however constitute any threat or danger to socialist system and country as a whole. In the following weeks and months, an unprecedented shake up took place in the acting government and the Central

Committee of the Polish United Workers Party. Numerous ministers and members of the Party resigned under pressure, or were replaced amid mutual accusations of incompetence, disloyalty, ideological corruption or outright subversion. The two distinct, competing and vying for greater share of power Party fractions were set for a showdown. One of Polish ethnicity, grouped around the General Secretary W. Gomulka and known in the political circles as the "Boors", were under attack from highly influential group of ardent Stalinists, trying to undermine them and wrestle control of the leadership and who were known as the "Jews" (Zydy). Ultimately the Polish communists prevailed in the much publicized and openly contested straggle for power and ideological supremacy within the ruling party. Normally tightly controlled state media were unusually transparent in their reporting, at least went significantly beyond the usual minimum or nothing at all on the inner workings of the Party apparatus. That was perhaps a purposefully created an atmosphere of liberalism for open debate and accountability, amid much speculation within all walks of society in the entire country, at least for the foreseeable future. Those who still didn't trust the country's media, were glued again to the favourite and widely considered as the most reliable source of information-Radio Free Europe, broadcasting around the clock from its German headquarters in Munich.

It soon became apparent, the personnel changes encompassed not only the ruling political elites, but also many university rectors perceived as too liberal, or those who deviated from the official communist academic curriculum, and therefore created fertile breeding ground for revisionist student activities and were promptly replaced with people sure to follow the official Party line. The purges swept through the justice system and numerous judges, prosecutors and internal Security Bureau officers, mainly remnants of the old Stalinist guard from the 1950's show trials, were replaced with members of younger generation with relatively clean slates. Also, the state radio, television, most daily newspapers and magazines of any significance lost a number of journalists, chief editors and managers. Liberals were equated with Zionists, and Zionists were equated with subversion, and therefore had to be relieved of their positions of influence and privilege. The stage was set for the biggest emigration of highly influential ethnic Jewish minority in the post- World War II history of the country.

Almost simultaneously the media devoted much of its coverage to continued political and social reforms, dubbed the "Prague Spring" taking place just south of the border, in neighbouring Czechoslovakia, initiated by the new communist party leader Alexander Dubcek. There was much excitement in the air, as the news of a radical political program called "socialism with a human face" was related by the media, passed on and debated by all who paid any attention to politics on both sides of the border. The new "Action Program" launched in April, announced far reaching liberalization of the most important aspects of people's lives, including freedom of press, freedom of speech and movement, with economic emphasis on consumer goods and a real possibility of a multiparty system. The program would also limit the power of secret police and outlined new foreign policy, including both, maintenance of good relations with Western countries and future cooperation with the Soviet Union and other communist nations. People's hopes were instantly revived, although subconsciously met with great deal of skepticism. The political turmoil in the highest echelons of power seemed so remote, and so far removed from the lives of ordinary people, that it all seemed surreal, almost as if it had nothing to do with the country itself. An isolated group of people, risen over the years to the ranks of mythical gods in the minds of the citizens, were not expected to relinquish their status, power or institute any tangible changes to the status quo. True to its popular saying, "nothing ever changes around here", or "change is a luxury we cannot afford", became a self-fulfilling prophecy. People resigned themselves to poverty, hardship, misery, and hopelessness as a fact of life, and learned to live with it and around it the best they could.

In the wake of increased tensions and occasional hostility in the community, as a result of continuous political upheavals in the country and abroad, ceaselessly broadcast by the media, the Brodski family, mother and son withdrew even further into their own, small world within the confines of the walls of their old, communal housing apartment, not much even by the standards of this town, but a little haven of their own. They had no television, but they had a good, large, cabinet style short-wave radio, several years old, but nevertheless it was probably one of the best in its class back then. It was manufactured in the country and could easily pick up many well-known radio stations across Europe. The other option was Radio Moscow, equally accessible but with its own agenda, closely aligned with the official government view on rapidly developing stories. For the first time Alek and his mother, sitting in a comfortable sanctuary of their home, heard a story of supposedly officially unreported, but eventually passed on to Radio Moscow by few surviving witnesses, who escaped the carnage of My Lai village massacre by the American troops of over 500 Vietnamese civilians. They were horrified by the news, although viewed it with suspicion, it just couldn't be the America they thought they knew from all the sources. Then surprisingly broadcast on all the national news outlets, they heard on the radio parts of translated Lyndon Johnson address to the nation, in which he announced concrete steps to limit the war in Vietnam and declared his decision not to seek re-election for the presidency, which was universally met with great relief.

The Passover holiday of Saturday, April 13, wasn't high on Mrs. Brodski's list, amid general apathy she and Alek increasingly felt, as their problems with limited resources and the daily grind of a hard life mounted, and with it a profound feeling of isolation and loneliness was creeping in. She had absolutely no intention of celebrating Passover for seven days in a town where they were the only acknowledged Jewish family, at least as far as they knew, and there were the usual obligations of school and work in an environment where probably nobody knew what Passover was, or even cared. It took Mrs. Brodski a considerable effort to prepare the traditional dinner the night before, or something that would at least remotely resemble what she remembered from her younger years. With difficulty, she made three pieces of unleavened bread, the matzo and separately matzo ball soup with parsley, supplemented with few boiled eggs and sweet salad of shredded apples with walnuts and cinnamon. Alek helped to set the table on a white tablecloth already in place and brought in plates, cutlery and cups for the tea, while his mom brought in the ready food from the kitchen. It was about thirty minutes before sundown, when she lit a single candle, and they finally sat down to eat the meal, but not before they both bowed their heads down, and she said a short blessing.

"Blessed art thou, Lord our God, Master of the universe, who sanctifies us with Your commandments, and commanded us to kindle the light of Shabbat and of the Pesach holiday. Blessed art thou, Lord our God, Master of the universe, who has kept us alive and sustained us, and has brought us to this special time."

Although it was a modest meal, they both enjoyed it immensely and took their time to savour all there was on the table, while talking and reminiscing the years gone by in this small town, where it would seem not much ever happened and every day was just like just the day before, yet there was still so much to share. The gradual adjustment to the new environment of mostly Christian population of this small community itself, where it was virtually impossible to be anonymous, was a great challenge in itself. They felt isolated here and lonely, despite the fact most people here seemed to know each other, or at least have met or seen somewhere certainly more than once. For Alek his school posed the biggest challenge, he just didn't fit in, not for the lack of trying. Eventually, he often found himself on the receiving end of crude and cruel jokes and horseplay.

CHAPTER 8

PREPARATIONS FOR THE annual May Day celebrations were in full swing around the county and around the town, although there was much uncertainty and apprehension among the people in the aftermath of the political turmoil in the capital, with ramifications felt across the country. The May 1, 1968 national holiday was preceded by a major clean- up and decorating operations by supposedly voluntary crews made up of anyone from elementary school children of higher grades, middle school youth to low-ranking employees of different government institutions. Within a week red became the dominant colour, the colour of proletariat, symbol of the blood spilled by heroic previous generations in their struggle to defeat the "bourgeoisie" and free the masses from oppression. The Polish flags made up of equally proportioned white and red longitudinal stripes, fluttered in the wind alongside red Soviet flags, adorned with a characteristic trademark, hammer and a sickle. They were placed virtually at every lamppost, prominent buildings, schools, and state businesses along the major streets. Red canvas banners extolling the virtues of socialism, communism and a leading role of The Party span between tallest trees, and aligned lamp posts on both side of the main street. The Town Hall and the bulletin board in the town's centre, exhibited black and white portraits of the movements three bearded ideologues and forefathers: Karl Marx, Fredrick Engels and Vladimir Lenin. By then Joseph Stalin was out of favour and resting eternally in obscurity. Even some fifteen years after his death, his name evoked terror and was seldom uttered. The town's poorly stocked main bookstore, proudly displayed thick volumes of "The Works of Lenin" and "The Communist Manifesto" in its front window. It did generate some curiosity, but little genuine interest. The main event was the parade, which ran through the main street and culminated at the old sports stadium, where the gathered crowd would be greeted by local dignitaries and minor Party officials from the district office, who descended here for the occasion. At the head of the parade, a goose-stepping battalion of the local army unit made its presence known, followed by a rather large contingent of uniformed railway workers with a band up front, mutilating their trumpets, horns, flutes, and a drum in a strenuous attempt at what seemed like the national anthem, followed by even more muddled version of "The International". Next in line was a small group of voluntary fire department unit on an old red fire truck, that gave out frequent muffled, sputtering sounds, as if in its last throes. Yet, it somehow moved along slowly, defying the odds and inviting some laughs from the onlookers along the way. There were other trades represented, but one of the most populous groups were the teachers with their pupils of various ages of the town's two elementary schools, and the middle school. There was Mr. Buzynski, the popular music teacher in the crowd of teachers, and nearby, but not together the young and pretty Ms. Lubinska, as always radiant with a lovely smile and clearly visible sense of contentment on her face. Particularly the teenagers showed little enthusiasm for this big event, and many seemed rather embarrassed to be there at all, but it was a common knowledge, participation in the May Day festivities were mandatory for all students. Alek was among the group of grade eight students, the last year of his elementary school, before going on to secondary school, right here in town. Either because of his height or by assignment, he was marching in the back of his class and on the outside of a loosely organized column. There was a rather serious expression on his face, while the other boys and girls seemed to be enjoying themselves without restrain, talking and interacting. For many boys it was a perfect and long-awaited opportunity to strike up an awkward conversation with a secretly admired girl or pull off some hastily arranged prank. Alek looked as if he'd rather be anywhere else but here. As usual, he was dressed in his customary black trousers, matching jacket, white dress shirt and black shoes. It all seemed to be at least a size or two too big, and hanged on his tall, skeletal figure like on a coat rack. Alek could have been easily mistaken for one of the teachers, but his face betrayed his real age, still in his teens. He didn't look sideways at the spectators, but straight ahead and down occasionally, making sure not to accidentally kick, trip or run into the boy in front of him, when the marching column slowed down its pace for no apparent reason. The citizens who didn't participate in the parade, as well as many visitors from surrounding villages lined both sides of the main street, and looked curiously at the passing procession, and great many of them tried hard to spot somebody they knew. Mrs. Brodski was there well in advance and stood anxiously on the sidewalk, close to the curb, for what seemed like hours, waiting to catch a glimpse of her son passing by with the rest of the festive crowd, just like many other parents, grandparents and siblings, restlessly awaiting their turn. Finally, Alek appeared in sight, and as the group came closer, his mother leaned over towards the street, to make herself even more visible, and started waving and smiling lovingly, as only a proud mother could. Alek was completely absorbed in his own thoughts within the confines of marching column, without even as much as a brief glance sideways, and would have passed his mom by, had she not shouted his name, when he was just few meters away. Alek immediately looked in the direction of the familiar voice, as if awaken from sleep walking, and smiled back timidly, and at the same time lifted his right hand slightly and made a waving gesture back to his mother. He kept looking her straight in the eyes for a few more seconds as he was walking by, and in just a few strides, left her behind still standing there and smiling. Soon the long marching throng spilled through the wide-open gate of the stadium, as the loudspeakers played instrumental versions of well-known revolutionary and patriotic songs. The parade participants all took their designated places as pre-determined well in advance by the event organizers, and directed by few volunteer crowd controllers right from the gate. Alek stood quietly among his classmates, on the green turf at the edge of his column, slightly aloof, almost as if he didn't belong there. No one seemed to pay attention to him anyway, neither boys nor girls. Alek was perceived as a loner who didn't talk much, engrossed in his thoughts who didn't bother them, and didn't want to be bothered, just kept to himself. That trait alone however, was enough to get him into trouble, when the school bullies wanted to know badly, what he was up to? What was he thinking about? That aloofness seemed to project the wrong impression, and aura of superiority or provocation, which didn't sit well with the local young thugs. Alek just stood there patiently, looking ahead at the centre stage, paying little attention to the commotion all around. He was thinking about his mother, if she was also here somewhere among the spectators, or went back home shortly after the parade went through the centre of town? He looked sideways, and even turned around quickly to see if she was standing somewhere nearby. With her height and distinct features, she would be rather easy to spot, but she was nowhere to be seen. For a moment though, he had a feeling someone to his right, about ten or so paces away was actually staring at him. Alek didn't like being looked at like that, it made him nervous, but curiosity prevailed and he turned his head slowly in direction of the onlooker.

He recognized the face, it was the same boy he had seen that fateful day of the attack, back in September, standing there at the entrance to the alley, just looking at the whole scene unfold, but with obvious fear and genuine concern in his eyes, it seemed. He looked rather short then, but about fourteen or fifteen years old now and much taller, standing with his classmates, but somewhat detached, and just like Alek, in the outer row of his group. Their eyes met for a few seconds, but the boy promptly lowered his gaze. This time Alek sensed strange concern in his rather sad eyes, and was puzzled by the unexpected encounter, and then quickly turned his face back towards the centre stage. Alek couldn't concentrate on what was happening in front of him but waited impatiently few more minutes looking absently straight ahead, pretending passive interest in the festivities, but soon instinctively turned his head back to the right again. Surprisingly, the boy wasn't there anymore, he just disappeared, nowhere to be seen. Alek looked around for several more seconds, but he was gone as mysteriously as he appeared among his peers, the group of students nearby, staring curiously at him just few minutes ago.

The dignitaries and important local officials including Commandant Sokolowski, alongside visiting minor Party apparatchiks from the district office stood on a specially constructed and freshly painted wooden platform, or rather large stage ready for the biggest spectacle this town has ever seen. The stage was adorned with few Polish flags, alongside equal number of Soviet red flags with the well recognizable emblem of hammer and sickle, conceived during the Russian Revolution of 1917. Over the years it became the most recognizable symbol of the communist movement, representing the alliance of industrial workers and their peasant counterparts, under one banner of dictatorship by the proletariat. The dignitaries stood on the stage without any particular order, mostly middle age and older men dressed in dark suits, few with nondescript female companions, most likely proud wives by their husbands' sides or assistants, occasionally waving their hands in friendly greeting gestures. It was quite a sight to see; their red, well-fed faces glistening in the hazy, mid-day sun. The town's folks looked with great curiosity at all the assembled, the visiting few and the vast majority town's own administrators and communist leaders, since they've never seen such numbers of them assembled here before, certainly never May Day festivities on this scale. For some it was yet another reason to speculate on the motives for this unusual presence, and for others, perhaps overly naïve, who took the spectacle literally for what it was, it must have given them a feeling of importance, and of the growing status of their town. The grand finale of the parade and celebrations has begun at last. The highest local Party official, the town's mayor himself, Comrade Kutasiuk stepped up to the microphone, tapped on it few times with his index finger, cleared his throat, and started to speak. First, by welcoming the visiting out of town distinguished guests and the local officials, the pillars of society as they say, dutifully gathered on the stage, all dressed in their finest dark suits and ties.

Then the mayor turned his smiling face to the gathered civilian crowd and the parade throng, now all standing in a relatively orderly groups of spectators on the large grassy field, opposite the platform. He sincerely welcomed all the gathered, especially emphasizing the young people, the students, as the torch bearers and the country's best hope for the future. Each time Mayor Kutasiuk mentioned a specific group of people, a somewhat timid applause followed from the crowd and visibly more spontaneous from the dignitaries. The mayor looked to his right, then to his left, bowed his head and with a slight had gesture introduced few closest comrades by name. He then repeated one of the names looking to his right, at a stocky, medium height, past middle age, bolding man with a reddish face, and let it be known that it was his rare honour, indeed a privilege to welcome Comrade Baranski, the regional Party Secretary. The mayor then enthusiastically announced that the distinguished guest would like to take this opportunity to speak to the citizens of this fine, historic town, and then slightly bowed his head again, and looking at Baranski, smiled invitingly, pointing to the stand with a microphone and stepped aside. Comrade Baranski elegantly dressed in a new dark suit, white shirt and a distinctly dark-red tie, slowly crossed the distance to the microphone in a few short steps, thanked the mayor for the introduction and pulled out a sheet of prepared notes form the right pocket of his jacket. He then scoured the crowd with his eyes, as if looking for familiar faces, and once satisfied, begun to speak.

"Dear comrades, distinguished guests, ladies and gentlemen and fellow countrymen! On this day we're gathered here to celebrate a very special occasion. Since the inception of People's Republic of Poland at the end of World War II, May 1 has come to symbolize the indelible spirit of our beloved country. It is that spirit which endured foreign invasions and occupations by our enemies, our immediate neighbours, who thought it could be extinguished, and the country permanently erased from the map of Europe. Over twenty years later, we can unequivocally state that neither the spirit has been extinguished, nor the country or its national identity erased. We have risen stronger than ever on the ashes of Nazi Germany and our own bourgeois aristocracy, which brought this country to the brink of existence in 1939. The brave army of the Soviet Union with Polish People's Army by its side, had liberated our motherland from the greatest evil humanity has ever known. Upon the unprecedented destruction, a new, free, democratic and socialist homeland was established. We are forever grateful and indebted to our Soviet brothers and sisters for the unimaginable sacrifice they paid to liberate our country and to build our socialist Poland. All along Polish United Workers' Party has been instrumental, and its leadership indisputable in their efforts to rebuild the country from the massive destruction inflicted upon us by Germany. The Party has been our guiding light in freeing ourselves from the chains of the old, decadent bourgeois order, and uniting all segments of society in our march towards justice and prosperity for all, under one socialist banner. Workers, peasants and working intelligentsia stand arm in arm as equals, united by a common purpose, and today we celebrate their day. This day was written in blood of the early socialist martyrs in the fight for better future for

all, so we can celebrate this day as a crowning victory of the working men and women across this country, Europe and the World. It's been 120 years since The Communist Manifesto was first published, but its resounding truth and credo that the proletarians have nothing to lose, but their chains, has finally been fulfilled, as demonstrated by the tangible achievements of our socialist country in the lives of its citizens, and your lives ladies and gentlemen standing here today. The victory over fascism and bourgeois capitalism has been achieved, and the rotten world order of social injustice, inequality and exploitation of men by men, has been buried in the dust heap of history. The rotten, inequitable capitalist system, which for centuries enslaved the societies of Europe by division and exploitation of the many by the few has been replaced by a new socialist order, as so rightfully stated by the immortal words of Karl Marx: "From each according to his abilities, to each according to his needs." Dear fellow citizens, I should mention, and as most of you know, this year, November 11 marks the fiftieth anniversary of our country's independence from 150 years of partition and foreign domination by three European empires of the old-world order, Russia, Germany and Austro-Hungarian Empire. The new socialist order of Marxism-Leninism built on the ashes of those empires in a spirit of mutual cooperation, respect and brotherhood of nations withstood the test of time and has become the envy of those still oppressed in every corner of the globe, and a beacon of hope, the new standard for all future generations. When the prophetic words of the Communist Manifesto "Workers of the world unite!" were first published in 1948, few knew that one day they would become a universal reality, and the most potent force in the world today, for united we stand, and divided we fall."

Comrade Baranski went on and on for several more minutes, extolling the virtues of socialism and dramatizing the battles and subsequent victories of the labour movement. His face turned red as a beat, his eyes inflamed with passion, as the lofty words were pouring out of his mouth like a torrent. Finally, it was impossible to tell, whether he was truly intoxicated by his own words of achievements and triumphs of socialism, or the vodka he drank shortly before the celebrations started to kick in and take over with clearly visible effects. He wiped his perspiring, low forehead with a white handkerchief pulled out of the right pocket of his trousers. On few occasions the speech was punctuated by a shrill, contemptuous whistle from one of the local hoodlums hiding in the rears of the crowd. One could see a determined uniformed policeman making his way through the throng in the direction of the source of the whistles, while the people weren't making it any easier, refusing to budge and move aside. Clearly frustrated policeman uttered some incomprehensible threats, slowly squeezing through the crowd, nevertheless. Meanwhile Comrade Baranski's speech took on a more sombre tone, and the crowd became impatient and visibly restless by the lengthy, tedious speech, as he continued.

"Comrades, my fellow countrymen, our work is not finished yet. There is still much to be done on our path to where we want to be. Sadly, there are those in our society, who would want to turn the clock back, to where things used to be. To those people we say, there is no turning back, so either join us, or step aside, because we'll have you moved. To those imperialist and bourgeois sympathizers, we had extended a conciliatory hand, but with much regret I confess, that our gesture was rejected. Therefore, we were given no choice, but to fight with unwavering determination the traitors and agents of the decadent, imperialist West, the saboteurs, agitators, and liberal Zionist scoundrels wherever they are. The enemy doesn't sleep, but is lurking in the shadows, trying to subvert our motherland and instill chaos and confusion in the minds of citizens. We must be vigilant and any attempts at subversion must be ruthlessly eradicated, and the perpetrators brought to justice. The role of ordinary people under the infallible guidance of The Party, is instrumental in protecting this country from domestic opposition elements, class enemies, spies and traitors. We must trust the Party and its policies as a crucial and indispensable force in our common struggle for a free, democratic,

just and prosperous socialist Poland. Working men and women from all walks of life, from east to west, and from south to north, unite! Thank you."

The dignitaries and The Party officials started clapping vigorously as soon as comrade secretary finished his speech, but the crowd stood unmoved and silent for a few seconds, but what seemed like minutes, which caused visibly uncomfortable consternation and a stir among the elites on the platform. The citizens were gasping in disbelief, they have never heard a speech in their town like this before; given with such passion and conviction, it rivaled or exceeded the best speeches on the radio and television given by the General Secretary, or the Prime Minister himself. Finally, few sporadic, single claps started it all, and more and more adults and children in the crowd joined in, to what became a rather lukewarm and scattered applause. The crowd's reaction wasn't received well by the comrades. Many were obviously bewildered, some visibly dismayed and agitated, looking around at themselves and back at the less than receptive crowd with anger and contempt. The people stared at the stage probably equally surprised by their reaction. Many in the group of ordinary onlookers, no longer timid and fearful, were encouraged by their numbers to express some derogatory comments about the speech and towards the comrades on the platform, as if in a collective hum, show of freely expressed indignation with anybody who happened to stand nearby. The disconcerted murmur turned into an unprecedented display of discontent, combined with muffled sporadic outbursts of hostile shouts, as if certain of assured anonymity and thus impunity in this large, assembled crowd, which otherwise would have been unthinkable for fear of serious consequences. Again, hecklers in the back started to jeer and whistle, the so-called local "criminal element", was in full force and doing their best to show what they thought of Baranski's speech and the dignitaries on the stage. Commandant Sokolowski's team moved in again, wielding batons, ready to strike, with the main law and order enforcer constable Kovaluk right in front. He was well known around town for his reliability and diligence in what he thought was fulfilling his duty towards socialist motherland. He was a frequent object of ridicule, as a perfect specimen for the job they thought. Middle height, a bit on a heavy side, yet strong and stupid. Some derisively dubbed him "the man of the cross" in reference you his apparent lack of education, some said illiteracy, and swore they had seen him sign his name with a cross on a dotted line. However, that was just a malicious rumour, for in fact Kovaluk could read and write, perhaps not proficiently, but nonetheless he survived with what he had. The accepted understanding was that The Party did not tolerate discontent, independent thought or divergent opinions among its ranks. In reality any opinion was viewed with suspicion, even that in line with the official Party position was suspected as not genuine or possibly sarcastic. They all had to be vigilant, as if there was always someone behind, watching. The preferred policy was to leave the thinking and formulating opinions to the leaders of The Party. This ever-present, omnipotent entity portrayed itself as the infallible source of wisdom and a torrent of profound ideas, which only they understood, only The Party held the secret to the ultimate knowledge, an exclusive monopoly on the ultimate truth, and the masses were there to listen, comply and obediently fulfill The Party's directives according to all those five-year plans in virtually every sector of the country's economy, the educational system, cultural and social life.

Mayor Comrade Kutasiuk again stepped up to the microphone and asked for attention, in fact he had to repeat it few times: "Attention please…attention, attention please!" Many residents and visitors from the villages did pay heed to the mayor's plea and turned their eyes to the stage. He announced the beginning of entertainment part of the May Day celebrations, mainly by the children and youth of both elementary and the secondary schools, interspersed by few words of introduction and praise from their teachers and principals. Proud parents were overjoyed by the performance of their pupils in choirs, trying their best at the well-known patriotic songs, solo performances and poetry reciting. Many people in the audience reacted with sincere appreciation, even those who had the most basic knowledge of literature were somewhat familiar with the heart-felt, timeless verses that suited the socialist agenda, of great poets like W. Broniewski, K. Galczynski or A. Slonimski. Of course, any event of this kind had to include some well-known Russian literary giants such as Alexander Pushkin and Vladimir Mayakovsky. For almost two hours the entertainment session continued uninterrupted in a well-organized and obviously previously rehearsed sequence, except for brief announcements from selected teachers or the principal. Slowly it was all coming to an end, and the people and children in the audience were all becoming tired and restless, and some already left. Many people began to move around the large grassy field, stop and talk to someone they knew or someone newly acquainted, and there were those individuals or small groups slowly moving towards the exit gate, and leaving the stadium inconspicuously. Alek didn't even notice when his mother approached from the back and stood behind him, slightly to his right side, making an effort not to disturb her son, but rather secretly observing him, with that seemingly ever-present gentle smile on her lips. After several minutes, Alek must have sensed somebody watching him, turned around and their eyes met, and he was quite surprised and greatly relieved to see his mother's familiar face, and smiled back. She squeezed his right arm gently, and with a little push forward, gave an unmistakable signal it was time to leave the stadium. He had no objections; in fact, it was on his mind since shortly after coming here. Alek had no patience for any public gatherings; they made him tired and uncomfortable. He just couldn't concentrate during official ceremonies, whether public, like May Day or those frequent school assemblies he so dreaded. Alek always had this uneasy feeling that he was observed, people stared at him for no apparent reason. He was well aware of some striking differences with other teenagers, and quite possibly most people in town. They all had distinctly Slavic features, and he had visibly Jewish facial characteristics. At times he felt like an unwelcome outsider, a foreigner with no permanent place to call home. Over the years however, some things didn't make much sense to him, as he witnessed numerous instances of thinly vailed animosities, and occasional hostilities among the Slavs themselves. It seemed to him there was no love lost between the Poles, Ukrainians and Russians either. Although on a surface, the town seemed to rest in a sleepy peace and tranquility, from time the true feelings would come to the surface, things were said and done and then back to normal, as people went about their business as the best of friends again. One thing Alek had also noticed, it was the older generations, the parents and grandparents that fed the fires of ethnic strife and resentment among themselves and poisoned the youth. The reasons for it were as foreign to him, as perhaps his own presence in this community to others. He overheard on few occasions passionately arguing men about historical wrongs unleashed by each of those nations on the other, about prolonged occupations, mutually committed atrocities and border disputes. However, what was probably most disturbing, was the fact that many kids and teenagers were already infected with the same venom, and like little vultures were running around, spreading the same animosities and resentments. Constant vigilance became Alek's daily reality at public events, school playground or the town's streets. He was also concerned about his mother; she was the only close person he had, and she was more than just his mother, she was his only loyal friend.

Mrs. Brodski and Alek moved swiftly, navigating through the crowd, trying to reach the gate of the stadium as fast as they could, hopefully without bringing too much attention upon themselves for leaving too early, well before the majority of the gathered crowd. Just behind the main entrance gate, Alek immediately noticed the same boy he had seen before, standing just outside the stadium gates, waiting and looking around. He immediately noticed Alek and his mother leaving, as if in a pre-planned, premeditated move to actually be there and to be seen when they were leaving. Their eyes locked briefly, and just as quickly the boy turned sideways.

"Mom look, there he is again," said Alek.

"Who is there?"

"The boy I told you about last fall. He was the witness to the whole scene, standing there and looking at us, just like now," said Alek, slowing down and pulling his mother by the sleeve.

"Are you talking about that boy standing by himself over there, to the right of the gate?"

"Yes, that's the one."

Mrs. Brodski briefly stopped and looked back at the boy with renewed interest, at someone who was a total stranger, and yet somehow became a part of their lives and by some inexplicable coincidence, a silent witness to its turning point. She looked intensely into the boy's eyes for a few crucial seconds, and he looked back at her with that same penetrating but a sad, almost anguished gaze of someone who was deeply troubled or suffering, someone painfully lonely. Despite his participation in the May Day celebrations, the boy seemed detached from it all, just an observer, engrossed in his own little world. Mrs. Brodski was suddenly struck by a distant memory of an obscure episode from the past and smiled warmly. He smiled back for a second or two, with that same faint smile she vaguely remembered from all those years ago. He then shyly turned his eyes away, and with a renewed impenetrable and placid demeanor, looked briefly sideways at someone or something, and then slowly walked away. Zofia Brodski suddenly realized she had seen those light-colored eyes and the shy boy before, without any doubt. It must have been several years ago, perhaps seven or eight years before, and now she was absolutely certain of it.

"I think I know him. I mean, I've seen him before, I'm sure. I can never forget those eyes and that face, although somewhat changed now", she said to Alek as they walked away.

"What are you saying, Mom? How do you know him? You never told me that."

"It was something that happened long time ago. At the time it was nothing to be concerned about, a trivial thing, and it had nothing to do with you. Actually, I had forgotten it, buried it deep in my memory until today."

Once outside and well on the main street sidewalk, Alek and Mrs. Brodski slowed down again, and walked at leisurely pace back home, sharing few personal impressions of the whole spectacle they just left behind, but mostly walked in silence for several more minutes. Alek begun to have a strange feeling of a most uncomfortable remorse, for he too realized had seen the boy over the years few times, as he was growing up and in most unexpected circumstances, when least expected. Whether by chance, coincidence or the boy was intentionally following him, Alek couldn't tell. As they walked enjoying a relatively fair spring weather, they held their heads up high, not as was their usual habit of mostly looking down, trying to avoid eye contact with strangers. The weather improved as the day went on, with occasional bursts of weak rays of sunshine between several scattered clouds. The temperature was still quite low, only around plus 16 degrees Celsius, but still it was a perfect day for an afternoon stroll. With all the visitors from the villages mingled with the locals, there was significantly more traffic on the sidewalks and the streets than usual on any given day, but perhaps not particularly because of the significance of the May Day, but rather people taking advantage of the statutory holiday. Although few precious hours were already "wasted" on the parade and festivities at the stadium, but nevertheless it was a much-appreciated day off work and equally cherished day off school. Alek and Mrs. Brodski were happy for a day, or whatever was left of it, at times almost elated, walking slowly, not in a hurry to go back home, savouring the moment, or quite possibly even to be seen or to meet someone they already knew. They looked at the buildings decorated solemnly with national and Soviet flags and mostly red banners with various slogans in large, white lettering, extolling socialism, its founders and The Party. The streets were much cleaner than usual, with freshly manicured lawns and new flower beds with variety of plants still in their infancy, all along the main street of town. The people passing by were dressed for the occasion in their finest clothes and all seemed absorbed in their own world or private conversations with their companions, paying no attention to the mother and son walking among them. On this particular day Alek wanted to be noticed and wished that someone would stop and greet them like an old, loyal friend, someone who even from a distance would smile, recognizing them at once. He would have been so truly happy to see them too, especially seeing others shower his mother with complements she's never had for many years now. There was a quite audible music coming through an open window from one of the old, wooden houses with front-yard gardens along the way, a rare tune on the radio, the unmistakable guitar sound of The Rolling Stones and poignant lyrics of "Dandelion", invoking strange nostalgia, distant imaginary images and mystique of the free West, somewhere far away, well beyond their reach.

"Prince or pauper, beggar man or thing
Play the game with ev'ry flow'r you bring
Dandelion don't tell no lies
Dandelion will make you wise
Tell me if she laughs or cries
Blow away dandelion…"

"Mom, tell me about him, tell me about that boy, I want to know. What happened several years ago?" asked Alek, breaking the moment of nostalgia and silence between them.

"Son, this is so insignificant, a child's play I'd say. I have almost completely forgotten it until today, and it just came back to me suddenly. I don't think it is even worth talking about."

"No Mom, you've got to tell me. I want to know. I want to understand why he keeps showing up? What is this all about? We don't even know who he is."

"Alek, don't take it so seriously, don't let it become your obsession. It's a small town, people bump into each other all the time. Somehow, we ended up here, although it wasn't our choice, and now living here we see the same people from time to time. In a way, we all influence each other's lives, whether we like it or not, and sometimes we don't even realize it. Look, we all live under the same sky, breathe the same air, attend the same schools and shops, and sooner or later our lives in a mysterious way are interrelated, we are dependent on others one way or the other, at least to some extent."

"Mom, please don't…What happened several years ago? Tell me."

"Alek, in all honesty, I never thought I'd ever be talking about this. It's just so irrelevant. Do you really want to know about something I only suspect is related to the young man we've just seen?"

"Mom, but few minutes ago you said you were sure your remembered him, and now what?"

"You know, I wish you'd drop the subject, but obviously it won't happen, you just won't let go off it."

"Mom, please don't make it any harder than it has to be. This is all quite bizarre, wouldn't you say?"

"Perhaps…"

"So, what's the story?"

"It's not much of a story, but subconsciously I guess, in a sense it probably had an effect on my thinking somewhat over the years. It was a summer vacation for the schools, nice and sunny day, seven or eight years ago. Some children gathered behind the big, wooden fence dividing our courtyard from the neighbours and the adjacent courtyard. You know, those few families of different ethnic backgrounds on the other side of the divide and as always, with several kids of various ages playing. Few of them approached the fence, and were taking amongst themselves.

I stepped out of the house, just few steps over towards the fence, and I overheard what they were saying. One of the boys apparently was visiting there, because I had never seen him around before, and the other kids were showing him around the courtyard. One of the boys said to the other two, just on the other side, and I could clearly hear them.

"Look, behind this fence that old Jew Brodski used to live," he said, someone whose voice I had heard few times before.

"Where is he now?" asked the new boy.

"Oh, he died not long ago in that big fight we had over here," answered one of the local boys and pointed to few sharp pieces of fire equipment displayed on hooks attached to the wooden, old shack several meters away, and added with pride: "All that was used in the battle."

"My dad fought in that battle too. It was our yard against them on the other side. It was a real war, I tell you", said the other boy with self-confidence.

"So, who lives there now?" asked the visiting boy.

"In that first apartment across, just behind the fence, only his wife and son Alek live there now", came a reply.

"Do you see them sometimes? Do they come out of the house at all?", asked the new boy again. "Oh yeah, for sure, but not very often. If you'll look through that hole in the fence, you might see the devils, if you're lucky."

"Why did you call them devils?" continued the visiting boy.

"Because that's what they are, my dad said", answered quickly one of the other boys with satisfaction and authority in his voice. The visiting boy approached the fence slowly and looked through the hole in the wooden plank for several seconds, looking around our yard. I was bent down, pouring water out of a wash basin, just few meters from our door. I caught a glimpse of the boy with those characteristic frightened and sad green eyes, looking at me, obviously expecting to see the devil. I smiled to him, and he was startled at first, but few seconds later he smiled back, and then quickly moved away, clearly embarrassed. Instinctively I stood there waiting, curious what would happen next, and again he stuck his face against the fence on the other side, with his eyes in the hole and looked at me again, just to make sure the devil was still there, I think. I smiled again and he smiled back for a second or two, and then frightened moved back, away from the fence. I didn't think much of it at the time and went back inside the house. That's the whole story Alek. I don't know why it stayed with me for all those years? I wasn't really thinking about it, not at all. I thought it was just child's play, although what the other boys were saying about us was not so nice; it gave me something to think about at the time. Nevertheless, it was one of those rare encounters, which for whatever reason remained with me."

"I really like the story Mom, especially that it is so strange. Is that what the people on the other side think of us, Mom?"

"No, not at all. There are many good families crammed together in those old buildings, and as everywhere most people are good, but just like everywhere there must be few rotten apples among them too."

"Do you know any of them personally?"

"Yes, of course. I know the tailor Kaminski and his wife. Very descent folks. Pious, friendly, always smiling and very helpful even without asking. They'd never say a bad word about anybody. Whenever they see me on the street, they stop and chat for a while. I've been to their home a couple of times, and Mrs. Kaminski has been here at our place too. You just don't remember or weren't at home at the time."

"I don't remember. Do they have any children?"

"No, they don't. They're childless."

"Anybody else that you know?"

"I know Mrs. Terpilowski and her husband Franek, who is a semi-retired electrician. They are older, but also very good people. They have three children, two daughters and a son, who is the youngest of the there. One of the daughters is married and lives in another city, in Lublin, I think. The other daughter is studying at University of Warsaw, and the son is now in the third year of the local middle school. All well raised, respectful children."

"Thanks, Mom, for telling me all this. I would have never known", said Alek with a hint of sadness, although visibly glad that the mystery of the wandering boy has somewhat been resolved.

CHAPTER 9

AROUND MAY 7, the national media and the Soviet Union's state radio and television stations as well as Radio Free Europe reported that, the so-called May Offensive was launched in the early morning hours of May 4, in which the North Vietnamese began the Phase II of the Tet Offensive by striking 119 targets throughout South Vietnam, including Saigon. By this time the prevailing mood and perception on the streets, was that America lost the war and there was no doubt, the communist North Vietnam won and with it, the entire block of communist countries in Eastern and Central Europe united within the Warsaw Pact alliance. Within the next two weeks and unexpectedly, a letter arrived from the Citizens' Militia station, which was handed to Alek by a mailman, when he just happened to be outside. Alek looked at it curiously and went right back inside, handing the letter over to his mother. She looked at it quite surprised, but immediately recognizing its source and flipped it in her hands, before tearing it open between her fingers and removing a single white sheet of paper from the envelope. I was an awkwardly typed two-sentence text by the undersigned, dated just three days' prior, addressed to Mrs. Zofia Brodski, stamped and signed by Commandant Sokolowski himself. Alek stood beside his mother, who visibly distraught sat on a chair at the kitchen table, sensing the importance of what she was holding in her hands. She looked at Alek for a few seconds and began to read.

"You are hereby requested to appear in person at 8 o'clock in the morning of Monday, May 20, 1968, at the office of the Citizens' Militia of the Polish People's Republic, at 195 Warynski Street. Failure to appear may carry serious consequences and result in legal action against you by the district office of the national government."

She finished reading, sighed and looked at Alek with a strained face but defiantly, as if trying to assure him with her demeanour, that there was nothing to worry about. Alek knew his mom well beyond the exterior façade she often projected, apparently in his best interest, as she was in a habit of saying. Alek was noticeably concerned, as to what it all meant for them, and asked exactly that. "What does it all mean, Mom?"

"I'm not sure what it's all about, but obviously they want me to appear at the station next week, on Monday. There is nothing you should be worried about. Maybe Commandant Sokolowski changed his mind about your case. I'll go there."

"No Mom, we'll both go there this time."

"I don't think it's a good idea to have you involved in all this. Besides, I've dealt with Sokolowski before, and I know what to expect. Actually, he seemed like a reasonable man at the time. Perhaps somewhat narrow-minded, but reasonable, nevertheless. I would not go as far as calling him a good man, but for a cop who is perhaps just following orders from the county headquarters, he has shown his human side, maybe even deviated from the protocol and possibly goes out of his way to at least look officially formal and authoritative, but fair and reasonable to the people in the community. He's stuck in this town as we all are."

"Mom, I'm going with you this time," said Alek again.

"Oh son, what about the school? Are you going to take time off school again? You've missed many days this year already, I'm really concerned."

"Don't worry, Mom, I'll make up those few hours; no problem."

"I don't want to sit here and argue with you Alek, but we'll see when the day comes."

On Sunday, May 19 Alek already couldn't concentrate on anything else, except the upcoming visit to the police station the next day, and was mostly silent, thinking what the next day will bring. His mother was probably equally apprehensive. She didn't talk much, unless absolutely necessary, and just went about her usual chores, quietly engrossed in her own thoughts. A summons to the police station was never good news, even a visit to this small local detachment. It was always better, if possible, to live quietly beyond their reach, not to give them a reason to contact. When the next day arrived, May 20, Alek and his mom were up quite early, long before it was needed to get ready, eat breakfast, and walk about ten minutes to the station. Naturally, they came to an understanding that they both would attend the appointment. Again, they didn't talk much, but knew well what each other was thinking. Both were calm and composed, without any visible signs of fear or apprehension. They dressed in their best clothes; Alek his usual black trousers, white shirt, and dark jacket, with a tinge of gray in it, and the same pair of black, worn-out dress shoes he has had for almost two years now, which used to be too big, but now fitted his feet perfectly. Mrs. Brodski put on her long-sleeved beige blouse, simple black skirt, dark-gray cardigan with front buttons, light gray trench coat, black shoes, and a simple black leather purse. Just before they left home, she looked herself over in the mirror, then at Alek from head to toe, and once satisfied she smiled approvingly, and they both left. They walked at a regular, average pace mostly in silence, passing several kids on the way to school, and few folks on their way to work or the stores. Two old delivery trucks whirred noisily by, leaving behind a trail of light-gray smoke. Mother and son covered the distance quickly and soon found themselves in front of the familiar high two-story concrete building, near the town's centre. Double wooden entrance door led to the building's vestibule, and then two flights of steep concrete stairs with rusting metal railings all the way up to the top.

Although there were no visible streaks of urine, or the filth Mrs. Brodski encountered on her previous visit, left there late at night by the drunkards spilling out onto the streets from the nearby restaurant at closing time. Doubtless, for some it was a perfect place to relieve themselves, with a dose of newly found courage, proportional to the amount of consumed alcohol, as to make a bold statement of what they thought of those communist guardians of law and order. This time the walls were reasonably clean, obviously refreshed for the May Day celebrations, but the characteristic foul, nauseating smell still persisted inside the building, especially on the ground floor, as if its essential feature, one could not be without the other.

Mother and son ascended the stairs slowly, carefully scaling each worn out concrete step, Mrs. Brodski first, with Alek right behind her. When they reached the second floor, they stopped for a few seconds looking at the door with a sign to the office of Citizens' Militia. There was not a sound coming from anywhere on the floor, not even from inside of the office they were about to enter, just eerie, unnerving silence. Mrs. Brodski pressed the door handle slowly down, pulled it and stepped inside, with Alek close behind holding the door ajar. At first, they didn't notice anyone inside, but the at the same time the officer present must have heard the door creaking and lifted his head from behind a large desk in the back of the room, leaning backwards and stretching out his torso, as if to let it be known, that he was ready and waiting for them. It was the Commandant Sokolowski himself in full uniform and alone in the office, looking intently at the guests, while puffing a cigarette. He got up from his chair quickly, greeted the pair from afar by waving his hand, and without hesitation approached the front counter where mother and son were standing. He walked around the counter, opened a small wooden swing door, and cordially invited them inside with what seemed like a sincere smile.

"Please come inside, I've been expecting you. We have a lot to talk about, so let's all sit down. At the moment there is nobody else here, just you and I, so we have this big room to ourselves, and we can talk freely without interruptions. As you can see, there is nothing to be concerned about."

Mrs. Brodski hesitated for a second or two, looked at Alek, but then stepped right through and followed Sokolowski inside the office. The room had its own distinct strong mixture of overpowering, stifling, putrid smells dominated by old wooden furniture and worn-out floor, tobacco, sweat and some cheap cologne in various proportions. The Commandant again took a seat behind his large, clattered desk and asked them to seat down on the two wooden chairs already pulled up on the other side. He looked at them keenly for a few seconds, as if trying to sense what they were thinking, and then quickly looked around the room. The Commandant looked tired and detached, mentally absorbed in other things and disinterested in the meeting, as if he'd rather be somewhere else. He rubbed his unshaven chin a few times with his left hand in an obvious struggle to regain mental concentration, looking for just the right words to begin. He then lowered his gaze onto some documents on his desk, took one more deep puff of his cigarette, and proceeded slowly to extinguish the butt smoldering between his fingers in a large overflowing glass ashtray. Once satisfied with newly regained focus, he looked at his guests with renewed confidence and began to speak in a quiet, almost subdued tone.

"I'm glad to see you both here today and thank you for coming. I realize the letter must have given you a cause for concern, but I'd like to assure you, there is nothing to be concerned about, or to be afraid. There is a certain protocol we must follow here and that's all. My colleagues are on duties in town today, and won't be back for a few hours, I think, so we can have some privacy."

"Yes, I must admit, we both were a bit concerned. I've never been summoned to the police station in my life before. It's all new experience to me," said Mrs. Brodski, visibly unsure what to expect, despite Sokolowski's assurances.

"Well, as I said, there is nothing to worry about and it has nothing to do with that unfortunate incident with your son Aleksander last autumn. What I want to talk to you about is an entirely different matter. You must have heard about the student protests in early spring, first in Warsaw, then around the country, and in fact in other European countries. It is not a secret, it's been reported extensively by our media, and of course by Radio Free Europe. I don't suspect you listen to that foreign propaganda bombarding our airwaves around the clock, but there are some that do, and we know it. There is some strong opposition to what we're trying to do in this country. The enemies of the state are trying to derail everything we've achieved so far since the end of the World War II. We all know that there are some changes taking place at the highest levels of the government, in the media and at universities around the country."

"Yes, I've heard something about that, although I don't pay much attention to politics, but people talk about it around town," added Mrs. Brodski.

"Let me just make my point here," Sokolowski began again. "Not only our country is going through this great transformational period, but other countries too. There were protests in countries like France and Germany and America. The protests in France were particularly violent and on a much larger scale, joined by trade unions, which eventually swelled to some eight million people on indefinite wildcat strike. Soon the demonstrations spread to provincial cities, and almost brought down the government of President Charles de Gaulle. I'm sure you know all about it. Our own media covered everything quite extensively. What happened here in Poland was completely different. We don't have those problems here in this country, and I'm sure you're aware of it. In Western Europe they have some fundamental socio-economic problems, which is only to be expected sooner or later under their capitalist system, which enriches few at the expense of the vast majority, as we all know. Nevertheless, it's not what I wanted to talk to you about. There have been some changes in our country too, as a result of swift political reforms, following the student unrests. Our borders have opened up for some people, they can now for the first time, as never before since the end of WWII obtain passports legally and without any problems, without obstacles, as was sometimes the case before, and they can go, they can just leave the country, if they don't like it here and if that's what they want."

"I don't understand Sir, who can go?" asked Mrs. Brodski, quite surprised by his monologue.

"The Jews, of course. They can go."

"The Jews?"

"Yes, the Jews can go or anyone else, if that's what they want. People who think life is better somewhere else in the West. They're free to go."

"Why the Jews?" asked Mrs. Brodski with genuine skepticism.

"Let's just say, there is suspicion, actually I should say, a reliable information that many Jewish activists and high-ranking politicians of Jewish descent are behind all those protests around the country, all that mass hysteria and subversion."

"They are? What that has to do with us?" asked Mrs. Brodski quite astonished by what she has just heard.

"Yes, they are. It's a common knowledge, it was in the press and on television. To make the matter clear, I have only the influential Jews in mind, actually a small minority even among them, probably a handful. Mostly the leaders in politics, the justice system, academia and those in mass media, like the leading newspapers and magazines. Please don't take it personally Mrs. Brodski, as far as I'm concerned, you're one of us, a citizen of this country. On the other hand, it might be your chance, your only chance. There is a unique window of opportunity as never before in our post-war history, and it would be in your best interest to take advantage of the situation."

"Are you telling me we should leave our country because of who I am? Because of some apparent or imaginary transgressions of certain individuals in public life, who happen to be of Jewish ancestry, and of whom I've never even heard of?" asked Mrs. Brodski quite shocked by Commandant's suggestion, raising her voice.

"No, I didn't say that. All I'm saying is, you're on your own, just the two of you, with hardly any friends and no extended family. This is a big chance for you two, a chance of a lifetime, while all those undesirables are leaving with a one-way ticket," continued Sokolowski.

Alek was completely lost and couldn't quite understand the conversation unfolding in his presence, but for whatever reason or no reason at all, he was at ease, and just listened to the Commandant's monologues and occasional mother's interjections. He had full trust in in his mom's judgement, a woman who has proven herself over the years that she could hold her ground under any circumstances. Alek has seen his peers on many occasions being embarrassed even to be seen with their parents in public, much less intercede on their behalf. At that age it was unthinkable, an ultimate humiliation. Alek was proud of his mother; he has seen her come out on top successfully in many verbal confrontations, when pushed too far. She could easily make fools of those who persistently tried, but she never purposely looked for a face-off herself. Quietly, deep down, he greatly admired his mother, she was above all those petty posturing, jostling for attention, recognition and social status even in this obscure, small town on the outermost eastern outskirts of the country.

"Sir, why are you telling me all this? I still can't understand what some Party bureaucrats in the government and all those others in positions you've just mentioned have to do with us? Just because I'm Jewish? You're implying something that I personally don't identify with."

"Yes, yes that's true, but this is a completely different matter, you don't seem to understand what I'm trying to tell you. I'm only telling you this out of the goodness of my heart. There is nothing in it for me, please believe me. This might be your best chance at a better life, somewhere else abroad. What's keeping you here?" continued Commandant Sokolowski.

"Sir, please tell me, where in the world can we go? Why would we even want to go leave the country and go somewhere else?"

"What do you mean where? How about Israel?"

"What are you saying, Sir? I was born in Poland, that is further east, what's now part of the Soviet Union, and so was my father, and my grandfather and God knows how many generations before them."

"You do as you please, but let me tell you, the time of reckoning has come," said Sokolowski emphatically.

"I don't understand you, Sir. I have no idea what you're talking about. This must be a misunderstanding. Why did you summon us here?"

"Mrs. Brodski, let me frank with you. My own father was in the AK, the Home Army during the war as a young man, fighting the Germans. After the war, he and thousands of others like him were persecuted by the new communist government. He, who so bravely fought for liberty of this country against the German invaders, was imprisoned in 1953 on false, totally fabricated charges of active subversion, as an alleged ardent oppositionist to the new system and colluding to overthrow the government. He was locked up on Rakowiecka Street in Warsaw, tortured by the UB, the notorious Security Bureau, tried and sentenced to death in 1954. The sentence was appealed, and almost a year later it was commuted to 25 years in prison by the Secretary General of The Party, Comrade Boleslav Bierut himself. Eventually my father was released, virtually on his deathbed several months after Bierut's death in March of 1956. He died shortly after. My father was a true Polish patriot, but not according to some overzealous party bureaucrats and the secret police, who branded him a traitor. Do you know who the interrogator was, or the prosecutor, or the judge at his trial, and everyone else in between, in the new justice system?" asked Sokolowski, visibly agitated.

"No, I don't," answered Mrs. Brodski without hesitation.

"Let me tell you then, Mrs. They were blood-thirsty monsters. There were of course some home-grown Poles and scoundrels of Jewish decent involved too. Oh yes, we had them all."

"I'm really sorry to hear that, Sir. I really sympathize with you, I really do. If what you're saying is true, then I have nothing but words of sympathy for you and your family, Sir. I believe the perpetrators must be held accountable, even now, if they're still alive."

"Wishful thinking, that's all it is. Those bastards are still untouchable. For your information, my father was a well-known commander in the underground with many successful actions against the Germans to his credit. He was best known by his pseudonym, "Falcon". Yes, he probably was against the new communist government the Soviets installed in the country after the war with the help of Polish communists, but so were most people at the time. That is not a reason to sentence a good, courageous and honourable man, a true patriot to death. Have you ever heard of Bloody Luna?"

"No, I'm afraid I have not," replied Mrs. Brodski

"Julia Brystiger, the interrogator, a murderous monster, that's who she was."

"Yes, yes, I'm so sorry to hear this, Sir. Such an awful tragedy, it's incomprehensible. Please accept my deepest sympathy for you and your family, Sir," said Mrs. Brodski, distraught by the Commandant's revelations.

"I deviated from the subject perhaps into personal matters which don't concern you in the least. We all carry things around that weigh heavily on our minds and hearts, and I'm no exception, and it doesn't take much for them to surface. I know you and your family have suffered terribly during the war, but my family had suffered not only during the war, but many years after, as I just told you. We all have our demons to contend with. Nevertheless, regardless of what you may think of me, or the work I'm doing here, I sympathize with you. If you ever need a good reference, that is if you'll decide to apply for passports of course, or anything else for that matter, you can count on me. Please do not hesitate to contact me. I'll be here to help."

"Thank you, Sir. I'll take your word for it, although I'm not sure what we'll do. We both know these are uncertain times, and things could change from day to day. Just a few months ago, who would have thought we would be talking about it?"

Commandant Sokolowski suddenly became restless, looked hastily around the room, as if trying to make sure they were still alone, pulled out a cigarette from a package on his desk and lit it up. He then looked at a clock on the wall, leaned back into his chair, away from his desk and turned to his guests with a penetrating gaze, taking few deep puffs, then blew the smoke above his head. Meanwhile a distant sound of footsteps outside, still at the bottom of the concrete staircase could be heard, the sound of which was getting closer and closer with each step. The Commandant hastened to explain: "I think one of my men will be here soon, so we must be just a little more careful what we say, but there is nothing to be concerned about."

Unexpectedly, Alek moved impatiently in his creaky, wooden chair, turning to his mother and visibly worried, despite Sokolowski's assurances, said:

"Mom, can we go now, please?"

"Yes, we'll be going soon, son. Don't worry, just wait," replied his mother.

"I haven't finished yet, please stay few more minutes," added Sokolowski, and lowered his tone, looking intently at Mrs. Brodski, then at Alek, and back at Mrs. Brodski again, and then begun with a feigned concern and sincerity.

"I hope that what I said to you today, stays between us. Please do not share it with anyone. You know, during the May Day ceremonies, as you had probably heard or seen, we had rare visitors from the regional Party office and the interior ministry district offices, some very important and influential people. I talked to them privately about the situation in the country, the changes that have been taking place in the highest echelons in the capital and spilling over to provincial capitals, and the challenges we're facing here, locally. It confirmed what I've known already myself. Some individuals are allowed to leave the country if they want to, the doors are open, and there are also some undesirables, who are advised to leave the country. This is a rare opportunity indeed. You might consider taking a trip to the district passport office and apply for passports for both of you. I'm telling you this out of my genuine concern for you, perhaps despite your misgivings, and you would be wise to take this opportunity, it might not come again soon, if at all."

The front door swung open, and a uniformed, middle-aged policeman appeared, with a rather cheerful look on his face. He smiled and greeted them all cordially from a distance, not a bit surprised by the company the Commandant entertained, as if he knew all about it, or it was a normal occurrence here at the station. He proceeded behind the counter, then a coat hanger nearby, and then walked over to the nearest desk and sat down as if with a well-rehearsed routine. Alek and his mother seemed confused by the sudden addition to the room. They both turned around and looked at the policeman curiously for a few seconds, unsure what to make of it, or if they should continue the conversation or leave. Surprisingly, Sokolowski's demeanor has suddenly changed again, from somewhat nervous and restless just few minutes ago, to noticeably relaxed and fully at ease. Mrs. Brodski took it as a good sign, as the Commandant had previously assured, there was nothing to be concerned about, and said:

"Sir, I'm sure you were sincere in what you've said to us today, and we do appreciate it. We'll certainly consider your suggestion and explore our options. I must confess, it was unexpected, but it is a very interesting suggestion, although I'm quite surprised by it. Frankly, never a thought has crossed my mind to leave my country, the country of my ancestors."

"I understand your apprehension, but it might not be as bad as it seems at the moment, Mrs. Here the possibilities, as you're well aware are limited for you in this town, just like most other people, but somewhere else they might be endless. I'm afraid that with your limited resources you won't be able to resettle somewhere else in the country without assistance," said Sokolowski.

"With all due respect Sir, perhaps that's all true what you're saying, but this town is our home. There is no doubt, life here is tough at times, and as you know, we have faced difficulties and some hostilities, but we know our way around here and also have few friends. Somehow, we've managed to survive thus far. It would have never occurred to me to leave not only this town, but this country. Is there anything else you'd like to tell us, Sir?"

"No, that is all I had to say. Please think about it. I thank you both for coming here today. I'm glad we had this conversation. By the way, I still feel somewhat guilty about that incident with Aleksander, back in September of last year. I hope nothing like that has occurred to you again, young man."

"No Sir, it has not, although I'm quite careful to stay out of harm's way," replied Alek confidently.

"Good for you, son, good for you… These things happen occasionally to other kids too. I don't think you were specifically singled out, because of who you are."

"I don't know, Sir", said Alek.

"Yes, unfortunately similar assaults happen to others too, and for no good reason at all", added Commandant Sokolowski. Alek became increasingly restless, and turned to his mother again, pleading.

"Should we go now, please?"

"On a different note, Mrs. Brodski, I've spent a considerable amount of time on matters that concern you and your son. It might raise suspicions among my colleagues, here at the station. We're quite busy here with our own work, which requires immediate attention, and we're understaffed. You must have heard what happened recently; the whole town is talking about it. It's actually quite funny," interrupted Commandant Sokolowski.

"No, I haven't heard anything in particular, especially something funny, but I'm not much around town, Sir. I don't know many people, just few neighbours and friends."

"I'm not even sure if I should go into this, but to end our meeting on a positive note, let me tell you, because as I said, the whole town is talking about it. Last week there was a break-in at the rectory of our Catholic church, and the thieves discovered that our good shepherd, Father Antoni Pukalski was actually a very frugal man, true to persistent suspicions. Supposedly, the box-frame of his couch was converted into a secret compartment, and it was at least half-full of money, literally filled with stacks and wands of cash. Apparently, it wasn't some loose change either, but banknotes, paper money and lots of it. How the thieves managed to uncover that, we don't know and neither does Father Antoni, but we're conducting our full investigation at this time. Allegedly, the thieves cleaned out most of his stash and left just some of it. Obviously, they came unprepared for such a big haul."

Here the Commandant burst with prolonged round of laughter, and then continued, once he managed to regain control of his emotions.

"The funny thing is, the thieves took their time and ate most of the torte Father Antoni had in his kitchen fridge, and to top it off, they drank two bottles of some premium red wine he stored in a cabinet in his study. The thieves had quite a party there", said Commandant Sokolowski and begun to laugh loudly, without reservations. The other policeman sitting in the front of the office must have overheard the conversation and also joined in and had a chuckle.

"Yes, that's very unusual for this town, and it is actually quite comical, I must admit. Do you have an idea who was behind it?", asked Mrs. Brodski smiling, quite amused by the story herself. Alek too couldn't keep his strained, serious demeanor and for the first time during the tiring conversation was quite entertained by the story and delivered a short burst of laughter.

"No, we have no idea who was behind it, but imagine Mrs., Father Pukalski wants us to pursue this matter at all costs, no matter what, until the culprits are found. The old cleric is a stubborn man, he doesn't want this covered up, although this whole thing is quite embarrassing for the church."

"Why would it be embarrassing? I'm not sure I understand", said Mrs. Brodski.

"Why? You know, I don't go to church, but everybody knows how Pukalski is always soliciting more and more money from the pulpit, whining how poor the church is and struggling, how there is always shortage of money to cover even the current expenses, much less plan for the future. Now, we all know where the money went, right into his old sofa. If his parishioners only knew about it…But is the good shepherd shamefaced about it? Oh no, not at all."

"Well, I'm not familiar with those things. I've never been to the church, or discussed matters of Catholic faith with anyone, so it would be inappropriate for me to comment on the subject," said Mrs. Brodski diplomatically, but smiling with apparent sign of being quite entertained by the story. Soon Mrs. Brodski got up from her chair almost at the same time as Captain Sokolowski, and with it, they gave a signal the meeting has come to an end. Alek was caught off guard, listening attentively to the incredible tale, but soon he too sprang to his feet.

The Commandant, smiling broadly, extended his hand to Mrs. Brodski, then to Alek and thanked them again for coming.

He led them slowly back to the front counter and the small gate on the side, swung it open and holding it, let them through. He then bowed cautiously, smiled and said "Good-bye!" They both turned to him just before the exit door, returned "Good-bye!" and equally politely nodded and smiled, somewhat relieved that the meeting finally ended. It was not what they expected, true to the Commandant's words, there was nothing to fear indeed. Once outside, they hurried down the steep flights of concrete stairs, as if afraid of being called back to the police station, feet stomping hard on the cold steps, waking loud echoes. They didn't slow down past the front door, but continued in a hurry for several more meters, before realizing they were actually outside, and already left the police station well behind. They walked in silence, still strongly under the impression of the meeting they just had left, oblivious of the traffic on the sidewalk and the vehicles passing them in both directions on the street, and strangely, they were sad. It was a relatively fair and warm day, with few gray and white clouds scattered against the otherwise mostly blue sky. Home was the only place they wanted to be, small and crammed as it was, yet it has always been a place of refuge, away from the often misunderstood and inhospitable world outside. Soon they reached the familiar courtyard surrounded by the old, gray, mostly single or two-story row houses. Every one of those dilapidated buildings, depending on its size was divided into few separate dwellings, each one with its own entrance, either from a common corridor, or direct entrance from outside. Alek and his mom lived in a small communal, corner two–room apartment with a tiny two-piece washroom, and a separate entrance from the inside courtyard, secluded at the back of the building and facing high wooden fence separating it from the adjacent courtyard. Their building and the adjacent courtyard with two similar buildings behind the wooden fence, running barely two meters away, parallel to their kitchen window and the front entrance, were a standard in this impoverished part of town. The old, worn-out fence over the years became recognized as a natural divider between two different worlds, inhabited by distrustful and often competing families, all living misery, yet engaged in senseless, petty feuding. Their attitudes were often passed on to their children, who carried on the same irrational traditions to the next generation. Each courtyard had a life of its own, which revolved around neighbourhood-specific and unwritten rules, implemented, and which surprisingly were never questioned, but universally understood and broadly implemented. Children and adults alike, although inconspicuously, liked to peek through the gaps between the wooden planks or holes left in place of missing knots. It was more a force of habit, a simple curiosity, than any particular reason to see what was going on in the world on the other side of the fence. Older folks, especially those who didn't work outside of their homes, drew a wealth of interesting observations, exchanged information, gossip and occasionally insults with folks on the other side of the divide. It was a curious routine indeed, which became an indispensable part of their everyday lives. Once outside the neighbourhoods, it was seemingly all back to normal, almost as between the best of friends; smiles, friendly gestures, courteous greetings, handshakes and even the customary kisses planted on both cheeks between female neighbours.

Alek and his mother spent better parts of the next few days pondering the future, trying to make sense of what Commandant Sokolowski told them about emigration with such certainty and conviction, and what they had no way of confirming to be true. He either knew something others did not, or was just mindlessly repeating and spreading some unsubstantiated rumours.

CHAPTER 10

OVER TIME HOWEVER, the rumours became a reality, confirmed repeatedly in conversations, initially mentioned in general terms by the major government ran media outlets, and in greater detail by the always reliable Radio Free Europe. In the meantime, Alek's restless imagination carried him away to some faraway places, perceptions of which accumulated in his mind over the years from stories he read or heard, and which now came back vividly to life again, and seemed closer than ever. Numerous discussions he had with his mother on the subject of potentially leaving the town, or perhaps even the country, failed to produce a consensus, much less any concrete plan of action. The subject of final destination was left open to further discussion and contemplation, subject to financial resources. Whatever the final decision, Alek had full trust in his mother's judgement. Time and time again, the experience has thought him she was right, even when he was posturing and defiantly arguing with her over little things, or at times what he thought were matters of great importance. Admitting his own errors and failures in judgement didn't come easy, since everything she said sounded so true and convincing, and certainly withstood the test of time. Occasionally, Alek tested his mother's patience and resistance level by venturing a little further in his arguments in an attempt to stake out his own sphere of influence. To his surprise, he found his mother to be a rather passive and reluctant participant in those verbal family confrontations, and thus withdrawing from conversations with clearly visible sadness, before any serious argument erupted.

June 5, 1968 became another extraordinary day in the state mass media, when the only subject of the news, analysis and around the clock speculation, was the assassination of Robert Francis "Bobby" Kennedy, United States senator, brother of the late president John Fitzgerald Kennedy, assassinated November 22, 1963 in Dallas, Texas. The sombre-faced television announcers anxiously read a short, prepared statement, and others repeated them countless times on radio waves.

> *"Today, at 12:15 in the morning American senator Robert Francis Kennedy was shot three times and wounded in Los Angeles, California at the Ambassador Hotel by a 24-year-old assassin, Palestinian – Jordanian immigrant Sirhan Sirhan. The senator was immediately transferred in a grave condition to Central Receiving Hospital, and later to the Good Samaritan Hospital for immediate surgery."*

The tragic event became a continuous story with photographs of the senator splashed across television screens, until a day later the same announcers read another brief statement.

> *"American senator Robert Francis Kennedy died at 1:44 this morning at the age of 42 of gun-shot wounds sustained a day earlier. By his side were his wife Ethel, his sisters Jean Smith and Patricia Lawford, his brother-in-law Stephen Smith, and his sister-in-law Jacqueline Kennedy."*

The senator's untimely death gave the authorities and the state media a unique opportunity to exploit the tragedy for their own purpose of emphasizing political violence and general instability of the American "pseudo-democracy", the rotten capitalist system with its prevailing and inherent decadence, and once again an unmistakable proof that the system ran its course and was undoubtedly in its last throes.

The beginning of June also marked momentous days in the Brodski household. Decision has finally been made, although with much intense deliberation. They would emigrate. It was agreed on a general concept of leaving the country for good, but the final destination was still left up in the air, and a subject of further numerous discussions in the following weeks which still failed to produce a consensus, although America and Israel figured prominently in their deliberations. Ultimately however, they were at a mercy of some yet unknown bureaucrat in the district passport office, who would undoubtedly expect at least some attempt at securing a visa to a country he would deem acceptable, and which in his mind would not compromise in any way the good name and security of the country. It has always been a common knowledge, that most passport applications were denied without any explanation, although with an appeal process in place, which was long and arduous, always leading to the same result, passport denied with a brief note attached, that the applicant had a right to appeal the decision further to the Ministry of Interior. Although, it was not recommended to pursue it, as not to bring unwanted attention to oneself, those who did appeal to the Ministry, were expected to receive a customary letter stating the obvious, that the office "upholds the decision of the lower administrative instance". This notification in turn dutifully informed the applicant of one final possibility, the appeal of the last resort, to the General Secretary of The Party himself. Those desperate and persistent enough to take that route, in the best case had never received a reply, or else had their place of residence exchanged for a period of "rehabilitation" in a reformatory, which in effect was a political prison, supplemented with a generous doze of indoctrination, or even in some rare cases, those particularly determined and unruly, craving attention, never to be heard from again.

Alek's mother harboured increasingly nagging thoughts of emigrating to Israel, a sense of adventure to live happily and work among their own people. Although Israel was a foreign country, somehow at times it seemed closer than the country they were born in, and so were many generations of their predecessors. She knew well, that since the end of World War II, remnants of the Jewish populace from across Europe, so horribly decimated by the Nazis, were settling in the newly established state of Israel in 1948. The Jews finally had a state of their own, a place where they could live in peace, and not be afraid where the next threat to their very existence was coming from, at least that was the prevailing hope and dream. Nevertheless, leaving Poland was an arduous and lengthy process shrouded in uncertainty. Obtaining the passports was dependent on producing a valid visa in the capital from the embassy of their chosen country. Visa application had to be supplemented by rigorous medical examination at a designated medical clinic. The trip to Warsaw itself was a serious undertaking, requiring careful preparations, time and a significant amount of money. What followed, was a flurry of activities in the Brodski household, during which it was ultimately decided, that to ensure any chance of obtaining the passports, Israel was the only reasonable option. Then followed two tiring trips to Warsaw to obtain the visas. The ventures were successful, resulting in obtaining immigration permits or promissory notes, as they were referred to, but still without the actual passports. The trip by train covering the distance of about two hundred kilometers, which took about four hours each way, with frequent stops along the way. It gave Alek a rare and only opportunity to see the country beyond his small town. He was glued to the window most of the time each way, as the new, fascinating world passed before his eyes. The train stations along the way were mostly old historical buildings, freshly painted white or beige with some decorative elements in gray or black, like the year it was built, right at the top of the building, high above the main entrance, and right below it, a big sign in bold, black lettering with the name of the city or town. An indispensable feature at every train station, somewhere on top of a secondary, or adjacent smaller building, was a specially constructed billboard with a familiar slogan in red lettering on white background, extoling the virtues of the ruling party, superiority of socialism and achievements of the new socialist motherland.

Every time the train slowly pulled out of the station, picked up speed and left the village behind, a whole new world opened up before Alex's eyes, unlike anything he's ever seen before, a beautiful expanse of pastoral countryside. Far at a distance, solitary or small clusters of predominantly gray and white houses with few old farm buildings dotted the horizon, surrounded by vast wheat or potato fields with new, lush vegetation all-around. The scenery changed seemingly every few kilometers, from farmlands and forests to rolling green meadows, with few scattered streams and ponds or patches of overgrown shallow wetlands, with a familiar presence of white storks, always migrating here every spring from Africa, and calling these areas home for a few months every year.

Two weeks later another day trip followed, by train to the district passport office in the nearest biggest city, population of about forty thousand, and which was just over 35 kilometers away heading west, but still took well over one hour each way to cover. The train stopped at every small, impoverished village along the way, just long enough to let few new travelers on board or off the train. Sometimes the train briefly stopped in between settlements for no apparent reason, as the track cut through the middle of vast agricultural lands on both sides. Inside the train travelers impatiently paced the corridors, smoked cigarettes, speculated on the reasons for the unscheduled interruption, looked out the windows. Few disgruntled men disembarked for a few or several minutes and looked ahead of the locomotive, trying to satisfy their curiosity for the cause of the sudden stoppage. Those occurrences were always a perfect occasion for widespread grumbling on the failures of just about everything in this supposedly socialist paradise, where in fact not even one thing seemed to work faultlessly. It gave Alex a unique opportunity to relax and immerse in thoughts and dreams of what was to come, oblivious of all the commotion around him. Quietly, he thought of Israel as just a temporary residence, a stop-over for a few or several months at the most, eventually ending up in America, somewhere in one on those big metropolitan centres on the east coast, the Atlantic coast. The American films he had seen over the years and the stories he had read, all implied life was good there, certainly better than anything it had to offer in this God-forsaken town and country, and until quite recently it seemed, there was no way out of the current situation. Suddenly, with all the political social turmoil, the meaning and implications of which he could barely comprehend, there was a glimmer of hope, a narrow opening to escape the confines of this isolated, dilapidated eastern town, right on the border with the vast, flatlands of the Soviet Republic of Belorussia, itself swept by the winds of communism and with it of wicked misery.

For Alex, the sudden prospect of a long journey abroad, and a new beginning became a source of rare, yet still officially concealed, and internally suppressed daily joy, regardless if it should all turn out to be just a wishful thinking, an elusive dream with not even the slightest chance of its realization. In the following days and weeks, the daydreaming became an increasingly frequent, almost routine escape into the unknown, magical world, which gave him a rare comfort, a sense of remarkable contentment and ever-growing hope, while the prospect and burden of dealing with the vast government bureaucracy in the district passport office fell on his mother. Soon it became apparent, the whole endeavour was so difficult, demeaning and time consuming, that at times they began to doubt the sense of the whole undertaking. First, there were the lengthy applications to be filled, few original documents to be submitted, such as confirmation of their residence from the town hall, document of previous residence, record of employment for Mrs. Brodski, and an enrollment confirmation from his school for Alek, birth certificates for both of them, death certificate for Jakub Brodski, photographs and finally processing fee, which in itself was a significant amount of money, at least in their household.

The passport office was conveniently located with various local municipal government offices in the most prominent building in the town's square, and most importantly, the district Party headquarters. It was a common perception, that entering that building was something one should do as a last resort, when all other options failed, or there were no other options. Clients, ordinary citizens were mistreated right from the front counter by rude, conceited, and incompetent personnel, usually young women with plain, average looks, but manners of spoiled princesses, with questionable education and embarrassing lack of knowledge on the whole range issues within the scope of their respective departments. Most of the women seemed to be in a permanent state of agitation, exceedingly impatient, and any prolonged or persistent questioning from a reluctant, cowering client, generally considered an intruder, would set them off, and certainly with assured impunity. The secretaries, clerks and most department managers were especially abrasive, often outright abusive, especially towards country and small-town folks or peasants, whom they usually considered lesser beings. The superficial reasons, real or imaginary pertained to such things as "intruder's" dress code, language skills, lack of good manners and overall personal hygiene. The prejudice was prevalent in most government offices, in fact it was an inherent part of the bloody communist system, and generally accepted as a sad fact of life. Openly challenging any of the government employees, from the lowest in rank to management was not recommended.

It could only guarantee an absolute failure of mission they tried to accomplish on their visit, not to mention a humiliating public lecture, right there on the spot, laced with an array of derogatory epithets. At best of times, to get anything done, usually meant two or three trips to that dreaded institution. Briberies, one of the greatest achievements of the socialist experiment, were the most common assurances of business done quickly and efficiently, usually on the first trip, unless some brazenly disappointed bureaucrat higher up the ladder thought the "voluntary donation" was not enough. The same rules applied to the small district passport office, serving the city, surrounding few small towns and villages within about fifty-kilometre radius.

Comrade Rakowski or simply "Rak", as he was commonly referred to, and of course Party member in good standing, was the head of the department with a staff of just a few employees, consisting of his deputy and four female clerks. Rakowski was a middle-age tall and rather slender man with a small moustache, which for some inexplicable reason was usually the norm for a male civil servant or a policeman. His services and favours were in great demand, and his powers vast. He knew it well, and used them to his best advantage, like an omnipotent God in matters of life and death. For many folks obtaining a passport to go anywhere beyond the country's western border, a trip sometimes meticulously planned for years, and quite often kept secret till the very end, was a dream come true, an opportunity of a lifetime. Comrade Rakowski was well known for his spiteful, malicious streak, apparent devotion to the socialist cause, whether genuine or pretended was rather impossible to tell. Undoubtedly, he had good connections, and must have served his masters well, since he was at it for over six years now, and as comfortable in his position, as anybody who knew how to play the game well. The whole bloody cancerous system in fact over the years became a perfect breeding ground for venomous, conscience-depleted bastards like him. His deputy Stasiuk, also quickly made a name for himself, closely following in his boss's footsteps; the familiar, proven path to guaranteed success in his career, Party rank and financial security. Almost all of the employees in the passport department, or any government office for that matter, right from the first female clerk behind the front counter, had an aura of superiority about them. They displayed total lack of understanding, sensitivity or empathy for the plight of often desperate clientele, some with serious family matters, or pressing administrative issues to be resolved. The clerks were immovable. The way they walked, the way they talked, even the way they looked at clients, would have been enough to scare off even the most determined, or the most desperate souls, if only there were other options. It was not uncommon to hear hushed profanities directed at those civil servants from around the corner, from the restless clientele waiting in the corridor. One could overhear the popular adage, especially among impatient men, who summed-up that particular brand of indolence in one sentence: *"They're like old bitter whores, not so understanding and sensitive anymore."*

Since there were no other options for those who decided to travel abroad, they all had to endure the indignities and abase themselves in highly deferential postures, preferably with unmistakable signs of profound veneration towards those superior beings on the other side of the counter, or any of the small private offices behind closed doors, where the second wave of scorn was waiting for them. As at all government offices, right across the double entrance door, on the main feature wall, hanged the familiar and ever-present three portraits. One was a sizeable black and white likeness of the First Secretary of The Party, Wladyslav Gomulka, then in the middle the white eagle on red background, the country's national symbol, and to the right hanged black and white photograph of perfectly bald Prime Minister Jozef Cyrankiewicz, both ardent communists peering down sternly from above, or "*red bourgeoisie*" as they and the top executives of The Party were often referred to by ordinary folks.

CHAPTER 11

AFTER INITIAL REGISTRATION at the front counter, the Brodskis were asked to sit in the waiting room, which was just outside the door, with several simple wooden chairs lined-up on both sides of a long corridor, along a nondescript, beige walls with few randomly spaced "No Smoking" signs. Most of the chairs were already taken up by other vividly tired and disillusioned people, silently waiting for hours for their turn to be served. They all waited, Alek and his mother and all those other strangers sharing furtive glances, rolling their eyes, exchanging seldom more than few words, but bound by common frustrations, disappointments and fear of the unknown. They already had the applications ready, which consisted of two double-sided pages of flimsy, low quality paper folded in the middle, the processing fee, along with two photographs each, and all the supporting documents. The whole stack was looked over by one of the clerks. The sluggish female clerk rather indifferently flipped the pages, with what seemed like an approving nod and few scant, barely comprehensible words, signed and stamped the applications at the top, and directed them to the waiting room. From time to time one of the perpetually irritated and callous female clerks came out from behind the counter and called out somebody's family name once, twice, or rarely three times if there was no immediate reaction, and the person called out didn't jump to his feet immediately. Strangely, many people were waiting there for hours, until growing increasingly restless and from time to time walking up in frustration to the front counter, angrily demanding to know what they were waiting for, the reason for the delay, or the status of their applications.

Among the clients was a middle-age tall and bearded man attracting much attention, pacing nervously back and forth with his head down, absorbed in his thoughts, and from time to time letting out an incomprehensible curse or several familiar profanities. He didn't elicit much sympathy, if that was his intention, on the contrary the folks looked at him with disdain and apprehension, perhaps afraid the man would unexpectedly turn his anger towards one of them, someone randomly chosen. Even that lone, disruptive client added to the dreadful atmosphere of the whole establishment.

The common understanding was, that every newly submitted application would be followed by a grueling interview, or those who had submitted their passport applications weeks before, were there on their second or third visit to finally pick up their new, long expected cherished document. The whole process was of course rigged and wrapped in a vail of uncertainty, from initial submittal of the application to finally receiving the ready passport, or official notification in the mail, that the application was denied without any further explanation, but always with an added brief note, that the negative decision could be appealed. In cases where the applicant chose to appeal and had to appear at least once more, it usually meant there were other expectations, past the front counter, in one of the offices somewhere in the back, which was an essential part of the whole process. Subtle, unwritten message was being conveyed to the applicant, that financial considerations were now at play; the great wheel of government bureaucracy had to be greased.

Those who knew the game well and came prepared with an envelope stuffed with some noteworthy banknotes, were usually the lucky ones, who would eventually leave the passport office with a smile on their faces and a passport in hand. Those who knew how to play the game, but refused to play it, convinced they had the law on their side, and approached the process with a dose of visible hostility, were doomed to fail or in rare cases even worse. There were stories passed around of such rebellious individuals charged with public disturbance, disorderly conduct or even subversion. The police station was nearby, and the lawmen ready to intervene. There were also people who were never truly exposed to any dealings with all those various government offices or agencies, and simply just didn't know how to go about it, or were too naïve thinking, all was well and in great order in the new socialist motherland with the ever-caring, benevolent government of the people, for the people and by the people. They would soon find out that naiveté or outright ignorance were not mitigating factors, they wouldn't get them anywhere, and the only option was to learn the game fast and play by the unwritten rules. Naturally, Mrs. Brodski and Alek were both very nervous about the whole affair, since they have never had to deal with any government authorities at this level, where everything seemed strangely foreign and overwhelming, permeated with fear and elevated to almost life and death significance. To make the matters worse, they certainly didn't know how to play the game, in fact they didn't even know such option existed in the first place. The relative comfort of waiting in the corridor for what seemed now like at least two or three hours was suddenly interrupted by a loud female voice: "Brodski!" People looked in the direction where it came from, but nobody moved. Alek and his mom were completely absorbed by their own quiet conversation, oblivious of the surroundings beyond their two chairs, as if forgetting the reality of life beyond.

The young female clerk who came out from the main office around the corner, stood at the head of the narrow waiting room, and looked impatiently over the two rows of people sitting along the walls on both sides of the corridor. Visibly unhappy about the lack of immediate response, she bellowed again:

"Brodski!", "Is Brodski here?"

Alek caught the sound of his name and sprang to his feet, still somewhat confused by the sudden, least expected interruption, followed by his mom, who also heard her name this time loud and clear. Mrs. Brodski surged forward first, and Alek followed right behind her towards the first office on the left side. As soon as the clerk saw two people respond to her call and up on their feet, she retreated promptly back to the office. They came through the door and remorsefully approached the long front counter. The clerk was already standing there impassively looking down at some papers. Instinctively she lifted her head, as if expecting the clients to arrive there on the other side at that precise moment. Mrs. Brodski began apologetically in a subdued voice.

"I'm sorry about it Mrs., but we didn't hear you call out our name, we were so distracted by the noise, all those people..."

"No need to explain Mrs. Brodski. I understand."

"Thank you, that's very nice of you. You must be so busy here."

"Yes, we're very busy. The summer season is near, so naturally people travel everywhere, and many more travel abroad than ever before, as people prosper and can afford it, or have relatives in other countries. Of course, nowadays we have many more clients like you, who would simply like to emigrate. It is written Israel in your applications. Any particular reason why you chose Israel? Don't like it here Mrs. Brodski?"

"Oh no, no, it's not that we don't like it here, not at all. We love this country, we are citizens, this is our home, the only country we've ever known. You see, there are just the two of us. My husband died several years ago, and it's been a real struggle at times. All my close relatives didn't survive the war, and the few distant cousins that I know of and are still alive, were caught in confusion when the border was redrawn just after the war. They just stayed there on the other side, in the Soviet Union."

"Are you Jewish, Mrs. Brodski?"

"Yes, we are."

"I'm sorry for being so intrusive, it's actually none of my business, but I'd like to ask you, just out of curiosity, and you might be asked this later by Comrade Rakowski, during your interview. Is the reason for your emigration to Israel to be among your own people? Do you feel alienated here? Did you experience any problems with the people that you live among?"

"You see, before the war my family lived in the eastern parts of Poland, but since the border was moved west, and the eastern parts annexed by the Soviet Union, we resettled on this side of the border, as thousands of other like us."

"Well, it's a matter of opinion whether it was annexed, or previously occupied by our country, but that's not for us to judge. So, when are you planning to travel Mrs. Brodski?"

"We're not sure yet, it all depends, if we'll be granted the passports, which I hope won't take long."

"Since it's a matter of emigration, not just a short trip abroad, as most people waiting here are planning to do, you'll have to see Comrade Rakowski, or his deputy Comrade Stasiuk. Yours is certainly a more serious matter, and in cases such as this, decisions are not taken hastily. It's a standard procedure and nothing to be overly concerned about. I'm afraid you'll have to come back here another time Mrs. Brodski."

"I'm sorry to hear that. I thought it would be just a simple procedure and all could be done in one day. We were waiting here for hours. I took a day off work and Alek a day off school, and now we are told we have come back another day?"

"I know, life seems unfair. Don't we all know that? Mrs. Brodski, it's not every day we have someone here, who for whatever reason wants to emigrate. These things are not taken lightly in our department. We'd like to know why? Why would anyone want to leave this beautiful, increasingly prosperous, and democratic country and go somewhere else?"

"I've explained it to you already Mrs. Of course, it's not all that simple, there are many other things at play, which we've taken into account. The decision didn't come lightly. It's our future at stake."

"I'm sorry for the inconvenience Mrs. Brodski, but you just might have to explain all those reasons to Mr. Rakowski. I have nothing to do with it. These are the procedures. You'll be notified in the mail when to appear next time."

"How soon will we receive the notice to appear?"

"You should be getting it within two to three weeks."

"So, is this all for today, nothing else that can be done?"

"Yes, Mrs. Brodski, this will be all for today. I'm sorry once again for the inconvenience, but we must follow some strict regulations here, especially if it's about more than just a passport for a short trip abroad. We don't set the policies here, we just implement them."

"Yes, I understand."

"Good day to you both!"

"Good day, Sir!"

Alek and his mom turned away from the front counter and just stood there in silence for a few seconds looking at each other, as if not quite sure what to do. There was a visible concern on their faces, a feeling of helplessness. Slowly, without a word, they began to move towards the door. Once outside the office, they both looked one last time at the people sitting on both sides of the corridor, waiting for their names to be called. Alek pushed the double, heavy wooden door open and they left the corridor, then descended few uneven, worn-out concrete steps down, then through the main entrance door and onto the sidewalk. Once outside, they stopped in front of the government building, appearing disoriented and sad. They looked around within the immediate vicinity of the city's square, then at each other, quite unsure of their next move. Passersby walked around them and hurried indifferently ahead, preoccupied with their own business. Alek, standing about three feet away from his mother, looked straight into her dark, tear swelled eyes, waiting for her to decide the next move. She reached into her purse with one hand and ran her fingers through the contents, and once satisfied, lifted her head up with renewed determination and looked around the city square. She noticed a sign "Dairy Bar" above the door of one of the businesses that filled this large city square on all four sides, with a narrow cobblestone exit-street in each corner. Mrs. Brodski quickly regained her composure, reluctant to show her weakness, pretended all was well and the minor irritable experience at the district government office should not consume their wellbeing and ruin the rest of their day. In retrospect, she was actually positively surprised by the overall treatment they received from the clerk, for she expected much worse. The employee wasn't overtly friendly, but she wasn't rude or particularly ill-tempered either, although certainly emotionless and formally detached. Mrs. Brodski then turned to her son.

"Alek, let us go and eat something. It'll do us good. What do you say?"

"Sure, mom. Where to?"

"How about that "Dairy Bar" on the other side?" She pointed with her finger to the left row of stores and small businesses.

"Sounds good. I'm hungry."

Without further hesitation they started walking silently in the direction of the bar, looking at the enticing sign at a distance, above dark-green wooden entrance door. Soon they found themselves right in front of it, with two large, misted over windows, one on each side, adorned with sagging, old, beige curtains inside the premises, marking the approximate size of the bar. Alek reached for the door handle first, pulled it and held it open for his mother. She walked right in, and Alek followed slowly behind. Once inside, they were hit by a strong, pleasing smell of cooked food. The bar was almost full, only few scattered seats remained vacant. The furnishings and décor were basic, but functional and designed for a high daily turnover of indiscriminate working-class clientele.

Several wooden tables with metal legs and glass tabletop covers were scattered around the sizeable room, each with four matching plain wooden chairs. Each table and every other piece of furniture had a rather old, overused and well worn-out appearance. The entire floor area was covered with white and dark-gray square porcelain tiles, with numerous cracks and chips, over the years filled with multiple layers of grime. Here too hanged the three familiar portraits of the country's "saviors" on one of the walls, the First Secretary Gomulka of United Workers' Party on one side and the Prime Minister Cyrankiewicz on the other and the white eagle in the middle, the country's national symbol, watching over the diners from above.

It was a self-serve restaurant. Alek and his mom approached the service counter, behind which two corpulent and rather busty, past middle-age women with rosy cheeks stood, serving the dishes, with a third younger and relatively slim, but pale women moving around behind their backs. The Brodskis looked up at the back wall, big part of which was covered with the establishment's menu on a large, plastic panel densely covered with black, removable letters and numbers. The menu didn't entirely or accurately reflect the restaurant's name, "Dairy Bar", but none of the items served were meat-based. The bar served two types of cereal with milk, potato and flour pancakes, cheese and potato filled pierogis, cottage cheese crapes, few varieties of egg dishes, baked goods, yogurt, coffee and tea. They both ordered potato pancakes, the "latkes" and the always popular grain coffee with milk, which in these parts has become a cheap, universally available substitute for the much more expensive real coffee, usually available only at better restaurants and cafés. Without much difficulty they were able to locate two vacant chairs at one of the far inside corner tables already occupied by two other people and sat down to eat. They ate in silence, evading curious, meaningless glances that usually followed newly entered customers. Mrs. Brodski avoided being drawn into sarcastic attempts at conversation from a young couple sharing the table with them, while Alek ignored them completely, devouring his portion rather quickly. His mother however was taking her time, visibly engrossed in thoughts, what he guessed must have been matters related to the passport bureau. Alek looked around the premises with great interest; the customers, the furniture, the décor and the three female employees behind the counter, since it was one of only few times in his entire life they were eating outside of their own home. He recognized that majority of customers were most likely out of town visitors, just like they were; few farmers from the villages on a business trip or shopping excursion to the district capital, intermingled with possibly few locals. The peasants were quite easily recognizable by the cloths they were wearing, and even by the way they were moving around and behaving, as opposed to the local residents, who were certainly better dressed and showed more ease of movement and confidence. The peasants were mostly dressed in oversized, dark, outdated, and well-worn out clothing, reminiscent of the 1950's style. The women had colourful scarves over their heads, some tied under their chins, and still other had them just loosely wrapped around. Most men wore old style, dark suites, usually with stripes and long, wide lapels. The matching baggy, turn-up trousers they were wearing, all seemed too long, with excess folding onto their black dress shoes. Some men were sporting a beret on their heads, which was often considered an indispensable part of any farmer's attire, completing the image, so easily recognizable by city dwellers, and what over the years became a frequent subject of derision, as expressed in the popular local saying:

"In summertime or fall, you can always tell a peasant by his beret from them all."

Alek couldn't help it, but smiled just thinking about it, while looking at the people all around. His mom noticed it, but didn't say a word, and also smiled warmly, without asking her son for details of his amusement.

"We have to go now, son. We must hurry back to the train station to catch the four o'clock train back home", said Mrs. Brodski

"Sure mom, I'm ready."

They both took the last few quicker sips of their grain coffee, got up, thanked the young couple and left the table behind without looking back. Once outside, Mrs. Brodski led the way out of the large city square, into some side streets and straight to the train station, which was in the city's southern district. Despite a considerable distance to cross, they walked briskly, and the march was most enjoyable. New imposing, concrete apartment buildings and mature, leafy trees lined both sides of the street, and green belts with equally spaced shrubs and occasional "Keep off the grass" signs separated the sidewalks from asphalt driveway. Somewhere halfway to the station, they crossed a small bridge over a narrow river, which ran through the south side of the city, with a wide strip of primal green meadow on both banks with multitude of colourful wildflowers, several children playing, happily running around, kicking a ball, and flying a kite.

Soon Mrs. Brodski and Alek boarded their train at the second platform from the old, historic station building, already almost filled with mostly commuting workers from the villages, and probably some travelers from all-around the area on a day trip to the county's capital. It was difficult to find two adjacent vacant seats, although there were few scattered single seats here and there, and Mrs. Brodski soon took up one of them. Alek preferred standing in the corridor to seating squeezed in a packed compartment with seven or more strangers, gasping for fresh air, and in time as the train pulled away, certainly someone among them, who would try to engage him in a meaningless conversation, and ask questions he didn't want to answer. Besides, he had this well preconceived idea of what it would be like. Seating in a compartment meant being exposed to all those foreign, foul smells emanating from a group of exhausted travelers, surely some industrial workers and peasants, many in their tattered clothing, and who were on their way back to distant suburbs and nearby villages. The contents of their belonging were spread out on the shelves above their heads, or in bulging bags at their feet, and once the sliding door of the compartment was closed, the commuters were exposed to the ever-present stifling air. It would somehow never occur to anyone trapped inside to open the window, or quite often the window mechanism itself was broken, and the window permanently shut, and travelers trapped in the stifling air for the length of the trip. Most passengers were reluctant to be the first to get up and struggle with the window for fear of failure, or inviting an unwelcome comment, in case the rest were happy with the way it was. It was all of a particular concern to young Alek. He was instinctively sensitive to all those inconveniences, growing up quietly in relative seclusion, rarely interacting with people beyond the circle of his peers at school and out of necessity, or few neighbours, perhaps just two or three he considered quite positively disposed towards him or his mother, with no overtly visible signs of prejudice. There were several passengers in the corridor of the train carriage, mostly men, some with their arms resting on the lowered windows, taking in the scenery passing them by, and some with their backs leaning heavily against the walls of compartments, looking impassively ahead, smoking cigarettes. The few partially open windows along the length of the narrow corridor created an unpleasant wind draft with the moving train, but also a surge of fresh air from the outside, clearing up the long interior from the clouds of cigarette smoke. The familiar whistle of the locomotive could be heard occasionally coming from the front of the train, ahead of every railway crossing along the way. Steam engines were still a prevailing sight in these parts, where distances were short, and the train covered this stretch of eastern track few times a day. Alek overcome by curiosity and nostalgia stood by one of the windows, looking at scattered farm buildings and residential houses along the way, some near the railway track, and some further out in the distance, nestled in a serene pastoral setting of variety of already cultivated farm fields, patches of green meadows dotted with colourful wildflowers beneath a boundless, still mostly blue sky, merging with the vast land on a blurred, distant horizon. The early evening warm wind, coming through the open windows was blowing at Alek standing near, and in its strange way it was a welcome relief, gently soothing his strained face, alleviating the accumulated pain of his tormented mind. Tears swelled in his eyes, and he was sad. The end of the school year was near, within days, and as every year at this time, a period of particularly stressful activities. The end of eighth grade for Alek also meant temporary freedom at last, but most importantly imminent application to a secondary or trade school, and where the final marks from elementary school were vital for acceptance. The two-year trade school was usually preferred choice for those somewhat less ambitious students, or still undecided and wavering "late bloomers" with limited academic background, and as a last resort or transitional period, when all other attempts failed. Entrance exams testing proficiency in written language, literature, and of course in mathematics were standard and compulsory at the only local middle school, although probably with a scaled down level of expectations, than it would have been at most secondary schools in larger metropolitan areas. Some students opted out for better, reputable boarding schools in the district or provincial capitals, which meant living away from families and only occasional visits home during major statutory holidays or family emergencies. Worst of all, a school away from home meant living with a group of teenagers one would have otherwise never met or cared to meet. Alek's academic performance thus far was mediocre, although he didn't find it exceedingly difficult, but rather overwhelming. The number of mandatory subjects and the volume of mundane, repetitive homework was more than he able to process and attend to at any given time especially when it so often interfered with his other interests and daydreaming. Currently in his life, the only logical choice for Alek was the local secondary school, although he was reluctant to pursue his further education in most likely similarly inhospitable environment, he was already so familiar with. The official end of school year celebration came and went, marking it the last day when mandatory attendance was closely monitored and expected. As always, certificates were handed out with a transcript of final marks, which for many students and their parents was a cause for celebration, but unfortunately for some, it was a day of complete disappointment, a failure, almost a disaster. It wasn't uncommon to see parents and their offspring from various classes huddling together and sobbing, or parents in utter despair confronting their children outright, scolding them and shouting. Few pupils were always found with their heads down, sitting somewhere in a secluded school corridor, while inconsolable, utterly devastated parents were nervously pacing around, asking helplessly: "What now?"

Failing marks those days, as all knew well, meant a grade holdback, a repetition of the whole schoolyear. It was commonly understood, that good secondary and then post-secondary education almost always meant success, future position, relative prosperity and a ticket out of this small, forgotten town to a new dream world of the country's large urban centres, where opportunities were knocking at the door, and certainly drastically increased for those who supplemented their education by joining the ranks of The United Workers' Party.

For Alek it was not so much about career anymore, but still gaining valuable knowledge and experience while waiting, just in the event they leave the country. In the worst case, a survival for at least four years at the secondary school, if everything goes well academically, enduring all the special attention from his peers, as can only be generously bestowed on the town's only known young male Jew. He would be within easy reach for all those who made it their life's purpose to relive their frustrations on an easy target, or brazenly show their contempt and hostility for no apparent reason, other than trying to impress others, similarly underachieving types, or just plain ignorance, in line with their only plainly visible quality. The act would make them feel good about themselves for few minutes at a time, an instant gratification, or otherwise they had little else to show and feel good about.

In the best case, the application for admission to secondary school was just a temporary measure, while patiently waiting for the passports from district office, but just in case it would take longer than they thought, the final, positive result was never in doubt, or so they thought. The anxiety was dispelled in the beginning of July, when a summons to appear at the passport office within two weeks came in the mail, typed on the same flimsy, government office standard sheet of paper, by the same obviously long outdated typewriter with clearly visible indentations around each letter. The note was without any additional explanation or a hint whether the passports were granted or declined. If it were not for the stress associated with the whole process, another trip by train to district capital would have been a welcome break from the too familiar, depressing, poverty stricken and perpetually hopeless surroundings of their obscure little town, if only for a day.

CHAPTER 12

ALEK AND HIS mom were back again in the same high two-story building housing the City Hall and few essential federal government offices, serving the city and the entire county. They were on time, as directed at 10 o'clock in the morning, but again at the front desk they were asked to wait outside the door, in the same long corridor with chairs lined up on both sides, serving as the waiting room. They spent the time looking at the people coming and going and all those waiting, until well over one hour later, a female clerk came from around the corner and called out distinctly.

"Brodski!"

Alek and Mrs. Brodski quickly got up, and headed in the direction of the female clerk, standing there, just outside the door to the passport office. Mrs. Brodski smiled and walked right behind her with Alek dragging his feet few steps behind.

"Please follow me. Comrade Rakowski will see you now."

Thy walked passed the front desk, then through L- shaped corridor to the very back, which housed few separate offices, each behind closed, heavy wooden door. The clerk stopped in from of the last door on left hand side and knocked. The man inside responded after a few seconds.

"Come in, please!"

The clerk opened the door, and let the mother and son in, then closed the door behind them. Comrade Rakowski who was sitting behind a large oak desk, immediately lifted his head up, looked over the visitors and respectfully got up and with a barely visible smile on his lips said:

"Please, sit down", pointing with his stretched out right hand to two wooden chairs on the other side of his desk, and then sat down again. Alek and Zofia pulled the chairs and hesitatingly sat down too, anxiously waiting for Rakowski's next move. He looked down silently at some documents scattered around his desk, for what seemed like a minute or two, while Alek quickly surveyed his rather sizeable office. There was one large, slightly open window with a long lace curtain, almost down to the hardwood floor, gently waving in the light breeze coming through. Distant, muffled street noise could be heard from the outside. The air in the office reeked heavily of tobacco with a mixture of cologne and characteristic smell of antique furniture and interior of an old building. There were several documents spread out across his desk and few piles of stacked papers on both sides, some pens and pencils and of course a crystal ashtray with several cigarette butts in it already. Directly behind Comrade Rakowski, up on the wall hung the ever-present three portraits, cultivating the cult of personality for many years now. The two highest ranking communists in the land, so concerned and obsessed with their infallibility and eventual immortality, must have sanctioned this distasteful, pathetic display themselves. Rakowski's office also housed a high brown wooden bookcase with several volumes of neatly stacked books, mostly bound in dark-red or brown hard covers, two matching filing cabinets, free-standing wooden coat rack, plain worn-out couch up against the wall near the entrance door, and small coffee table beside it. Comrade Rakowski was wearing a white dress shirt with sleeves rolled up halfway to his elbows, with a slightly loosened navy-blue tie around his neck, and without a jacket, which was hanged on that ornate coat rack in the corner, next to the bookcase. Comrade Rakowski lifted his head up, looked over his visitors, and began in a slow, measured tone.

"I've looked at your passport applications carefully. It says here that you're a widow Mrs. Brodski, and there are just the two of you in your family from what I can see. You have also indicated that you're planning to emigrate to Israel. Why do you want to leave the country, and why Israel?"

"We are Jewish, Sir."

"I know that, but why do you want to leave this country?

"We want to settle in Israel. I think it will be good for both of us in our circumstances."

Rakowski looked at them with his piercing, steely blue eyes and a little smirk in the corners of his lips and continued.

"Are you not happy here in Poland, is that the reason?"

"Sir no, it is not the main reason, or should I say it is not the reason at all. I'm a single mother with a son fast growing up, with limited resources, a job at a fruit and vegetable processing plant with hours cut at least in half every winter and spring. We have no immediate or extended family in this country that I know of, very few friends and no possibilities for any improvement in the near future, as far as I can see. As a mother I have to think not only about my own future, but primarily about the future of my son."

"You think that Israel is the solution to your problems, Mrs. Brodski?"

"I think living among our own people would certainly open up new opportunities for both of us. I've heard that the government is letting people out, all those who want to emigrate."

"Actually, is not that simple Mrs. Brodski. I don't know where you've heard this, or who told you this story, but that's not exactly the whole truth."

"Mr. Rakowski, there must be something to it, because even our media were alluding to this, and people are talking."

"People are talking? And what are they saying?"

"That the Jews and others can leave, if they want to."

"Let me tell you Mrs. And I'll be frank with you. Of course, some of our citizens of Jewish descent and others, those from the east can leave the country to reunite their families, if they wish to. In fact, many have already left, but those were different people."

"What do you mean by different people, Sir. I don't understand."

"What I mean is, those are people who occupy or occupied high positions in the country, mostly in the government, academia, judiciary, and mass media. In essence, privileged members of our society, who were still dissatisfied or disillusioned with what the country has given them. Those are the most ungrateful, subversive scoundrels, I dare to say traitors, who now spit at our motherland, and who were secretly trying to subvert the socialist order and structure of our society, because they had their own egotistic ideas, as to what the socio-political system of the country and their own role in it should be. It must be said, those corrupt enemies of the state and of the people, wanted to gain even more power and control for themselves, as if they haven't had enough already. After all, at one time or another, many of them were at the forefront of the revolutionary movement. And now they don't like the system they were instrumental in creating. Do you realize what the cost of their experiment was in human lives?"

"Sir, we are not interested in politics, or what happened in the highest circles of the government and all those other institutions you've mentioned. That's something I've never really understood and haven't followed closely the current events. For us, it is the everyday life, but mainly our future as the motivating factor, nothing else."

"Mrs. Brodski, you sound very naïve. Are you trying to tell me, you've never heard about the student protests instigated by the sons of many prominent Jewish individuals?"

"I've heard about the protests of course, it's not a secret anymore, it's a common knowledge, which was covered quite extensively by our own media at the time, but I don't know much about the background of those unrests. Actually, I'm not interested in those unrests, that supposedly shook up the whole country. As I said, we both have our own concerns, far removed from what's happening in the capital and other big cities."

"I see your point, but as I said, those are the people who are mostly leaving the country now. If they don't like it so much here, and their goal was to subvert all that we've worked so hard to build on the ashes of World War II, then let them go. We'll be better off without them."

"Mr. Rakowski, I really don't know much about politics, nor do I want to, for me the most important thing is the future of my only son Alek, and my own, of course."

"Please don't make it sound like it's been such a tragedy for you here in our democratic, increasingly prosperous, socialist country. There are opportunities here for everyone, if one only tries."

"Sir, believe me, we've tried everything."

"Perhaps you haven't tried hard enough. How do you get by then, if you're saying your hours at work are severely limited during winter and spring?"

"I do some housekeeping."

"I don't mean to pry into your private life, but what happened to your husband, if I may ask?"

"Jakub died of leukemia about eight years ago."

"I'm sorry to hear that. Have you ever considered re-marrying, Mrs. Brodski? I hope you don't mind me asking this, but you're still young and an attractive woman. "

"I've been asked this before, but to answer your question, no I have not considered re-marrying. I'm quite happy the way I am."

"I respect that. It's your choice, but things would have been much easier."

"Perhaps, but not necessarily. My options are rather limited in that small town. There are no Jewish men that I know of, and as I said, I'm not interested anyway."

"How about you, young man, why would you want to go abroad, and to Israel of all places? Rakowski turned suddenly to Alek, when least expected. He became confused, clearly caught by surprise.

"I don't know. As mom said...", answered Alek with uncertainty. In the presence of his mother, he learned to rely on her to take care of family business, and knew well, she would never disappoint. Faced with direct confrontation he was lost for words, especially in matters he knew very little about, although they discussed those topics previously at length. Better life abroad was still a product of their hopes and imagination, rather than actual, verifiable fact.

"What do you mean you don't know? You must have thought about it. You have no family there, no friends. You've never been to Israel before. Why the hell would anybody want to go there? That country is quite unstable, practically in a permanent state of war, with enemies all-around, especially after the Six-Day War just over a year ago."

"I have no friends here either," answered Alek quietly.

"Oh, I don't believe that, young man. Everyone has friends at your age. Maybe not always the kind of friends you'd like, but friends nevertheless."

"I don't. I used to get picked on sometimes at school, and I'm glad that is over. I was harassed on the streets too. I think, it would be nice to see other countries too."

"Yes, we all do. We live in uncertain times now, and this country while not perfect yet, we all know that, but certainly is an example of peace, economic stability, relative prosperity, equality, justice and social progress, and the so-called West can only dream about. You must know by now what's happening around the world, even in America."

"Not really, I don't know those things, but from what I've read, seen in magazines and heard on the radio, it all looks good," responded Alek assertively.

"Mrs. Brodski," Rakowski turned again to Alek's mother, "I don't know what nonsense you've been feeding your son with, but you both should think long and hard about your emigration plans. There is no better place for both of you, than our country, I assure you. There have been enormous opportunities created for women here, as never before in history, thanks to our superior social and economic system, guaranteeing full employment, as opposed to the Western economics, social and moral decadence. Which seems to me, is still stuck in the XIX century mentality and with no way out. Let me cite to you one of my favourite quotes from Karl Marx:

"*Social progress can be measured exactly by the position of the fair sex in a society, the ugly ones included.*"

After saying this, Rakowski burst with a brief laughter, visibly proud of himself, and then quickly reached out for a package of cigarettes on the right side of his desk, near the ashtray. He pulled one out and lit it up, inhaling deeply, and then releasing a big cloud of white smoke above his head. Meanwhile Mrs. Brodski listened carefully to his monologue and watched his every gesture, and finally retorted with a surprising frankness.

"Personally, I don't know about that, perhaps you speak from the experience of your position and environment you've been working and living in, but I haven't been exposed to all those opportunities, or seen much progress, if any, in the last few years, certainly not in these parts. Our position is not something to be envied."

"Well, maybe you haven't been looking in the right places or hard enough? Have you thought about upgrading your skills or learning something new? Like a new skill or a trade?" Comrade Rakowski was now clearly content and in total control of the conversation, visibly enjoying his arguments and impunity which his position guaranteed. It entitled him to say whatever and how he wanted. He didn't miss an opportunity to use it, in fact he seemed to relish every minute of the conversation. After a few seconds pause, like a well indoctrinated, professional propagandist, he looked at Mrs. Brodski and added with a cynical smile:

"Again, Karl Marx quite accurately also said: *"From each according to his abilities, to each according to his needs."* And then he quickly added: "Wouldn't you say it's true?" Mrs. Brodski and Alek didn't say anything to that, just sat there impassively, looking at Rakowski with further anticipation. Momentary silence enveloped the room, except for a gentle rustle of paper between Rakowki's fingers, as he began to flip slowly the pages of their passport applications. He lifted his head up, took another puff of cigarette, and then looked at Mrs. Brodski and Alek with a visibly changed expression on his face. Few drops of perspiration appeared on his forehead, and suddenly he appeared tired and disinterested, almost impatient, in unmistakable sign, the appointment over which he was presiding and in total control was coming to an end. He looked out the window for a few seconds, and said:

"Mrs. Brodski and you Alek, thank you for coming here today. I sympathize with your plight, however I'm not the sole decision maker in cases such as this. I make recommendations, send them to Warsaw to my superiors, and they either approve the applications, or they don't. It's a chain of responsibilities to assure the system is fair for all and serves what's best for the country."

"When can we expect to hear from you, Sir?", asked Mrs. Brodski.

"You'll definitely hear from us. I'd say within a month you can expect something in the mail, but one way or the other we'll let you know," said Comrade Rakowski. Although his answer was vague, it didn't sound entirely promising, or entirely pessimistic. The was no other option, but to wait patiently for what he just said: "something in the mail."

Rakowski got up behind his desk, which was a clear sign the meeting was now definitely over. Alek jumped to his feet, Mrs. Brodski followed suit, and the three of them walked slowly to the door. Rakowski seized the handle, opened the door and asked them to follow him back to the front office through the narrow corridor they came from. Once they reached the familiar large room, he turned around and in a very cordial, but official manner, slightly bowed his head, shook their hands, and assured them once again they'd be getting a response from his office in the mail within few weeks, without giving a slightest hint of what it might be. Mother and son then proceeded towards the exit door, passing few workstations and the front counter along the way, and once again into the long corridor serving as the waiting room, then few steps down and out through the heavy, wooden main entrance door and out onto the sidewalk. As the first time around, once outside, they seemed somewhat disoriented and stopped for several seconds to look around for an exit street out of city square. They soon found themselves underway to the train station, and this time well before the rush hour and ahead of the throngs of passengers filling in every possible seat, with only standing room in the corridors, as was the case before, on their first trip. Nevertheless, there were many passengers, just like they, coming back from a daytrip to the city, usually on business to government offices or shopping excursion, as was evident by baggage many of them carried. Although Alek was naturally uncomfortable in all crowds, or even small groups of unfamiliar people, he was greatly intrigued by the mostly working-class men and women and the peasants who in such large numbers traveled regularly to the city and then back home. He found them irresistible to look at, at their behaviour, manners and attire, it all had a special allure to him, almost as if observing a distinct, unfamiliar species. Years of hard, exhausting labour left its indelible mark on those people, evident on their bruised and scarred, somewhat disfigured hands, with vividly protruding veins, and those tired, burnt by the sun faces, covered with deep and premature farrows. It was often perceived by the city dwellers, that there was a characteristic smell emanating from the peasants, a mixture of the outdoors; the wind, the soil, the vegetation, and perhaps a trace of farm animals, as suggested, which only added to the widespread, but disguised resentment of the visitors on a daytrip from the villages. Yet, despite all that, whether justified or not, there was an unmistakable look of dignity, determination and resilience in the eyes of the farmers, and strangely, easily discernable politeness, one might say, almost apologetic expressions in their words and behaviour, as if a humble gratitude for just being allowed to be there. There was never any noticeable sign of anger or slightest irritation in those folks, on the contrary for the most part, they seemed good natured, almost serene in overall demeanour. It could have derived perhaps from the essence of their existence, resigned to their fate of hard, moderately rewarding labour, but often misunderstood temporal life in quiet anticipation of life everlasting one day, when the good Lord decides it's time to go. After all, everything was in the hands of God; the weather, the harvest, the fortunes and misfortunes, trials and tribulations of everyday life, and of the very nature of life itself, that mysterious, subtle force from birth to death.

The summer was in full swing. Second part of July was marked by particularly warm weather, with temperatures around plus 20 degrees Centigrade already by 9 o'clock in the morning, and by early afternoon hovering around 30 degrees and rising. The town folks were out on the streets going about their business, or in front of their houses tending to their flower beds, or in the back, working in their lush gardens and proudly looking at the new, plentiful crops of fresh fruits and vegetables. There were also many people just standing idly around on street corners, or on the sidewalks in front of their houses, talking cheerfully to neighbours and friends with renewed hope, despite and oblivious of the ominous, disturbing international and domestic news, incessantly proclaiming the world at the crossroads in the wake of massive socio-political upheavals and well-organized, massive protests across the European continent and around the world, especially the United States. Here, in this small town, life had its own pace, far removed from worries of politicians, who feared the latest, even the smallest developments in some regions as an existential threat to their rule, the deeply entrenched power brokers in the capitals. The far greater number of those who were ruled, the subservient, restless, working-class masses, perceived this as unique opportunity for a long-overdue and much-anticipated change at last. It was time to have their voices heard, and a profound transformation to the unjust social-economic status quo finally established, just short of revolution. In these parts, the eastern peripheries, the latest political developments were so far removed from the reality of people's simple lives, that strangely for many, the perception of reality was quite often closely aligned with the official communist government's position. Whether out of ignorance, true conviction, or just for argument's sake, the events were still frequently seen around here as nothing more, than *"a foreign, hostile, capitalist bourgeoisie propaganda."* The seemingly justified mass labour movements were taken with a dose of skepticism, as with just about anything else in life, except the final judgement by the Almighty God, whom they feared the most, and who undoubtedly presided over what would be in the end the ultimate equalizer, either the happiness of everlasting life, or eternal condemnation to the depths of hell, regardless of political convictions, position, material or social status.

The centre of town at this time of the year was bustling with activity, mainly due to increased volume of people, locals out on the streets, or visitors from the villages and other small towns, either on shopping trips, visiting friends or relatives, or for entertainment whatever little of it there was. The few cafés and restaurants along the stretch of old, dilapidated two and three-story adjacent concrete buildings, of about three hundred meters long, or about three city blocks, were often packed with customers, especially in the evenings. The Town Hall offices were strategically located at one end, followed by variety of small stores, eating establishments, and at the very far eastern end of the row of buildings, also known as the "halls" was the police station. They buildings were all in various stages of disrepair and neglect, most with patches of discoloured peeling paint or falling off plaster. The "halls" were separated from the tree-lined main street by a wide green belt, which was one of the main features and attractions of the town, carefully tended to by few part-time seasonal landscapers. There were several different shrubs and flowers planted in a carefully arranged rows, starting with colorful tulips in the early spring, then later on daffodils, pansies, geraniums, mallows, at least three colours of narcissus, and few species of roses. Close to the major street intersection in the geographical city centre, right in the middle of the green belt, stood a large stone monument with a pointed top, crowned with a prominent, metal red Soviet star, commemorating the town's liberation by the advancing Red Army from a small German garrison stationed here until early months of 1944. The front metal plaque, facing the sidewalk was engraved in Russian, and in the inaccessible back of the monument, there was a comparable plaque in Polish, the order of which was a contentious issue in itself. On weekends, this area was coming alive, as young men and women from the villages were arriving in groups by train, by bus, on motorcycles, bicycles, or even few lucky ones in their own little cars, looking for entertainment, looking for fun. It wasn't long before minor disagreements with the local, easily irritable young men and women looking for action, escalated into full-blown fist fights, spilling from the establishments onto the sidewalks. Those dustups between the locals and the villagers were always an integral part of town's landscape, almost a tradition, and for many young men of both affiliations, a rite of passage, ascendency into real manhood, when honour is fiercely defended and respect is gained or just as easily lost, at least till next time. It was not uncommon to see men with bloodied noses or blood-splattered shirts stagger around, proudly displaying them like badges of honour, and walking back into the smoke-filled, packed restaurant, looking for some more action. The town's inconspicuous bootlegger Ivan Kurvichenko, or jokingly "Ivan the

Terrible", as he was most commonly known, was always prepared for the "invasion", and kept his shack well stocked with his finest hand-crafted "refreshments" mostly for the after-hours crowd, those who just never had enough.

It was Saturday, and a rare long weekend, culminating with a national holiday on Monday July 22, commemorating 24th anniversary of Polish Committee of National Liberation, proclaiming establishment of a new provisional government of Poland on the heels of retreating German army, and advancing Soviet Army at the end of World War II. On special occasions such as this, usually associated with notable dates in the history of the socialist country, a live band was playing its best renditions of the most popular domestic and international pop hits, while drunken, sweaty patrons were shaking rhythmically on the small dance floor, or in between the tables for lack of a better space, but closer to the action, doing their best to impress their partners, or complete strangers of both sexes, who were too drank to notice, or didn't care anyway. The booze was low-priced, but selection limited to two or three kinds of vodka, brandy and champagne from the Soviet republic of Georgia, two kinds of wine, red and white, and always one kind of beer, a cheap swill at a room temperature, barely fit for consumption. Although the food menu suggested a reasonably good selection of dishes and appetizers, the patrons were quickly confronted with a stark reality, when the waitress once again, in a well-rehearsed line and a facial expression of utmost innocence, convincingly informed the bewildered patrons, one after another:

"I'm sorry, but we've just ran out of it."

In the end it didn't really matter, as long as there was something or anything to eat at least, and the booze was flowing uninterruptedly, a package of cigarettes was within easy reach, the band was playing and the ladies were sending all the right signals, life was good for the moment, perhaps for the night. It was time to forget the politics, glorious achievements of the socialist motherland under the ever-vigilant United Workers' Party, increasingly menacing veiled threats from the ever-concerned Big Brother to the east, and the grueling everyday life here in these parts in general, dispensing its own cruel, unforgiving dose of reality.

On evenings like these, Alek was usually out, pacing around the town's centre, or somewhere nearby, against his mother's best advice, curious and fascinated by the rare display of its nighttime recreational side, however small it was, unlike the usually sleepy and uneventful most days year-round. He clearly kept within safe distance of all the commotion, on the other side of the wide, dividing green belt, just watching the local nightlife unfold, right in front of his eyes. There were times when he had to retreat, when the rowdies were getting too close for comfort, perhaps looking for just anyone within close vicinity to unload their frustrations.

CHAPTER 13

THE WELL-KNOWN LOCAL courtesan Anka, a familiar presence on a warm night like this, was also out, walking slowly in pair with her friend and aspiring hustler Elzbieta, or Ela for short, eager to learn the tricks of the trade from the pro herself. Anka wasn't a beauty in any sense of the word; worn out and with visible signs of neglect in overall appearance, but surprisingly still in a considerable demand, if the price was right, and it usually was. Ela was decidedly much younger, more attractive and desirable of the two, who still managed to maintain an aura of youthful innocence about her. Nevertheless, their services were in demand, mostly among the young, sex-deprived studs of the local army unit, or the visiting village boys, whose only chance to see a piece of naked rear end, were the free-grazing cows in their natural environment of the green pastures. There was a saying around town: *"In the absence of fish, even crab is a fish"*, a perfect metaphor for those two ladies of the night, especially the elder one, who from early adolescence must have decided that school was just too challenging, too demanding, and there certainly had to be an easier alternative, or quite possibly there was more to her decision than that. Ela, being relatively recent addition to the night trade, had dropped out of school just few months into her second year at the local middle school. For Anka and Ela, the significantly less experienced of the two, business on weekends, particularly on Saturday nights, especially for the elder one was brisk. Ela was still wavering and letting some opportunities pass her by. Anka however, over time even managed to acquire some steady clientele. The rumour had it, even some prominent local public figures were seen with her, when swiftly disappearing into a dark alley or the small park behind the "halls." Surprisingly, it was all viewed with a great deal of tolerance and understanding, all within acceptable limits of course, as somewhat of a "desperate times call for desperate measures" doctrine, and a good topic for street-corner conversations and gossip at any time. Some would argue with unshakable conviction: "I don't blame the man. Have you seen the hag he's married to?"

The town's official slut and her faithful apprentice Ela, over time became so indispensable, that neither the mayor, Comrade Kutasiuk, nor the police Commandant Sokolowski did anything about their activities. But it must be said for the two entrepreneurs of female gender, they worked hard at it. After all, in spite of all the communist rhetoric, it all came down to the old capitalist principle of "supply and demand", and who in his right mind could argue with that? Behind the row of buildings, the so called "halls", there was a small city park with few tree-lined alleys and wooden benches, almost completely drowned in darkness, except for few light posts at the perimeter of the park, casting feeble light over the treetops. Some patrons used the park as a last resort to relieve themselves, or a quick stop for sexual activity due to lack of a better place in the vicinity, and best of all, the outdoor locale was absolutely free.

Anka was seen making at least two or three trips to the back and disappear into the darkness for at least half an hour at a time, and then mysteriously reappear again, as if nothing happened. Ela followed in her mentor's footsteps only once on that particular night. It didn't escape Alek's notice, as he was watching it all from a distance, patiently waiting and for whatever reason, something he could not quite explain, but it hurt him personally. After seeing Ela only a couple of times before, Alek quickly developed a keen interest in her, an infatuation of sorts, and he made sure to be out on those specific days during holidays, or just an occasional Saturday night, when the town was in such a celebratory mood, despite the always possible danger of running into a group of thugs. He was almost sixteen, but because of his height, the way he dressed, and his serious demeanor looked more like eighteen. In September he was set to go to the local middle school, that is if the whole emigration business wouldn't work out by then. Ela was still very young, perhaps just a year or two older than he was, possibly not even quite seventeen. Alek's impression of Anka however, was quite different. The well-experienced local whore was in her late twenties, but if one was to judge by her unsavoury appearance only, mid-thirties would most likely be her real age, he thought. Ela on the other hand was blonde, slim and rather tall, and also definitely better looking of the two, with proportional, shapely lower body, long legs and delicate, thin arms. Alek was envious of all those times when she stood there smiling in the twilight of the evening, wearing her best summer dress with flowery pattern, or a pair of tight jeans, standing in the shadow of a large leafy tree, or in a nook of a building, talking to a group of young men. Few of them familiar local thugs, perhaps only little older than he was. Alek watched from a distance, imagining himself being the object of her attention, just being in her presence, to feel her close, the way she stood close to and touched the other men, with sincerity and innocence of a young woman, who possibly still felt out of place in her new role. Nonetheless, most likely she was there because she wanted to be, and not only for financial gain, but just like the men she was courting, she wanted to be touched, she wanted to be noticed and loved, and who was there to judge her, because for Ela, there was not much to go back home to. The Bible summarizes it perhaps best in The Gospel According to John: *"Let him who is without sin, cast the first stone."*

Alek walked anxiously up and down the main stretch of sidewalk, trying to get a glimpse of coquettish Ela in the midst of a group of young people in front of the restaurant, absorbed in a light conversation, frolicking, visibly delighted, as the sound of music spilled outside through the open windows, into the warmth and stillness of a perfect summer night. There was an intense aroma all around, emanating from the multitude of flowers in full bloom in the nearby flower beds, mixed with perfume of few other young women standing outside, the smell of cigarette smoke and alcohol, adding to the unique atmosphere and enticing mystery of the night. The policemen were nowhere to be seen, perhaps conveniently absent, hidden away at the station and reluctant to get too involved, unless things really got out of control, and somebody rushed into the station screaming for immediate intervention. In fact, they preferred to stay out of sight for the most part, only occasionally venturing outside, making quick rounds, and going back in for a little celebration of their own. Commandant Sokolowski was always restrained in his enthusiasm for excessive indulgence in alcoholic beverages on the job, and tried to keep his deputy Kovaluk, an unrepentant boozer and the two other brutes in uniform under his constant surveillance. But he did allow a couple of shots of vodka on special occasions, such as this one.

Although, it was quite late already, past 10 o'clock, and his mother was certainly worried, Alek just couldn't resist the allure of what was happening right in the centre of town. After all, in just over a month he was scheduled to attend the local middle school, crossing the once unimaginable threshold to a totally different world, a strange world of almost adulthood, something he's been waiting for with great anticipation for a long time. It was very seldom that he was still out past nightfall, even during the middle of summer vacation. Alek didn't want to go home, not just yet, not before Ela at least looked at him, or before she would tell him she didn't care, and it was all in his imagination, if somehow he managed got close enough. Despite the fact she actually looked at him a few times before, for a second or two, when on the streets, both going about their own business, he wanted to know if it meant anything, if she at least noticed him, or it was only his fantasy, and she was completely indifferent like towards many other young men she has seen, vying for her attention? Foolishly, the temptation was too great, and Alek moved closer and closer towards the restaurant, out in the open, within just several meters of the group of young people, where he could be easily seen and recognized. It didn't take long before Alek was noticed, but not by Ela, the person he wanted most to be noticed by, but a young man in his late teens, whom he'd recognized at once. He would never forget that face as long as he lived. It was one of the men who attacked him on that fateful day in September of the previous year, and that other hoodlum was with him too, but Commandant Sokolowski's son Adam was visibly absent. In fact, since that time Alek has never seen him out about town again. The two thugs were among a group of young men in their early twenties, all clearly intoxicated, smoking cigarettes, flirting and evidently trying to hook up with the girls loitering around there on the sidewalk. The man turned towards Alek standing several meters away in a hazy light of a nearby streetlamp, and pointing with his stretched-out arm said:

"Look, it's that Jew again."

Two other man and Ela immediately looked in Alek's direction, staring back at them motionless, as if rooted to the spot. The man started walking slowly towards Alek, and was soon joined by few others, including Ela, who seemed hesitant at first, but reluctantly followed nevertheless, swept by the group. The men surrounded Alek unceremoniously, each one of them nonchalantly took his place in a circle, and the young women stayed few steps behind, unconcerned, still all with smiles on their faces, most likely curious what this was all about? The man whose face was forever etched in Alek's memory approached him slowly, as if dragging his feet, with a characteristic swagger of a typical punk with his backers closely behind. He stopped perhaps within just several centimeters of Alek and looking straight into his eyes with a derisive smirk, blew cigarette smoke in Alek's face. Unprepared, Alek jerked his head backwards, took a step back and momentarily covered his eyes with one hand. The other men in the group burst out with laughter. Alek was terrified of what might come next. He felt trapped again, a dreadful feeling he was already well familiar with. Again, he didn't look for it, all he wanted, was to look at people enjoying themselves, listen to the music, savour beautiful summer vacation night without another unpleasant incident. Going out, Alek thought that he might run into people on a day like this in town's centre, without the need to be on high alert, to be constantly vigilant, but if an opportunity should arise, he was prepared to readily extend his friendship to anyone who'd take time to even notice him, or better yet to exchange few words. For once in quite some time he ventured beyond the safe streets and alleys and immediately regretted it. Alek suddenly realized, what a mistake it was to go out and stay out so late, there were neither those who paid any attention to him, or cared to meet him, much less talk to and spend any time with him. The stranger stood right in front of Alek and there were two others behind him, and one on each side, not in any particularly organized or intentional order, more as a result of curiosity inspired, spontaneous following of the leader. The young man looked intently at Alek with an aura of superiority and the ever-present insidious smirk on his lips, then turned to Alek with a contemptuous grimace.

"Do you remember me?"

Alek didn't answer, just looked back at him with anticipation, as did all the others gathered around them. The man grabbed Alek's arm with his left hand, and squeezing it tightly pulled him in closer with the same provocative sneer.

"So, you don't remember me, but I remember you quite well. What have you been doing here at this time? Sneaking around? Shouldn't you be in bed by now?"

"I'm sorry, I was just about to go home," uttered Alek, his voice trembling.

"I saw you standing around here for quite some time, watching us. Were you waiting for somebody? What were you looking for?" continued the man.

"Excuse me, but I must go now. It is late, indeed; my mom must be waiting," said Alek, trying to free himself by stepping backwards and pulling his stranded arm away. However, the man held him back and squeezed Alek's arm even tighter, then threw the still smoldering cigarette butt down and said:

"No, you're not going anywhere, not yet," and emboldened, turned to his mates, still with the same derisive, contemptuous smirk and added: "Did you hear this? The Jew wants to go back to his mommy. What should we do with him?"

There was no answer, no emotion and the incident attracted little attention, beyond just those gathered around Alek, despite of the few other small groups of young people standing around nearby, socializing, sending indifferent glances, seemingly too absorbed to pay any attention. Yes, the hoodlums always need the presence and support of their chums to exist, they need the assurance of "we", as if there was a group complicity, and in that, a personal exoneration.

"Please let me go. I'm sorry if I caused you any trouble, I didn't mean to," pleaded Alek with increasingly desperate tone.

"You've been talking to the cops. What did you tell them?", asked the young man with visible hostility.

"I didn't tell them anything. Please believe me, I didn't. There must be a mistake."

"Don't lie to me, you were seen more than once going to the police station with your mother." There must have been a reason. So, what was it all about?"

"Oh, it was nothing, nothing to be concerned about, a private matter."

"A private matter with the cops? How interesting? What possibly would you want to talk to them about?", persisted the man, getting increasingly agitated. Suddenly, unexpectedly he sent a short, stiff jab into Alek's rib cage. Alek yelped, let out a shrill cry of pain, bending his body forward, under the brunt of the hard blow, burying his face in his hands, as if expecting a barrage of punches to follow. Ela, who was standing silently, watching the whole scene unfold, immediately surged forward, pushed herself through and stepped right in the middle of the unfolding drama.

"Tolek, what are you doing? What was that for? Leave him alone, do you hear? Leave him alone! What's the matter with you?", she said with disgust and grabbed the man's hands, forcefully separating him from Alek. She then stepped right between them. The man stepped back but was visibly stunned by the young woman's bold reaction and looked at her in disbelief. They all have known her; she was part of the bunch. The man then turned sideways and looked at his friends confused, suddenly uncertain, as if seeking support among them. There was no reaction, not a word said. They all just stood there stunned, reluctant to join in on either side. Alek was still mortified, but somewhat relieved by the sudden, unexpected turn of events. Ela was right there in front of him with her tantalizing presence, just several centimeters away, such as he's never seen her before. Alek could literally smell them both, especially the repulsive man reeking of tobacco, alcohol and perspiration, mixed with a subtle, sweet smell of perfume emanating from Ela. He was repulsed by Tolek, but was strangely drawn to Ela, inexplicably prepared to endure even more indignities, as long as she was near, on his side. Despite her well-known about town dissolute lifestyle, and a somewhat distant or detached and seemingly indifferent demeanor, or perhaps a well-concealed pretense, she seemed kind and affable. Here she was bound and restrained by a strict, unforgiving and unwritten, but commonly understood code of the street, and in her trade, even in this obscure little town, which she must have known all too well. They all had to maintain an appearance of association and unity.

"You stay out of it", said Tolek to Ela.

"What was that all about? What has he done to you?", she asked him forcefully.

"It's none of your business. I said, stay out of it!"

"It is my business. You just hit an innocent schoolboy for no reason at all."

"The Jew knows bloody well what he's done. He talks to the cops, and one should not talk to the cops," said Tolek with increasing impatience and agitation.

"I don't understand. Talking about what? What does it have to do with you? How do you even know him?", persisted Ela.

"Listen, I know what I'm saying. It's none of your business, do you understand? Just stay out of it. Go and screw somebody. Go on, get out of here."

"How dare you? You know, you're such an idiot. I thought you were a real man, a friend, but you're not. You're a coward, that's what you are. If you're looking for a fight, then go and find yourself somebody like you or a little older, an then we'll see what a man you are", and she pointed to group of men standing near the entrance to the restaurant, then continued with a visible indignation, "Let him go, or I'll talk to the cops myself."

"What are you talking about? Is there something going on between you two I should know about? Tell me, have you fucked him too?"

"You're a sick man. There is nothing going on between us, but there might be, and it would be only my choice, not yours. You're drunk!"

"Oh, I see what's going on; you've switched your interest to kids now. You want the first crack at his virginity, is that it?"

"You're such an idiot, you're embarrassing yourself. I don't want to talk to you and I don't want anything to do with you.

Yes, I'd rather talk to him anytime. He's probably more of a man than you'll ever be."

"Oh, how soon you forget, Ela. That's not what you were saying last night. Remember, you slut?"

"Why don't you piss off and leave us alone? You're a total loser. Let me tell you something, at least I work for my money when I need to, and you're steeling and robbing people and waiting for somebody to buy you a drink or threaten innocent people to buy you a drink, because you can't afford your own. That's the kind of man you are, a total looser."

"I've had enough! Get the hell out of here and take the boy with you." Alek was in total shock at the unexpected turn of events. Never in his wildest dreams he could have anticipated this young woman, he's barely seen fleetingly a few times on the streets, to stand up for him, in his defense and so bravely against this well-known thug. Ela looked defiantly right into Tolek's eyes for a few seconds, then slowly turned around to look at his gang, few mutual acquaintances and gawkers, who were equally stunned by what had just happened. Tolek stepped back two steps and with the characteristic, derisive smirk on his lips, as if trying to show he was still firmly in control, awkwardly turned sideways and looked at his friends sheepishly, somewhat embarrassed, but still trying his best to project a triumphant image. They all stood in silence for a few seconds, but what seemed like minutes, then muttered something amongst themselves. From a distance, a muffled sound of music could be heard coming from the restaurant and distant voices of several patrons standing near the entrance. Ela, without hesitation, took Alek by his right arm and squeezing it gently, turned him around and shoved along, right out of the spot on the sidewalk he was reluctantly rooted to, leaving the crowd behind. They walked briskly without a word for several meters, before Ela slowed down noticeably and looked back once, when certain they were already within a safe range. They walked east, in the general direction where Alek lived, as if she already knew, before she asked unexpectedly.

"Where do you live? I'll walk you home."

"Oh, you don't need to do that. Don't worry about me, it's not very far."

"I don't even know your name. So, what is your name?"

"It's Alek. And you?"

"Ela."

"Thank you for standing up for me."

"Oh, don't mention it, that was nothing at all. You knew my name of course. You've heard it many times just a while ago."

"Yes, in fact I did. Nice name."

"So, tell me, what were you doing out so late. Isn't it past your bedtime?" she said mischievously, smiling.

"Just hanging around. Summer vacation."

"I'm sure your parents were worried."

"It's my mom only. What were you doing out so late?"

"Same as you. I'm sorry to hear that. So, you only live with your mom and no dad or siblings?"

"No, just the two of us."

"I'm curious, why?"

"Long story."

"How long?" persisted Ela.

"Oh, longer than the time we have."

"I understand. Maybe some other time?"

"Maybe?"

"We'll see, Let's leave it at that. I don't usually plan things far in advance", she said.

"Do you know him well?" asked Alek.

"Know whom?"

"Tolek."

"Why do you ask?"

"Just curious. It seemed like you've known each other for some time and quite well."

"Yeah, I've known him for about two years, maybe longer, but sometimes I wish I'd never met him."

"So, why do you hang out with him?"

"It's complicated."

"Is it true what he said?"

"Said what?"

"You know…you and him, last night."

"I don't want to talk about it."

"All right. Tell me Ela, where do you live?"

"North, on Pulaski Street. Not very far from the centre either, just different direction."

"You know, I've seen you a couple of times before," said Alek

"Don't be silly. I'm sure you have. This town is so small, everybody must have seen everybody here at least once before. I've probably seen you too, in fact I'm almost sure I have."

"You probably have, although I do my best to stay out of sight," said Alek and laughed timidly.

"Really? How so?"

"Never mind. How about your parents?"

"It's a long story."

They both burst out laughing. Alek slowly regained his confidence as they walked along the dimly lit sidewalk. The street was almost completely deserted; only occasionally a hunched, black figure moved swiftly on the other side, hurrying back home. The air turned colder by the minute, with sporadic light gust of easterly wind and with it, sparse drops of summer rain falling gently and dotting the dark pavement. Alek wanted to say something, but couldn't find anything sensible to say, as not to embarrass himself, and they walked in silence, arm in arm, so close to each other, and yet so far, engrossed in their own private thoughts. He glanced secretly at Ela's strangely sad face whenever they moved out of the shadows, and into the range of each weak light cast by the tall, curved at the top steel streetlamps, spaced equally at long intervals along the street. At the next intersection Alek turned left, and Ela followed him into a narrow, dark cobblestoned street emanating a surreal, eerie feeling, as if lost in the comfort of its perpetually dismal existence of the past decades and forgotten by the world outside. Oddly, it too had its own distinct aura and a unique, inimitable smell. There was a long row of old, decrepit communal housing apartment buildings drowned in total darkness, with only few windows with sagging, nondescript simple linen curtains, behind which a stream of heavy, yellowish light betrayed any signs of life.

"I live over there," said Alek, pointing to one of the dark buildings, just ahead.

"I'll walk with you right to your door," said Ela.

"You don't have to."

"But I want to. Do you mind?"

"No, I don't mind. My entrance is from the back of the courtyard and it's completely dark there."

"So, is that a problem? asked Ela.

"No, not a problem, but it's not a very nice place."

"Don't worry, mine is not so nice either. My parents are not rich. Why do you think I would stand there in front of the café on a day like this?"

"I don't know. I guess we both don't have much to brag about," said Alek.

"At least we've got something in common", added Ela.

Soon they were both in the back of the building, standing in front a single wooden door, with a high, worn-out threshold and two large gray concrete tiles below it. The small kitchen window right beside the door, and one just around the corner to the right, revealed no sign of life. It was all dark inside.

"This is it. Once again, thank you for everything," said Alek with a low voice, almost a whisper, standing with his back close to the door.

"You know, I'm glad I've met you. You're a nice person," said Ela.

"Thanks! You're nice too. I'm happy to have met you too."

"I hope you don't mind me asking, but how old are you?"

"I forgot. Stress, you know…"

"Yes, yes of course, I know all about it. Most of the time I don't remember my age either, and who cares?" she said and laughed quietly.

"Right. Well, good night! I must go now. Thank you so much."

"Good night, Alek. Thank you too! Next time try to avoid that place at this time of night at least."

"I will, but where can I see you?"

"Why would you want to see me? You don't want to know someone like me."

"Why not? I'd like to."

"I'm not sure. We'll see. Good night!"

"Good night! Be careful on your way back, Ela."

"Don't worry about me, I'll be fine."

Ela leaned forward and gently touched Alek's right hand with the tips of her fingers, looking at him motionless for a few seconds, straight into his eyes she couldn't see in the darkness.

She then turned around and slowly walked away into the night, towards the distant, hazy streetlight. Alek just stood there for several seconds, thinking about all that had just happened and listening to her departing steps, until he couldn't her them anymore, and he was sad.

CHAPTER 14

THE INEVITABLE LETTER from the district passport office came in the mail in early August, as expected, and in just two sentences changed the plans Mrs. Brodski and Alek so carefully devised and nurtured for the past several weeks. It simply said:

> *"We regret to inform you that, by decision of Regional Passport Bureau, in the name of and according to the laws of Polish People's Republic, your passport applications for the purpose of emigration to Israel have been denied, based on arguments you had provided. You may appeal this decision to the Ministry of Interior, at Warsaw, ul. Nowy Swiat 6, within 21 days from the date of this notification."*

The letter was sealed with an official stamp and the well-known communist bureaucrat's Comrade Rakowski's signature. Mrs. Brodski has always harboured doubts about the whole procedure, with little trust in the integrity and fairness of the system itself. If the bureaucrats expected and were so used to receiving bribes as indispensable part of the process, she would not conform, for she had nothing to give. She found it hard to comprehend, how the fate of two ordinary, harmless people from the peripheries of Eastern Poland could have any impact on the ountry such as this? By denying permission for a single mother with a son to leave the country for destination of their choice, what was there to be achieved or gained by the vast, out of control, communist bureaucracy? Doubtless, it was all mandated from the top down to finally rest in the hands of overzealous, greedy politicians at local and provincial level, common swine with a vengeful streak and insatiable appetite for power, free to interpret the law as they wished, and perhaps in a way it was all directly attributed to their level of political indoctrination in the communist ideology, as prescribed by the protocols. The most credible option however, and possibly the most credible of them all, was that such decisions were solely the work of corrupt district passport authorities, local brazen opportunists, far removed from any superior scrutiny at national and provincial level, well entrenched in their beliefs that, at least for a foreseeable future they can extort money as they wished and with impunity, unapologetically and without remorse. Mrs. Brodski announced rather reluctantly, quite aware of the impact it might have on Alek, that they will not be appealing the decision of the Passport Bureau to the Ministry of Interior. She just didn't have the energy, time or money to pursue what she thought was obviously a lost cause. They'd have to make the best of whatever life they had here, at least life that was quite predictable. Certainly, there was the accompanying misery at times, but never an extreme destitution, and the present reassurance, as it played out within the boundaries of all too familiar surroundings, of knowing they were not in it alone. Most working-class people here were in similar circumstances, and not better or worse. It was a strange, unspoken understanding, possibly the only common thread that bound them together more than anything, unity of people in misery.

Alek was inconsolable for a few days, as his hope of travel abroad and an adventure of a lifetime was dashed, and with it his dreams of a new, better life somewhere, anywhere but here. It was difficult now to literally change the entire perspective on his future life, after all this time he has spent cultivating an imaginary, splendid existence in an unknown dream-world only he knew, where life was beautiful, where life was good. He withdrew into solitude, didn't eat much, spent his days thinking, reflecting, reading, flipping pages of a geography atlas, listening to music on their old, cabinet-style radio, writing something, or just lying on the sofa and looking aimlessly at the ceiling. Eventually, after about a week or so of soul-searching convalescence, without any pressure from his mother, Alek began to show some signs of interest in the world outside of their home. Although still somewhat reluctantly, he agreed to go grocery shopping with his mother, who convinced him to go outside under a pretext she needed help to carry it all, in case they'd buy more than just bare necessities.

It was Saturday, early afternoon when they stepped outside. The air was still, and the sun high up and not a single cloud to be seen on a perfectly blue sky. On their way out of the courtyard, they greeted two women from the neighbourhood, standing there chattering while their small children were playing nearby. Alek had light white cotton, short-sleeved shirt and black trousers on, and a pair of black, worn-out leather shoes; his favourite attire. Because of the way he looked, he was often mistakenly taken for being dressed up for some special occasion, or celebration nobody else seemed to know about, but in fact he was not, it was just his preference. Since the end of the school year his black hair has grown much longer, now completely covering his collar. Alek didn't pay any particular attention to it, and now was finally free of the constant nagging, harassment and reprimands from teachers, who supposedly were trying their best to enforce an imaginary, non-existent school protocol regarding length of one's hair, where apparently short hair was a must. In the past Alek had seen on few occasions, but luckily never experienced himself the wrath of a particularly obsessed teacher, trying to stop "bad influences", or teach the "rotten apples" a lesson, by pulling a poor pupil by the hair with such force, as to almost lift him off the floor. One other popular form of punishment for overgrown hair, was ear tweaking. Equally effective when especially forcefully applied, the punishment would sometimes make the little recipient wet his pants. Such was the joy of education at elementary school level in a communist motherland, and for many little rascals not to be forgotten anytime soon, if ever.

In the early afternoon Alek and his mom walked leisurely towards the main street, enjoying every step of the way, straight on to town's centre, where most of the stores were located in relative proximity. It didn't take long before the heat and the sultry, stagnant air was becoming barely manageable, having a visible effect on the pace of life all-around. The already sleepy town became even more lethargic as the time went on, with listless people moving sluggishly, apathetically, or some frantically looking for cover in the shadows of trees or nooks of buildings, if they had to go out at all. People in these parts were accustomed to a rather cold climate for at least four months of any year, with a steady whiff of unforgiving, frigid air from the east, courtesy of the vast, open steppe of the Soviet Union. When finally, the summer came with its full intensity, and with it a sudden upward surge in temperatures, many people were naturally not prepared for the drastic atmospheric change.

Surprisingly, there were some folks gathered here and there in the vicinity of the town centre, which Alek and his mother reached within ten to fifteen minutes from their home. They could hear a distant sound of orchestra, getting closer and closer with each passing second. There soon appeared at a distance a throng of several dozens, mostly black-clad people, marching slowly, right in the middle of the main street, with the orchestra up front, all dressed up in characteristic black uniforms of railway workers and the rest of the people, family, friends and neighbours right behind it. The orchestra consisted almost entirely of brass wind-instruments, with a short, fat man in the middle of the first row with a large, round drum strapped at a skew over his torso, banging at it with regular intervals and gasping for air. The all-male band, as it seemed most at a brink of total exhaustion under the mercilessly burning sun, but determined, strenuously blowing and marching forward, while some musicians wiping off their perspiring foreheads from time to time with white handkerchiefs in between the notes. Only employees of certain position, stature or those with over twenty-five years of distinguished service were given the full honours of an official funeral. The resident National Railways' band in traditional black garb accompanied the deceased on his last journey to the church, and then on to the cemetery, to be laid to eternal rest in a two-meter-deep pit. The funeral procession was a rare and sombre event, that stirred the town's otherwise uneventful days, with residents stopping, looking and reflecting on the life of the man who just passed away, who most of them knew, some quite well, and related to their own fragile existence, while still glad to be among the living. Right behind the orchestra, repeatedly playing few mournful renditions of the standard, classic funeral marches, followed four strained, heavily perspiring pallbearers carrying an ornate, dark-wooden casket on their shoulders. Then closely behind, the distraught wife of the deceased in the middle, wrapped in black headscarf and a lace veil over her face, accompanied by their three grief-stricken adult children linked together by arms, walking slowly with sullen faces, staring down at the pavement under the burden of grief, following the sudden death of their beloved husband and father. Behind them, without any particular order, were members of his distant family, friends, neighbours, and just ordinary townsfolks feeling the need to pay respects to the popular and likeable man they knew and respected. Alek and Mrs. Brodski slowly followed the back of the funeral procession alongside the sidewalk, while they were passing the town centre, and on to the Catholic church under the patronage of Saint John, standing about half a kilometre to the west. Along the way, Mrs. Brodski had a strange, nagging feeling to move closer to the front, to see the grieving family in the first raw behind the casket. About fifty meters from the church the band stopped playing, and the old, hunched woman in the centre of the first row behind the casket briefly lifted the vail off her face to wipe the tears and perspiration. Mrs. Brodski stopped in her tracks in shock and Alek with her, unable to move and utter a word. It was the dear, old woman Maria Pavloska , slowly walking behind her husband's casket being carried by four men, with an expression of utter devastation on her pale face. All three children were dressed in black, two daughters and a son walking together in the first raw holding their mother under both arms, all family with expressions of such profound sadness and suffering, that it was painful to even watch them passing by. The grandchildren, ages six to thirteen, also visibly distraught and somewhat confused by the whole procession and attention from onlookers on both sides of the street. They were walking behind in the second row with their parents, accompanied by husbands of Pavloska's two daughters, and Pavloska's daughter-in-law, the wife of her son Marek, her eldest child. Mrs. Pavloska has been the closest to a true friend Mrs. Brodski had in this town, and grew quite fond of the kindly old woman over time, although their home visits were rather rare, they occasionally met in town. Mrs. Brodski, still in disbelief, motioned with her hand to stop a passerby, and asked someone for confirmation of what she already knew.

"Is that Maria Pavloska?"

"Yes, it is," she answered.

"And that is...," continued Mrs. Brodski, pointing to the carried casket, without finishing her sentence.

"Yes, I'm afraid that is her husband, Stanislav Pavloski," answered the woman with a sigh, and curious herself, asked Mrs. Bradoski.

"Do you know them?"

"Yes, especially Mrs. Pavloska. What happened, do you know?"

"Heart attack, I'm told," answered the woman quickly and walked away.

Mrs. Brodski and Alek looked at each other stunned. Both were still in total shock and lost for words. They took several steps towards the church, as the procession of mourners moved along, and then watched the throng of people from a distance for several more minutes, as it stopped at the wide entrance to the church courtyard. The parish priest, Father Antoni Pukalski was already waiting, and after some words exchanged with few people from the crowd, he bowed cordially and spread his arms in a most inviting, utmost sincere gesture, asking them all to proceed to the church for the final funeral mass, but without the band of course. Mrs. Brodski and Alek looked at the whole ceremony with genuine interest. Most people there seemed to know each other rather well, and the priest himself, although with a serious demeanour, behaved like an old, much revered friend who has always been there in their lives for better or worse. The truth be told, Father Antoni in fact was always there, like a dear, trusted friend, a confidant and an advisor, a part of their lives for many years now, through baptisms, first communions, confirmations, marriage vows and unfortunately funerals.

Mrs. Brodski and Alek were soon drawn closer to the courtyard entrance, marked by a large square concrete pillar, one on each side, and each one connected further in opposing direction to almost two-metre-high, thick, solid concrete wall surrounding the entire property in what seemed like a perfect square, broken up by two narrow openings along the way on opposite sides, serving as additional exits and entrances. The whole structure, the church and the walls were all off-white, relatively freshly painted and glistening brightly in the intensity of the summer sun. The church dated to beginning of the nineteenth century was not an architectural marvel by any standard, rather modest and plain in its design inside and out, but revered, nevertheless. Along the perimeter wall, inside the courtyard were growing equally spaced, mature chestnut trees that over the years became a permanent home to few species of birds.

After several more minutes, Alek was growing increasingly restless. He couldn't quite understand his mother's prolonged interest in the funeral, the whole commotion, or whatever there was that caught her attention. He didn't like the strange curiosity and mysterious look on her face, afraid that she might become personally involved in the funeral activities, yet he quietly waited and followed his mother's every step. The funeral procession, almost the entire throng of people soon disappeared inside the church, except the band along with several other people, who for whatever reason opted to stay outside, in the shade of the large, leafy chestnut trees. There were few wooden benches spaced along the fence walls, in between the trees, perfectly located for all those who decided to rest, protected from the afternoon sun for the duration of the inside funeral ceremony. Alek and his mom stood around the entrance for few more minutes, then slowly edged forward beyond the walls and inside the courtyard, without arousing any suspicion or attention among the several people lazily loitering around the church grounds, looking for relief from the burning sun against the backdrop of a perfectly blue summer sky. Mother and son walked leisurely around the church, right to the back and then to the other side, along the west wall of this much respected, historic house of warship. They looked with utmost interest at the surroundings, and every detail of the church structure itself, the tall stained-glass windows, the roof and the bell tower. There was a profound sense of peace about the entire compound, an undisturbed atmosphere of special, soul soothing sanctuary, as if a sublime, mysterious, overpowering spiritual presence hovered above, wrapping its arms around the structure, and all the little earthly creatures, those hidden in the trees and the people scattered around, all silenced for fear of disturbing what most believed to be sacred grounds.

CHAPTER 15

AUGUST 20, 1968, was a day unlike any other since the end of the II World War, a day of unusual activity in the sky, with dozens of large Antonov transport planes streaking across the sky almost uninterruptedly, one after another at regular intervals, in close formations with a continuous, distant drone throughout the day and overnight. They were all flying at very high altitudes and coming from the east, the Soviet Union, and headed south-west. People already out in the streets stopped, many more came out of their homes, and looked up at the sky with bewilderment, quietly speculating on the meaning of the sudden, massive air force mobilization by the "Big Brother" to the east. Alek couldn't satisfy his curiosity enough and was outside a few times throughout the day and well into the evening to look at the great formations of airplanes passing by overhead, until they couldn't be seen anymore as the night was setting in, and only distant, roaring sound of the engines still reached the ground below. He overheard the neighbours in the courtyard and across the dividing wooden fence, feverishly discussing, speculating and arguing over gravity and significance of what they've been witnessing. Whatever was behind it, the people were sure, nothing good would come out of it, and a prospect of yet another war, just over twenty-three years later was a real possibility once again. The world was clearly at the crossroads; upheavals in the capital re-shaping the whole political landscape, student protests across the country still freshly resonating and similar spontaneous uprisings across the continent, giving rise to militant student activism. The Vietnam War still raging in spite of anti-war protests in America, civil rights movement and assassination of Martin Luther King Jr., constant turmoil in the Middle East, the Cold War intensifying and now what seems like a beginning a new, major armed conflict. The media were initially eerily silent on the unusual, dramatic events unfolding right in front of people's eyes, and conveniently didn't report anything out of the ordinary. As was always the case in times of uncertainty and abnormal activities, Radio Free Europe was always there to fill in the gaps, and although there was a renewed and intensified jamming of the waves, soon the announcements got through, transmitted incessantly with constant updates on the latest developments.

"On the night of August 20 and continued through the day of August 21, army of the Soviet Union supported by armies of three other Warsaw Pact countries, namely Bulgaria, Poland and Hungary have invaded Czechoslovakia with an estimated 200,000 troops and about 2000 tanks. It is suspected that Alexander Dubcek, the First Secretary of the Central Committee of The Communist Party of Czechoslovakia and leader of the country, has been removed from power and his fate is unknown at this time. Most likely comrade Dubcek was placed temporarily under house arrest. There have been numerous independent reports of spontaneous uprising of ordinary citizens of Prague against the foreign invaders, however nothing is known of any resistance by the regular Czechoslovak army, or its whereabouts. Numerous sources, domestic and international have confirmed several casualties, as well as acts of sabotage and peaceful resistance in the capital of Prague, as well as other areas of the country to a lesser degree. The volatile situation is being closely monitored by the governments of major Western countries, who have publicly expressed their outrage and unequivocally condemned the invasion, demanding immediate explanation from Moscow. It is widely seen as a first implementation of the so-called Brezhnev Doctrine, by which

the Soviet Union reserves the right to intervene in any Warsaw Pact country to subordinate their national interest and, or supposedly hostile anti-socialist internal factions, to those of the Eastern Bloc as a whole and through military force, if necessary."

Mrs. Brodski was unusually quiet, although in good spirits on Saturday afternoon, as the month of August and the summer was coming to an end, marking the fast-approaching end of summer vacation and the beginning of new school year. For most students it was a much-dreaded time, when the looming end of freedom, as it was commonly perceived, was a time of heightened anxiety, when every passing hour brought them that much closer to the ultimate calamity, back to the hated classroom. In the end, they resigned themselves to the inevitable fate, and spent the last days dejected, wasted on worries, rather than unhindered, light-hearted enjoyment till the very end. The hardest hit were the children born into dire poverty, whose parents grew fruits and vegetables to supplement their meagre incomes and had their offspring toil in the garden for hours each day, digging, planting, weeding out, picking the crops and taking it to the market in town or the district capital any way they could. Thus, went by their summer vacation. The sons and daughters in the surrounding farmlands and villages had it even worse, for their days were filled with never-ending hard labour from dusk till dawn, not only in the gardens and fields, but tending to the herds of farm animals and flocks of domestic fowl. Sadly, all that effort elicited very little sympathy among their peers, those who were better off, who at least had a semblance of summer vacation, on the contrary, it evoked frequent scorn and contempt, as supposedly they had nothing to be proud of, and no interesting stories to tell.

Mrs. Brodski was busy in the kitchen, hurriedly preparing food while humming some unknown, barely audible tune. She was all dressed up as if going to attend a special event or an important meeting, with a subtle aura of secrecy, adding to the mystery of this fine, late Saturday afternoon. At last, she looked at Alek with a prolonged and loving gaze and her familiar serene smile, and said:

"I'm going out, but I'll be back soon."

"Where are you going, Mom?"

"I'm meeting someone. No need to worry, just a social get-together."

"Social? Is it he or she?" asked Alek with a hint of sarcasm.

"Why do you ask? You know I seldom go out, but this is one of those rare times. Just relax son, stay home, or go for a walk in the meantime."

"Is it he or she?" persisted Alek.

"It's hard to say. It's rather two people that I'll be seeing tonight."

"Why can't you just say it? What's all this secrecy about?"

"Alek, I'll tell you all about it when I'm back. Nothing to be concerned about. As I said, a social kind of meeting, nothing serious, without commitments."

"Mom, it's just weird, the way you're acting. What's the big deal?"

"It's not a big deal at all. Just drop it, son. You're tiring me."

"Does it have to do anything with me?"

"Maybe, we'll see. I'll let you know."

"Fine. You don't want to tell me, I don't want to know."

"I've got to go now, Alek. I'll be back later."

Mrs. Brodski looked at Alek with sign of exasperation on her face, shook her head, but managed to smile one last time and left home quickly, locking the front door behind her and hurried west, towards the main street. The weak rays of the setting sun, barely visible just above the horizon, pierced brightly through few remaining vacant spaces between low rooftops of adjacent houses and dense tree branches along the way, casting long, distorted shadows, and then slowly disappearing from sight with every passing minute. There were already some noisy groups of young people gathering in front of the always popular two nightspots for the only remaining entertainment in the town's centre. The men were standing there in the company of young, local and out of town women, talking, laughing and smoking cigarettes, while waiting for the live band to arrive, and kick off the night with its easily recognizable repertoire of the most popular pop hits of the last few years. The same band was a familiar presence in town with numerous appearances, but the patrons never seemed to tire of them or their music, and always gladly listened and danced to it, as if for the first time, as long as the guitars played. From time to time the band added a song or two to their repertoire, as a new widely popular domestic song was released, or an international hit found its way to the country, and all those most devout followers waited for it with great anticipation, regardless how bad the rendition was. In time, the four members of the band became well-respected and admired local celebrities.

Mrs. Brodski passed the town's centre without paying much attention to the gathering of locals and out of town revelers, quickly crossed few hundred meters west and only slowed down when she reached Saint John's parish. She looked at the church with apprehension, as if trying to adjust to the new surroundings in front of her and reconcile with her persistent thoughts and nagging doubts of what she was about to do. She looked at the church from the bottom up to the steeple, and the metal cross right at its peak and rested her gaze there for a few seconds. She stopped and hesitated for a moment, then proceeded cautiously further to the side of the church and on to its adjacent rectory. It was a single story, gray building with a wide, wooden front door with a narrow, rectangular stained-glass window at the top, and few concrete steps leading to the front door. The main building elevation had few windows, all with curtains drawn, but no lights in any of the rooms, or any visible sign of life, except one, a dim, yellowish light in the corridor, just behind the front door, illuminating a small stained-glass pane just above. Mrs. Brodski walked up to the door, and just stood there motionless for several seconds. She looked up once at the light coming through the coloured glass, and then pressed the doorbell on the right side of the door frame and waited. Only a prolonged period of silence followed, but no sign of life from inside of the compound. She pressed the buzzer again, held it for a few seconds, then released it and stepped back. This time, after a while she could hear a distant muffled noise coming from somewhere deep inside, but quickly approaching, and finally clearly audible footsteps just behind the front door. Soft, pleasant and quite youthful woman's voice behind the door was heard.

"Who is it?"

"Good evening, madam. I'm Mrs. Brodski. I was here few days ago and made arrangements to see Father Antoni, if you recall."

"Good evening! Oh yes, yes, I remember now, Mrs. Brodski", said the woman inside. Miss Klementyna, the cheerful parish housekeeper promptly opened the door, and standing to one side of the corridor, bowed and with a good-natured smile on her face, invited the guest in.

"Please come in. Father Antoni is in his study; he's been waiting for you. Please follow me, Mrs. Brodski."

"Thank you. I hope I'm not taking him away from some important matters."

"Oh no, no…as I said, he's been expecting you."

They walked in semi-darkness to the end of the corridor, and then turned left into another corridor, running in opposite direction towards the back of the building. There was a total, undisturbed silence in the building. The air was stuffy, but of rather pleasant smell, a rich combination of antique furniture, floor polish, incense and freshly extinguished or burning candles. At the end of this somewhat shorter, but wider corridor, they came to a small vestibule with floor-length, dark and heavy curtains, hanging on a semi-circular metal rod suspended from the ceiling. Miss Klementyna stopped in front of the curtain, and said in a whisper:

"Please wait here." She then slid the curtain open to one side and knocked gently on the door.

"Come in, please," answered a pleasant, male voice from the inside, few seconds later.

Miss Klementyna gently pressed on the door handle, pushed it slightly ajar, stuck her head in, and announced the visitor.

"Mrs. Brodski is here to see you, Father."

"Come in, come in," the same male voice cheerfully responded.

Miss Klementyna swung the door open and delicately pulled Mrs. Brodski by her arm, right behind her inside the spacious room, where the parish priest, Father Antoni Pukalski was already waiting. The priest was sitting at his desk, but quickly lifted his head up, got up and hurried towards the door to meet the guest. He crossed the distance in just a few long strides, and with a restrained smile and a cordial nod, stretched out his right hand to greet Mrs. Brodski and introduced himself.

"Good evening, Madame! I'm Father Antoni Pukalski."

"Zofia Brodski," she said, holding out her right hand.

"I'm happy to see you. My good woman Miss Klementyna told me you would be coming, so I was expecting you", said the priest and quickly measured the visitor with his lively eyes, unabashedly from head to toe, and then smiled mischievously after what he saw. Naturally, It didn't go unnoticed, and for a moment Mrs. Brodski felt a flash of discomfort.

"I'm sorry for taking up your valuable time, Father."

"Oh, not at all, not at all…good that you came. I'm at your service."

"Thank you, Father. I'm so glad you agreed to meet me."

"My pleasure. If I can only be of help. Please sit down and make yourself comfortable, right here or wherever you like. Miss Klementyna, would you be so kind to bring us some tea and biscuits?"

"Yes, of course. I'll be back shortly," said the housekeeper and left the room.

Father Antoni first pointed to one of the two chairs near the coffee table, then to a sofa on the other side. Mrs. Brodski chose the chair, while Father Antoni waited, and then unexpectedly started slowly pacing around, with his head down, looking at the floor and hands crossed behind his back. The priest, wearing a traditional long, black cassock, white clerical collar and black leather shoes, barely visible from under the robe suddenly seemed tense and uneasy, as if he'd rather be alone or somewhere else. He was absorbed in his thoughts, obviously trying to find appropriate words to begin the conversation, or was still under the impression of whatever he was preoccupied with before Mrs. Brodski came in. She looked around the rather large room filled with interesting, eclectic collection of old furniture and decorations; a table with six chairs, a large wooden desk with high-back ornate chair, a bookcase filled with several rows of books of all sizes, neatly stacked, mostly in brown or dark-red hard covers, a three-seat gray fabric couch, a small coffee table and two more wooden chairs with thick red, worn-out cushions beside it, all in the same outdated, but comfortable and functional style. The wooden, spotless and perfectly polished floor was partially covered by two colourful and somewhat dated area rags, reminiscent of those of Afghan or Persian origins, most likely not authentic. One rug laid under the desk end extended beyond it on all sides, and the other, a smaller one, under the coffee table. The walls were decorated as expected, with three crosses in various places, and the iconic large picture of The Black Madonna, also known as Our Lady of Czestochowa, a faithful reproduction of the famed and venerated painting housed in Jasna Gora monetary in Czestochowa in Southern Poland, a revered place of constant pilgrimages. Also, as in every building of Catholic religious order, an ornately framed, medium size colour photograph of the current Pope Paul VI. The other immediately noticeable decorative objects included two vases with freshly cut flowers, one on the table, and a smaller one on the desk. Then there was a three-armed silver candelabra, with partially burned candles and dripping, congealed wax, that prominently stood on the table. One corner of the room was entirely taken up by a large, almost up to the ceiling exotic plant in a large, brown clay pot, that stood right on the bare hardwood floor. Undoubtedly, another curiosity and imagination-stirring object for any visitor, was the glass enclosed middle section of the bookcase, filled with variety of glasses, and among them few exquisite, cut-crystal wine glasses. Mrs. Brodski couldn't resist the sudden, nagging thought of what Commandant Sokolowski once told her about the break-in to Father Antoni's quarters, and the sofa box frame full of money discovered and cleaned out by the thieves. She wondered, if that was the actual sofa in front of her, and if so, was it replenished with money again? After a brief mental straggle, she abandoned the thought and tried to concentrate on the purpose of her visit. Except for the priest's steps, there was not a sound to be heard, either from the street or inside of the rectory, as if it were completely deserted.

"Mrs. Brodski," began the priest suddenly, "what is it that brings you here?"

"Oh yes, it is rather hard to convey without being misunderstood. Actually, I've struggled with my conscience, if I should come here in the first place. I have thought about it for quite some time, actually. It was not an easy decision."

Before the conversation went any further, there was a gentle knock on the door and without waiting for an answer, radiantly smiling Miss Klementyna walked in and announced herself. She carried a tray with a tea pot, teacups, two small porcelain dessert plates and a plate of butter biscuits. She quickly crossed the room and cheerfully set the tray on the coffee table, then removed all the contents, placed them on the table, bowed, excused herself and just as quickly and quietly left the room, closing the door behind her. Once the door closed, Father Antoni proceeded to sit on the sofa, close to the chair Mrs. Brodski was sitting on, and with his penetrating, lively eyes and a slight, but sly smile looked at his guest. At first, she felt most uncomfortable under his steady gaze and somewhat provocative demeanor, but quickly managed to regain her composure again and waited for the priest to initiate a conversation in this unexpectedly informal setting.

"Dear Mrs. Brodski, you need not worry, I'm here to listen and if there is anything I can help you with, I won't hesitate. Please tell me, what is it that brings you here?"

Before Mrs. Brodski was able to answer, Father Antoni poured the tea, and with seemingly naturally sincere gestures of his hands invited her to taste the beverage.

I've heard a lot of good things about you Father, about the parish and the good work that you've been doing in the community, but I must admit I've never been to the church before. I'm not even sure if you know who I am?"

"Let's just say, I have a pretty good idea who you are, madam. Let's not forget, this is small town, and sooner or later the word gets around."

"That makes it easier. I and my son Aleksander as far as I know, are the only Jewish family in this town. That's where the problem is. We don't go to church on Sundays like most people around here do, we don't celebrate the usual holidays, like Christmas and Easter, or anything in between. God knows we've tried our best to assimilate, and on some occasions yes, we celebrated with our neighbours, when invited. They're all very nice people, I cannot say enough, very nice, and yet we struggle to be accepted here. In this town it's either you're part of the Catholic diocese or the Eastern Orthodox at the other end of town. We're part of neither, but why should it be a problem living in peace, side by side with all those who do go to church?"

"I see. I understand what you're saying. I sympathize with you, I truly do. We're all one people in the eyes of God, we're all children of the Almighty, regardless of whether a Pole, Russian or Ukrainian or what church you go to, I assure you. It is the people who make those differences and distinctions along ethnic, religious and national lines. The good God does not, in fact God's message is universal for all the people regardless of their superficial or imagined differences or affiliations. You cannot find even one verse in The Bible to the contrary."

"Father, have you ever had people come to you, unbelievers in a sense, or the Orthodox Christians who wanted to join the Catholic Church?"

"Oh yes, of course I have. You know the war had displaced a lot of people and thrown many of us where we would otherwise never be, if we had a choice, and myself including. Are you thinking of joining The Church?"

"No. I'm here about my son."

"Your son? Tell me about it."

"It's about my son Aleksander, not so much about me anymore. He's struggling at school, wherever he goes he has to look over his shoulder for fear of being harassed one way or the other, or even assaulted. They just won't leave him alone. I'm talking about the band of idle, young hooligans roaming the streets, bullying and pushing around innocent people, even beating them up."

"Has your son been a victim of those attacks?"

"Yes, he has, a few times. Since Alek has really grown in the last two years, somehow he became more visible in their eyes, and one of their targets."

"I'm not sure if there is any way I can help you with this, Mrs. Brodski. This is not something I deal with, as you well know. Have you talked to their parents or the school?"

"Yes, I've tried to find who their parents were, at least of three particular delinquents. Their parents apparently are all busy working and don't know what's going on, or even care. They don't want to listen to these stories and are always quick to defend their children. Frankly, I don't think that they actually have any influence over their own children anymore, even if they try to intervene."

"Have you talked to the police?"

"Yes, I have. It was a waste of time. One of those hooligans was Commandant Sokolowski's son. Of course, the son and the father deny his involvement."

"Mrs. Brodski, it seems you've done whatever you could. It's really unfortunate and I sincerely sympathize with you. I'm sorry, but I just don't see there is anything more I could do for you."

"Father Antoni, I've also been an object of some harassment in public places, but nothing serious. The neighbours tend to avoid us too. There is very little interaction, so we just keep to ourselves. It's not easy for us to live in that old housing complex, with a constant feeling of isolation, being singled out for no apparent reason, other than who we are. We are Jews and always will be, we don't have it written on our foreheads, and we don't behave or live differently than anybody else. We do look somewhat different, but there are others from the east that resettled here after The War. I never thought it would be such a problem, but obviously I was wrong. In this small-town mentality, nothing escapes people's notice. I've been thinking about it for quite some time now."

"What about, Mrs.? Tell me."

"Father Antoni, what would it take to have Alek baptized?" said Mrs. Brodski unexpectedly. The priest was visibly surprised by what he's just heard and looked at her with disbelief and a hint of suspicion with that characteristic, penetrating gaze, as if trying to test her sincerity.

"I must confess, I'm quite surprised by what you've just said. I've never dealt with such a case before. If I understand you well, you want Alek baptized in our church, you want him to become a Catholic Christian."

"Yes, that is our intention. I want him to have the same opportunities as everybody else. He has a whole life ahead of him and as long as we stay here in this town. I see that the only way forward is to take that step, to blend in. It seems to be a very important aspect of life around here, where much of it evolves around the Church and many Christian celebrations."

"Do you think that it will solve your problem? How about you Mrs., do you want to join the Church too?"

"I personally don't want to go through all this at my age. I'll live the rest of my days just the way I am. But baptizing Alek at least, I think might definitely help us to be become a part of this community in a way that everybody else is, as it seems is expected of us."

"Dear Mrs. Brodski, I must tell you, it is a serious matter and a life-long commitment, a matter of faith, and it should not be taken lightly. I don't want to discourage you, but I also don't want to think that it is only about resolving your personal issues by using The Church as means to do it, as part of some larger scheme. Do you realize the ramifications of such an undertaking? Baptism is a life altering experience."

While saying this, the priest moved closer to the edge of the sofa, leaned forward and gently laid his right hand on Mrs. Brodski's knee, as if trying to emphasize his point in a personal gesture of understanding and sympathy, while looking straight into her eyes with a suspicious mixture of empathy and a hint of naughtiness on his pale, clean-shaven face. She was momentarily startled by his unexpectedly bold venture, stiffened and straightened her back, but otherwise kept her composure intact, and with just a quick glance at his right pudgy paw firmly on her left knee, without any further sign of movement, she displayed no immediate and obvious symptoms of disapproval and decided to ignore it and continued.

"Yes, I know, and I agree. As I said, I have thought about it for quite some time now, actually ever since our applications for passports to emigrate were declined. I've talked to Alek about the baptism in general terms a few times. Surprisingly, he had expressed genuine interest in The Church and its teachings."

"You were planning to emigrate? What in the name of God compelled you to seriously consider emigrating? When? Where?"

"Yes, few months ago. We were thinking of Israel. I've heard there was a unique opportunity for us now, with in all that political turmoil in the government. The doors appear to be open for a time, if only briefly, I'm sure. Sometimes there are days, that I realize there is nothing that keeps us here, and for Alek's sake, for his future, emigration would have been the best option, I thought."

Father Antoni appeared to be taken by surprise by what he's just heard, briefly wiggled his fingers on Mrs. Brodski's knee, and then abruptly took his hand back. He sighed, whispered few incomprehensible words in what seemed like Latin, raised his eyebrows, took two sips of tea, looked around the room, and then back again at his guest without saying a word for several seconds, and finally asked: "Does your son know you are here?"

"No, he doesn't, but he wouldn't object, I'm sure."

"Do you think we could all meet and discuss this further? I'd like to hear from the young man himself, in case a concrete decision has to be made. Tentatively, I agree with your intentions, and I do not personally object."

"When is it convenient for you to see us, Father?

"How about if we all meet in a couple of weeks, in the evening, at 6 o'clock or so? It should give you some more time to discuss and think this over. If you'll ever happen to be in the area, please drop in and let us know exactly when you wish to come. There is no pressure, you must feel completely comfortable about your decision."

"Absolutely, we'll be here. Thank you so much for your generosity and understanding. I'm very grateful."

"Let me ask you, do you have The Bible at home, the New Testament?"

"No, we don't, but I'm somewhat familiar with its contents, as most people are. I do however have a copy of the Old Testament."

"Good, but let me give you one," said Father Antoni and sprang to his feet without hesitation. He walked over to the bookshelf, looked up and down the shelves, then sideways, and quickly noticed what he was looking for, then pulled The New Testament from one of the lower shelves, brought it back to the table and handed it to Mrs. Brodski.

"Here it is, please take it. It's yours. This particular one is not entirely new, but has not been used much at all."

"Thank you. I certainly appreciate this, but let me pay for it," she said and began to open her purse. Father Antoni immediately stopped her, leaning over and touching her hand.

"Oh no, no, that's not necessary. It's a gift. We have many spare copies around here. I hope you'll find it useful. Please look it over at home, and have your son study some parts that interest him, or he's not familiar with, if this is something that suits him, before we meet next time. I'm certain this has a potential to open up many possibilities for the young man, a new path in his life, but most importantly, towards the Almighty God and the eternal salvation. Will it be something he would want to adopt for the rest of his life? It remains to be seen. Undoubtedly it is a weighty commitment and should be taken very seriously."

"Once again, thank you so much. I'm really grateful for your generosity, and as a mother, I hope that you'll be able to help him, kind of like taking him under your wings. Alek can be difficult at times, but he's a good boy. You know, it's that age when he questions everything. He can be rebellious and often thinks he knows everything, and doesn't seem to recognize any authority, but at least he's thinking and searching."

"I understand, most of us went through all that once in our lives. I think we'll get along just fine. I'm looking forward to meeting your young man."

Soon Mrs. Brodski visibly delighted with the outcome of her visit, got up from the chair and made a motion that she was ready to make her way towards the door. Father Antoni was already standing nearby, looking at her expectantly with a slight smile of contentment and equally happy to be a host to such a refined, dark-haired beauty. He too was ready to walk her to the door. One could only guess what tumultuous thoughts ran through the mind of this small-town parish priest, with insatiable appetite for temporal adventures, well beyond the strict confines of The Church doctrine. Despite his age, he considered himself a rather progressive messenger of the word of God, guidelines and directives of The Vatican, but felt at liberty to keep it somewhat open to personal interpretation, best suited to the environment he worked in, especially those vague parts related to spreading universal happiness. He walked two or three steps behind Mrs. Brodski while admiring her slim and shapely figure. He just couldn't take his eyes off her bottom, but it should not be held against the amiable cleric, for it is doubtful if any man could, walking behind this admirable woman. She slowed down by the door, as Father Antoni leaped forward to open it, and let the lady through. Without looking back, she proceeded hesitatingly along the long, dimly lit corridor towards the front exit door and stopped at the end. The eager priest once again leaped from behind, quickly grabbed the door handle and opened the door. Mrs. Brodski turned around to bid him good night, and the shrewd priest was right there, within just several centimeters of her, looking at the beautiful woman intently with his piercing eyes, smiling mischievously. She stepped back quite surprised at the priest's audacity.

"Good night! It was a pleasure meeting you. Thank you for your time and The Bible," she said.

"Good night Mrs. Pleasure was all mine. I'm glad I could be of help," said the priest and politely nodded his head. She crossed the threshold and stepped outside into the perfect, late summer night. The air was still quite warm, with a strong aroma of chestnut trees surrounding the church compound, and a most pleasant mixture of flower scents carried over from the gardens of nearby residential dwellings.

"What a beautiful night it is! Please be careful…," exclaimed Father Antoni cheerfully and with a genuine concern, as he stood on the front steps for several seconds, inhaling the fresh air and looking wistfully at the quickly departing slim silhouette of Mrs. Brodski, and God only knew what he was truly thinking about.

CHAPTER 16

THE SCHOOL YEAR began on Monday, September 2. It was a mostly sunny, but noticeably cooler day, with temperature hovering around sixteen degrees Centigrade at its height in the early afternoon. It was Alek's first day in the middle school, a day of hope, but perhaps equal amount of anxiety. If the elementary school was any indication, there was little to look forward to. Mistreatment and abuse from seemingly always angry teachers and those few rude, offensive brutes in the ranks of peers, especially of higher grades, was to be expected, at least as far as he was concerned. Over the years he has seen many others, just like him fall victim to this senseless culture of power play at the expense those, the thugs knew well would not challenge them, because they just couldn't. Who could ever forget Mr. Fedoruk, the physics teacher, who seemed perpetually angry and ill-disposed to everyone and everything around him? He was often seen walking around the school with a sturdy oak pointer-stick and wielding it at the slightest sign of purported or imaginary transgression. Alek too on one occasion felt his unrestrained fury on the palm of his right hand, when Mr. Fedoruk decided to administer his brand of justice for accidentally running right in front of him and crossing his path. He considered it an intentional attempt to cause a collision and a premeditated effort to knock him off his feet. Alek took the punishment like a man and hid the swollen hand from his mother for a few days, soaking it in cold water whenever he could, to alleviate the acutely burning sensation, at least for the first two days, and eventually decided not to mention anything to her about it, for fear of a well-intentioned motherly interference, and then most likely further wrath from that cruel barbarian of Ukraininan descent. Needless to say, Mr. Fedoruk's reputation quickly spilled around town, beyond the confines of the school and became a subject of occasional derisive speculation on the reasons behind his constantly sour mood and aggressive behaviour. The story often repeated, which soon became the universally accepted truth, as the only plausible explanation for his out of line, sadistic conduct, was his sexual frustration. It had to be.

It was said by those who claimed to know the subject well, that when the bitter man after several weekly unsuccessful attempts to mount his unresponsive wife, brought to the brink of total exhaustion by the sheer load of housework, shopping and raising their three children, running around and the brats causing mischief, the man then unloaded his frustrations on those around him. The story was, when the nights came, the poor, dejected woman lay down like a dead fish. It went on for months on end, and months turned into years, and eventually the desperate physics teacher was becoming more and more despondent and irritable, looking for an outlet, anything to alleviate his pent-up stress and anger. It didn't take long, before even the older kids picked up the story from adults embellished it a little, and repeated often enough, that when it eventually reached Fedoruk himself. He was literally beside himself and vowed to catch the culprits, like a wild beast on a prowl, administering his revenge indiscriminately and with renewed vigour each time. Alek's only hope was, that at the new school things would be different, and what happened in the elementary school was a thing of the past, never to be repeated again. After all, he was not a child anymore, but a young man now and expected to be treated with respect he deserved.

The highlight of the day on this first day of school was a general assembly of all the students and teachers in the large adjacent courtyard, which started around 10 o'clock in the morning. The students were assembled in orderly rows by classes, with a help of few teachers walking around with sheets of paper in their hands, assigning students to their proper places. For many freshmen it was the first opportunity to meet fellow classmates, size them up, strike up a conversation and get the early feeling of a potential future friend or a foe. However, the first impressions were usually wrong, with a lot of posturing on all sides. As always, there were few pranksters in each class, attracting attention, vying for an early position of a class clown, and of course few more serious, sombre types with annoying self-confidence, self-usurped leadership impulses, perceived inherent right to scold others and preach their brand of wisdom without solicitation. Many of those were usually eager candidates for membership in the Socialist Youth Association, the first-tier breeding ground and a springboard for future membership and leaders in The Party. Alek was careful to not to draw attention to himself and was not looking to engage anyone in a conversation either, but preferred to quietly keep a low profile, unnoticed in the crowd, avoiding or dismissing even slightest overtures from those around him, as difficult as it was for about ninety minutes of this spectacle. The teachers, assistants and administrators were proudly seated on wooden chairs assembled in several rows, facing the students on opposite side of the courtyard. However, due to the large number of students, squeezed in a semi-circle in rows and columns separated by classes, the closest were within about ten meters of the school staff. The event began when the school director, Comrade Dymalski dutifully and sullenly called for a minute of silence, commemorating the 29 anniversary of the breakout of World War II, which began at 4:45 in the morning, when Germany treacherously attacked Poland on September 1, 1939. Then the silence was interrupted by the national anthem played through loudspeakers, as everyone was standing at attention with sincerely somber expressions on their faces. Then, after a minute or two of another period of brief silence, followed a general informational session, and finally the assembly culminated with a lengthy, monotonous speech by the school director Comrade Dymalski, a well-known bureaucrat, educator and a notable Party member. As expected, he reminded all those gathered of importance of good education, extolled the virtues of the socialist motherland, where for over twenty years now, people enjoyed free, unfettered access to schools of their choice. He then introduced the teaching staff and praised the facility and newly acquired equipment, and finally went on a passionate rant about the ruling party's role and merits in the indisputable achievements of the socialist country.

"It is an unprecedented achievement of our socialist country under the guidance of Polish United Workers' Party and its infallible leadership, which made mass education its priority. It brought the country back from backwardness and staggering rate of illiteracy under the previous bourgeois dominated, class divided society and the horrible destruction of World War II, to current highly educated population in a free and democratic country, with equal opportunity for all people regardless of ancestry or descent. Today, our socialist country has emerged as one of the leading nations among the progressive and fast developing nations of the world. Illiteracy, which was a norm under the bourgeois and aristocracy, is now, as are they, a thing of the past, and we can say will absolute conviction, they have been successfully eradicated. We encourage our youth to study and work hard, to follow in the footsteps of our great socialist leaders and pioneers in science, industry, medicine, education and politics, and when the time comes, to eventually take their places and continue the great revolutionary tradition of unparalleled achievements in all aspects of our lives, that we all can be proud of."

Later, after the official opening ceremony, the day was filled with mostly organizational matters, classroom assignment, weekly course schedule, supply lists, buying and swapping books with students of higher grades, eager to get rid of their old books and make some money in the process. Again, many opportunities presented themselves to mingle with other students, and to get the overall feeling of potential for a closer relationship or even friendships. Alek continued to stay clear of any engagement, in fact went out of his way to avoid any face-to-face contact, preferring his own comfort zone on the first day at the new school, although he noticed few students he had seen before, either at the elementary school or on the streets. In the next day or two, as every year, it was expected to commemorate the beginning of World War II by a field trip to the grave of an unknown soldier on the outskirts of town. In the meantime, the corridors were alive, full of students, boys and girls from around town and the villages, walking around in different directions, standing alone or in groups, engaged in lively conversations, laughing and telling stories of the past summer vacation, of the care-free world left behind. One could see teachers hurriedly crossing the corridors with intensity and seriousness on their faces, peeking inside the classrooms, paying little attention to the crowds of students loitering around. There was a different feeling to the middle school, not only the exterior of the building itself, the surrounding grounds with well-maintained landscaping, mature trees and shrubs, but inside as well; the floors, walls, doors and windows, even the smell of the air was different, as if aged with the school, trapped inside and assimilated. It was impossible not to notice the stark contrast in the actual interior appearance of the school, to the one so admiringly described and praised by director Dymalski in his opening speech. The long stretches of plain, worn-out PVC tile flooring with cracks and missing pieces under the glare of dim, outdated, low-wattage incandescent light bulbs. The dark-beige walls were long overdue for a fresh coat of paint, with clearly visible numerous chips, pen and pencil marks, carved in little hearts and initials of unknown lovers, and crude attempts at mural art, or just signs of unloaded anger and frustration on the walls everywhere. Many wooden classroom and storage doors were met with similar fate, and showed unmistakable signs of deliberate abuse, beside their considerable age. Some sections of the walls displayed galleries of black and white large, framed photographs of graduating classes from the years past, posing with their teachers, seated or standing in multiple rows, with sullen faces and looking ahead. Alek looked at the old photographs with much interest when passing by, imagining his own class there one day forever immortalized for future generations to see. One of the feature walls displayed a large, red banner proclaiming the leading, indisputable and infallible role of the socialist Party in guiding the nation toward its glorious future. He glanced at it quickly and moved along the main corridor, looking for his classroom, according to the schedule he had received from the administration office. He recalled when that fateful snowy December night he stood outside, beneath a windowsill, secretly peering inside into one of the rooms with the lights on, when by chance he came across a revealing, intimate encounter between Mr. Buzynski and lovely Ms. Lubinska, the math teacher. He remembered it well, it was one of the first classrooms in the south end of the school, seemingly just like any other, but right across from it, on the east side of the courtyard there was a windowless garden tool or equipment shed. It had double wooden doors, facing that memorable window, and must certainly be seen from inside now, through the same classroom windows. Alek quickly reached room number 103, hesitatingly pressed the door handle and opened the door. The classroom was already filled with students, but with few desks in the back still left unoccupied, and he was obviously late. The teacher, whom Alek did not recognize at first, a middle-aged man walking between the rows and talking, who did not immediately react the sound of opening door, but when several heads turned in that direction, he too noticed Alek standing there, unsure of himself.

"Come in, come in, don't be afraid. Are you in the right class? Have you looked at your schedule?", asked the teacher.

"Yes, I think so. I'm sorry I'm late," answered Alek.

"What's your name, young man?"

"Aleksander Brodski."

"Brodski? Let me see...," and the teacher walked over to his desk in front of the class, took a sheet of paper in his right hand, and looked at it for a few seconds. He quickly picked out the name Brodski listed in alphabetical order, near the top of the sheet.

"Yes Aleksander, you're at the right place, although late, but we won't be concerned about it today. Please take a seat in one of those vacant chairs in the back. By the way, as I've already told the rest of the class, I'll be your music teacher this year. Today we're just having a general informational session, and it just happens that I'm here with you today. Tomorrow you'll start your regular classes according to the schedule. I know you're all eager to get out of here as soon as possible, so I won't keep you much longer."

Alek still felt out of place here, with an awkward expression of embarrassment on his face for being late, and now being the object of attention, as all eyes were on him for much too long to feel any comfort in the teacher's rather friendly and inviting overtures. He then walked towards the back and took a seat on a vacant, old and creaky wooden chair, at one of the double, wooden desks, supported on four wobbly metal legs, in the outside row, parallel to the windows. There were two chairs to every desk, and both of them were vacant, as were few other desks and chairs in the vicinity. All the furniture showed signs of age, and just like the walls and doors and just about everything else in this school, displayed legacy of previous generations and were covered with all sorts of pen and pencil markings, scratches, carved out hearts, scrawled initials, few partial little figurines with extremities vaguely resembling intimate parts of human anatomy and engraved words, not normally found in school curriculum, but certainly an indispensable part of any student's repertoire. The teacher started pacing again, and now was heading straight along the outside alley between two rows of desks, with his head held high, and talking about the challenges facing the school, because of oversized classes, and not enough space to accommodate all the students comfortably, inability of teachers to adequately convey the information, hence the resulting poor performance of students. Suddenly Alek looked startled, as if he had seen a ghost, and looking at the teacher with all intensity, walking in his direction, towards the end of the classroom, he uttered to himself: "Buzynski!" Yes, he was sure of it, the music teacher and a quite well-known local cultural celebrity, a man entrusted with the entertainment part of many official celebrations, either by his students, or himself playing the accordion or upright piano. Mr. Buzynski was best known among the students as "Nightingale", dubbed perhaps quite appropriately so by someone several years ago, and the name stuck ever since. He was certainly the man of that memorable night back in December, when perhaps for a few magical minutes for Alek the time stood still. He lowered his head down, pretending to look at his class schedule, afraid to be recognized, although he was sure, he couldn't have been seen outside the window in the darkness of that winter night. He couldn't quite understand, what it was in that brief moment in a life of two people he didn't even know, although had seen them separately a couple of times, that stayed with him for all those months, and sure to remain in his memory perhaps for the rest of his life? What was the reason for that, now seemingly insignificant event, which evoked in him such nostalgia and sorrow and it wouldn't let go?

Why was he still strangely drawn to it when it had no meaningful effect on his life, and yet it remained a part of him? Why was it tormenting him after only few minutes of a chance encounter of an event in which he had absolutely no part, but was merely an unintentional observer? Those questions Alek couldn't answer. He still remembered vividly Ms. Lubinska sitting on the desk with her legs crossed in a beautiful red dress, as Mr. Buzynski stood in front of her and played the accordion with such devotion, as he's never seen anyone play before. Their eyes were locked in a rare moment of pure loving embrace, or so it seemed, and she was blushing. This picture forever etched in Alek's memory for some inexplicable reason, always evoked a strange feeling of sadness and nostalgia in him, although with a lingering remorse of being an accidental witness to a private moment in two people's lives he was not supposed to see.

Buzynski walked to the end of the classroom, without paying much attention to any of the students, but rather concentrating on his impromptu lecture and the floor below his feet, then turned around and walked slowly back to the front of the class. Alek looked outside the window, and there it was, about twenty-five or thirty meters away, straight across, the tool shed he remembered well, when hiding below the windowsill over nine months ago, with his back against the cold, concrete wall of the school, and he was profoundly sad.

CHAPTER 17

SUNDAY, SEPTEMBER 8, marked a statutory national holiday, and an annual harvest festival, celebrated throughout the country in countless official observances with participation of the highest local and regional Party dignitaries, activists and the military. In the capital Warsaw the ceremony was held in the biggest open-air sports arena in the country, the 10th-Anniversary Stadium, opened in 1955 and commemorating ten years of the Polish People's Republic under the rule of the socialist party, and ten years since the end of World War II. The event was televised on national state television, transmitted by the state-controlled radio waves, and was attended by the highest national government dignitaries, scores of ranking politicians, ruling Party bureaucrats, highest army officers and visiting guests from other communist countries of the Soviet Block, but mainly from the Soviet Union. The stadium was packed and overflowing with about 100,000 spectators from Warsaw and visitors from other cities, towns and villages, as well as numerous performers in the entertainment part of the whole spectacle. The tragedy struck as the cameras were rolling, although few noticed at first, or paid any close attention to a lonely man, a solitary black figure engulfed in flames in the bleachers, amid the noise and commotion of the festivities in full swing, thinking the self-immolation of the man was an integral part of the entertainment segment. Soon however, many people in the surrounding seats recognized the human-torch, as a deliberate and premeditated act for all to see, as they quickly dispersed and cleared the area, but few threw themselves at the man, desperately trying to extinguish the flames with their jackets, and rip the man's burning clothes off his body. The police and security agents quickly moved in and cordoned off the section and forcibly escorted the man down, before he collapsed to the ground and was rushed to the hospital. In the following days and weeks, the state media were totally silent on the tragic story, and managed to effectively suppress it, but it quickly spread nevertheless, at least to some parts across the country, as radio Free Europe, in spite of the incessant jamming of the waves by state security apparatus, filled the gaps with details of the tragic event, with periodic updates as more facts were coming in from witnesses, family and friends of the man in the stadium, which in part read:

> *"Ryszard Siwiec, 60-year-old accountant, husband and father of five children from south-eastern city of Przemysl, and the former member of the resistance in the Home Army during World War II, had poured inflammable liquid over his body at the Harvest Festival in Warsaw on September 8th, and lit himself on fire. The tragic act of self-immolation in the presence of almost 100,000 spectators and highest government officials in the stands, including the First Secretary of the Polish United Workers' Party, Wladyslav Gomulka, Prime Minister Jozef Cyrankiewicz, ministers, regional Party secretaries, all high-ranking army officers and foreign guests. The details of his sacrifice were apparently well planned in advance and done in protest of the recent invasion of Czechoslovakia by the Warsaw Pact counties, including Poland, and an act against the Polish communist government. He was rushed to Warsaw Hospital, where he received a brief visit from his wife, but died from his injuries four days later, on September 12".*

* * *

Mrs. Brodski with Alek by her side, stood on the same steps in front of the door to the church rectory, pressed the doorbell and waited. There was no sound coming from the inside, just undisturbed, total silence all-around, captured within wall of the compound, lined with chestnut trees all around, with gently waving branches and a delicate rustle of leaves already changing colours, and glistening at the tops in low, weak rays of setting sun. This time Alek pressed the doorbell twice in succession, and they waited. After several seconds they heard a distant sound of footsteps fast approaching the door, and finally a familiar, cheerful voice of Ms. Klementyna.

"Good evening! May I help you?"

"Good evening Ms.! I'm Zofia Brodski with my son Aleksander, here to see Father Antoni."

"Oh yes, of course. Please wait a minute."

Then followed a sound of a brief struggle with a slowly turning key inside the old lock and the door opened. Ms. Klementyna stood at the threshold with a radiant and inviting smile.

"Please come in. I'm happy to see you again Mrs. Zofia. It's been few weeks, but I'm really glad you decided to come back. Your son, such a handsome young man. You must be proud of him. Father Antoni will be delighted to see you both. Please follow me."

"Thank you for your kind words, Ms. I'm also delighted to see you."

They all walked in single file along the familiar, dimly lit corridor to the back of the building, with the same characteristic smell of antique furniture, incense, burning candle and fresh wooden floor polish. Finally, at the end of the second, shorter corridor, Ms. Klementyna stopped in a small vestibule, at a door shielded with a long, dark curtain suspended from a semi-circular, metal rod. She parted the curtains and knocked on the door.

"Please come in," responded the priest almost immediately. Ms. Klementyna swung the door open, took few steps inside and Mrs. Brodski with Alek followed right behind her. Father Antoni, lifted his head from behind a large oak desk, sprang to his feet and in a few quick strides crossed the room to greet them. In a most cordial manner, he then bowed his head slightly and stretched out his right arm in a sincere gesture, but with a somewhat restrained smile towards Mrs. Brodski.

"Good evening Mrs. I'm happy to see you again and glad that both of you could come here tonight. You look lovely this evening, Mrs., if I may say so."

"Good evening, Father. Thank you. This is my son Aleksander," she said, feeling uneasy right after hearing the rather unexpected compliment coming from a parish priest. Father Antoni nodded and firmly shook Alek's hand with a genuine expression of interest and satisfaction that he managed to come, despite his doubts that the young man was serious about religious conversion.

"I'm glad I can finally get to meet you Alek. Your mother told me good things about you. Please do not feel uncomfortable or intimidated in anyway."

"Good evening, Father," answered Alek politely, but timidly, looking shyly into the priest's eyes, visibly unsure of himself, despite Father Antoni's friendly, inviting manner.

"Let us all have a seat", said the priest pointing to a couch and chairs around a coffee table, and turning to Ms. Klementyna, added: "Could you bring us something to drink? I think it's about teatime now."

"Yes, of course. I'll be back shortly."

Mrs. Brodski seated herself on the sofa this time, and Alek took a seat on one of the two comfortable, cushioned chairs by the coffee table. Father Antoni also took a seat on the sofa, but at the other end and looked at his guests for a few seconds with a penetrating gaze, as if trying to guess their thoughts. They sat silently and looked at him with anticipation. The parish priest once satisfied that his guests have settled in comfortably, mentioned something about being extremely busy, his very hectic, tiring schedule, frequent trips to the villages, meeting families in great need and distress, and overall prevailing pessimism in these parts and perhaps the country as a whole and abroad. It wasn't long before Ms. Klementyna was back with a loaded tray of white porcelain teapot and cups, butter biscuits, dessert plates and napkins. She then briefly turned to the guests, smiled with her characteristic warm smile, bowed and left again.

Alek looked around the room curiously, and it seemed like everything in it was uniquely interesting, emanating a feeling comfort and serenity, and as if there was a certain mysterious meaning, a sense of belonging to all the objects around the room, which must have been in their original places for decades, and could not be anywhere else. Like the oak desk drenched in a dim light of a desk lamp, or the ornate four-armed chandelier, hanging from a ceiling above a wooden table on the other side of the spacious room. Although interior of the room itself; the walls, floors, one sizeable window and the furniture clearly showed all the characteristics of an advanced age, as if they belonged to a different era, they were all still in a very good condition, or nicely restored and maintained, and most likely destined to serve well for many more years. Everything here seemed to convey a feeling of serenity, durability and permanence, like The Church itself, which certainly withstood the test of time.

Father Antoni like a good host poured the tea, invited his guests to sample the biscuits, and without further delay got right to business.

"Please try some tea and biscuits. They're splendid. As I said before, I'm glad both of you are here, and that's good news. The fact that you've returned, tells me that you've given the matter some thought, and are here to tell me all about it, otherwise you would not bother to come back at all. Am I right?"

"Yes, you're right, Father. We've talked about it indeed," said Mrs. Brodski

"Are you ready to join the Church?" asked Father Antoni bluntly.

"As I said during my first visit, it is only for Alek. I'll live out my life just the way I am. Alek has his whole life ahead of him, and it is his future I'm mostly concerned about."

"Alek, let me ask you then, are you ready to be baptized and accept Jesus Christ, the Son of God as you Lord and Saviour?"

"Yes, I am," answered Alek emphatically, without hesitation.

"That's good, that's really good, I'm glad to hear that. The sacrament of baptism is the most important decision in one's life, young man, especially at your age. You probably know, this holy ceremony is usually done at infancy, when the parents decide, but in your case it's a little different, but as they say, better late than never."

"Yes, I know."

"I assume you realize that it all comes with certain responsibilities. The baptism is just the beginning, next comes the First Communion, then Confirmation, then possibly marriage, etc. That's not all, in between there are numerous holidays, religious celebrations and periods of special prayers leading up to important dates in the liturgical calendar year, which The Church dutifully observes, and as a good Christian and a Catholic, you'd be expected to attend many of those. Not to mention, you'll need to study the Catechism and attend our weekly classes for young people like yourself, leading to The First Communion, here in one of the two rooms adjacent to this building."

"That sounds like a lot, but I think I'll manage. Actually, I'm looking forward to these new responsibilities and a new life."

"That's good to hear Aleksander. There are some technical issues involved in this process as well. Frankly, I've never had to deal with a situation like this before, where a parent is not a Christian, nor anyone else in the immediate family. I will have to consult our diocese's bishop Modlinski. Mrs. Brodski, I'd like you leave me your full names, dates of birth and your address before you go. There could be other information required, of which I'll let you know. I don't see any obstacles, but we must follow proper procedures. It might take few weeks."

"We understand, that's not a problem. We've waited this long, we can wait a little longer.

"It is rather unusual situation, perhaps even implausible, I must admit, when a Jew comes in and says of his own free will, he wants to be baptized in the Catholic church by a priest," said Mrs. Brodski with a big smile."

Father Antoni burst out with a brief laughter, then got up from the sofa and walked over to his desk, where he picked up a pad of lined paper and a pen, and quickly returned back to his seat, handing them to Mrs. Brodski.

"Please write down your full names, dates of birth and your current address for me," he said.

"Of course, I'll be happy to. I hope we'll hear from you soon."

"I promise you, as soon as I hear something from the bishop, I'll let you know. It will be just a formality, I think. I do not anticipate any problems. It is always good when new faces want to join our growing congregation. As they say, the more, the merrier."

Suddenly and unexpectedly the engaging conversation was interrupted, as the old, wooden entrance door creaked and slowly opened. Quite surprised, the three of them instantly turned their heads in the direction of the door, but it took few seconds before a male figure appeared leaning inside halfway through the door. The intruder instinctively looked towards the sofa, chairs and the coffee table where they all sat, and with a reserved, but slightly mischievous smile he waved his right hand and said: "Good night, Antoni. I must be going now. Take care my friend and see you soon. Good night madam, and you too, young man. Please don't get up Antoni, I'll find my way out."

Father Antoni immediately jumped to his feet nevertheless, but barely managed to take few steps around the table, and towards the man peering inside, when the door closed, and the visitor without even waiting for answer, quickly disappeared and only the receding sound of each step could be heard behind the wall, separating the long corridor, leading to the exit door. Father Antoni took two more short steps towards the door, but abruptly stopped in his tracks with an expression of slight embarrassment and disappointment.

"Good night, Vladimir", he said quietly, as if to himself, and then slowly turned around and returned to the sofa. Again, he looked at his guests with that characteristic, penetrating and scrutinizing gaze, as if probing for secrets of their thoughts. Once satisfied with what he managed to observe, and reassured there was nothing to be concerned about, he made few strange, undefinable facial contortions, sighed and then smiled with a good-natured smile, as if signaling the end of the momentary disruption.

"That was my good friend Father Vladimir from the Orthodox Church, as you may have noticed. He was just visiting briefly. Have you met him before?"

Alek just shrugged his shoulders indifferently, without a hint of awareness of who the man was, but the question certainly caught Mrs. Brodski's attention.

"Yes, I've seen him before here and there, and I've heard about him, but I've never met him personally," she said.

"I'm curious, what have you heard about Father Vladimir?" pursued the priest.

"Nothing in particular, I think. Otherwise, I would have remembered it quite well, but since I can't really remember anything of significance, then I guess it was just that, nothing in particular", she answered evasively.

"I see…I've heard rumors around town, but regardless of what you've heard, let me assure you, those are just rumors, there is absolutely no truth to them whatsoever. Father Vladimir is the most decent man and God-fearing apostle of Christ you'll ever meet. But let us go back to our business, shall we? Tell me Mrs., from what I understand there are just the two of you, right? Family of two?"

"Yes, just the two of us. My husband Jakub died several years ago, after a lengthy illness. Ever since we're on our own and struggling, I must say. We don't have any close family in Poland or The Soviet Union that I know of, only few distant cousins on both sides of the family in the old, eastern territories, before the border was moved west. Now it's all Soviet Union. Quite possibly few relatives who somehow survived the war could have emigrated to Israel, Western Europe or United States, but it's just my speculation. Most died during The War in the camps, as far as I know; Auschwitz, Janowska, Sobibor, Belzec."

"I'm sorry to hear that, it breaks my heart. That's really tragic. I sympathize with your plight Mrs. Brodski, I feel your pain. I meet a lot of people, and trust me, there are many who struggle with the past and under the current system with personal tragedies, in most tragic and unfortunate circumstances. What happened during World War II was horrible; whole communities wiped out, millions of people as we know now, most families were affected. We've been living in peace now for over twenty years, but it's not a paradise either, we all know that, regardless of what the government is telling us."

Father Antoni leaned over to Mrs. Brodski at the other end of the old sofa, and with what seemed like a genuine concern and empathy, touched her hand and held it for several seconds, as if trying to console her, to soothe her pain. She didn't shy away or resist the priest's unexpected gesture but seemed rather comforted and relieved. Alek didn't make much of it either, and found the priest's action to be sincere and reassuring. After all, he was a man of God, well known in the community and respected by most, and such expressions of sympathy from the parish priest were not unusual. In fact, among most devout parishioners of female gender, such warmth and compassion were much appreciated.

"Thank you so much Father for understanding. We really appreciate your kindness and support," said Mrs. Brodski in a rare moment of revealing personal story. It was more than she wanted to say and has said in a long time to anyone, but most surprising of all, she told it to a man she hardly knew, a small-town Catholic priest. The thought that it will stay with him forever, never to be passed on any further, was reassuring enough to convince her, this was a man she could trust. After all, he was bound by secrecy in most aspects, like the sacramental seal of confession.

"Dear Madam, it is my pleasure, you can always count on me. I'm a priest first, but I am a human being, and I know what's happening in this country. Frankly, I don't see much prospect for drastic improvement in the quality of life here any time soon. I'd argue, that there is no hope at all. I understand and I don't blame you for looking at ways to improve your family's situation, it's only natural."

"I think I told you before, during my first visit, that we tried emigration, after all nothing really keeps us here, at least not much. We were advised by someone knowledgeable and of considerable authority around here, that particularly the Jews were allowed to leave the country, whoever wanted to, of course. Unfortunately, we were turned down. I don't even know on what grounds, but whatever it was, the decision forces us to make the best of the situation we're in right now and in this town," said Mrs. Brodski.

"Without getting too much into politics, which is not my specialty obviously, from what I know, the emigration policy is aimed primarily at the elites of this country, those in politics at the highest levels, academia, industry, mass media and possibly judiciary, but not ordinary people, Mrs. Brodski."

"Well, at least we've tried, and should things change, we'll be ready to try again. In the meantime, we'd like to really become part of this community, as opposed to being the outsiders we're perceived and feel to be now."

"I understand. I think you've made the right decision, and this is the first step towards your goal by coming here. Before I'll get a reply to my inquiry from the bishop, in the meantime it would be a good start to give more serious thought to Alek's baptism, do some real planning, make preliminary preparations, like choosing your godmother and godfather. I also think that it would be beneficial for the young man to familiarize himself with the New Testament even further."

"That's what I intend to do", said Alek.

"Good. It might prepare you for what's ahead of you in terms spiritual commitment, our church activities and celebrations throughout the year. I have no doubt, it'll have a positive effect on both of your lives. It'll set you on a new path, it'll add meaning to your life. You'll meet new people, might even find new friends and of course you'll gain wider acceptance. It will change your life, believe me. Let me ask you Alek, do you have any personal interests or hobbies? What do you do in your spare time?"

"I read, listen to the radio and sometimes draw and write."

"What do you read, if I may ask?"

"Anything really; books, newspapers, magazines. The public library is only about two hundred meters from our home."

"That's very interesting. I'm curious. What do you draw?"

"Mostly ordinary people with pencil, ball-point pen or fountain-pen."

"I'm impressed. Now you've got me really interested. How about your writing? What do you write?"

"I should have said I'm trying to write; poetry and short stories, but I know, I'm not that good at it. It's not anywhere near as good as what I read", said Alek shyly.

"That's wonderful, I'm really impressed. What an outstanding young man you are. Mrs. Brodski, you must be proud of your son."

"Yes, I am, although he spends too much time by himself. It troubles me. I wish he'd go out sometimes and interact with his peers, but he's just not close enough with anyone to keep in touch after school or on weekends. This is one of the reasons we're here, we'd like to change all that, to get him involved with other things beyond our home."

"Aleksander, I hope it's not too much to ask, but could you recite one of your poems to me? That is if you remember it by heart. I must admit, I'm really interested. Literature is something that I myself immerse in. You're a very creative young man."

"I'd rather not. It's not worthy of your time, Father."

"How do you know?

"That's what I feel."

"Don't worry about that Alek, you're being too modest. And I have a feeling, your writing is really good."

"I doubt it, but I like doing it. I still have a lot to learn."

"Alek, if you remember one of your recent poems, please recite it, don't let Father Antoni keep asking you," interfered Mrs. Brodski.

"Listen to your mother," added the priest.

Alek's options ran out; he didn't expect such outcome. He was asked to recite one of his poems, in fact to reveal his innermost thoughts in the process, which he was guarding so meticulously. He looked at them as if pleading for mercy, but there was none to be found. His mother only smiled with a look of pride in her only child, and Father Antoni was anxiously looking with anticipation.

"Fine, it won't be long, but please don't laugh. I'm warning you, it's not any good," said Alek and got up from his chair, stepped back from the table few short paces, hunched and looking at an unknown, distant point in front of him, with a sullen, almost mournful expression on his pale face began.

"Speak to me"

"Speak to me Father of All
Devine voice touch my soul
Your strong, merciful hand
Lift me up above despair.
Years of shattered dreams
Grief-stained path impressed
Tear-soaked ground beneath
Will you burry me?
I've walked for years alone
Eternal truth eluded me
Quest for reason ran its course
Only faint hope still remains.
In the ravaged body's shell
My pain-scarred naked heart
With relentless throbbing pain
Aches for your healing voice.
Hear its agony's sacred cries
Speak to me, Father of All."

When Alek finished the recitation, he seemed visibly moved and exhausted, and just stood there for a few seconds, swaying slightly amid total silence. He then slowly returned back to his chair, with his head down, quietly waited for reaction. Father Antoni looked at him with astonishment, lost for words, and his mother seemed equally bewildered and truly concerned about her son's very personal, painful confession through his writing, and how little she actually knew about his fragile state of mind.

"Wow! Astonishing! I must say, I'm pleasantly surprised at the quality and maturity of your poem, Alek. Next time I'd like to see more of your writing and few of your drawings too. The poem was very revealing, a personal plea to God to hear you out and to speak to you, unlike anything I've ever heard before from someone of your age, or anyone else for that matter. I'm beginning to understand better your decision to come to know God through Jesus Christ."

"It is still hard for me understand, that being somewhat different would be a reason to feel so isolated and ostracized in this town. It never occurred to me that Alek had suffered to such a degree, although I always thought we both had a good, close relationship", said Mrs. Brodski.

"You must understand my dear, it's all this small-town mentality, cultural divisions and even ethnic differences that come to surface from time to time, despite the impression of peace and tranquility. One common thread here is Christianity, besides the widespread misery of course, whether Roman Catholic or Eastern Orthodox, but it binds these people together, it gives them hope. To tell you the truth, some district Party bureaucrats are trying to discourage people from going to church, and yes, even in this small town those few apparatchiks are quoting that old, worn-out phrase of Karl Marx: *"Religion is the opium of the masses."*

You would be surprised by the rampant hypocrisy I'm sometimes faced with. Some of the same people who preach that stupid communist propaganda, come secretly at night to have their children baptized, or to make arrangements for their loved ones with the last rites, or to perform Christian burial. Oh yes, yes... over the years I've seen it all. Nothing surprises me anymore."

"How interesting, I would have never thought. I think, under the circumstances people do whatever it takes to get ahead, to live a relatively normal lives, and I guess for some The Church and Karl Marx can get co-exist. We all know what life is like around here."

"Let me tell you something about Commandant Sokolowski, just between us, something I just can't get over, something quite disturbing. Few weeks ago, it was brought to my attention, that the Commandant was shooting at birds around the church, nestling in those big trees with a small caliber KBKS rifle. As you know, lots of birds, mostly crows nestle in those tall chestnut trees around the entire compound. That man just stood there on the west side, behind the concrete wall separating us from the adjacent empty lot, and was brazenly target-practicing, lead ricocheting in all directions. I wasn't here at the time, but apparently a lot of children gathered and witnessed the whole incident, as he was shooting indiscriminately for what seemed like an hour, I was told. The children were naturally horrified. Miss Klementyna and others, who happened to witness the whole scene later related to me, that the terrified, disturbed birds were circling around in flocks, and many sat on the cross on top of the bell tower. Even to the cross the very symbol of our faith, Sokolowski showed no respect. The lead hit the cross several times according to the witnesses. He killed several birds. Some fell on top of the metal roof, some on the ground below, few behind the perimeter concrete wall, and scores were badly injured, still struggling to escape. Please imagine, all of those poor helpless God's creatures had to be picked up later up on the roof and around the church and disposed of. Horrible, absolutely horrible! Such cruelty…I was so shaken up, and till this day, weeks later, I still cannot get over this."

"I'm shocked. As you say, absolutely horrible. Who would have thought? To me Commandant Sokolowski seemed like a relatively decent, reasonable man, doing whatever he had to do as part of his job. I've never sensed in him any deviations, evil intentions or extreme tendencies of any kind, on the contrary he seemed like a level-headed, rather helpful and understanding man, whatever his motives were at the time, at least in my dealings with him," said Mrs. Brodski convincingly, but visibly disturbed by Father Antoni's revelation.

"I'm sorry for straying from the subject with this terrible story, but it has affected me deeply. When you would least suspect, people you think you know and respect show their true colours in the most unlikely circumstances. I'm happy to have met you and to get to know both of you. I know you're good people, who found themselves in this often inhospitable, God-forsaken town, and are just struggling to live your lives, to survive. I assure you, you've made the right decision about baptizing Alek. It will certainly help you, and in time you'll meet many good people like yourselves."

"You've convinced us Father. We'll certainly wait with anticipation for news from the bishop. As you suggest, we'll start preparations. Thank you so much for your time, generosity and support, Father. We must be going now, we've already taken-up too much of your precious time.", said Mrs. Brodski and rose from the sofa with a visible expression of satisfaction and newly found inspiration. The priest and Alek, rejuvenated in his decision to become a Christian, sprang to their feet almost at the same time, exchanged few words while standing, and then all of them headed for the door. Father Antoni again walked behind, with a mischievous smile on his face, as part of his compulsive habit of admiring his female guest's shapely, slim figure. Along the way towards the front exit door, they walked in silence, perhaps reflecting on the meeting and all that was said. At the end of the corridor, Father Antoni leaped forward and opened the solid, wooden door and let them out. They stopped just outside into a twilight of September evening, with a gentle, cool breeze bringing with it a distinct smell of a changing season, the unmistakable scent of approaching autumn. They looked at each other for several seconds, as the parish priest in a fatherly, sincere gesture of kindness, put his arms around their shoulders and said:

"I truly believe and as most people like to think, there is more to life than this temporal existential misery, but beyond it, there is life everlasting."

Father Antoni bowed cordially with a warm smile bid farewell to his quests, shook their hands, and promised to be in touch either by mail or through his indispensable assistant Father Feliks, or wouldn't even mind if Mrs. Brodski just dropped in in a couple of weeks for an update. Then they all parted with a good feeling of time well spent in mutual respect and appreciation.

CHAPTER 18

THE SECONDARY SCHOOL under the patronage of Roza Luksemburg was not exactly what Alek had expected, although there were few noticeable differences, and the distance from his home was about the same as to the elementary school he had gone for the previous eight years. He noticed that initially the teachers treated the students with much more respect, in fact some, mostly male teachers made a point of occasionally referring to students as Mr. and Miss., followed by their family name. It wasn't always taken seriously however, sooner or later the sarcasm became plainly apparent, once the curriculum was well under way and the usual problems came into play, like the first poor marks on tests and essays, homework not done, habitual lateness or disruptions in the classroom. One thing was certain, there were never any overtly aggressive verbal outbursts, name calling or threats from the teachers, as was often the case in the previous school. Alek did not fall into any disorderly category of students to invite public scalding or be reprimanded. He consciously was always on time, had his assignments done, was reasonably well prepared for the tests, although his first marks were rather low, but within a passing range, and seldom participated in any class discussions or interactions, as much as he could, as not to draw much attention to himself. Generally, he preferred to keep a low profile, unless specifically asked or challenged by the teacher or one of his peers, something he could not avoid. One of the negative aspects of the new school, was the frequent changing of classrooms. There was a physics lab, chemistry lab, biology lab, one for both geography and history classroom, one and the same for mathematics, Polish and Russian language, and of course the dreaded gymnasium. For him perhaps his most despised place in the entire school.

Alek did not like sports, particularly in the setting of this old, decrepit gym in urgent need of repairs, and in it, any of the individual exercises or group games, like volleyball, basketball or indoor football. Not only that the gym needed renovations, but it was badly lit and relatively small for what it was designed to be, with a somewhat reduced size of basketball court, serving also as a court for other games, then the small and crammed change rooms, making it a perfect place for those few nasty characters of male gender, whose only purpose in life it seemed, was to make the whole experience of physical exercise on and off the court, the most unpleasant and miserable for others, especially those most vulnerable, which somehow those tormentors easily identified. There were two gym classes a week, the last hour of the school day on Tuesday and the last hour on Friday. The Friday's session was exceptionally stressful. It was co-joined with a different class, with all the male students from the second year, all of them about a year older, and for Alek it was a dreaded, torturous experience. The horrible commotion, shouting, running around, pushing and shoving, the ball flying in different directions, the piercing whistle of the teacher, and before long, he could hear somebody's voice calling: "Get him, get him!", which for those ruffians was enough to send the ball flying at great speed in Alek's direction, or bump into him with full force and knock him down, and then laugh uncontrollably, as if it were the most hilarious thing in the world. Another place in school that required special attention and vigilance was the school cafeteria, and it too wasn't planned for future expansion and could not receive the volume of students descending here for the lunch break, but it had to. Just like most of the school facilities, it was allowed to deteriorate over the years far too long, either due to lack of funds or mismanagement. Regardless, for Alek it was not the most inviting environment for a meal or socializing. Around noon, a single file line-up of noisy, restless students stretched from the front counter to about half the length of cafeteria. There was the usual pushing and shoving, jumping the queue, general disruptions and intimidations from the usual, easily recognizable few older underachievers, who commanded the most attention and exerted their self-usurped power at will, and ready to unleash their brute force if challenged. Over time, it became an accepted fact, just the way things were, and most others learned to live with it rather quickly, without provoking anything more serious, beyond occasional exchange of verbal insults. Behind the counter were two sluggish, middle-aged female servers with and aura of superiority, who looked like they'd rather be anywhere else but there, and that attitude only added to the overall resentment of this still popular establishment. Although the cost of food was just a nominal amount, the cafeteria had little to offer; just a few bare basics, like ham and cheese sandwiches, or plain Swiss cheese sandwiches, butter buns, tea biscuits, and of course tea, or a hot liquid product known as grain coffee and one kind of soda. Many students usually brought their own food and used the cafeteria to sit down and interact with their friends. Alek seldom ventured into the school cafeteria. He usually had his own lunch brought from home, unless on one of those rare occasions he didn't have anything with him, or one of his classmates insisted he should go to keep them company and convinced, that it would be beneficial for his own sake to show affiliation and loyalty to the class, rather than roam the corridors alone in the meantime. Once Alek found himself inside the cafeteria however, he still tended to stay aloof from the biggest crowds, patiently waiting or rather slouching in line for a cup of tepid grain coffee, looking ahead, seldom sideways, as not to invite unnecessary stares, or so he thought. He wore his customary white dress shirt, black, baggy trousers and old black, worn-out shoes. In this school his unusual attire didn't attract much attention, as it did in the elementary school, where all those spoiled, mean little brats noticed even the slightest peculiarities about everything and everyone. Here it was different, much more serious attitude prevailed, not many cared and surprisingly there were few others with much the same predicament, who thought they didn't fit in and kept aloof. The curriculum was more serious, something to contend with and not to be dismissed lightly, and the teachers were bloody serious about it too, as if the subject they thought was the most important, above all others. Alek eventually joined a hardly occupied two tables pulled together in a far corner, with two loners like himself. They never received any attention, except occasionally for all the wrong reasons, when eventually noticed by one of those burly underachieving types, looking for cheap entertainment at their expense. Isolation however, was a sure way to lose a popularity contest among the girls, who tended to group around the more outspoken, athletic and seemingly constantly joking, funny types, whose main mission was to be the centre of attention at all costs. The few quiet, withdrawn smaller groups were perceived as a bunch of boring losers, generally treated with disdain by the popular crowd, and who permanently resigned to the fact that, none of the coveted school beauties will send as much as an accidental glance in their direction. For Alek it was an infrequent chance to interact with few like-minded colleagues, share some stories like anyone his age would, at times even ordinarily silly things, and yet in their own way much more than that. From current and recent political or cultural events, or impressions of the latest music hits from Western European and American pop charts to the latest, most talked about foreign and domestic films, opinions on books, magazine articles, shared interesting stories from other people and of course occasionally even discussions about God. Rarely Alek had a nagging need to disclose and elaborate on his newly arrived at conclusions, after hours of thinking and pondering the meaning of temporal life itself, the sense of human existence. Those often came late at night, lying in bed on his back, blindly looking at the ceiling in total darkness of the room, and asking himself:

"Why am I here? What does it all mean? Why is life such a struggle, even for those who seem to have it all, but who cannot buy themselves out of terminal illness or the inevitable death, and neither can they take their riches with them? If good, virtuous lives were to be rewarded, why was there so much misery, so much suffering in this world? Certainly, disproportionately more among the downtrodden, poor, yet earnestly religious, God-worshipping people, than among the well-to-do, often selfish, immoral and wicked, at least so it seemed. Alek, recently being strongly under the influence of reading The Bible he received from Father Antoni, was further thrown into doubt and confusion. He reasoned, if Jesus Christ's horrific death was the ultimate price paid as redemption for humanity's sins and its ultimate salvation from eternal damnation, then it was certainly a waste of a good man. Not only the people were not redeemed and delivered from evil, if anything, the world has gotten gradually much worse and worse, and the three decades between 1914 – 1945 encompassing the two World Wars were the best testimony to his startling conclusions. The evil triumphed on such unimaginable scale, that all the previous centuries from the death of Son of God, were just the beginning, a prelude to a gathering storm, slowly increasing in intensity, and culminating without precedence in such mass destruction and loss of human life, magnitude of which had no equal in the history of human race. Barely out of the ruins and ashes of World War II, the specter of communism descended on Europe like a plaque, to draw more blood and tears, to sow more misery and torment, especially among those nations of Eastern Europe, which in the previous conflicts suffered the most. Alek's Mom did not always openly agree with all his gloomy and pessimistic views but expressed her skepticism about the contents of The Bible often enough, that it only added to his own internal struggles. Although at times their conversations turned into somewhat bitter arguments, he was just as exasperated by her frequent reluctance to even engage in those exchanges, her purposely condescending tone, occasional outbursts of laughter, and ultimately giving up too easily. On the other hand, Alek's few new colleagues, who dared to delve into the subject when confronted with his unexpected digression into matters of philosophical nature, trying to explain all that is going on in the framework of religious beliefs, for the most part had a much simpler view of the world around, or simply didn't know what the hell he was talking about. Although, he's heard it in the past numerous times, all evil in the world was somehow always easily explained by The Church, and then repeated endlessly by those who listened and readily believed it, that it was all justified and benevolent God's retribution for people's sins. Regardless, it all didn't make sense to Alek at all. The Christian doctrine was all a nonsense, an insult even to his somewhat limited capacity to reason incisively at such a young age. Because, if that was the case, then God in its insatiable lust for vengeance, craving for blood, perpetuated the never-ending cycle of violence, misery and suffering, instead of alleviating it. If *"man was created in the image of God"*, it is therefore fair to conclude and it must be true then, they all are the same, equally vicious, blood-thirsty entities. To Alek, at this stage in his life it seemed increasingly natural to question the established truths and universal interpretations. Why was it, that during The War, all those helpless people by the millions, who must have prayed earnestly for their lives, for a miracle, when they saw a German soldier's gun pointed at their head, and nothing happened? Then in a split second, the words of prayer froze on their lips, as the soldier pulled the trigger with typical German efficiency, the gun went off, and the eager German moved on to the next victim, and the next, and the next…, as bodies were falling into the ditch dug up previously by the victims themselves, and the supposedly good, merciful God was looking on. Nevertheless, Alek was certain he was right, especially after he has given it so much thought, the arguments were plainly obvious and irrefutable, he insisted. The Bible wasn't his only source information; after all, the town's library was just a short walk away from his home. He must have read a significant portion of its contents already, and increasingly more and more serious literature, that others of his age would not even consider, he thought. The new course at school, called "Introduction to Marxism and Leninism," which rejected all the supernatural and blamed much of the humanity's ailments on the bourgeois capitalism, religious beliefs and superstations, imposed for centuries upon the uneducated masses by the deeply entrenched ruling classes and the influential Church with its multiple layers of enforcers, from Vatican down to local clergy. The Marxist realism proclaimed the new truth and was here to enlighten the general populace enslaved in religious dogma, break the shackles that kept them in bondage for centuries, empower and set them free. Rational, as the new school curriculum seemed to Alek, in reality it had not convinced him, he remained skeptical. In fact, he could not recall a single person he knew or ever met, who could say anything positive about life under the supposedly liberating "dictatorship of the proletariat." Even Father Antoni Pukalski himself was highly critical of the new communist reality, although himself largely immune to the dismal world outside his church. Personally, the parish priest had no reason to complain. On the other hand, The Church did not offer a tangible alternative either. If the common tenets of religious beliefs postulate the fatalistic, pre-determined nature of life, being the central part of the Christian doctrine, then what good is a prayer, if it won't change the outcome anyway? Naturally, it would seem completely useless, futile, even an utterly foolish practice to attempt to influence the laws of nature in one's favour by reciting imaginary lines of prayer to some elusive, invisible entity. Even more problematic to Alek was the Catholic certainty of the Holy Trinity; the Father, the Son and the Holly Spirit, which seemed to defy logic completely, and that's something even his mother agreed on, but as usual with her characteristic, condescending tone, or suspicious smiles. Alek reasoned, *"Since Jesus Christ died on the cross, then who actually died? Only the son, or the Trinity, three of them at once? Is God dead?* Then it leads to a fundamental question: *What father would sacrifice his only son in the name of some elaborate scheme to save the people, his own imperfect creation, and supposedly within just the narrow confines of the lands around Mediterranean Sea? He certainly could have done a better job in the first place, and no wonder, whenever the time comes for God's immediate, decisive intervention, he cannot be relied upon, he is in hiding, nowhere to be seen. Was this plot devised only to save the Israelites and few other nations in the neighbourhood, because in all the rest of the world, people didn't know anything about the story, and missed out on the offer, and by all indications till this day have no regrets."*

The one thing Alek dared not to share with anyone, was his mother's idea and ultimately his recent decision, originally suggested by her old friend Maria Pavloska, to be baptized in the local church and become a Christian. The closer it was to the already set date of Saturday, December 7, few weeks after All Saints Day, mutually agreed with Father Antoni, following a rather prompt and positive response from the bishop, the more apprehensive and withdrawn Alek was becoming. His doubts and increasingly frequent regrets have intensified, turning into an obsession, taking up most of his time, incessantly occupying his fragile mind and relentlessly tormenting him. *"What have I done?"*, *"How did I get myself into this?"*, *"What's wrong with me?"*, he asked himself repeatedly.

At times he felt like calling off the whole arrangement. After all, nobody can force him into something full of contradictions, something he's not sure about and most likely doesn't even want, except on those rare occasions when confusion set in, when suddenly, out of nowhere he had a renewed surge of longing and hope for that mysterious something of which Father Antoni said with such profound conviction: *"It will change your life."*

CHAPTER 19

ELA, THE PRETTY girl Alek met the past summer at night in front of the restaurant, who so courageously saved him from inevitable beating, appeared suddenly and totally unexpectedly. The crowded school cafeteria was the last place he expected to see her again. She had her life well planned out at the time it seemed, and the street was to be her life, at least for a foreseeable future, since things were not going well in her family with her habitually drunk father. Apparently, she dropped out of the second year of school the year before, and was not planning to return anytime soon, but here she was, standing near the entrance, just inside the cafeteria, looking around. She was wearing a tight navy-blue skirt, significantly above her knees, borderline acceptable in this environment, or possibly even beyond acceptable school limit, challenging the norm, and a light-blue blouse with a large collar and a gray cardigan over it. From a distance she seemed anxious and out of place, although evidently looking for someone, or otherwise, she would have not come here, or would join the queue. Ela didn't notice Alek, but he being so vigilant, with his eyes often fixed on the entrance door, noticed her immediately.

"I know her", he said to his lunch companions and pointed with a quick movement of his head in the direction of the door. They both looked up startled and immediately turned in her direction.

"No, you don't", said one with absolute conviction.

"I don't believe you", said the other with dismissive smile.

"You want to see? Just watch me", said Alek and jumped to his feet and then quickly strode across the room, and within seconds was right beside Ela, who was already turned around as if ready to leave the cafeteria.

"Hello Ela!", said Alek, standing two paces behind her.

She slowly turned towards him and looked at the young man in front of her with bewilderment, which quickly dissipated, and a smile appeared on her face. She looked at Alek intently with a penetrating gaze for a few seconds, and then said:

"Oh, hello Alek. What a surprise!"

"I'm just as surprised as you are."

"I didn't expect to find you here."

"Neither did I. Where you looking for me?" said Alek with a playful smile.

"I mean, I knew you were coming to this school. You told me, remember? Still, somehow I didn't connect."

"Yeah, I remember well what I told you. What are you doing here? Are you back in school now?"

"Surprise! Yes, I am. I decided to come back. Let's move away from here, shall we? There is just too much noise in here. Do you want to go for a walk?" she asked.

"Yes, of course. Let's walk around the corridors, if you don't mind."

"You haven't changed. You're just like the day I met you."

"Is that good or bad?

"It's good, of course."

"You look great Ela, I must say."

"Thank you. I'm happy to see you."

"I'm so happy to see you too. I've been thinking about you."

"I don't believe you', said Ela with a radiant, coquettish smile, as they were slowly walking down the long, ground floor corridor, from one end of the school building to the other.

"Would I lie to you? Look at me, could these eyes lie?"

"No, not your eyes for sure, but your mouth probably could", and she burst out laughing.

"So, tell me Ela, why did you decide to come back? What year are you in now? If I'm not mistaken, you dropped out in the beginning of your second year, right?"

"Yes, you're absolutely right, so I'm back in second now."

"Why?"

"What do you mean, why? I wanted to learn how to read and write a bit better, you know, a literate hooker sounds better to potential clients, doesn't it?"

"What? Don't say that. Read and write? Wasn't that supposed to be long behind us, like grade three or four at the latest? I didn't know you somehow slipped through the cracks until now, but as they say, better late than never."

"Hey, don't be mean."

"I'm just kidding, you know that."

"Of course, I do, don't be so serious. So, do you want to know the real reason I came back here?"

"I'm dying to hear. Surprise me."

Ela, looking at Alek with a mischievously wily smile, slowed down her pace, looked around and said: "the real reason I'm back at school is…because I knew you'd be here. I wanted to see you and as often as I could, at least in this school. Education is secondary."

"Oh, now that's a good reason. Finally, you're making some sense. Ela, do you really think I'm so naïve to believe all that? Now, try again."

"I just told you. That's the truth, Alek. Now, you look me in the eyes. That's the truth, but please don't make me repeat it again, or I might change my mind."

"No, no, I believe you, I do. I'm sorry, I just wanted to make sure."

"Forgiven, but only the part about education wasn't entirely true. Actually, I'm in here for more than just improving my reading and writing skills. I started late, two weeks into the year. Problems with admission; they did me a favour I guess. That's what the director said, but it's behind me now, and I'm glad to be here."

"You know, somehow I've always known that you are here for more than just reading and writing, you're much more than that", said Alek with a big smile, truly amused by the conversation.

"Well Alek Brodski, I wish I could talk to you longer, but I must be going back to class now; it's math. That's not something I'm looking forward to. By the way, how is your math?"

"Sorry, can't help you with that, if that's what you mean. I'm struggling myself. For me it's history now."

"So, what's your thing? Anything you're good at?"

"Oh yes, you can count on me with Polish, all the required reading, Russian, history, geography, biology, even introduction to you know what. Count me out with chemistry, physics and math of course."

"Oh good, I might find you useful after all."

"Yes, I'll be at your service. Is there anything I can count on in return?"

"Of course, a lot, but what do you have in mind?"

"Oh my god...What a day! I can't believe it, it's a dream…a beautiful woman is offering me her services. I knew I could count on you. You've proven it once before by saving my life," said Alek completely at ease and laughing."

"Now, I must go. As much as I'd like to stay and talk to you, I must go," said Ela equally delighted.

"So, till tomorrow?"

"Till tomorrow."

Alek stood in the corridor by the wall, looking at Ela departing quickly, navigating between students rushing back to their classrooms. She turned around once, looked at him one last time, and disappeared around a corner. Alek waited for few more minutes for much of the foot traffic to pass, and he was somewhat sad. He was still strongly under the impression of what has just happened and couldn't quite get over the effect Ela had on him and when least expected, right here in this school, where he'll spend almost the next four years. This girl was certainly something else, unlike anyone he's met before, it all seemed almost too good to be true. What was it about this young woman than made him react as never before in his life? There had to be something he didn't understand yet, a completely new experience. Way did she stand up in his defense back there on the street, in the summertime? Why did she really get enrolled in this school? Was it really true what she was saying that she wanted to see him? Did she really give up what she was doing when he met her? He still had doubts. One thing he was certain of, whenever he was in her presence, he was a changed young man. From a quiet, shy and withdrawn teen, with Ela he was completely transformed, at ease and confident, as if he had known her for at least few years, almost as if she were his sister or a soulmate. Was this just a passing dream, an infatuation or was it real? How long will it last, will she eventually get bored and move on? What about that crowd she was hanging out with? She can't just give up and cut off all her connections and relationships? They wouldn't let her even if she tried, Alek thought, but she has shown to be most determined, if she wanted to be. He was definitely impressed by Ela's fearless attitude, unlike his own, meek and timid, perhaps even cowardly, which he could not control in face of adversity, real or imagined danger. A year before, he was confronted with exactly that, the danger was real, and he could not stand up to the thugs, did nothing to fend them off, or even attempt to defend himself, he just gave up without a fight. Unlike the old, overweight woman Pavloska, who happened to walk nearby, who showed instant, unrestrained courage and saved him from most likely more verbal, humiliating insults, tousling around or pulling at this clothes or hair, and sent the thugs running.

CHAPTER 20

TUESDAY, OCTOBER 1, at sundown, and the tenth day of the month Tishri marked the beginning, of the holiest day in the Hebrew lunar calendar, Yom Kippur, the "Day of Atonement", preceded by a period called as the "Ten days of Awe", Rosh Hashanah. The holy days since September 12, leading to Yom Kippur, were not particularly celebrated by Alek and his mother, and as for the personal reflection, self-examination and repentance, they thought they've done it year-round, and possibly even too much of it. However, on the day of Yom Kippur, Alek took a day off school, as did Mrs. Brodski, a day off work, and they just stayed home, especially that it was such a miserable day outside, and they both fasted for most of the day at least. Alek spent many hours thinking about his decision to convert to Christianity, straggled with it, and as a precaution prayed earnestly and asked God for forgiveness, in case he committed a serious transgression, begging for guidance and enlightenment, and hoping the upcoming year, would be indeed a turning point in his life. After all, God, or the Son Of God Jesus Christ was a Jew too. In the near future, in his new life as a committed Christian, he expected to seek the glory of God through his actions, and ultimately salvation in the afterlife, but in the meantime, a universal place in community he felt excluded from. He and his mother didn't talk much throughout the day, but mostly kept to themselves. By the end of the day, in the evening, she occupied herself with light household chores, and Alek tried to catch up on his homework.

As the time went by and well into the autumn, the school was increasingly becoming a fight for survival, where one had to spend so much time, despite it being a much-dreaded place. Many teachers, who initially displayed a well-maintained composure of civility and restraint, eventually dropped their facades, and by November, just like the change of season had shown their true colours. It seemed that for some educators, those particularly malicious, teaching through terror, threats and intimidation was the norm, the only path to attaining good education. They relished the unconstrained power and tolerated no dissent, just because they could, knowing well they wouldn't be challenged, and that's how the system has always worked, terror from the top down. The unreasonably heavy load of homework, on top of workshops, lab classes, experiments with old, outdated equipment, and then numerous assignments, group projects, required reading, followed by periodic quizzes and tests, for many students was the end of any positive notions of the middle school they had. Those, who since early childhood harboured with them noble dreams and hopes for better future with education, as most of them did, had to abandon them along the way, adapt and burry them deeply in their already severely strained minds, and quickly realize, it was mostly about day-to-day survival. For few especially sensitive and vulnerable, the dream was dead; they just couldn't take it and dropped out. By now, relatively closely guarded friendships, networks of support groups, and cliques of like-minded students were well-formed. Alek found himself mostly on the sidelines, increasingly isolated, except for occasional interactions with few students, who like him, were generally perceived as misfits, for their lack social skills or athletic abilities, unappealing physical looks, their attire, or just general tendencies towards scholastic achievement, despite the highly hostile, stressful environment, hugely regimented and overloaded school curriculum. Ela became

Alek's most frequent and faithful companion. They met few times a week in the cafeteria, although reluctantly, as not to attract too much attention, but preferably in corridors of the school, and occasionally walking back a short distance from school, before they both turned off in a different direction and headed back home. Their trysts didn't go unnoticed, and soon became just another reason for resentment and escalating harassment by the popular school "elites", or the tough guys, who were setting the tone for general prevailing atmosphere and governing conduct, beside the official rules set out and strictly enforced by the school administrators. Just to be seen with an attractive girl like Ela for those few "strong, but stupid types" was more than they could quietly take, and surely invited fits of jealously spiteful comments: "*Have you seen who that Jew is going out with? Can you believe that?*", thinking, they themselves deserved and had an exclusive right to the prize, but unfortunately had to settle for second best, or even further down the ladder, when compared to Ela. No, they wouldn't miss an opportunity to let their resentments be known, by intimidating, disdainful stares, vulgarities, blocking the path, or "accidentally" bumping into Alek from time to time, when their frustrations boiled over, assuming and rightly so, he would not defend himself. Yes, he just stood there, looking and waiting with bewilderment, unable to move, expecting the worse, which never came, luckily something always happened. The traffic flow, the bell rang, too many witnesses, someone intervened, teachers approached and eventually they all scattered in different directions.

The weather was increasingly and noticeably colder by the day, with gusts of chilly, easterly air, a mixture of freezing rain and early snow rushing from across the border, the vast flatlands of the Soviet Union, and as always inviting sarcastic, familiar remarks from the locals: *"Nothing good has ever come to us from the east."* In the gloom of daylight, the school became even more inhospitable with its dim lighting, dingy, decrepit, poorly heated classrooms and corridors, with old, outdated, notoriously failing radiator heating system, fed by coal or metallurgical coke, shipped from the southern mills of the country. When and if delivered, large pile of coal was a permanent feature in the back of the school, by a set of small, rectangular, just above the ground windows, with direct access to the basement boiler room. The fuel was shoveled inside through the low windows by a well-known to all older man, the boiler room operator. The short, skinny man in tattered clothing, with blackened, stringy hands and arms, smeared with ash and coal dust, and a perpetually tired face densly covered with wrinkles, has been around the school for as long as anybody could remember. Mr. Anastazy Kotlinski was a good-natured chap, a widower who kept to himself, but had much sympathy, natural affinity and understanding for the students, seeing them come and go over the years, striving to gain education against all odds, under the most unfavourable conditions. Mr. Kotlinski himself had very little formal schooling and was clearly ashamed of that. It was a common practice by the school administrators and many teachers, as a form of punishment for many infractions to send male students, the troublemakers, "the rotten apples" to help the old Kotlinski shovel the coal. Anastazy was delighted to to see the students, to be temporarily relieved of the most arduous task of his thankless and lonely job, when eager, equally delighted young men, were only too happy to get away from the stress of classroom. They dropped in unexpectedly from time to time, when ordered to do so, or at times it was a perfect place to skip the hated classes, to give the old man a hand, keep him company and smoke a cheap cigarette the boiler attendant generously shared with them during a well-deserved break from the heavily loaded shovels. Infrequently, Anastazy didn't show up for work, as if reminding all those ingrates, school administrators, teachers and students alike, not to take him for granted, fort he deserved respect, regardless of the rampant, malicious speculation that the previous night he must have overdosed, self-medicating again, simply got sloshed and couldn't drag himself out of bed. The old school without heat was freezing; fogged up windows, unbearably cold walls, desks and chairs, one could hardly sit on, but preferred to stand or pace around. The scene was striking; students and teachers wearing their outdoor coats, groups of girls huddling together, gnashing their teeth, surrounded by clouds of vapour, and it became unbearable to participate in a class setting, much less to have any meaningful work done. Eventually a word came in the late morning from the school director Comrade Dymalski, that the classes would be dismissed for the rest of the day. The well-known saying, commonly used around town, specific only to this small community, if one was to pay attention to all that was thrown around: *"It is cold like an old whore's heart"*, was an expression often repeated by men, who thought it was a perfect metaphor for chilly and miserable days like these.

It was a rare opportunity for Alek to spend more time with Ela and walk her home, which she didn't object to this time, unlike his few previous attempts, citing a variety of often trivial reasons to cool off his enthusiasm, just in case he expected to be invited inside the house at the end of their journey. Despite the dreary day, they both were quite excited about having most of the school day off, a rare opportunity, but something they both strongly agreed on, perhaps for different reasons, that the school was not a place they enjoyed spending their time in.

It was Saturday, the sixth day of the week, and it meant all schools, offices and government businesses worked till one o'clock in the afternoon, which was generally recognized as one of those few tangible achievements of socialism. The Party never failed to remind the populace and frequently promote the act, as their benevolent gesture for the benefit of the working classes, while reminding them that on the other side of the Iron Curtain they were still all stuck in the age not much different from that of the Industrial Revolution, when twelve-hour workday was the norm, and child labour was as common, as child education nowadays. Alek and Ela walked slowly, enjoying every moment, paying little attention to the light, cold drizzle mixed with swirling sparse snowflakes, quickly melting mid-air and disappearing before reaching the ground. As much as Alek tried not to think about possibly being invited inside Ela's home, he was increasingly apprehensive. What will he say, how will he behave if she introduces him to her parents?

"What are you planning to do for the rest of the day?" asked Alek along the way, trying to test her intentions.

"I'm behind with my studies, in fact with almost everything, and you're going to help me", she said without hesitation.

"Am I?" asked Alek caught off guard.

"Yes, you will, won't you?"

"Oh yes, of course."

"I'm glad to hear that, or you'd regret it."

"I would? What would I regret, if I may ask?"

"You would regret all the missed rewards."

"Rewards? Now, you're making things interesting. I can't wait."

"Another good trait you have that I like; you're so agreeable."

"You're too kind, my dear", said Alek and burst out laughing.

"Don't laugh, Mr. Brodski. You must understand, in the end a woman always gets what she wants."

"How prophetic…and what is it that you want?"

"In the immediate future my homework done, tons of it, and as for the rest we'll see, it will depend on the academic results first. You mentioned on few occasions in the past, that literature and history are your passions, and apparently, you've read most required books till the end of the fourth year already. Well, you're just who I need right now, because as you well know, literature is not something I'm crazy about. I have other worthwhile, less time-consuming and more pleasurable passions."

"My understanding is, you desire my invaluable services with writing essays, summarizing books of prose and poetry, making outlines, conveying to you what they're all about, and preparing you for the tests, so you don't have to spend too much of your precious time on those tedious tasks, right?" asked Alek.

"Right, very nicely said. I knew you were the perfect man for the job."

"It looks to me that our cooperation will undoubtedly flourish, under the circumstances, and let me assure you, I'm committed, but let's just go over the details of our agreement one more time. What's in it for me?"

"Oh, my dear prince wasn't paying attention…I thought I made myself abundantly clear."

"No, not so, please repeat it princess, if you don't mind."

"Not at all, I'll be happy to. Tell me, when you're with me, what's really on your mind? What is it, that you want most? What's your greatest desire?"

"Oh my God…you reading my mind? It's a deal."

"The question is, are you up to it, Alek? I just might test your commitment sooner than you think."

"Don't worry about me, just make sure you don't renege on your end of the bargain, my dear."

"Alek, I'm not sure what's really on your mind, but don't get carried away. Aren't you more concerned about winning all those wars you've been waging with your toy soldiers?"

"Ela, for your information, all the wars have been won long time ago. Now it's time for consolidation of power that come with the territories and to collect spoils of the wars."

"Let me just ask you, seriously now; does you Mom know about me?"

"Yes, she does."

"What did you tell her?"

"You have no reason to be concerned. Actually, I told her about you the day after that night near the restaurant last summer. I didn't say everything of course, but enough to let her know that you're someone special."

"Could you be more specific?" continued Ela with her usual playfulness.

"Well, she knows you're my friend, and you've got guts, you're witty, smart, sweet, fun to be with, and of course very pretty," replied Alek, taking on a more serious demeanor.

"That's all? Do you always lie to her like that?"

"What do you mean, that's all? Those were not lies. I told Mom all she needs to know from me. The rest you can tell her yourself."

"It sounds like an invitation to me. So, when will I meet your mom?"

"Actually, it up to you, no pressure. I'm open to suggestions. Whenever it's convenient for you, is fine with me, or should I say, us."

"I'll let you know."

Ela and Alek were both unusually at ease and happy, walking slowly and laughing, as if nothing else around them mattered, or even existed and time stood still, and they didn't mind, in spite of the heavy overcast and gloomy weather. They were fast approaching Ela's home in an old and poor neighbourhood, just like almost any other, on the outskirts, but still relatively close to the town's centre, a long walking distance one could say. They passed few ordinary people on their way, going about their business in both directions, without paying any attention to the world around them, just scurrying along the wet sidewalks with their heads down, shielding faces from the biting, cold drizzle. Alek and Ela were already almost completely drenched, bent over, carrying their heavy, dripping bags full of books and school supplies, and it all didn't matter, at least now, for a few precious moments under the gray, heavy sky. Before they reached the door of Ela's house, she already pulled a key from her trench coat pocket, and without hesitation opened the door. She pulled Alek right behind her, before he even had a chance to utter a word, still thinking about the conversation they had along the way. Once inside, she quickly took off her coat, hanged it on a free-standing wooden coat hanger in the foyer, just inside, took her wet shoes off, and literally ordered Alek to do the same. She pulled on the sleeves of his wet, black overcoat, one by one, while he struggled to free himself from it, and then once off, threw it on top of the already overloaded hanger, and his wet hat up even higher. He left his school bag on the floor, by the wall, right beside the coat hanger. Alek didn't even had time to think, to say anything or resist when he was pulled by the arm from the foyer and into the kitchen, leaving several drops of rainwater behind. Ela's mother stood inside the kitchen and at first seemed rather startled and uncomfortable seeing Alek, standing right behind her daughter, something she was obviously not prepared for.

"Mom, I want you to meet my friend Alek", said Ela without hesitation.

Mrs. Nowak stretched out her hand to greet Alek, but their eyes met only for a split second, as she almost instantly lowered her head and turned sideways, but it was still long enough for Alek to notice what seemed like bruises on her sullen face.

"Mom, the classes were dismissed for the rest of the day. There was no heat in school, it was freezing, so we came home. I invited Alek to help me with some studies and homework. He's really good at many things."

"It's probably an exaggeration to say I'm good at many things, but I try", said Alek, somewhat uncomfortable in the strange surroundings.

"Don't mind me, do what you have to. Please go right inside the living room", said Mrs. Nowak dismissively, without looking, and with her back to them.

"Good, follow me Alek", said Ela, pulling him behind her to the next room.

Once inside the living room, Alek couldn't resist the temptation to look around, although tried to do it most discretely. It was only on few occasions he had an opportunity to be in other people's homes in his entire life. He and his mother just never went anywhere, beside few visits to the neighbours inside their communal building. It was extremely seldom that anyone invited them, and even if they were invited on rare occasions, his mother usually turned down the invitation, using all possible excuses she could come up with.

Ela's living room was of average, mid-size, but crammed with all kinds of old, outdated furniture accumulated over the years, but all the pieces probably had their purpose. One thing was certain, definitely it was not a household of affluence, on the contrary, of rather modest means, to say the least, if one was to judge by its contents, and like most families in town, they were caught up in the never-ending cycle of grinding poverty and misery, out of which there seemed to be no way out. Although the room had two windows, it was relatively dark in it, which Ela knowing it well, immediately remedied the gloomy interior by turning on the light switch near the entrance door. The three-bulb chandelier, centered on the ceiling above instantly lit up the room, casting a weak yellow light over the entire area.

"Have a seat Alek, wherever you want", said Ela.

"Thanks!" and he sat on the sofa, up against one of the walls.

"You must be cold. It's not very warm in here, but at least not as cold as in the school. How about if I'll make some tea?"

"That would be nice," said Alek.

"Wait then, feel yourself at home. I'll be back shortly", said Ela and hastily left the room. Alek while waiting, looked around with genuine interest, further exploring the room, its every corner, the floor, and every piece of furniture and decoration there was. Naturally, there was no luxury here, just simple basics all around, which withstood the test of time, badly outdated, but still functional. Even the smell inside the room seemed old, as if well established, but delicate and pleasant, an integral part of the surroundings, not at all offensive to a new visitor, unaccustomed to the strange home. Although his first impression upon entering was that of a very old, cluttered, and disorganized mess, he came to realize on a second look, it was actually quite functional. Everything here had its place and purpose, and above all, the place was tidy and clean. Ela was back soon with a blue towel over her shoulder, two mugs already filled with fresh tea, sugar bowl with a spoon in it, two napkins, and set it all on the table. Her hair was already ruffled up and dried with the same towel, which she handed over to Alek.

"Here, dry yourself up," she said.

"Thanks," he said and rubbed the towel quickly and vigorously over his head, face and neck.

"Let's sit at the table, Alek."

"Are you sure everything is all right?"

"Yes, of course. Why do you ask?"

"Maybe this is not the best time for my visit?"

"Oh no, it's just as good as any."

"Doesn't your mom mind? She seemed unwell. I had a feeling she was distraught."

"No, she doesn't mind at all. She already knows about you. Have you noticed she was upset?

"Yes, I have."

"What else have you noticed?", inquired Ela.

It was obvious to Alek that she was referring to the clearly visible bruises on her mother's face and decided to avoid the subject.

"What did you tell your mom about me?" he asked.

"Don't worry, nothing bad. I mean just look at you, you're a walking virtue."

"What? That means you don't know me at all."

"I know you well enough, Alek. I think you're a good, clever young man, unspoiled by the world around us yet. You seem so innocent, almost like someone from a different planet, not to take anything away from your exterior appearance."

"Well, my dear, that's all very interesting how you see me, but I wouldn't entirely agree with your assessment, and neither would my own mother, I assure you. Anything negative about me?"

"Yes, but I'm not sure it can be called negative. I get the impression you're a little naïve at times, that you believe in a world which doesn't exist. You think following the Ten Commandments will guarantee you success in our worldly life, and eternal salvation in the afterlife, you might be disappointed."

"Naïve? You must be joking. I disagree again with your opinion. As for the afterlife, I have my doubts about the whole Christian doctrine. How about my looks? My hair, my eyes, my dark complexion, which all seem to be a problem for some people. I look different, unlike the people around town, wouldn't you say?"

"What looks? Don't be silly. If anything, you're rather good looking, but don't let it go to your head."

"I'm a Jew, and I look like a Jew. Everybody knows that."

"So…it's not written on your forehead that you're a Jew. It shouldn't make any difference, certainly not to me."

"I never told you this, but just over a year ago I got beaten up pretty badly in the alley, just off the main street. I think exactly for that reason."

"That's horrible! What happened?"

"I'm sorry Ela, but I'd rather not talk about it. It's all behind me now."

"Why won't you tell me? Who did this to you?"

"Really, I don't want to talk about it, or my whole day will be ruined."

"No problem, but at least tell me who was it? Anybody I know?"

"Believe it or not, it was Commandant Sokolowski's son with two others you must have seen here and there. The old woman Pavloska, who happened to walk by saved my ass."

"Did you report it to the police? Did you tell Sokolowski the elder about it?"

"Yes, my mom went to the station, and then again both of us, but as expected, it was a total waste of time. Sokolowski said he conducted an investigation, and denied his son had anything to do with it."

"Of course, he would deny it; that bloody bastard. I hate them. They all think they're above the law. They're all crooked. They've been taking kickbacks from my friend Anka, whom you must have seen on the street last summer, just so they'd leave her alone. I won't even mention what else they wanted from her, but I'm sure you can imagine. Of course, they've been hustling that old man Ivan, the bootlegger for many years now. They want a cut from the liquor he sells. Everybody knows they buy from him after hours too, especially that fat boozer Kovaluk, Sokolowski's deputy."

"I didn't know all that. I don't know much what's going on around town," said Alek.

"Now you know. How are you supposed to know, if you're stuck in the house most of the time with your mother?"

"Those kinds of things wouldn't interest me anyway. That's something I don't even want to know."

"Fair enough. So, how did it all end with Sokolowski's son and the assault?"

"Nothing came of it. He denied everything. My mom didn't want Pavloska, who witnessed it all, to get involved any further, and of course Sokolowski didn't want to do anything about it either. That's all in the past; let's not talk about it anymore."

"Right, let's talk about homework, shall we? I need an essay done on Renaissance. Jan Kochanowski and his literary works."

"Have you borrowed the book of his poetry from the library?"

"Yes, I have."

"Have you read it?"

"Not all of it, only about two thirds."

"And what do you think about it? What parts do you have problems with?"

"I don't understand a lot from his writings. It's all written in this old XVI century language that I don't quite understand, much less any profound ideas or feelings he's trying to convey."

Ela pulled out the book of poetry, some notebooks and pens from her schoolbag, spread it on the table and looked at Alek with anticipation. He glanced at her and all her school supplies on the table, smiled and slowly took a sip of tea, as if gathering his thoughts. They both sat in silence for several seconds, visibly enjoying each other's company, as if time was of no essence, and the more it dragged on, the happier they seemed to be. Alek momentarily had the impression he's known Ela for a long time, as if they've always known each other, but waiting only for the right moment, for the right time to finally meet and fully appreciate the friendship. What happened on the street the past summer, had to be a destiny fulfilled, although under rather dramatic circumstances. Occasionally, Alek caught himself on being carried away by excessive imagination and silly, youthful notions of future life together, joy, happiness and possibly even family life. The fact that Ela wasn't fond of literature or history didn't bother him at all, on the contrary, he found it that much more interesting, an opportunity for him to shine. Ela had undoubtedly other positive qualities and attributes he found most compelling; she was bright, quick witted, courageous, mature well beyond her years, loyal, undoubtedly ambitious and pretty. Despite her young age, she already had a past, although not to be proud of in a strict moral sense, and for a time, until quite recently had an enviable reputation in the town's nightlife circles. Nevertheless, Alek felt that to be seen with Ela, one would not be compromised, despite her past, but most certainly it could be a reason to provoke jealousy, possibly leading to open hostility. She had the admirable looks, wits, charm and manners like no one else he's ever seen or been around before. To him she was irresistible, even knowing her questionable past. At times Alek was overwhelmed with a persistently nagging questions: "Why are our lives so unexpectedly intertwined? "What is the meaning of this relationship?

Alek took the small book of poetry by Kochanowski into his hands, and slowly flipped several pages, pausing from time to time, and reading few verses here and there with a barely audible murmur, while Ela watched his every move with genuine curiosity. Soon Alek stopped scanning the pages, took one of Ela's notebooks with lined pages, turned it to the back with an obvious gesture of attempting to tear out few clean sheets, and asked:

"May I?"

"Be my guest," she answered.

"I will write a general outline, analyzing his major pieces, what the author is trying to convey, his impact and place in Polish literature, because those will be the only ones most likely discussed in class. Jan Kochanowski's poetry is unique in a sense that it introduced new forms of writing, never before seen in our literature, and now are considered indispensable classics. Probably his best-known works are the threnodies, a series of elegies he wrote after the death of his beloved two-and-a-half-year-old little daughter Ursula. His other highly regarded works are the epigrams. I'll write for you also some general conclusions that the teacher will probably place particular importance on, and you can expand it in your own words. I think you have to read the book too, at least large parts of it, and if you'll read it more than once, you might find the old Polish quite comprehensible. You should also read the introduction in the beginning of the book, if you haven't already. It practically covers everything. In fact, you could almost get away with reading only the general introduction and the analysis of his most important works. Promise me you'll read it."

"I promise," said Ella with a big grin.

Alek begun to write, quickly filling the first page, occasionally making some verbal comments and referring back to the book, then filling in the second blank page of paper in much the same fashion, and stopped half-way down the third page, lifted his head up and looked at Ela, satisfied with his accomplishment.

"I was only going to write an outline, but it turned out to be almost the whole essay. As I said, you've got to read this thing, it's not that much. You could probably read it in a few hours, I'm sure. I went through some of his most popular works already in the eighth grade of elementary school, so not that long ago. We had to memorize one of his poems and recite it in front of the class."

"So, which one did you recite?"

"Threnody number seven, a rather short piece. How about you?"

"Impressive. We had the same thing in our class, but I'm sorry to tell you, I have nothing to brag about. I couldn't remember a thing."

Suddenly, a distinct, muffled sound of doors being slummed reached the room, followed by a commotion in the corridor, which seemed to have moved quickly into the kitchen, and then a hostile exchange of words between male and a female, who most certainly was Ela's mother. Alek sat motionless and looked at Ela with a profound concern, as her demeanor suddenly changed. She too sat and listened intently, without uttering a word, waiting for the incident in the kitchen to unfold, or just die down on its own, without further escalation, or her need for intervention. The male voice turned into incoherent shouts, interspersed with only few brief conciliatory words in a much more subdued tone from the female.

"My Dad is back from work," said Ela with tear-welled up eyes.

"Should I leave now?" asked Alek

"No, please stay."

"I'm afraid to ask, but is there a problem?"

"Yes, there is a problem, almost every time he comes back from work there is a problem, and on weekends there is a problem too."

"I know it's none of my business, and I feel sorry for you and your mom, but what is it about, if I may ask?"

"He comes back drunk, that's what it is all about, and if he's not, he comes back with a bottle of vodka and starts drinking."

"How long has this been going on?"

"Almost as long as I can remember..."

"I'm really sorry to hear that. Does it turn violent?"

"Of course. You've seen the marks on my mom's face, haven't you?"

"Yes, unfortunately. That's so sad, I feel for both of you, but I think I should be going now, just in case things get out of control."

"No, please stay Alek, exactly for that reason. I want him to realize that other people know what's going on too."

The sounds from the kitchen were getting louder and louder by the minute. Unmistakably, there was an all-out argument, with Ela's mother no longer in a pleading, subservient tone, but forcefully confronting her husband, perhaps encouraged by Alek's presence. Ela got up from her chair and started to move haltingly towards the living room door, when suddenly the sound of objects shoved around reached the room, followed by a loud bang, and a piercing noise of shattered glass. Ela grabbed the door handle and stormed out of the room, leaving the door ajar, no longer trying to conceal what was happening.

"Let go of my arm! Let go of me!", shouted Mrs. Nowak.

"Dad, please let go of Mom," said Ela.

"You shut up! Don't interfere! Stay out of it!" shot back Mr. Nowak in a slurred speech.

"No, I won't shut up. You should be ashamed of yourself," continued Ela.

"You get out of here, it's none of your business!" her father shouted back.

"It is my business. I won't let you hit Mom again, I'm not afraid of you anymore."

"Just look at yourself, you have no shame. You're completely wasted," said Mrs. Nowak in a contemptuous tone.

"I said shut up, both of you! I'll do whatever the hell I want!" shouted the father again.

"Oh no, you won't anymore. Get out of the house, you hopeless drunkard!" added Mrs. Nowak, confronting her husband up close.

"What did you say? Get out of my way, you bitch, or I'll…I'll…,"

"If you ever lift your hand at Mom again, I swear to God, I'll go to the police, or I'll kill you myself!" shouted Ela.

"What did you just say, you little whore? Get out of here, both of you, get out! Get out of my house!" shouted Mr. Nowak, swaying on his feet, struggling to pronounce the words.

"For your information, it is as much our house as it is yours, if not more, in case you haven't noticed, being drunk all the time," added Mrs. Nowak.

"I make the real money around here, and you two spend it," he shouted.

"You've lost your mind. What is there to spend? Most of the money you make, you spend on booze. You have no clue what we do here to put food on the table and pay the bills," said the mother.

"You both have no clue what I do, how hard I work, what stress I go through to make some money, and it's never enough. What the hell am I supposed to do? Steal? There is no hope in this fucking country, no hope in this bloody system that was supposed to take care of its working class. It's all a big lie, it's a fraud! I can't expect any help from you either. Oh no, just never-ending complains. So, what is a man supposed to do? I can't get another job. I may as well drink and forget."

"Where is any logic to that? To drink and forget? Do you ever think about your wife and your daughter? Do you ever think how we pay for food, fuel and electricity? Do you, you pitiful drunkard know, that the last time I bought something for myself, was probably three years ago?" agitated Mrs. Nowak continued with a trembling voice.

"I've heard enough! Clean up the broken glass, you useless bitches!" shouted Mr. Nowak, swaying on his wobbly legs.

"You broke it, you clean it up," said Ela with a raised voice.

Mr. Nowak begun to pace around the kitchen with his head down, shattered glass crackling under his shoes, slowly moving towards the door and then the living room, glancing back at his wife and daughter with his fogged-up eyes and disdainful sneer on his lips.

"Don't go there!" shouted Ela with a hint of panic in her voice. He didn't react but barged noisily into the living room and just as fast stopped in his tracks, once he noticed Alek standing next to the table, looking frightened, waiting with anticipation, as if expecting a storm to unleash its fury.

"Who the hell are you?" asked Mr. Nowak, surprised by the presence of an unexpected visitor. Ela and her mother, who followed him into the living room, quickly moved between them to prevent any escalation, or should matters get out of control, they were ready to react instantly.

"He's my friend, just visiting us," explained Ela.

"What is he doing in my house?" asked her father, pointing at Alek, visibly surprised by his presence, realizing he must have heard the whole commotion.

"As I said, he's visiting. We were doing some homework," replied Ela.

"Why is he in my living room? What's going on here?" continued Mr. Nowak with increasing agitation.

"I ask you, in the name of God to leave him alone. This nice young man is Ela's good friend from school. They were studying, that's all. Just leave him alone and get out of here," said Ela's mom forcefully.

"I want him out of my house!" shouted Mr. Nowak taking two steps forward towards Alek. Both women immediately moved in, one on each side, grabbed him forcibly by his arms and blocked from going any further. The man was swaying on his legs, breathing heavily, and staring menacingly at the young man in front of him. Suddenly in a most strenuous effort to free himself, he twisted his body to the right, swung his right arm above his shoulder pulling his wife with it, trying to loosen the restraint, while Ela still held on to his left arm. Alek in a split second decided it was time for him to leave. He leaped to the side and out of the way, and hurriedly retreated into the corridor leading in a straight line to the exit door. Without hesitation, he jumped into his wet boots, threw on his heavy, dump coat and hat, bent over and grabbed his packed school bag, looked back one last time and pressed the door handle. Ela rushed out of the living room and with tears in her eyes, threw her arms around Alek's neck.

"I'm so sorry about this," she said trembling.

"Don't worry about me, I understand. I'm sorry for you and your mom," he said with sadness in his voice, looking straight into her tear-filled blue eyes.

"Thank you for your help, I wouldn't be able to do it myself."

"I'm happy to be of help. I'll see you on Monday. If anything serious happens, you can always come to my home. You know where I live," said Alek

"Thank you. See you," said Ela with sincere gratitude.

They stood motionless for several seconds, embracing and without words, when renewed commotion coming from the living room told them it was time to part. Alek opened the door slowly, quietly, as if trying not to disturb Ela's father any more than he already was. They were hit by a strong gust of wind with droplets of cold rain resoundingly falling all-around, stirring the surrounding trees. Alek stepped outside, turned around, and looked one last time at Ela standing in the doorway, with a feeble, yellowish light in the corridor of her house behind her. She waved delicately, and he responded with his own slight hand gesture, then bowed his head nestled between a large upright collar of his coat and holding his sagging school bag in his right hand, he then quickly departed.

CHAPTER 21

ALL SAINTS DAY of November 1, 1968, was a day of much increased activity in town, just like the weekly open market day, except it was a day free of school and work, and like a national holiday celebrated across the country. It was a chilly overcast day with gray, shifting clouds stretching right across the sky, and as expected, there were no break in sight for a foreseeable future. Sporadic gusts of wind brought with it cold showers, adding to the gloomy, unpleasant atmosphere and somber mood, which like a dark veil shrouded the town. Despite the dismal weather, hundreds of visitors descended for the yearly commemoration, filling the streets, the church, the restaurants, and the three cemeteries, alongside the locals, out in full force. The Catholic cemetery was by far the largest, covering a wooded area of rectangular shape, surrounded by a high, white concrete wall, located in north-western part town, a considerable walking distance from town's centre. The cemetery was well organized with several alleys crossing the grounds in different directions, and rows upon rows of graves. Some marked by simple crosses or tombstones of different sizes, or numerous other, more elaborate large monuments bearing inscriptions of the name, date of birth and death of deceased person and an epitaph in memory of the loved one. At the wide, double metal entrance gate, few small vendors, always in search of ways to make some extra cash, were peddling their home-made candlesticks, and the always popular candles in small, thick, coloured glass containers. Two older women, just inside the gates, were selling few varieties of potted flowers, in brown terra-cotta clay pots at very reasonable prices. An elderly beggar in tattered clothing, without a left leg, sat nearby on a small folding stool, shivering and whispering something, perhaps words of prayer, occasionally lifting his head up, looking at passersby and pleading. His hat, with several small coins in it lay on a bare, wet ground beside him, and right behind his stool there was a pair of wooden crutches.

The Eastern Orthodox cemetery was much smaller, surrounded by an old, rusty chain-link fence, but nicely settled on a west side of a picturesque, secluded pond, in the vicinity of the Orthodox Church. The cemetery was overgrown with mature trees, leafless bushes, withered weeds and several scattered, evergreen shrubs. Next to the Orthodox cemetery, on even smaller plot, was tiny Jewish cemetery, surrounded by its own broken and rusted chain-link fence, with few sections between posts entirely missing, and at the entrance, at the end of a narrow, dirt and gravel pathway, equally badly damaged stood a permanently wide-open, leaning iron gate, made of long, two-metre-high square rods, welded up together with cross bars. The small cemetery contained perhaps few dozen upright tombstones, scattered over most of the area, without any particular order, many of them leaning, as the ground beneath them eroded over time. Almost all the tombstones were severely weathered and blackened, few crumbling by the effects of changing weather over years and decades, and surrounded by high, dense grass and bent, withered and discoloured common weeds.

Alek and Mrs. Brodski took advantage of the solemn occasion, and the official day off to visit the grave of Jakub Brodski, their husband and father. In the early afternoon they got dressed in their best autumn attire and walked several blocks to the site of his burial. The tombstone of Jakub Brodski, made by a local mason, was only one of perhaps three relatively new, and they had no idea who they belonged to; they didn't recognize the names. Most of the people there were buried before World War II, few during the war, and few in the years since. The little plot that included the tombstone of Jakub was the best maintained of them all, in fact it was the only one which had signs of regular upkeep, the other two more recent graves, possibly erected sometime in the last decade, seemed to have been visited at least several months before, suggesting that the family of the deceased were not local residents, but live out of town, and for reasons that will never be known, buried their loved ones here, in this small town, on the border with the Soviet Union. The rest of the tombstones were neglected, abandoned, forgotten, and eventually overgrown, without any recognizable path leading to any of them. Alek and his mom each placed a candle in a small, blue glass container, as was a common practice on this particular day and lit them up. They also laid a pebble that each picked up on the road to the cemetery, on both sides of the arched top of the headstone with a Star of David in the centre, and which flattened into symmetrical stone shelve on both sides of the middle part. They stood in silence, looking at the familiar simple inscription in Polish and the dates that meant only one thing, the beloved man died too early, he died too young.

Jakub Brodski
Beloved Husband and Father
17.IV.1924 – 28.X.1960.

They prayed earnestly in silence in their own ways, standing close together with their heads bowed for several minutes, before they noticed an elderly man in a long, gray trench coat, tending to one of the graves, pulling at the weeds and flattening the old, dry grass and withered branches of low shrubs on all sides. Mother and son looked at the man working with considerable exertion, care and dedication around the grave of presumably his loved one, and reflected on their own lives, full of loneliness, uncertainty, pain and grief. On this day, they both in their own ways missed Jakub more than ever, and were again cruelly reminded life was unfair, for some more so than others. It was futile to endlessly speculate, as many have before them for generations on the mystery of life, the pain of death, and the sense of it all. For Alek, every year set him apart even further from the cherished memory of his father, and increasingly he had to make even greater effort to cling to whatever was left of it, to preserve the remaining scattered, precious pieces of his presence in his fragile mind. At a corner of his eye, to the left, Alek noticed his mom pulling a white handkerchief from her purse, and with delicate touch drying her eyes. Soon he couldn't restrain his own tears rolling down his cheeks, and could barely control his pent-up emotions, as not to sob openly in the wake of increasingly surging unbearable grief with each passing second. The gloomy weather, the surrounding eerie silence with infrequent, indiscernible voices coming from adjacent Eastern Orthodox cemetery, and occasional gusts of wind bringing with it smells of autumn leaves mixed with distinct smell of burnt candles, evoked a strange feeling of despair, hopelessness and obscure, lingering memories. The dark, low-hanging and shifting clouds above the town, the cemetery and adjacent patch of wooded area of the Eastern Orthodox cemetery, with candles flickering between the gently swaying low branches and skeletons of bushes in the cold wind, only magnified the mournful mood of the somber occasion, commemorating and honouring the deceased, who lay there undisturbed for years in eternal sleep. Alek's mother without looking, sensed her son's internal straggle to control emotions, moved closer and placed her right arm around his shoulders. Alek, suppressing his emotions, could barely maintain the outwardly placid composure, and shivered momentarily from her unexpected, motherly loving gesture and under the weight of her embrace. Reassured, yet barely holding back tears, he slowly moved closer, leaned his head to the side, towards his mother, and he was profoundly sad.

CHAPTER 22

DECEMBER 6, AS every year marked the St. Nicholas Day, which happened to be Friday, and not celebrated in any meaningful way in the Brodski household, although Alek was very much under the influence of his school mates and activities of the closest neighbours, some of whom celebrated in their own ways, or not at all. Alek and his mother were all consumed with preparations for Saturday, the fateful day they've been waiting for a long time, the day which according to Father Antoni was supposed to change his life, the baptism. All the arrangements were already in place, after two additional trips to the rectory of St. John's Church, during which the ever-attentive priest was by then completely charmed by Mrs. Brodski, as much as she tried to keep the distance and concentrate on the business at hand. It soon became impossible to tell, whether it was just Father Antoni's seemingly selfless support and unmitigated enthusiasm was for Alek's baptism, or his now apparent infatuation with his mother.

Nevertheless, Father Antoni was impressed and pleasantly surprised with Alek's overall progress in knowledge of The Bible, his maturity and renewed enthusiasm and commitment to life as a Christian in the near future. The priest no longer questioned their decision to have Alek baptized, and to take that fateful step to become a member of the congregation, but accepted their initial explanation as sufficient and justified reasons to become fully integrated in the local community for years to come, if they decided to stay in town for good. It was universally understood, life in these parts was hard and centered around work, seemingly never-ending chores and daily struggle for basic necessities. The Church gave people hope, that there was at least something better awaiting them in heaven, an eternal joy and happiness, a paradise and life everlasting, as proclaimed by Jesus Christ, the Son of God. To get to the promised land, all one had to do, was to believe, to follow the Ten Commandments and pray diligently, observe the Christian holidays and rituals, practice the weekly generous offering, preferably a tenth of one's income, or if indeed unable to, The Church was flexible in that too, whatever one could afford was good enough, when the collection basket came around during Sunday mass. All those who were deprived, wronged, mistreated and abused in their temporal life here on Earth, would be abundantly rewarded by the Father in heaven, and their tormentors would certainly be condemned to eternal fires of hell, for death is the great equalizer and God is just. It was said: "*It is easier for a camel to go through the eye of a needle, than for a rich man to enter the kingdom of God,"* and further according to the Gospel of Luke*: "Whoever is the least among you all, is the greatest."* For most people those words were the ultimate consolation, after all who else to believe, if not the town's highest moral authority, the parish priest, the undisputed messenger of God in these parts, here on Earth, Father Antoni Pukalski.

It was already dark outside with a light snow falling from the sky, reflected in the dim light cast from the tall lampposts, lining the main street on the north side, slowly adding to the already thin layer of the white blanket covering the streets and sidewalks, with few freshly impressed tire tracks in both directions, and scattered footprints of various sizes, quickly disappearing under the new, gently falling white powder. The temperature already hovered around –13C, and as expected at this time of the year in these eastern outskirts, perhaps colder than in most other areas of the country, being heavily influenced by the unforgiving, bleak, often much colder weather patterns to the east, of the neighbouring vast, flat stretches of the Byelorussian Republic of the Soviet Union. It was almost 5 o'clock in the evening and Alek and his mother were running late, but walked slowly hunched together, and mostly in silence towards the St. John's church, taking cautious steps, as not to slip and fall. They were both wrapped in their heavy overcoats, with collars turned up, looking down at the slippery path in front of them, Mrs. Brodski holding tightly onto Alek's right arm, trudging along the almost empty main street, with just a few lost souls along the way, scurrying for cover. They passed rows of familiar old houses drenched in darkness, except for scant yellow lights, as if framed in small rectangular windows, trapped behind shabby, sagging curtains, as the only visible signs of life, sheltered from the inhospitable, desolate world outside. Alek recalled all those times in the past, when late in the evenings he had a habit of taking lonely excursions around town, along the streets he felt were safe enough to roam undetected, approaching the houses and peering inside through the ground-floor windows. Many homes still had the curtains drawn apart, with unsuspecting dwellers clearly visible from the outside, going about their lives under the glare of weak, incandescent light bulbs, inadvertently revealing secrets of their private lives. He felt guilty about being a witness of things he often didn't want to see, and on many occasions regretted looking inside, but was still mysteriously and irresistibly drawn to this strange habit of inconspicuously peering into people's homes. He had seen abject poverty and indescribable misery, people at their best, in their most intimate situations, and at their worst. He had seen households permeated by peace and love, but also those dominated by hostility, senseless violence and brutality against helpless wives and children, whose screams could be clearly heard even outside, all at a mercy of drunken, out of control husbands and fathers. Particularly vivid in his memory was the Krinski household, a family well-known in the community for all the wrong reasons, an example of extreme adversities, combined all in one. Mr. Krinski, a foul-mouthed, short and scrawny man with a volatile temper, was a low-ranking employee of the National Railways. His wife Halina Krinski, a rather tall, malnourished woman, was a housewife taking care of their five children, occasionally employed as a housekeeper for wealthier families. The family living in appalling poverty, was dominated by constant strife and violence, perpetrated by the man of the house. Mr. Krinski was seldom seen sober outside his work, a state which combined with his explosive temper, made their lives a living hell. He terrorized them all to a point of outside intervention on many occasions. Alek inadvertently witnessed their small children unattended, three dressed in rags, two half-naked, standing on chairs and sitting on the flimsy kitchen table by the window, somberly looking outside with their big, frightened eyes. The youngest three sitting on the table, were taking their turns in dipping their moist index fingers in a sugar bowl, then fervently licking them off, for apparently there was nothing else in the house to eat.

Alek and Mrs. Brodski entered the church from the back, left side door and right into a cold vestibule, which was almost completely dark, except for a solitary short, thick candle flickering in a metal holder affixed to a concrete wall, under a large painting of Virgin Mary and baby Jesus. Another heavy, wooden door led to inside of the main church nave, just barley warmer, filled with rows of wooden benches, split in the middle by an aisle, starting from the back of the church and right up to the front quarter of the entire length, near the front altar. The floor was covered by interlocking white and black ceramic tiles, except the front of the church, a wide area of few steps cascading down from the altar, covered by a bright-red carpet, and which ended about three meters before the first pews. The altar was dominated by a golden tabernacle right in the centre, and a large cross with a life-size figure of Jesus Christ affixed to the back wall, surrounded by an ornate wooden framework. On the left side wall in the front of the church was a dark-wooden pulpit, embellished with meticulously carved decorative elements and a dome over it, also adorned with symbolic religious ornaments, raised about two metres above the floor, with a narrow flight of steps leading to it. On each side of the church, closer to the back was a meticulously decorated with elaborate carvings dark-wooden confession booth. The high concrete walls of the church contained five large stained-glass windows on both sides. The most prominent features on both side walls however, were the Stations of the Cross, a series of framed, three-dimensional statues of Jesus Christ on the day of his crucifixions, a replica of Via Dolorosa in Jerusalem, believed to be the path Jesus walked to Mount Calvary on that fateful day, almost two thousand years before. Only front of the church was illuminated by a large chandelier suspended from the ceiling, with several small light bulbs and numerous crystal pieces, which like precious jewels reflected the light in a kaleidoscope of colours. There were also two burning long and thick candles set in tall, heavy wooden holders, one on each side of the wide steps leading to the altar, casting weak rays on to the first few pews on both sides, and the small group of people already seated there in anticipation of the ceremony about to begin. Alek and his mother quickly joined the group and were very happy they all came and excited to see them, since they didn't know many people in town, and probably the only person they could call a true friend was a recent widow Maria Pavloska, despite their significant age difference. Two of her three children with families also delighted Alek and Mrs. Brodski with their presence for this special occasion, and all just like their beloved mother Maria, seemed good-natured and most pious people. Also present, was Mr. Kaminski with his wife, the poor tailor who lived on the other side of the dividing fence, in the adjacent cluster of decrepit communal housing. Over the years they both expressed many friendly overtures and gestures of support towards the Brodskis, and the last few years even offered few goods and deeds, selflessly and without expecting anything in return. They led a rather private life with little interaction with the neighbours on both sides of the wooden divide, beyond the daily preoccupation with a steady stream of small sewing jobs for people from the neighbourhood. They both worked side by side, out of their living room, with his wife assisting with less demanding and complicated sewing tasks. Unfortunately, sometimes in the end it turned out the customers had no money to pay right at that time, or just a portion of it, and in return offered their own labour, or something they could spare out of what little they had. Sitting quietly in the second pew were two invited neighbours from the same building, both were middle aged women of struggling working-class families, who occasionally visited Alek's mother for tea or coffee, neighbourly gossip, or just to share their personal stories and comfort each other in the miseries of their lives. More than once the women sought temporary shelter from their husbands on a drunken rampage, if only they managed to take the children and escape in time, and then shivering inside with fear and the children crying, as the men went door to door staggering, looking for them, shouting obscenities, pounding madly with fists and threatening to break down the doors, if the occupants didn't open them immediately. Thus, relatively good neighbourly bonds were formed over time, perhaps out of necessity, rather than anything in common. Sadly, misery being the only tangible, common bond. They all waited in anticipation, sitting close together, wrapped in heavy winter coats in semi-darkness of the scantly lit, cold church, mostly in silence out of respect for the House of God, as was the custom, but even more so, the low, just above freezing temperature made it difficult to talk without a considerable effort. The payment for performing the baptism has already been made well in advance; the parish priest wouldn't have it any other way, and although it was a significant amount by any measure, about a half month's salary, he preferred to call it a "donation". Father Antoni was late now, but they all could hear distant noises and subdued voices coming from the sacristy. Finally, he emerged in his black frock and a white cape over it, with The Bible in his left hand, in the company of his assistant Father Feliks and a teenage altar boy with a silver tray in his hands, carrying two glass containers, the larger one filled with Holy Water, and the other with Sacred Chrism, a mixture of olive oil and sweet perfume, along with a neatly folded bright, white cloth. Both priests approached the pews cheerfully, looking at all the gathered and greeted them cordially. The guests all got up when the clergymen were just few meters away, and almost in unison answered: "Good evening!" and few, who were familiar with The Church tradition, joyfully added: "Praise be to God!"

Father Antoni, looked at all of them again from left to right, bowed amiably, and with a genteel smile replied: "Praise the Lord Jesus Christ!" He then approached the first pew and extended his hand to each and every one of them, with a particular emphasis on Alek, whom he greeted especially warmly, and his evidently happy mother. Then he leaned over to the guests in the second row, and they all, one by one leaned forward and met him halfway, extending their hands to the priest, smiling sincerely. He seemed in a particularly good mood, despite the cold, full of energy and beaming, as if a good, old friend met once again. Father Feliks, seemingly in a well-rehearsed manner followed similar routine, and greeted everyone cordially, and then moved to the side, to allow Father Antoni to take the centre stage, who promptly began with a short, introductory speech.

"I'm happy to see you all tonight, on this cold but special day, and because it is already close to Christmas, it makes it even more special. We're gathered here in this small group of family and friends to celebrate the sacrament of initiation, Alek's special day, his baptism, a day that will leave an indelible mark on his entire future life from this day forward. We will welcome him to our Christian family, which undoubtedly will be a turning point of his life, and a fulfillment of his dreams, as related to me over the course of many months, during which I got to know him and his beloved mother quite well. Although very small, but what a wonderful family they both are. From this day forward, Alek will be free from the power of darkness, and cleansed of the stain of humanity's original sin, and he will access God's gift of salvation, bountiful grace, his limitless generosity, and his profound, unconditional love. I know that Alek is already quite familiar with the New Testament and the Catechism of the Catholic Church, of which we've talked about in the past. While we're standing, I'd like to propose that we begin with the Lord's Prayer; shall we?" They all proceeded to recite the prayer, following Father Antoni and Father Feliks.

Alek seemed quite uneasy about the absence of his friend Ela, although she assured him, she would definitely attend, and somewhat intimidated by all this attention, even by his name being pronounced among the group of people he hardly knew, except perhaps for Mrs. Pavloska, for whom he had a special affinity and considered her not only a family friend, but more than that. By extension, her grown-up children somehow projected an impression of being close to him, although he didn't know them well at all. Alek met them only twice before at their mother's house, when he was there with his mom visiting Maria Pavloska. After finishing the recitation of the Lord's Prayer, Father Antoni, again looked over the guests with a smile, then Father Feliks and his altar boy, and asked the guests to sit down. The priest then turned his attention for a few seconds to something out in a distance, somewhere at the end of the church, gathering his thoughts with a serious expression on his face. Then he announced that he'd like to say few more words before the actual ceremony of baptism begun, and that he was aware how anxious they all were to start and get it over with, but he felt obligated nevertheless to fulfill his pastoral duty, as expected of him, and touch on few related issues, so vital to the ritual of baptism itself.

"I'd like to repeat what the Catechism of the Catholic Church says on the subject, which summarizes it quite well, that the sacrament of Holy Baptism imprints on the soul an indelible spiritual sign, and is the basis of the whole Christian life, the gateway to life in the Spirit. Through Baptism we are freed from the sin and reborn as sons and daughters of God, we become members of Christ's family. Baptism is the sacrament of regeneration through water in the word, and renewal by the Holy Spirit. It derives from Greek word *baptizein*, which means to *plunge* or *immerse.* Our Lord Jesus Christ gave himself to be baptized by Saint John the Baptist in Jordan River. I'd like to read to you now a passage from the New Testament, which Jesus said after his resurrection."

Father Antoni slowly flipped the pages and opened The Bible he held in his left hand to the Gospel of Matthew, verse 28:19. He then looked again at the gathered guests from left to right, with a more solemn expression on his face, and began to read in a deliberate, steady tone, emphasizing key words: *"Go therefore and make disciples of all nations, baptizing them in the name of the Father and the Son and of the Holy Spirit, teaching them to observe all that I have commanded you."* When finished with the verse from The Bible, the parish priest turned to Alek.

"Now, I'd like to invite our fine, young man Aleksander Brodski to come forward and stand here, in the centre, facing the altar and the light, and his beloved mother, Mrs. Brodski to stand to his left, and both godparents to join them, slightly behind Alek. Please, please come forward, and let us begin."

Alek with some hesitation took off his coat, left it on the bench and slowly, with obvious uneasiness came forward, as requested by Father Antoni. He was wearing slightly oversized black suit, white dress shirt, a black tie, and nicely polished black shoes. His mother followed right behind him, keeping an eye on her nervous son, and put a hand on his shoulder, once he reached the designated spot. The godparents, Maria Pavloska and Mr. Kaminski, the tailor, with some initial difficulty shedding their heavy overcoats and getting out of the narrow pews joined them several seconds later and took their places behind Alek and Mrs. Brodski. The priest quickly joined the group too, standing with his back to the altar, looking at them all intently for a while, as if trying to read their thoughts, and beckoned to the altar boy to move closer to his right side. He then turned to Alek, standing about a metre or so in front of him, towering above them all. Father Antoni also acknowledged with a nod of his head the presence of Mrs. Brodski and the godparents, each holding a hand on Alek's shoulder, and without further delay begun reading from a large, hardcover book, bound in dark brown leather, held out by Father Feliks, standing on his right side. Alek looked back hesitantly once again and noticed Ela, who came in late and was just settling in further back, away from the main group, in an empty pew, somewhere in the middle of the church, as the priest spoke with a calm, but resounding voice.

"Let us renew the promises of the Holy Baptism, by which we renounce Satan and his works and promise to serve God in the Holy Catholic Church, so I ask you, Aleksander Brodski, do you reject Satan?"

"I do," replied Alek.

"And all his works?"

"I do," he professed again.

"And all his empty promises?"

"Yes, I do."

"Do you reject sin, so as to live in the freedom of God's children?"

"I do."

"Do you believe in God, the Father Almighty, creator of heaven and earth?"

"I do."

"Do you believe in Jesus Christ, his only Son, our Lord, who was born of Virgin Mary, was crucified, died, and was buried, rose from the dead, and now is seated at the right hand of the Father?"

"Yes, I do."

"Do you believe in the Holy Spirit, the Holly Catholic Church, the communion of saints, the forgiveness of sins, the resurrection of the body and life everlasting?"

"I do," came a reply.

"God, the all-powerful Father of our Lord Jesus Christ has given us a new birth by water and the Holly Spirit and forgiven all our sins. May he also keep us faithful to our Lord Jesus Christ for ever and ever."

"Amen," they all said in unison.

Father Antoni put his hands together with utmost concentration and intensity in his voice, and pronounced few incomprehensible sentences in Latin, and when finished made the sign of the cross with his right hand directed towards Alek. He then turned to the altar boy standing to his right and took from the tray he was holding a transparent glass flask filled with Holy Water, approached Alek, and gently laid his left hand on top of his head, and with a slight push downwards inclined him to bow down, due to his considerable height. Once again, he looked at Alek's mother and the godparents standing near him, and then back at Alek with a most serene, genuinely sincere and saintly expression on his face and solemnly said:

"Aleksander, Jakub, I now baptize you in the name of God, the Father," and the priest carefully, but skillfully poured the first part of the Holy Water over the top-front of Alek's head, and continued emphasizing each word, "and of the Son," and poured the second, small part of the water, and then added: "and of the Holy Spirit," and poured the third part of water over the top of his head. A faint smile appeared on the priest's face, as he placed the glass carafe with about half of the Holy Water left in it, back onto the tray held by the altar boy. Alek slowly lifted his head up, looked at Father Antoni with a sincere gratitude, and then at his mother, smiled and in his whole demeanor there was an unmistakable appearance of a true satisfaction and a great relief, for he seemed a changed man indeed. The priest, without a word handed him a folded, white linen cloth from the tray, which Alek immediately understood was to dry his wet hair and face, which he did without delay. Then, with just a slight, agile movement of the fingers of his right hand, hastily fixed his ruffled hair. Father Antoni once again turned to the altar boy standing to his right, and dipped his thumb in the other open, small glass container with Sacred Chrism, a perfumed olive oil consecrated by the bishop, and anointed Alek's forehead with a sign of the cross, while bowing his head and whispering something in Latin. Unexpectedly and suddenly, the light in the back of the church high above the balcony, housing the pipe organ lit up, and someone invisible from the floor started to play the most profoundly pure and beautiful music; quietly, gently, and with such lightness, as if barley touching the keys, and yet touching the souls of all those gathered and listening below. They all turned around, looked up in the direction of the sublime, sweet sound, and they were stunned by the beauty, listening motionless, seemingly mesmerized. Unmistakably, it was the resident organist, a well-known and respected town's musical genius Mr. Kopytko at his best. He lived just outside the walls of the church compound, in a little old, wooden cottage, surviving modestly on a meagre pension allotted by the church, the ever-frugal Father Antoni. The organist supplemented his income by giving piano lessons to few students, some musically deaf, but of families with higher expectations, who had the ambition and money to spare and wanted their children to go beyond just the regular school curriculum. Mr. Kopytko was a rather short and chubby fellow, but a kind and deeply pious man, with the most agreeable, gentle and disarming disposition, who would most likely play for free if asked, just for the love of music and mutual enjoyment. He was known to deviate on occasion, possibly only few times a year from the religious repertoire, especially after the late-night mass, and with uninhibited enthusiasm delve into classics, like Bach, Beethoven or Chopin. Sadly, very few in town recognized his skills, much less what he was actually playing. Father Antoni was very proud of the organist and his services, or as he preferred to call it, his mission. The priest considered him absolutely indispensable, despite the fact this older man lived in a relative poverty, and the church coffers were full, which only he knew. However, Father Antoni found it particularly hard to part with money, but somehow diligent collection of this precious commodity came to him naturally.

Now Father Antoni stood there with the rest of the baptismal guests, with apparent contentment, and listened attentively to his resident virtuoso Mr. Kopytko. The priest, without attracting any attention, approach Alek, patted him on the back, shook his hand, congratulated him warmly, wished him well in his new life as a Christian, and expressed his sincere hopes that they'll be seeing each other more often form now on. Alek was visibly emotional with tears in his eyes, and his usually hunched over, lanky figure was now fully upright with pride, and certainly newly found great upsurge in self-esteem. Father Antoni then approached Mrs. Brodski and congratulated her on her son's life-altering experience, and expressed his high regard for the young man, how proud she should be of her son, and his hopes to see him more often in the church from now on. The priest also took his time to whisper, that he wished to see her as well, perhaps in not-too-distant future, although of course not in the church, in the front pews and down on her knees, but rather in a more informal setting, "to get to know each other better." After all, privately he was a self-professed connoisseur not only of good wine, but of beauty and fine things in life, and she was certainly both, beautiful and a fine woman. Father Antoni spent little time on the godparents, Mrs. Pavloska and Mr. Kaminski, just a quick handshake, and traditional: "Keep warm!", "Sleep well!" "Thank you for coming," and "Good night!" Unceremoniously moving on to the rest of the guests standing near the benches, the priest ran through them all even faster, with even quicker handshakes, and again: “Thank you for coming” and “Good night!”

Father Feliks followed suit, and cordially shook everyone’s hand, then bowed, extended his best wishes, especially to Alek, and said goodbyes with a sincere smile. No one paid much attention to the altar boy, and his presence would have been completely forgotten, had it not been for Mrs. Brodski, who turned around amid the whole commotion, and noticed him just standing there, exactly on the spot where they all left after the ceremony. She approached the teenager and said farewell, also on behalf of Alek, who at that time was preoccupied with the quests, who showered him with attention and best wishes. Of course, they were all invited well in advance to the Brodski household for an official reception, and now the invitations were enthusiastically re-affirmed once again. Alek did his best to maintain respectful façade, while furtively looking at Ela sitting in the back, and she looked back at him with a sad, withdrawn expression. The uneasy, but inspiring baptismal experience unquestionably had a positive effect on spirits of the entire main group of guests, despite the cold temperature outside and inside of the old St. John’s Church. They all became quite animated, almost exuberant as they were slowly edging towards the exit door through the dimly lit church, along the main aisle through the middle, and as the organ virtuoso Mr. Kopytko played his heart out, adding to the feeling that this was truly a momentous occasion. Alek stopped suddenly by the pew Ela was sitting in, and hesitantly sat beside her, at the edge of the bench, and looked her in the eyes. All the guest passing by turned around and stared at the young couple with bewilderment.

“I’m sorry for being late,” she said with sadness.

“Don’t worry, it’s all right. I’m glad you came,” said Alek.

“Congratulations!”

“Thank you.”

“You must go now.”

“Not without you.”

"I can't come."

"Why not?"

"I don't feel well," she said.

"But you must, if only for a little while."

"Some of those people, your guests know me. I don't think they'd like me being there."

"I don't care. I'd like you to come to my house, please."

"You know I can't. Besides, as I said, I don't feel well, and I'm not in a good mood tonight. I don't want to spoil the celebration. You must go now, Alek.

"Promise me you will come later, just drop in. They all probably won't stay long because of the children."

"We'll see, I can't promise. Please go now, Alek."

Alek looked at Ela, at her beautiful face; she had tears in her eyes, and quickly lowered her head, as if embarrassed or trying to conceal something. He touched her clasped, trembling hands, got up and hurried to join the group of guests, leaving Ela behind.

In the back of the church, just before leaving, almost all of the guests turned around one last time, looked at the well-lit altar in the distance, crossed themselves, some knelt down in reverence, paying homage to the Almighty God, whose presence they felt with renewed intensity. The main entrance vestibule at the end of the middle aisle was drowned in a feeble light of two candles burning on opposing walls. One near a clay, almost life-size figure of Jesus Christ on the cross with his nailed feet, low enough above the tiled floor, as to become over decades a revered shrine for the throngs of faithful on their way in or out, to stop and plant a quick kiss on the bleeding, cold feet, and perhaps a fearful glance at the horrific wounds of the Son of God; his head with a crown of thorns tilted to one side, with permanently closed eyes and a pale, lifeless face. Nearby, within easy reach, affixed to the wall, was a carved out, stone basin filled with Holy Water for the patrons to immerse the tips of their fingers and with the sign of the cross solemnly recite the timeless line: *"In the name of the Father, and of the Son, and of the Holy Ghost, Amen,"* just before stepping outside.

The guests, except the children, all lined up dutifully to perform this long held tradition, dipped their little fingers in the Holy Water, crossed themselves, and then slowly left the church into the darkness of the night, to be immediately struck by the cold, evening air of the early winter, which in these parts, and as expected, always advanced from the east, with its merciless ferocity, courtesy of the Soviet Union and sooner than anywhere else in the country.

The weak light from inside of the church shone through the tall, colourful stained-glass windows, casting feeble rays in the immediate vicinity, barley illuminating the nearest perimeter of the building. They could still hear the organ music, as they descended the wide, but slippery stone steps of the main church entrance, thinly covered by a layer of fresh snow, and walked through the open gate, marked by two massive concrete pillars, one on each side, and onto the sidewalk of Warynski Street. The street was named after the famed, late IXX-century notorious socialist revolutionary Ludwik Warynski, whose likeness also adorned one of the country's banknotes.

They all walked slowly along the almost completely deserted main street, crossing dark and empty side streets drenched in strangely soothing silence and mystery of the special night, leaving a trail of shoe marks imprinted in the fresh layer of the white powder. The group moved in a loose column, headed by Mrs. Brodski alongside Alek, with her right hand under his left arm, followed by the rest of the guests huddled together, without any particular order. Some engaged in a light-hearted conversation along the way, expressing their admiration for Alek, his tireless, loving mother and their dear friend Zofia. They were still deeply moved and under the impression of the just concluded baptism ceremony and all its participants; Father Antoni Pukalski, Father Feliks, the altar boy, and finally the irreplaceable organist Mr.

Kopytko, whose heart-warming, inspiring music still resonated in their hearts. The guests, being witness to this rare, soul-enriching ceremony had a profound feeling of spiritual renewal, a feeling of inexplicable lightness, as if they too reaffirmed their Christian vows, and committed their lives again to the timeless teachings of Jesus Christ. Alek thought of Ela when passing the deserted, familiar streets lined with leafless, ghostly skeletons of trees, and scarcely lit, old houses, the long stretch of central shopping plaza, known as "The Halls" with all the lights already out and windows boarded up for the night. Further down was the memorable bistro, where Ela so bravely stood up in Alek's defense, and then perhaps one hundred metres or so further down the road to he east, another one, the most popular drinking establishment in town for older patrons, the only two places with visible signs of life in town's centre. With a gentle, light snow falling, subtle smell of burnt wood in the cold, wintry air, feeble lights, occasional distant barking of a dog and barely audible chatter among his group of people, it all evoked in Alek a surreal feeling of nostalgia, loneliness and sadness.

The group soon reached the Brodski home, stomped their feet in front of the door and just inside the foyer to shake off any traces of snow off their shoes, and one by one stepped inside, hastened by Mrs. Brodski, who led the way. The host ushered them through the kitchen to the living room, which also served as a bedroom for the family. She encouraged them to take off their coats, keep their shoes on, if they wished, and sit wherever they could. It was quite chilly inside the home, although before they left the large, tiled stove in the corner of the room was filled with fresh coal, hoping it would still retain the heat when they'll get back, taking the risk of leaving it unattended. Alek looked inside the chamber, and threw few scoops onto the few remaining, but till glowing little lumps of coal. Soon after, the guests showered Alek with attention again, presented him with a variety of practical gifts and envelopes with wish cards and modest amounts of banknotes in various denominations, few books, a fountain pen, and a sketch pad with a charcoal pencil set. Again, a renewed flood of best wishes followed, hand shaking, hugs and atting on the back, making him most uncomfortable, awkwardly trying to maintain his best omposure, reciprocating kindly with words of gratitude for their generosity, and smiling shyly as best he could. Meanwhile Mrs. Brodski threw herself into serving food and drinks with help of Mrs. Pavloska and Mrs. Kaminski, the wife of the tailor. All was ready in advance, in fact Zofia had worked for the past three days, running to the stores a few times for missing ingredients, which were not always available, or exactly what she was looking for, and eventually as a last resort, had to borrow few things from her closest neighbours, or modify some recipes to suit what she had, or even giving up on some of the planned dishes all together.

It didn't take long, before the food begun to arrive on the fully expanded living room table, covered with a white tablecloth. Two additional chairs were brought in from the kitchen, and squeezed between all the others. The plates, cutlery and glasses were already there, set before they left for the church, and now just moved around, to make space for two more sets. The children were intended to sit on the sofa and eat with plates held on their laps. There were traditional, common hot dishes, appetizers and some cold cuts, and of course a bottle vodka to wash it all down with. For the children or those who abstained from drinking alcohol, there were few bottles of soda. Later tea was served with few choices of pastry, and more vodka flowed with occasional exclamations "Na zdrowie!," literally "To health!," and all along a lively conversation accompanied the feast. Alek struggled to maintain his interest in the topics discussed, most of which were of little interest to him, anything from bits and pieces of the country's politics and recent international events, as related by the government media and compared to what supposedly Radio Free Europe was broadcasting. Some also touched on the local news, Christianity and its essential role in the community, the local church and its colourful representative, Father Antoni Pukalski, and of course, the widespread gossip surrounding his alleged "wild side" of the parish priest. The subject always managed to elicit interesting comments and laughter. The priest's friendship with Father Vladimir, the well-known parish priest from the Eastern Orthodox Church, whose presumptive double life was now legendary in the entire county, also came under scrutiny. It was duly established, with much friendly deliberation and laughter, that friendship between the two clerics was no accident, as the old proverb rightly stated: "Birds *of a feather flock together.*"

Throughout the ordeal Alek hoped that they would just leave him alone, and did his best to avoid the conversation. Even if he tried to excuse himself from the dinner table, there was nowhere to go, nowhere to hide inside the home. He thought about his friend Ela. She seemed in obvious distress in the church, and although she didn't categorically turn down his invitation to attend the post-baptismal reception in their home, he had a feeling she had no intention of coming. The more he thought about her, the more he had a nagging, persistent thought that something grievous must have happened to her, most likely another violent confrontation at home with her father came to his mind. Everything else now seemed secondary, even the baptism itself was of little importance. Then came momentary, inexplicable flashbacks to the time just several hours before, when he was free of all the additional burden, free of doubts, which were now invading his susceptible mind with increasing intensity, tearing him apart, and like a swarm of stinging bees, attacking from all sides. The noise, the incessant chatter, the occasional bursts of laughter and the whole sumptuous feast was becoming a suffocating nuisance, a burden, at times even a torturous affair. In time a stream of regrets followed, weighing heavily upon Alek's conscience for his lack of gratitude to his mother, for her unwavering dedication, all the hard work she put into preparation of his baptism and this reception with what little she had and the invited guests, to make this day truly memorable for him. What he dreaded most, eventually happened, his restlessness was noticed around the table.

"Alek, tell me what you want to be when you finish your school?" he was asked unexpectedly by someone.

"I'd like to continue my studies at university, preferably Lublin or Warsaw," he answered politely, once he realized the question was directed to him, when startled out of his temporary oblivion.

"What would you like to study there?"

"I'm not sure yet, but possibly journalism or literature."

"Oh…is that so? Do you want to be a journalist or a writer?"

"Possibly, one or the other or both."

"It all sounds interesting, but how are you going to support yourself?"

"Exactly by that, working for some national newspaper or magazine."

"Very good. Good luck with that. So, you're already planning to leave this town in not-too-distant future?"

"No, not so soon, but if everything goes well, in about three or four years."

"You're not thinking of leaving your mother behind you, are you?"

"It might be necessary, but only for a few years."

"Then what?"

"Once I finish my studies and get a good job in one of those cities, she would join me of course."

"Sounds like you've got it all figured out, down to the last detail."

"Not quite, but I hope to start a new life eventually somewhere else."

"Alek, you've never shared those plans with me before," interrupted his mother, visibly surprised and confused by her son's decisive answers.

"No, I have not and I'm sorry, but these are only plans, just my imagination, my dreams, too distant to be taken seriously at this time."

"All right, fair enough, but I'd like to be informed in advance, what my only son is planning. Is that too much to ask?"

"Of course not, I promise I will, when the time comes."

"Who was that young woman in the church, Alek?" asked Pavloska's son, who already displayed all the signs of intoxication, and increasingly becoming a nuisance to all, with his intrusive questions and confrontational attitude.

"That was my friend Ela form school. She was invited too, but unfortunately, she was late and couldn't come to dinner tonight. She had some important family matters to attend to," answered Alek evasively.

"Are you sure? It seemed to me, she was more than just a friend from school," he continued.

"As I said, she's just a good friend from school. Sometimes we do homework together."

"Alek, I'm just asking. In the church it looked like there was more between you two, than just homework."

"I'd rather not talk about it," cut off Alek.

"You wouldn't want to be like that Jesus Christ's apostle Peter, who denied him three times, would you?"

"I'm not denying anything, I just don't want to talk about it."

"You know, I have a feeling, I've seen that young woman somewhere before. In fact, I'm sure I have," persisted Marek Pavloski.

"This is a small town, I wouldn't be surprised if you've seen her somewhere at least once," countered Alek.

"What I mean is, I think I've seen her walking the streets, or rather working the streets, I should say."

"Marek, I think you had too much to drink. How can you say such a thing? Please drop the subject and leave Alek alone," sternly interrupted Maria Pavloska in Alek's defense.

"All I'm saying, is that the young man is not telling us the truth," continued her son with the same derisive tone and sarcastic smirk.

"Marek, I'm asking you to stop this nonsense right now."

"Mom, I'm just saying the obvious."

"Marek, please stop it. Mom is right," added his sister Martyna.

"I'm afraid, I have to ask you to leave. Please just take your wife and daughter and go home. You had too much to drink. You are embarrassing me, your family and making a fool of yourself," added Mrs. Pavloska with even greater passion, now supported by her daughter.

"What's wrong with you all? I'm just talking to the young man," retorted Marek Pavloski, reluctant to give up easily.

"Yes, Mom is right Marek, we must go now," added his wife, Joanna.

It was almost 10 o'clock, when Marek took another shot of vodka, looked at the people seated around the table, murmured something to himself, grudgingly got up, walked slowly over to the coat hanger near the kitchen door, put on his heavy winter coat, and said: "As you wish, I'm ready. Shall we go?"

Before he stepped out the door, nudged by his wife, he offered Alek what sounded like an apathetic apology, to which Alek didn't respond at all, but was nevertheless glad Marek Pavloski was leaving. Shortly after 10, Pavloska's daughter Martyna with her husband and their two exhausted children also moved towards the exit door, escorted by Mrs. Brodski and disheartened and tired Alek. It wasn't long before Mr. Kaminski, Alek's baptismal godfather and his wife Amelia, who lived nearby, just across the dividing fence, decided it was time to head home. Although the tailor didn't miss a round of frequently replenished vodka glasses, he hanged in there remarkably well, was exceedingly well mannered and polite to the very end, and even offered to walk Maria Pavloska home. She promptly accepted his offer, and soon the three of them were standing at the door, all bundled up, hugging and kissing as the best of friends, promising to get together in the near future, since Christmas was just around the corner, giving plenty of opportunity to forge even closer bonds. Once again, they offered Alek their best wishes. The two remaining female neighbours from the same housing complex were the last to leave, since they didn't have far to go, just on the other side of the same old building, with entrances from a common corridor on the north side, just off the street. They left their children supposedly in the company of their husbands, under care of older siblings, and felt it was a rare opportunity to leave it all behind, even if it was only for a few hours, hoping "the house wouldn't fall apart," as they said. Alek was by then was completely tired, couldn't sit straight and alert after a long and an exhausting day and evening, full unprecedented events and drama. He got up from his chair at the table and moved to the sofa, visibly irritated. The two women were still in no hurry to leave, perhaps overstaying the hospitality of the hosts, and risking the wrath of their husbands. But as long as Mrs. Brodski was patiently listening to their stories of misery, how life had dealt them the wrong cards and there was no way out, but to carry the cross, but they showed no signs of being in a hurry to go anywhere. If one was to believe their narrative, each one had an appalling story of mistreatment at the hands of her often drunk husband on regular missions of expressing his brand of "marital love," by dispensing at will his strict measures to maintain the unwritten domestic code of discipline and justice for purported or imaginary infractions, "to set her straight," or "to keep her on a short leash," whenever the incensed man of the house felt his wife "stepped out of line."

Finally, the two neighbours left reluctantly, but it was obvious to the very end, they'd rather stay even longer but must have finally realized it was time to go, as not to make the matters worse, and certainly invite their husbands' wrath. They said their farewells with teary eyes but were grateful for the honour of being invited to the baptism ceremony and the reception. The women sincerely hugged Mrs. Brodski, and once again extended their best wishes to Alek and left. Suddenly, a profound silence befell on the Brodski home, almost eerie, uncomfortable, as some invisible, but deeply felt spirit left the room with the last of the guests. The baptism, followed by the celebration, which was supposed to mark Alek's new beginning, a turning point in his life, a promising new and joyous life as a Christian and his mother along with him on this journey, now seemed fictional, an outright illusion and a weighty, unnecessary burden, too late to unload.

Mrs. Brodski was tired too, but soon begun to clean up the table and take things back to the kitchen, making several trips back and forth, while Alek sat impassively on a sofa, in a strangely pensive mood, looking at his mother bustling about, and he was profoundly sad.

CHAPTER 23

DESPITE THE HIGH hopes for dramatic changes in his daily existence, not much has changed in Alek's life, and soon almost everything went back to normal, much as life used to be. He continued to see Ela occasionally at school, usually during lunch breaks, which naturally raised suspicions, unwanted attention, gossip and resentment. Sometimes they met after school, if the end of their classes happened to coincide, and walked home together as far as they could, till they parted ways just past the town's centre, and walked the last stretch of the way in different directions. Even less frequently they met to study or do their homework together, since Ela's father, Mr. Nowak regularly intoxicated, continued to display his usual hostility towards his wife and daughter or Alek if he happened to be there on a rare occasion, or just about everybody else who visited them. In turn, Ela was reluctant to visit Alek's home, despite his insistence and repeated invitations. She didn't feel comfortable in his mother's presence for fear of being asked about things in her past, or her complicated family life, which she didn't want to talk about either. For Alek, the supposedly new life came with added responsibility of attending regular church mass every Sunday, a schedule which in time became rather impossible to maintain, eventually turning into more feasible arrangement, every second Sunday and weekly or by-weekly attendance at the practically obligatory New Testament indoctrination, known as "religion classes." Those were held regularly once a week on Thursdays, in one of the specially converted bleak, poorly heated and badly lit rooms at the church rectory, equipped with several rows of wooden desks and chairs and a blackboard, similar to those in his school, but perhaps in a little better condition. It was the beginning of a new experience, a long and winding road towards the First Communion, reception of the Eucharist, and possibly the third of seven sacraments, immediately preceded by the second sacrament, the Sacrament of Penance, his first confession. When it finally arrived with a series of preliminary meetings, Alek again felt out of place in a group of about forty mostly second grade children and their intrusive parents, involved in all the preparatory activities of their little pupils, constantly showering them with unwanted attention. Alek was mostly alone throughout the rudimentary exercises, old enough to be trusted with preparatory regiment on his own. He preferred it that way, away from his mother's prying eyes and all the uncomfortable meddling, that others in a group had to endure. Alek attended all the preparatory sessions leading to the scheduled Sunday, May 18, 1969 ceremony all by himself. A trip to the district town was necessary to buy the customary white suit and matching shoes, a required part of a standard attire, which for many generations meant to symbolize purity.

Alek found the first confession to be the biggest challenge and couldn't imagine standing in a long line to the confession booth among the restless little children, most of them second-graders.

With his mother's assistance, he had a prior arrangement made with Father Antoni for a separate confessional session, just for him. It still posed a problem of honestly confessing his sins to the priest he always had reservations about. In the end he decided on a much scaled down list of his sins, whispered to the ear of Father Antoni or his assistant Father Feliks, whoever it might eventually happen be, and just enough to sound credible, without arousing the priest's suspicion and letting him go with a reasonable penance in the end. Alek knew well in advance from his school friends, who had it all long behind them and were well into their teens, what the inquisitive priest wanted to hear, especially from those who continued to confess regularly into their middle school years, although with reoccurring, mounting apprehension every next time. One of the customary first question was about the "first experience," and which meant only one thing, the first sexual intercourse and of course related other activities, and that for whatever reason was something the cunning priest seemed to be mostly interested in, and wanted to hear more than just the act itself quickly spitted out among all the other presumed sins, oh no. The priest wanted to hear all the sordid details from an already terrified teenager. However, if there was not much to confess in that respect, the priest felt obliged to continue the interrogation "in the name of God," as if on a mission, and drilled the young man about the next horrible deed on the list of grave sins, and that was masturbation. "When?", "Where?", or "How many times?" the priest wanted to know, and then in a spirit of understanding and compassion, graciously assigned penance, but surprisingly came just short of condemning it or banning the *"unhealthy"* and *"sinful"* practice altogether. Needless to say, the attitude of the clerics raised suspicions among the general populace and left many unanswered questions. It became a well-known fact, the priests had a particular interest in *"sins of the flesh,"* almost an obsession, while supposedly maintaining their own strict celibacy.

The weather was exceptionally nice on Sunday, May 18, 1969, with spring already in full bloom, the people dressed accordingly in their best and unusually cheerful. It was one of the first truly warm and windless days of spring, perfectly coinciding with a special mass and the church packed full of people; the communicants, parents, extended family, guests and unrelated church goers, who just happened to be there and thought there would be greater value in the once-a-year event, the First Communion mass. It was all that and more, in fact one could hardly imagine a more ceremonial, festive and celebratory event, greatly exceeding Alek's and his mother's expectations. Following the official reception of the Eucharist, the body of Christ, the concluding prayers and hymns with lively accompaniment of the in-house organist, always jovial and enthusiastic Mr. Kopytko, the whole group spilled out of the church and assembled on the prominent front steps, in front of the massive, wooden, wide-open main entrance door. Father Antoni took the central position in the back row, just in front of the double door leading to vestibule and the main church nave. The children were carefully assembled in ascending rows on the wide, gray stone steps by assistant priest Father Feliks, and an official local professional photographer hired by the church to commemorate the occasion. Of course, relatives could take group photographs of their children standing somewhere among the assembled, as they wished, but ultimately most parents were reluctant to take chances, and decided on the officially sanctioned commemorative, large size, but much overpriced photographs to be received in about two weeks.

Alek stood in the same back row as the priest, towering above all, with a serene and confidant expression on his face, despite a rather odd assembly of much younger, restless children, each holding an official commemorative framed picture of Virgin Mary with baby Jesus in her arms, stamped with The Church seal, date and the parish priest's signature in one hand, and a celebratory candle in the other. Meanwhile Mrs. Brodski stood in the back of the large, gathered crowd of associated family members, close and distant, and ordinary gawkers near the entrance to the church courtyard, by one of the large concrete pillars, that marked the wide entrance on both sides. Mother looked proudly at her only child, her son Aleksander, standing on the top landing, just off the centre, close to the parish priest, Father Antoni Pukalski. She marveled at the increasing resemblance of her dear son with every passing year to her late husband Jakub, and not only in physical features, but also his voice, character and manners. That only added to her sense of everlasting connection to her beloved late husband, now so perfectly reflected in her son standing there on top of the church steps.

Few meters away, surrounded by a large throng of gathered people stood Ela, Alek's friend, looking on with mixed emotions at the young man on the church steps, she still so cared about and who made such indelible impression on her, as no other young man she has met in her short life thus far. Despite his young age, she thought Alek was mature well beyond his years, defying the common perception of a vain, immature teenager without a clear sense of direction. On The contrary, he was a young man of good character, strong principles and convictions, and fascinating personal interests. Inexplicably, Ela had a profound feeling for quite sometime now, their friendship would not last. As much as she liked it to endure, she felt elusive forces at work beyond her control. Their respective family environments couldn't be more different, the influence and expectations of the local small community with some hostile, intrusive elements, and similarly contentious conditions created by a small group of students, who constantly incited animosities, and whose only purpose seemed to be making lives miserable for others, the most vulnerable they didn't like for whatever reason.

While study came to Alek relatively effortlessly, despite his habitual procrastination, Ela on the other hand struggled with almost everything, falling behind the fast-paced program of the school curriculum, much of which could be attributed to her difficult, endlessly adverse environment and family situation at home. It seemed though, that increasingly her determination to finish the middle school wavered, and it was just a matter of time before she dropped out again, perhaps this time for good.

Ela stood there barely visible, perhaps intentionally determined to be inconspicuous, as if she didn't know Alek at all, just a coincidental observer, obscured in the crowd. Outside the church courtyard, along the wide, tiled sidewalk, a teenager was passing by in a hurry on his way to the train station, quite oblivious of the ceremony in progress. Suddenly he looked sideways, and as if startled, noticed the large celebration, the commotion, the overflowing crowd of people and stopped as if frozen in mid-stride, as if time stood still. Unknowingly, without any preconceived idea, as if by inexplicable stroke of fate that was meant to be, he looked at the assembled group on the church steps and immediately noticed Aleksander Brodski standing by the priest, near the middle of the back row. Coincidentally, their eyes met briefly, mutually recognized, as if in a gesture of reciprocal understanding, like all those times in the past and in the most unexpected places, and mostly in traumatic circumstances. At once Alek recognized in the passing teenager the same boy he had seen many times before, who was curiously watching him from a distance, seemingly without any particular reason, but with a sense of strange, heart-felt concern and empathy emanating from his sad face, and yet as if curiously detached and fearful, full of apprehension and uncertainty. Still rooted to the same spot, the teenager then instinctively turned halfway around, with his eyes transfixed further to the side where Mrs. Brodski was standing by the concrete pillar, smiling warmly, looking at her son with apparent pride and simultaneously eagerly observing the people all-around, as if desperately seeking signs of approval, recognition or a trace of appreciation and long-sought acceptance from the townsfolks. Ultimately, Aleksander paid the price of assimilation and acceptance by being baptized and now taking the First Communion in the name of God. The Catholic Church sacrament was normally given in the early grades of elementary school, most often at the age of eight, but under the circumstances, Alek took a leap of faith in his mid-teens. Isn't that what they all wanted, he thought? Wasn't that the price he had to pay?

Sadly, no one seemed to care or perhaps even notice the overjoyed mother, or the towering teenager on the front steps of the church. The gathered were absorbed in their own affairs, likewise beaming with pride, keenly concentrated on their own children and accompanying relatives for this momentous occasion in the lives of their pupils. Strangely, the passing teenager's and Mrs.Brodski's eyes met for just a few seconds, as all those years ago, when he was just a child, staring through a hole in a wooden fence dividing the two adjacent courtyards, and as back then, without words. He was struck by unmistakable warmth and affinity emanating from the good woman's face, as if they have always known each other, almost as if she were his own mother, and now they inevitably met again, although briefly, after a long but prescient absence. The scrawny teenager, Dominik Poleski slightly nodded his head and smiled back timidly, and thus acknowledged Mrs. Brodski. He hesitated momentarily, then lowered his head and quickly resumed walking to the local train station with renewed haste, to catch the next train to the provincial capital Lublin, and as fate would have it, never to come back here again.

THE END

www.ingramcontent.com/pod-product-compliance
Lightning Source LLC
Chambersburg PA
CBHW071417200726
48294CB00002B/426

* 9 7 8 1 9 6 0 1 9 7 7 3 3 *